Praise for *Finding Napoleon*

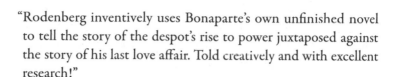

"Rodenberg inventively uses Bonaparte's own unfinished novel to tell the story of the despot's rise to power juxtaposed against the story of his last love affair. Told creatively and with excellent research!"
— STEPHANIE DRAY, *New York Times* & *USA Today* best-selling author of Historical Fiction, including *America's First Daughter* and *The Women of Chateau Lafayette*

"Napoleon's last years, awash in intrigue and poignant with loss... by Rodenberg, who deserves kudos as a rigorous researcher and gifted writer... this intricate tapestry... brings to life the twilight years of a captivating historical figure."
— *KIRKUS REVIEWS*

"*Vive l'Empereur!* In *Finding Napoleon*, the Bonaparte endgame becomes a new beginning—and a rousing, delightfully peopled adventure. Margaret Rodenberg's superior scholarship, exquisite scene-setting and crackling storytelling mark her as a historical novelist to watch."
— LOUIS BAYARD, *New York Times* notable author of best-selling Historical Fiction, including *Courting Mr. Lincoln*, and *The Black Tower*

"From the first words, *Finding Napoleon* by Margaret Rodenberg enchanted me. Exceptionally well researched, the writing is vibrant, the details evocative. The story of Napoleon's final years is conveyed with moving compassion, humor and wit. I love Margaret Rodenberg's writing and I look forward to reading more by her. Highly recommended!"
— SANDRA GULLAND, author of *The Josephine B. Trilogy* and *The Game of Hope*

"Napoleon Bonaparte's life was an incredible, inspiring, and ultimately tragic epic. In *Finding Napoleon*, readers enter deep into both the beginning and the end of that exceptional drama, as Margaret Rodenberg brings to life the inner circle of the ailing emperor as he spends his final years in exile on the remote island of St. Helena. No one is more qualified to tell this sweeping tale than Margaret Rodenberg — her research is in a league of its own, and her writing is beautiful and poignant."

— ALLISON PATAKI, *New York Times* best-selling author of *The Queen's Fortune*

"Margaret Rodenberg has an outstanding knowledge of and empathy for the life of Napoleon Bonaparte, especially his time in exile on St. Helena. And unlike many, she has actually visited that remote island and seen the actual conditions of his captivity. In *Finding Napoleon*, she combines that knowledge and empathy with her exceptional ability to weave her imaginative story of Napoleon and Albine de Montholon. In so doing she leaves readers greatly entertained and, I hope, wanting to read more about one of history's most fascinating personalities. I highly recommend this fine book by an outstanding author."

— J. DAVID MARKHAM, President, International Napoleonic Society; Knight, Order of the French Academic Palms; Author of *Napoleon for Dummies*, and *The Road to St. Helena: Napoleon After Waterloo*

"*Finding Napoleon* is a fascinating look at Napoleon as a writer of romance, a tender father, and a mature lover examining happier times amid the trials of his life in St. Helena—a side to him not often explored, and one I found completely enrapturing. His forgotten lover, Albine de Montholon, adds an intriguing dimension. Rodenberg's sense of revolutionary culture and period detail sparkle and her storytelling is truly absorbing. A winner!"

— HEATHER WEBB, coauthor of *Ribbons of Scarlet* and author of *Becoming Josephine* and *Rodin's Lover*

"A tale within a tale, *Finding Napoleon* by Margaret Rodenberg creates three vivid characters - Napoleon in exile, Napoleon becoming a young military hero, and Albine de Montholon, the emperor's last love. Through superb writing, the author brings history to life while offering insights into the passions that drove this man to greatness. Highly recommended."
— M.K. TOD, author of *Time and Regret*, and
the blog, www.awriterofhistory.com

"In her haunting historical novel, *Finding Napoleon*, Margaret Rodenberg bookends the Emperor's life. She enlarges upon his own semi-autobiographical novel, giving us insight into his early days, contrasting them with the contracted, duplicitous court that accompanied him into captivity on St. Helena after Waterloo. And yet, it is through unexpected friendships forged on the island, his tumultuous final love affair with Albine de Montholon, and a longing for the son he's lost that we truly do find Napoleon during these, his last days. Highly recommended."
— MICHELLE CAMERON, award-winning author
of *Beyond the Ghetto Gates*

"*Finding Napoleon* reimagines three powerful turning points in the romantic life of Napoleon Bonaparte—childhood, the young military hero, the still-passionate man in exile. With finesse and deep insight, Margaret Rodenberg delivers a masterful tour de force. A must for historical fiction bibliophiles."
— KATHRYN JOHNSON, author of *The Gentleman Poet: A Novel of Love, Danger, and Shakespeare's The Tempest*

"With a cast of authentic and vibrant characters, including a heroine who is every bit Napoleon's match, *Finding Napoleon* explores the gray landscapes of interpersonal relationships. This, the reader will feel, was Napoleon, and these were the characters who populated his later years. *Finding Napoleon* belongs among the best of historical fiction—present, alive and real, rendered with the touch of a poet and masterful storyteller. A delightful, informative page-turner."
— SCOTT G. HIBBARD, author of *Beyond the Rio Gila*

FINDING NAPOLEON

FINDING NAPOLEON

A Novel

MARGARET RODENBERG

SHE WRITES PRESS

Published 2021
Printed in the United States of America
Print ISBN: 978-1-64742-016-1
E-ISBN: 978-1-64742-017-8
Library of Congress Control Number: 2020919842

For information, address:
She Writes Press
1569 Solano Ave #546
Berkeley, CA 94707

Interior design by Tabitha Lahr

She Writes Press is a division of SparkPoint Studio, LLC.

This is a work of fiction. Names, characters, places, and incidents either are the product of the author's imagination or are used fictitiously. Any resemblance to actual persons, living or dead, is entirely coincidental.

"Gaston the Eccentric," from *Bratsk Station and Other New Poems*, by Yevgeny Yevtushenko, copyright © 1966 by Sun Books Pty. Ltd. Used by permission of Doubleday, an imprint of the Knopf Doubleday Publishing Group, a division of Penguin Random House LLC. All rights reserved.

To my beloved husband, Bert Helfinstein
Without whom these pages would be blank
and my heart empty

Power is only
       a small blessing,
bad for the nerves,
We should be creating masterpieces,
masterpieces!

— YEVGENY YEVTUSHENKO

A note to readers ⁓

Years ago, when I learned that Napoleon Bonaparte tried to write a novel, I vowed to finish it for him. That brief handwritten manuscript still exists. In the "Clisson" sections of *Finding Napoleon*, I draw upon its words, ideas, and characters and expand it fivefold. So, while the story herein is mine, I like to imagine young Napoleon, all elbows, lanky hair, and ambition, in a cold, candlelit apartment near Notre Dame, scribbling my source material.

⁓ Margaret Rodenberg

Prologue

Albine

UNLESS YOU TOO STITCHED A white gown for the guillotine, do not judge me. But if you'd faced the terrors I have—if you were Empress Josephine herself—I'd accept your judgment on my morals. If you were Napoleon's second wife . . . No, let's not talk of Marie Louise more than we must.

Since you're not Josephine (and likely an ember to her bonfire), I beg you to listen. Within these pages, learn secrets about Emperor Napoleon, whom I loved. He and I were of a piece, our hungers rooted in a bog of family, ambition, treason. We both had children to lose. We both had trust to betray. We both had seen better days. I expose our frailties for your entertainment.

Oh, I don't pretend to be his equal. The Emperor inhabited a grand stage. I was a creature of the boudoir. History will remember me as a tendril in the forest of his life. Yet when we intertwined, one could break the other.

I warn you: some of this is hearsay from people with tarnished reputations. Much came from the Great Man's lips when his body lay naked at my side. Part is from a novel Napoleon wrote about himself. I add spice to the stew.

So know my Napoleon, know me, and I shall love you for it. For what but love matters? It is the holiest, costliest, easiest thing to give. I gave mine freely, as Napoleon gave his to me. I was the last woman he loved.

Vive l'Empereur!

— ALBINE, COUNTESS DE MONTHOLON

Chapter 1

Napoleon

"BORN FOR WAR, MY SON." Napoleon Bonaparte buried his nose in his boy's auburn curls, feasting on child scent, milk and mash, perspiration and chamomile.

Outside in the Tuileries courtyard, a drummer beat *rat-tat-tat*. Another, another, dozens more joined in, until the call to arms rattled the windows that ran the length of his son's cavernous bedchamber.

A shiver, absent in war, twitched the Emperor's shoulders. Fifty-four battles, and he'd never been afraid to die. Until he had this child. Until he had his Eaglet.

The boy squirmed. "Papa Papa?"

He kissed the Eaglet's fingertips one by one. "Born for war. Come, I'll read you what that means." He shifted his manuscript out of the shadows. Not that he needed light. He'd memorized his faded scribbles years ago. He deepened his tone to an army timbre. "*Once more, you seize the tattered battle flag. You yell, 'Hoorah!' from smoke-seared lungs. The cavalry, sabers drawn, thunders in your wake into the cannon fire. Your horse's hooves crush bones of fallen men. All at once, a musket blows a thousand arrows through your chest. Your horse wheels, collapses. Earth soaks in your blood.*"

His voice broke.

Around him, the palace bedroom loomed, desolate as an empty church. A crib occupied a corner, but his wife, always the proper empress, insisted their three-year-old sleep in the gold-draperied bed. How far from the straw pallet the Emperor and his brother had once shared. He stroked his child's linen gown. "When I come home from war, *mon petit*, we'll play outside. I'll get the two of us good and dirty."

The Eaglet giggled, his cheeks tiny peaches. "Now, Papa-Papa? Play now?"

A gangly schoolboy clutching a toy soldier scrambled from behind the sofa. "*Moi aussi, mon cher oncle?* I play, too?" Louis-Napoleon asked.

The Emperor straightened an epaulet on his nephew's uniform. "But of course, Louis-N."

Outside drums beat *rat-tat-tat, rat-tat-tat, rat-tat-tat*.

The Emperor twisted his stiff bulk, bound though it was with ornamental sashes and stuffed into the lucky green military jacket that had grown too tight. He squinted through a window into the palace courtyard, where soldiers gathered under the winter sun. He counted the gold eagle standards held aloft.

All the troops hadn't arrived. But even with the stragglers, he'd never have enough. And every day more foreign soldiers surged over France's border, screaming for his blood. He hugged the wriggling Eaglet to his chest. "Be still, royal squirmer. Don't you want to hear more of Papa's story? Before I say goodbye?"

"Bye? Bye, Papa?" The Eaglet's heart-shaped mouth, a miniature of the Emperor's, quivered, gaped, and exploded in a howl. Louis-N covered his ears. The Emperor leaned in, absorbing the wail. He lifted the screaming child above his head and lowered him bit by bit until they met nose to nose, openmouthed, swallowing each other's breath.

"No bye, no bye-bye," the Eaglet whimpered.

The Emperor slumped into the velvet cushions, the Eaglet pressed between his knees and chest. There he rocked, his body aching to absorb the child, like a mother in reverse. Anything to hold him always. Louis-N huddled at his side.

The chamber door opened. Marie Louise, the Emperor's young wife, swept in, centuries of imperial ancestors floating in the wake of her silk shawl. Her auburn hair twisted beneath a diadem, emeralds swathed her regal neck, and her china-blue eyes glared down her thin nose. On a table beyond her husband's reach, she tossed a folded paper, its imperial Austrian seal broken.

"News?" he said. "From your father?"

She pointed at Louis-N. "You—out!"

Louis-N shrank against the sofa cushions.

The Emperor tousled his nephew's hair. "Find Marchand. He'll take you to admire the soldiers." He waited until the door shut behind the boy. "That's beneath you, Marie Louise."

"The brat carries tales to his mother." She reached for their child.

The Eaglet batted her away. "Eaglet stay with Papa-Papa."

The Empress's pretty dimples hardened. "Colonel von Neipperg brought the message."

"What? Him again?" The Emperor plopped the Eaglet on the carpet among his toys. "Stay away from that one-eyed Don Juan."

"Too late, my dear. I've passed an amusing hour listening to his gossip. Everyone in Austria thinks you're sure to lose." Marie Louise tapped the letter. "As one emperor to another, Father demands your surrender."

The Emperor half rose from the sofa, but the twinge in his side recalled the odds against him. His anger faded. Anyway, they were wrong. He had a chance if he could catch the enemy unaware, divide them up, skirmish them into chaos.

Outside, drumming rose, fell, peaked again.

The Eaglet lifted his plump hand in salute. "Papa-Papa! Play soldiers?"

The Emperor returned the salute. "*Mon Dieu*, Marie Louise, some French empress you are. Think of those men outside. Josephine would have—"

"Josephine? Bah!" She bared her perfect white teeth, a stark contrast to his first wife's blackened nubs.

He grabbed a fistful of her silk shawl. "Look at you, mimicking her style. Toothless, divorced, Josephine's still more France's empress than you'll ever be." A petty attack, instantly regretted, but he'd had so little sleep and his stomach ached. He released the shawl and retreated. Everywhere he was on the defensive—with his wife, with his ministers, with his enemies swarming the French borders. Now the Eaglet was crying. He caressed the child's hands. When he looked up, Marie Louise had crossed to the fireplace.

She threw the shawl onto the flames. "So much for Josephine and her fashions. I'll be in Vienna for the spring balls. Where will you be, eh?"

"Go ahead. Run home to Austria, but you're not taking my son."

"Of course I am. I'm his mother."

"You're also a monarch. Bred, reared, sold to be a queen." He lifted the child and stalked to the door. "Now, leave this room with dignity, like the empress I made you."

She raised her mulish chin.

He wondered if she might kiss him farewell, but no. He'd lost her months earlier, when the tide had first reversed against him. Strange he felt so little. They'd been in love. Or so he had thought. He waited on the threshold.

Her gaze lingered on their son. For once, her voice was soft. "When you're around, he doesn't want me."

He touched her bare arm. "You are young, and I am sorry." He shut the door behind her.

The Eaglet patted his cheek. "Maman mad at Papa?"

"Yes, mon petit. Maman, the British Empire, the Russians, the Austrians . . . The whole world's mad at Papa." He brushed a curl from the boy's forehead. The skin seemed too delicate. Did they give him the right things to eat?

In the courtyard, voices shouted. The last of the soldiers must have arrived. He scooped up his manuscript. He'd have it sent to Josephine at Malmaison. Still loyal, she could be trusted to hide it until he returned—and to destroy it if he didn't. He smoothed his uniform, put on his bicorne hat, and stepped onto the balcony with the Eaglet perched against his shoulder.

"*Vive l'Empereur!*" The cry traveled through the field of men. "*Vive le petit roi!*"

He scanned the troops, calculating. The Old Guard, the V Cavalry, the raw recruits of the Young Guard. Red jackets of the Hussars, green of the Chasseurs, blue and white of the infantry. Tattered plumes on tall hats, proud sheen on worn boots. Everywhere ferocious mustaches. More horses than he'd expected. The odds were moving in his favor. They had a chance.

He was still Napoleon, after all.

A fresh cry erupted from his soldiers. "*Vive l'Impératrice! Vive Marie Louise!*"

His wife stood next to him, her graceful head on its long neck tilted to his army. She pulled the screaming Eaglet from his shoulder and backed away.

He stood alone on the balcony, empty arms locked to his sides. Still the soldiers cheered. They hadn't seen. They didn't know. They thought he wept for them.

Albine

NO DWELLING ON BATTLES, IF you please. Suffice it to say, my Emperor plunged into desperate war against foreign troops on French soil. At first, he won. Then he didn't. For pity's sake, even Napoleon couldn't hold all Europe's armies at bay. You probably know what happened. They exiled him to the Isle of Elba, two days' sail from France's southern coast. Now, whoever thought he'd stay put?

Meanwhile, I holed up in a dank, low-ceilinged flat in Paris with Charles de Montholon—aristocrat and general, my third husband since my debut marriage at seventeen. While I scrounged the streets for food, Charles grew adept at tossing our son Tristan's cloth balls into teacups. (Except when saving his own skin, the man was as indolent as an overfed cow, though that made no sense, since he hadn't a spare ounce of flesh on that long, bony frame of his.)

For ten months, foreign troops roamed the city, the cost of bread skyrocketed, and King Louis (XVIII, this time) plunged into pre-Revolutionary extravagance. Marie Louise, the traitor empress, stole home to Austria with the Eaglet. She and Colonel von Neipperg waltzed at all the Vienna balls that spring. And poor, sweet, divorced Josephine died of a cold.

Finally, one bright day in March, Paris's streets erupted in celebration. Napoleon had made a glorious cunning return to France. As he marched five hundred miles to the capital, never firing a shot, the army and the people rallied to his side.

I shook Charles by the ears. "I told you so! Napoleon's a genius. Now, on your way to join him!"

Charles raised his aristocratic nose (giving me a most unpleasant view). "You forget Napoleon doesn't like me. Not since the incident. Don't look at me like that. The old matter, the soldiers' pay."

I pressed a finger to his lips. "Well, we needed that money. And besides, Napoleon forgave you. It's forgotten."

"Bah! General Bertrand will remind him."

"That old rump! Fling yourself at Napoleon's feet. If he wins, he'll reward us. On the other hand, if he loses, we'll follow him into exile, where no one can hound us for our debts. Perfect either way."

"Either way, disaster." My husband's long arms closed around me. He pressed close, but I shooed him out the door before he could unbutton his breeches.

Alas, while France rejoiced, the rest of Europe geared up for war.

Three months later, as I dabbed crushed cucumber on oh so faint wrinkles above my lip, Charles burst into our apartment.

I spilled half my precious paste. "*Zut!* Dearest, how came you here? Is the war over? Is Napoleon in Paris?"

"You and your damned Napoleon." Charles's uniform reeked, but the blood on it apparently wasn't his. "The British, Austrians, God knows who else, are at the Paris gates."

I bolted to the window. No marauding soldiers. Charles must have deserted his post to reach Paris before them.

He tugged his smoky curls. "Get packing. Take only valuables, do you hear?"

I chuckled. "Valuables? Nothing's left. The silver sent Tristan to Switzerland. Enough to pay the school for two years."

"My God, you paid two years at once?" He flung open the empty cupboards. "Nothing? Nothing left for us?"

"But, Charles, think. Two whole years. Our boy's safe." My fist closed around the bread crust in my skirt's secret pocket. Small comfort, that leftover prison habit, but my throat reopened to let words escape. "Where's the Emperor?"

"On the run. Malmaison by now."

"Then that's where we'll go." I resorted to my old refrain. "Napoleon rose like a star—"

"And he's crashing back to Hell. Aha!" He dragged a plain blue jacket from a trunk. "Put on a fancy, low-cut dress and a white scarf. We must look like Royalists."

"No, no, everyone knows you've been with Napoleon. It's Malmaison or a firing squad for you." I yanked at the jacket, tearing loose a sleeve. "And God knows what for me."

We locked eyes. He let the jacket fall.

I stretched to kiss his stubbly cheek. "Thank you, love, for coming back for me."

"Fool that I am. Could've gotten shot for deserting." His voice rasped against my ear. "At least Malmaison postpones the firing squad. Bring bread, dried meat. No time for your panics, do you hear?"

We threw a few possessions in a sack and joined the throngs escaping Paris. Somehow, we'd get to Malmaison and the Emperor. I'd missed out on his first exile. Napoleon Bonaparte wasn't going to escape me again.

Chapter 2

Napoleon

BEHIND MODEST CHÂTEAU DE MALMAISON, the Emperor shuffled his boots along a pine-needled path, his bicorne hat clutched against his aching stomach. As he rounded a bend, his momentum faltered. His tiny mother, in her widow's high-necked black, her spine as erect as the wall behind her, presided over Josephine's garden from a stone bench. Cataract eyes, once sharp steel like his own, now dull oysters, marred her handsome Roman profile. A breeze rustled the garden's pink roses. His mother's hair didn't stir beneath the lace shawl; her blue-veined hands remained as immovable as granite.

He wet his lips. Shifting his hat from hand to hand, he wiped each palm on his white knee breeches. He tiptoed forward, knelt, and laid his head on the stiff black silk that formed his mother's lap. *Ahh!* escaped her lips. Her dry fingers caressed the bridge of his nose, stroked his cheeks, tangled his thin hair. The cedar scent she'd worn as long as he could remember mingled with Josephine's roses. A warmth washed through him.

She jerked her hand away. "Napoleon? I thought you were your brother."

His jaw tightened. "No, it's me, Maman."

"Home already? Too soon for good news, I'd say." His mother pouted, her short upper lip identical to his. "So. How was it, my boy? That place the servants whisper about? That Waterloo?"

His face sank into her black silk as her words carried him back to the knoll overlooking Waterloo's plain, where the French army collapsed in blood and mud as his screaming soldiers scrambled backward, trampling fallen comrades' shredded flesh, while on the left, British shot raked their chests, and on the right, British cavalry swinging sabers half severed French limbs and heads, and all the while, as if from God above, cannonballs pelted down, tore into French backs, and, bursting through the fleeing soldiers' chests, ripped out their hearts.

Ripped out his.

Now, as then, his bowels threatened to let go. His jubilant escape from Elba, the fruitless maneuvering for peace, the French army who rushed to his call, the chance to recover his crown and his little son: all lost on an overcast June afternoon.

Above that battlefield, beyond the rising smoke, amid the heavy clouds, a patch of blue beckoned. In answer, he dug his spurs into his horse's flanks, but as his mount leapt battleward, into Glorious Death with his men, General Bertrand's sturdy gray wheeled into his path. When he swung his horse left, General Montholon, a saber arched above his head, blocked the way.

Montholon, eyes raw from cannon smoke, dark with fury, pointed his saber at the Emperor's heart. "No, you don't. They'll hang you on the nearest tree, let English soldiers take potshots. Where's France's glory then?"

The Emperor thrust out his chest. "*Eh bien!* Do the job yourself."

General Bertrand knocked Montholon's sword aside. "Haven't the British had enough victory? Your Majesty, save yourself, for your son, for our Eaglet." Bertrand's weary eyes brightened. "Thank God! Here's Marchand with fresh horses. We ride for Paris. Let politics decide our fate."

But if the battlefield at Waterloo was a disaster, the situation in Paris was worse. Those who had curried favor now maneuvered at the farthest distance. He didn't blame them. He'd failed. Still, he told his valet Marchand, politicians' betrayal stank worse than battle carnage.

So he signed the abdication, left Marchand to gather supplies, and, with a dozen guards at his heels, rode to Malmaison, his country home, to bid goodbye to his mother.

The story floated out in bits and pieces, in a voice not his own, the speech flowing against his will. "And so, Maman, it's over. I should have died in battle."

"You pushed your luck too far. *I* was happy on Elba." She took his cheeks between her palms and lifted his head to confront her clouded eyes. "But you, my boy, you had to pick up the crown again."

"Always the comforter, eh, Madame Mère?" He strained to rise, but his cursed legs had no strength: too many hours in the saddle, too much girth around his belly. He gripped the stone bench and struggled to his feet. "Farewell, then."

She flailed blindly. "Have patience with an old woman."

He caught her hand.

She drew him down beside her. "Out with it! What plan's rattling about in that head of yours?"

He twisted a rose from its branch. "British sanctuary."

She gave a cackle of laughter. "Of all things, not that."

"Of all things, yes, that. They'd have hanged me if they'd caught me on the battlefield. In peace, protocol demands they welcome a deposed sovereign. I doubt the French king will be so kind." He stripped the rose of its petals and grabbed another. "No, I'll live retired outside London, write my memoirs, raise the Eaglet. Join me?"

"A fairy tale! The British may take you in, but they'll never give you the boy." She smoothed her skirt, erasing the depression where his head had lain. "Still, thank you for the invitation."

"Come, come, they can't keep holding the Eaglet, now, can they?" The second rose met its fate in his hands. "Marie Louise—damn her—has all but deserted him."

"Are you destroying flowers? Stop that, do you hear?"

He brushed the rose dust from his fingers. "Take my word: if they don't return him to me, I'll make a stir like they've never seen. I can do it, too—none better."

Her smile was grim, her waved hand dismissive. "Leave the boy in Austria. It's safer for him. But tell me, son, who stays with you? Who's loyal at the end?"

He hesitated. "Generals Bertrand and Montholon, with their wives in tow."

"Generals? Ha! The first is a martinet, the second a louse married to that hussy Albine."

He bit back a retort. "And Las Cases comes as secretary."

"A squirrel with a quill in its paw." She bobbed her head, an awkwardness acquired with the cataracts. "What? No Cipriani? That devil would follow you into Hell."

"Franco joins us on the road."

"Well, then." The muscles around her mouth hardened, stretching her lips into a skeletal smile. "Better than being alone, I suppose."

"When I get the Eaglet, I won't be alone."

"Let me tell you, you'll not recover the cost of begetting that child."

In the fading light, his mother's beauty flickered between what she'd been and what was to come. A chill washed over him. "That doesn't matter. When I think of his sweet round face, when I remember—feel—his little arms around my neck, smell the milk on his breath . . . no, Mother, the cost doesn't matter." He stroked her dry knuckles. "I recognized the Eaglet's destiny the moment my lips felt his heartbeat." He stared into her opaque oracle eyes. "As you did with me."

Her mouth opened. She laughed.

He winced. "How can you mock when that's how you raised me?"

She rose, swaying. "Corsica was different."

"Different?"

"There, you knew who you were. I warned you none of this would last."

Fatigue clouded his head. When had she become so old? When had he? Yet the old puppeteer could still pull his strings, as she had when he was a child. "Come, Mother, remember what you always told me. Born for war? Destined to save Corsica?"

"You think I don't remember?" Her breaths were shallow. "Your dreams, too, will fade."

"My dreams don't matter anymore." He clasped her shoulders to steady her. "I'll risk everything for my son. You have no idea."

She slapped his cheek. "How dare you preach to me what a son can mean?"

He kissed the palm that struck him.

HE SPENT THE REST OF the evening wandering the small chateau's elegant rooms, recalling the early, tumultuous, happy years with Josephine. Oh, the price of that gold-leafed harp, that exquisite Sèvres plate. Josephine had pleaded forgiveness on her knees for buying them when they could not afford such things. And how sweet she'd tasted between the sheets afterward. Then, everything seemed possible, nothing certain.

But dead these thirteen months. A simple cough, and she was gone.

At his order, servants had filled her boudoir with cut roses.

"Ah, my friend. A perfect Adam and Eve, we two," he whispered to the pillow where her soft brown curls used to spread. He smoothed the red silk bedcover. How many men had she entertained on that mattress during his absences? No matter. She'd learned her morals from the Revolution, and reticence had never been her nature. Yet, for all that, she'd stayed loyal through their divorce. The woman understood—breathed—politics. If only she'd been able to give him children. She'd cooed over the Eaglet when he had smuggled the infant out to meet her. He'd wrapped his arms around them both and let their sorrows mingle. Josephine had been the first to pull away, the one to say, "Enough, Bonaparte. You have a new wife now."

But that "new wife" had her one-eyed Austrian lover. He withdrew from his breast pocket the note that had arrived the night before the disastrous battle. He reread the words he'd had too much pride to tell his mother.

Whether you win or lose, I'm not returning to France. My father forbids a divorce, but I am no longer your wife. Marie Louise

He hid his face in his hands. So many lessons to teach his son.

He touched Marie Louise's letter to a candle flame. No one need ever know.

In the hallway outside Josephine's boudoir, he rolled his forehead against the closed door, brushing his lips on the cool paint, willing his murmurs to seep into the wood, to search out Josephine's spirit, to bind once more with her.

"Without you, better to walk alone," he repeated, until his mouth grew dry.

Downstairs, his library, its dark oak a masculine reserve in the otherwise feminine chateau, appeared untouched. A key stashed on a top shelf released a drawer in the wide mahogany desk. He pocketed a red silk sack of diamonds and retrieved the metal box that held the novel he'd started writing as a lovestruck twenty-six-year-old desperate to understand life. His Josephine had had a fine laugh when she discovered those secret pages two decades earlier. Now she was dead, the ink was fading, and no one else knew he had written them. Even the Eaglet and Louis-N had probably forgotten the bit they'd heard.

He fingered the manuscript's soft white pages. The only hands to have touched the papers were Josephine's and his. Her light flickered in his chest. A surge of youth burned through him. What a thing to be once again the young character in this novel, to have destiny's path stretched before his feet, not strung out behind him.

Like the Eaglet.

The papers crumpled in his fist. His own chance to die in glory had slipped away.

Yet a new path might be blazed for his son, the rightful Napoleon II.

He smoothed the pages against his thigh. With an addition here, a twist there, the story could turn into a lesson for his little boy. One day the Eaglet would open the metal box, thumb through the pages, search for his father among the scribbled words, and find the Napoleon he himself must grow to be. As the end approached, how fitting to recall how it all began. He lit another candle, sharpened a quill, and marked up the first page.

CLISSON: THE EMPEROR'S NOVEL

By Napoleon I, Emperor of the French, King of Italy, Protector of the Confederation of the Rhine, etc.

(The Emperor still liked the old title—the name of an ancient French general, and better not to use his own name for a character in a novel.)

Part I: On Destiny Discovered
Corsica, 1769

Clisson was born for war.

Rebels chanted the child's first lullabies. "*Guerra! Libartà o morti!* Four hundred years enslaved by Genoese. Are we Corsicans sheep to be sold to a French king?"

Clisson's father, a tall man with wild chestnut hair, led rebel troops over the island's mountains. His tiny mother, her belly stretched around unborn Clisson, rode a donkey among the women at the militia's rear. His brother Joseph clung to her breast. Inside her womb, Clisson's fingers grew toward the stiletto at her waist.

His father ordered the militia into French cannon fire on a bridge. Within an hour, their bullets spent, the rebels cowered behind fallen comrades' bodies. The dying threw themselves upon the bloody heap to raise a barricade, but soon the battle cries switched to "Run!" His father spearheaded the retreat.

His father, mother, and a ragtag hundred more escaped to the slopes of Monte Rotondo, where snow chilled rivers in July. On a sunless afternoon, the rushing Liamone swept the mother's donkey into its torrent. Her skirts sopping, she clutched the reins in one hand. With the other, she lifted her toddler above the froth. Her heels spurred the donkey against the churning current. When at last the shivering animal clambered onto the embankment, Clisson's mother collapsed.

Clisson was fighting to be born.

The rebels doled out their remaining gunpowder and shot. A few circled back to ambush the French. The weaker, blood-soaked ones blocked the path while the women struggled on with the father to find a cave. Gunfire muffled the mother's moans.

"Hold fast, brave love." The father's voice quavered.

His little wife's bright eyes shamed his fear.

After dark, a campfire delivered warmth. His mother bit a rag and strained for the birthing. Torches danced shadows on the cave walls as the people's shout of "Born to liberty!" greeted the boy's first cry. They swaddled him in Corsica's Moor's head battle flag and christened him over a bloodied drum. His parents gave him the name Clisson, after an uncle lost to French artillery on the bridge.

His mother raised her moist head from the donkey blankets. The shadow of her Roman profile filled a cave wall. "This son's born to be a hero," she told the women.

A cousin, blessed with second sight but marred with a birthmark on one cheek, dropped to her knees. "Clisson will cross rivers with impunity."

"Beware the sea," whispered a crone.

The mother spat on the baby's forehead. All the women, except the crone, formed a line to do the same. Such a boy, conceived during rebellion, born to the battlefield, his first cries echoing gunfire, was destined to be a soldier. But his Corsican homeland begged for peace. Clisson's father numbered among the first to swear loyalty to the French king.

His mother bit her thumb and cursed. What to do with a boy born for war?

THE EMPEROR EXTINGUISHED HIS CANDLE. Yes, that captured his own beginning, at least the way he liked to tell it. He'd take these papers. He'd ready the stories for the Eaglet. If all went well, they'd read them together, he and his son, in England. But come morning, he'd best be on his way before the French king caught up with him. Then it'd be death or, worse, prison.

The library door opened, and Louis-N peeked in. "Grand-maman said I wasn't to bother you."

The Emperor opened his arms.

The boy ran to him. "Uncle, dear Uncle, take me with you. Please."

He held Louis-N at arm's length. The boy had the Bonaparte strong nose, soft mouth, and determined cleft chin. His high spirits would be welcome, but no. It would break the boy's mother's heart. He kissed his nephew's cheeks. "Your destiny lies here in France. Those words are a gift. They were once told to me."

Albine

CHARLES AND I ARRIVED AT Château de Malmaison in a stolen wagon drawn by a hack we liberated from a butcher's yard. As it was too late at night to demand entry, we slept outside the iron gate. In the morning, the Emperor's greeting broke our slumber.

"My dear Montholon! My dear Albine!" Napoleon exclaimed. "Such a night you've had. All on my behalf? Yes, yes, you may join us. We leave in a quarter hour. Forget this wretched cart. You shall ride with me."

"I told you so," I mouthed to Charles, who pinched my bum.

All day, our entourage of coaches rattled through French countryside. As we rolled over roads Napoleon had paved in better times, under the shade of trees he'd planted, and alongside canals he'd dredged, I wept over my Emperor's accomplishments. While he watched, I stashed his loan of a handkerchief between my barely veiled breasts. When he wasn't looking, I twisted my hair into a dusky blond knot high on my head, à la Marie Louise. That coiffure, the fullness of my cleavage, the eagerness in my voice, all conspired to evoke a happier time. I pressed firmly on the bag under my feet so the candlesticks I'd stolen from Malmaison didn't clink.

As sun warmed the fields (and my husband moped in his corner of the coach), my admiration warmed the Emperor. His posture straightened, his gestures took on their old decisiveness, his speech grew more clipped as he pointed out a new bridge, improved canal locks, a school for poor children.

I recounted the time I'd met the Eaglet and how the sweet boy had kissed me. "On my cheek, just here." Tears (real ones, I swear) lingered on my lashes as I fondled the handkerchief the Emperor had given me. He plucked it from me and dabbed both our faces.

Charles, staring out the coach window, startled us with an oath. "Look. Versailles," he said. "Damn those royalists. Probably already obliterated every Napoleonic 'N' on the walls."

I twisted in horror to the Emperor, hoping he would at least slow the coach before ejecting us from it. Napoleon stared unspeaking at the huge chateau, where undoubtedly workers were painting over the symbols of his reign (damn Charles for saying it).

As Versailles disappeared from view, Napoleon retreated into a corner of the chaise. For the next three days, he banished us from his carriage. I banished Charles from my bed.

Chapter 3

Napoleon

A BRICK OF PRIDE HAD been forming in Napoleon's chest until the shadow of Versailles reminded him that an older dynasty than the Bonapartes had reclaimed France. His flickering optimism extinguished, he fell silent, contemplating his mother's aspersions on Albine, refocusing on looming threats, composing speeches in his head.

As night fell, they arrived at the military academy of Saint-Cyr. He brushed aside the offer of the headmaster's quarters in favor of a cadet room that reminded him of his school days.

He slept fitfully in his clothes. At first light, he stepped over the guard who slept across his doorway, stifling the urge to berate the snoring fellow for dereliction of duty. From there, he made his way down the dark stone corridor and into the crisp air to enjoy the solitude of the garden and the woods beyond, surprising a doe and its fawn sipping at a creek. He'd forgotten how much he liked to be alone in nature. Someday he'd take the Eaglet on forest walks. He followed the *dee-dee-dee* of a nuthatch but couldn't spot the bird among the dense tree limbs.

Leaves rustled behind him. Perhaps a squirrel. Or another deer. Perhaps not. He hid behind a tree.

Another rustle. The rhythm of footsteps. An assassin? Or a kidnapper. More likely an enemy than a friend. His hand eased inside his jacket. He pulled out a folded knife, pressed the release, and flicked the old stiletto open. Its sharp point and razor edge would stop at least one assailant. If there were more . . . He felt for his poison vial. No, Marchand had that. If they tried to take him prisoner, he'd slit his own throat. There'd be no public hanging to satisfy a vengeful king. Poor Eaglet, left alone.

The footsteps approached, stealthy as a spy.

Almost at his tree.

He whirled. The stiletto sliced air.

No one.

From behind, his wrist was wrenched. He lost the knife. Someone knocked him to his knees. A yank on his hair, a blade at his throat. His head snapped back.

Franceschi Cipriani's lean, leathery face hung over him.

The Corsican pulled him to his feet. "Piss in a chalice, Master, what're you doing out here? I coulda killed you."

The Emperor embraced Cipriani, squeezing the man's fleshless ribs against his own well-padded chest. "Ready to carve me up, were you, Franco? You son of a butcher."

Cipriani held him fast, then pushed him off. The Corsican stooped to search the ground. "How was I to know it was yourself invading my campsite? Got here late. Your precious academy locked tight. Like to get shot if I broke in. Ah, here it is." He compared his stiletto with the Emperor's. "Still got your mother's, eh?" He handed it over. "Lost my old knife long ago in that British prison."

They touched their blades tip to tip.

The Emperor stepped back. "Mon Dieu, Franco, you look like a beggar. Smell like one, too. Where'd you get those rags?"

The Corsican sniffed at a stained sleeve. "Won this nice bit of cloth at dice."

"Explains why you're late. No matter. Marchand'll fix you up with servant's clothes." He shook Cipriani's arm. "We don't want the British questioning you."

"Off to London, are we?"

"That's the plan."

"Too bad. Place's nothing but bad wine and worse women. Not to mention that sewer of a river. What's the mission?"

The Emperor grasped the Corsican's thin shoulders. "We're going to recover the Eaglet from those damn Austrians. You with me, *o amicu*? No matter what it takes?"

Cipriani laid his open palm over the Emperor's heart. "Together at the start. Together at the finish."

They both spat on the ground.

THEY TRAVELED THREE MORE DAYS under cloudless skies. In the countryside of loyal France, villagers kissed their Emperor's hand, sang him songs, and hung on his carriage while he waved farewell. At Poitiers, he took time for an extended bath. Along the way, he slept in the best beds. His horses were always fresh, his chicken dinners simple, the way he liked them. No matter the danger—he lectured to his nervous companions—they'd make a dignified, not a scrambling, retreat.

He caught glimpses of Cipriani asleep in the luggage cart. Mostly, he rode alone, having banished the distracting Montholons to General Bertrand's carriage. If he didn't think too far into the future, if he ignored Bertrand's and Montholon's long faces and their wives' bickering, it was easy to pretend all was well.

Until they reached the Atlantic coast. There, grim Frenchmen draped a longboat in funeral crepe and rowed him out to a British frigate. The Emperor climbed the ship's ladder and raised his sword in salute, saying, "Take my boot upon this deck as testament to the esteem in which I hold the English people." A pretty, almost spontaneous speech he'd devised some days before. What was in it to make the captain blush?

Around him, British officers and sailors stared, some open-mouthed, some with derision. One made a vulgar motion at his crotch. Another splashed a bucket of stinking slop near his boots.

He stood immovable, above insult. But beyond the rail, wave trailed monotonous wave toward the gray horizon. A darkness spread through him. He recalled why he hated the sea: the utter isolation. As long as the British held him on their ship, he would have no means to communicate, no way to negotiate his future, no path to recover his son.

A hateful choice, but better than the French king's scaffold.

They sailed from France's Atlantic coast into the English Channel. There, they hugged the shore but didn't land. The ship's hold grew rank, the sailors surly. Salt wind and daily tears scalded General Bertrand's wife's pretty cheeks. Her stout husband, scratching at his saber-scarred chin, vowed not to polish his sword until he could plunge it into English soil. While Albine rubbed her Emperor's white hands with lavender oil to ward off the sun, Charles de Montholon lost to him at chess.

The sea was calm the evening Montholon rapped on the Emperor's door. In one long stride, the lanky general pushed past the valet, Marchand, to enter. The narrow, pine-walled captain's cabin, surrendered to the Emperor's use, was crammed with Napoleon's books, clothes, and personal mementos. The Emperor himself, reclining on his old, collapsible iron camp bed, smiled dismissal to Marchand. He indicated the valet's empty stool. Montholon ambled past it, his loose limbs reminding the Emperor of a wooden puppet held together with string.

The general stationed himself at a porthole. "This voyage, sire, is monotonous. A man like you isn't accustomed to inaction."

Napoleon sighed. "No prepared speeches, Charles. What's on that devious mind of yours?"

Montholon hitched a shoulder. "If the British were going to let us ashore, they'd have done it by now."

"And so we should vanquish a hundred sailors and set sail for America?"

Montholon gave a thin smile. "Bertrand disapproves of suicide charges. We'd never convince him to do his part. On the other hand, my wife and I are willing to do ours."

"Come, I gather this isn't a general profession of loyalty. Be specific."

Montholon wet his lips. "A man has needs, sire."

"Many." The Emperor sat up. "Which are we discussing? Yours? Mine? Sit. Pull up that stool so I can see what's in your face."

Montholon balanced on the stool, his knees spread apart, his feet tucked to avoid the Emperor's slippered toes. He took a deep breath. "I wish to offer my wife to satisfy your . . . your manly needs."

The Emperor lifted his brows. "I'm touched. And how does Albine feel about this service? Or should I say sacrifice?"

Charles leaned forward. "She suggested it."

The Emperor sniffed. Cognac had boosted the man's courage. "And you? How do you feel?"

Montholon lowered his eyes. "It's an honor to give one's wife to the king."

"How pre-Revolutionary, but I forget you're an aristocrat." His smile faded. "Does she know I opposed your marriage? Predicted she'd play you false, didn't I, and here we are."

Montholon's jaw clenched. "Sire, I'm trying to help you. No, I never told her."

The Emperor relaxed against the bulkhead. "Keep it that way. No reason to hurt her pride. Listen, I won't say no. Let's say instead the need doesn't arise at the moment. No, no, that wasn't a jest. Truly, I thank you both." The Emperor put out his hand.

Before taking it, Montholon wiped his damp palm on his breeches.

After the general left, the Emperor stood at his porthole, watching the procession of gray waves. Charles de Montholon had always been a scheming, thieving fellow, but he'd never before considered the man perceptive.

Albine

THE SHIP ROCKED. I CAUGHT my mirror as it tumbled from its ledge. A month already on this hulk. My forehead throbbed with every lurch, every bob, every dip, till I swore my skull would split. And, oh, my stomach ached from acting cheerful. Why wouldn't these damn British allow us onshore? If my lavender oil ran out, I couldn't rub the Emperor's hands.

Most of all, I yearned to walk a mile in a straight line, my feet on grassy land that didn't pitch and yaw. But in that tiny cabin, where I couldn't escape my own stink, where I could fling out my arms and press my palms against opposing walls (or, as the Emperor insisted I call them, "bulkheads"), I could take but five measly steps before I had to turn around.

A veritable prison.

Better not to think on that. I adjusted a dangling lock of hair to conceal the scar on the back of my neck. Opening the small porthole, I gulped salt air to stave off my trembles. This wasn't the Revolution. I wasn't in a cell. I'd boarded the ship willingly, purposefully, making its confines the opposite of a prison. I felt the several pockets I had sewn into my dress and found a comforting crust of bread to chew.

Out the porthole, almost within earshot, lay the English town of Torquay. Somewhere among those dull, huddled buildings were hat shops, gloves for sale, laundresses who washed clothes in a boiling kettle. Somewhere in that town, women like me schemed to ensnare a man. How many would dare to use her own husband to lay the trap?

All for a good cause. Our son would join us here in England. Napoleon would sponsor him at their military academy. How fine Tristan would look in a cadet uniform.

Returning to my mirror, I stuck in the last of my hairpins, securing the knot I'd twisted on my head. Not a style that suited me. I preferred something looser, more coquettish. But from the moment in the coach when I'd improvised a coiffure à la Marie Louise, a decided gleam had entered the Emperor's eye. (After all, every man craves what he's been denied. And when denied, he snatches at any shadow of his desire.)

The cabin door opened.

Charles, at last. Our eyes met. His were wary, raw, triumphant.

"It's done?" I blurted. "You made the offer?"

He nodded. Pressing his long, thin body against the wall (that damnable bulkhead), he avoided touching me as he brushed through the narrow cabin. From a clothing pile in a corner, he unearthed a cognac bottle and, holding it high above his head, drank its dregs.

"Accepted?" I asked.

"The thought's planted. Give it time to take root." He wiped his lips on his sleeve.

I wished he wouldn't do that. We didn't have a maid or many clean clothes.

Despite the cognac, his hands trembled. I took the bottle from him and placed his hands on my breasts. While he explored, I pulled out the hairpins to become his Albine again. No more Marie Louise. I guided him onto the narrow bunk. His mouth sucked my skin, licking the tender spots, reasserting his property rights.

While he strained to enter me, my mind wandered. Mostly, I hoped the Emperor wouldn't wait long to claim me. Ashore in England, even secluded on some genteel estate, other women were bound to present themselves to him. I wasn't one to overrate my charms. But if I got there first . . . well, once ensconced in the Emperor's arms, I'd be difficult to dislodge.

Charles finished.

I whispered, "For our son, for our future, my dearest."

In that moment, as eager as I was to give myself to the Emperor, I swear I loved Charles all the more.

Napoleon

WHILE BRITISH POLITICIANS ARGUED OVER what to do with him, the sea grew rough. Still Napoleon was not allowed ashore. Instead, a haughty, red-haired British admiral boarded, assuming diplomatic duties, insisting he (the Emperor Napoleon) be called General Bonaparte.

His meager court—Bertrand; Montholon; their wives, the pretty, sunburned Fanny and earthy Albine; his secretary, Las Cases, whom Madame Mère had likened to a squirrel; Las Cases's English-speaking, sixteen-year-old son; and the somber, pock-marked valet, Marchand—gathered in the officers' squat wardroom. Cipriani remained below, in the ship's hold, deep in dice with a clutch of sailors.

Admiral Cockburn unrolled a document. "From the First Lord of the Admiralty, translated into French." As he read, the muscles in his long face twitched to suppress a grin that nonetheless disfigured it. *"It would be inconsistent with our duty to this country, and to His Majesty's allies, if we were to leave to General Bonaparte the means or opportunity of again disturbing the peace of Europe. It is therefore unavoidable that he should be restrained in his personal liberty . . ."*

The Emperor clasped his hands behind his back and squeezed his fingers numb.

Despite Cockburn's atrocious French, the meaning of his words was clear. No sanctuary, no genteel retirement outside London, no reunion with the Eaglet, no, no, no—nothing except a six-week sea voyage into the South Atlantic to exile on the remotest island in the world.

Cursed St. Helena.

At the island's name, Fanny Bertrand's sobs filled the low-slung room.

The Emperor yearned to plug his ears. Instead, he pointed at the admiral, only to withdraw his hand to conceal its shake. "I demand direct communications with the Regent."

The admiral, allowing his grin free rein, swept a bow. "Impossible. This ship's underway to the southern hemisphere."

Sailors' footsteps pounded overhead. The vessel lurched as unfurling sails caught air. Fanny writhed in her stout husband's arms while Albine, breasts spilling from her low-cut dress, waved her handkerchief to cool Fanny's manic flush. Las Cases and young Emmanuel Las Cases fidgeted in a corner, inching forward, drawing back, whispering. Montholon slumped into a chair and laughed, his high pitch tainted with hysteria.

The Emperor's mouth opened. He clamped it shut. St. Helena. Exile five thousand miles from France. With these people. He should have died in battle. Or did Marchand have that vial of poison? He could save them all a pile of trouble.

His son's "Papa-Papa" echoed in his mind. The familiar pain in his side struck deep as a dagger. He struggled to remain upright. No. He'd not bend. He'd not stumble. No matter where they sent him, he'd find a way to rescue his boy. At least his enemies held the Eaglet in a golden cage. His own upbringing had been far worse.

CLISSON: THE EMPEROR'S NOVEL

Ajaccio, Corsica, 1777
Clisson Is Eight

"Clisson!" Inside the house, his mother banged a broom against a door. "That boy had better show at school today."

"Gone," the maid, Camilla, called from within.

His mother leaned out an upstairs window to search the narrow street. "Clisson!"

Clisson, toes perched on the alleyway's foul gutter, flattened against the house's stucco wall. He held his breath against the sewer stench. When the window slammed, he gulped for air, slapped the stucco from his hands, and surveyed the street.

All clear of Mamma's spies for now.

Sprint to the corner, turn to the right.

The citadel loomed two blocks away, the harbor just beyond. Ahead, the baker's wife swept a stoop and glowered, "Clisson, get to school or I'll tell your mother."

But no schoolroom could compete, no mother's whipping could vanquish the lure of soldiers' muskets and cannonballs. He dashed past the bakery. His running feet drummed in his head: "Learn what soldiers do. Mamma says I was born for war."

On the parapet, French guards in uniforms of white and blue and red stood out against the sky. His own clothes, the color of dirt, made him disappear into the street. He ripped off his shirt and pulled it on inside out. Bright ribbons snipped from his mother's skirt streamed down his chest.

The season was dry. Donkeys grazed in the citadel's moat. At the iron gate, the sentry towered over him, poking at his homemade military decorations. But bring soldiers bread, and the Enemy welcomed a boy into its ranks. Clisson delivered his lunch to the man's outstretched hand.

Today's guard was named Jacques. That one spoke Italian and could be kind when Clisson traded olive bread for the soldier's rationed brown. The entrance was gated shut. Clisson peered between the crossbars into the army universe. In the courtyard, an officer commanded soldiers to break what had been a man. Clisson turned to Jacques.

"A thief," the guard said. "You're too young to watch. On your way."

A hammer crushed the man's fingers; another broke his wrist. A wheel groaned, tightening ropes, extending the man's arms. The screams did not stop. Clisson's stomach rose into his throat.

Giovanni, the butcher's oldest son. A brand seared a hole through his cheek. Two of the French soldiers, showing big teeth, laughed with the lieutenant. They stuck Giovanni in the side.

Clisson flinched and sidled to Jacques's hip. "Why?"

"They say he shorted our supplies and stole a gun."

Clisson tugged Jacques's sleeve, bringing the soldier's ear to his lips. "In town, they whisper that the lieutenant dishonored the butcher's daughter."

"Better not to say it, child." Jacques stared into the distance.

In the courtyard, the screams turned to groans. A soldier led a saddled white horse for the lieutenant to mount. Two guards winched open the portcullis. The guard Jacques, with Clisson cached behind his legs, snapped to attention. The lieutenant thundered through the tunnel, galloped out the gate, and disappeared down the promenade along the crescent harbor.

Clisson ducked under the grille before the bars dropped. He crept along the mossy wall and peeked into the courtyard. The guards had turned from monsters back into men. A young one on his knees vomited in a corner. Two older soldiers shielded the sick one from view; a third patted his back. Clisson would have done the same, if they had let him.

From his satchel, he pulled his lunch pouch of water tinged with wine. He caught a guard's attention and pointed to the prisoner on the rack. The guard turned his head. Clisson scanned the yard. *All clear.* He tiptoed forward.

The blood smelled stronger, flowed redder, than inside the butcher shop. The man's hands had turned to meat. Clisson forced his stomach back in place. "Giovanni," he whispered into a tattered ear. "*Sii pazienti, o amicu.* We'll avenge your death." He could taste the blood. With shaking hands, he raised his water pouch to the man's lips.

Foam from Giovanni's mouth bubbled pink. "Poc . . . ket."

Clisson glanced around. No one had heard. He felt for a pocket in Giovanni's pants.

"Back . . . under."

Clisson pushed his hand under the man's waist into a slick of blood. Giovanni's eyes widened in pain. Clisson's fingers found a folded knife in the waistband and eased it out.

"Give . . . Franco. Use in . . . my name."

Clisson stuffed the knife into his shirt and brought his pouch to Giovanni's lips, but the man's eyes rolled to the white and his mouth flopped open.

Clisson jumped back, splashing water on the dead man's chest.

Two soldiers approached: François and Alain. They'd let him hold their bayonets and carry cannonballs for their practice shots into the sea. They'd taught him military words in French.

Clisson gripped Giovanni's arm.

They were the Enemy. They must not, would not, see him tremble. Clisson denied the heaving of his stomach, the shaking of his knees. He steadied his hand to comb the dead man's hair between his fingers.

When a boy has been born into war, childhood goes missing.

Chapter 4

Napoleon

THEY ENDURED SIX DREARY WEEKS on the ocean, broken with a grog-filled celebration when they crossed the equator into the South Atlantic. Mornings, days, weeks blurred into a lifetime of salt spray, bad food, and rolling motion.

The day the voyage drew to a close, the sky was gray, the Emperor's narrow cabin too dark to read Franco Cipriani's features. More than ever, the wily jack-of-all-trades—a minor servant, as far as the British were concerned—resembled a shadow. Ocean sun had parched his face into cowhide that drooped beneath his brows and jaw. The dear fellow had lost what little fat he had. His black jacket hung loose, and the Emperor had lent him a sash to hold up his breeches. It might have been a trick of the light, but at times his Corsican compatriot appeared two-dimensional.

Marchand's voice, as precise as the black-suited valet himself, penetrated the closed door. "Sire, we're rounding the island into the harbor. Doesn't Your Majesty wish to come on deck?"

The Emperor's back muscles tightened, squaring his shoulders. He maneuvered past his tented camp bed, steadied himself against the roll of the ship, and opened the door to grimace into his servant's pockmarked face. "Tell me, what kind of man rushes to see his prison?"

Marchand flushed.

The Emperor, relenting, squeezed the valet's arm. "You go, my friend. I'll follow in a moment."

Albine de Montholon, her blue-striped dress faded from weeks at sea, elbowed past Marchand. Her smile crinkled her skin where it showed a bit of age. "May I join you, sire? To celebrate our arrival?" She curtsied to show off her thick auburn hair, dressed à la Marie Louise. She couldn't guess how much that style annoyed him.

The Emperor blocked Cipriani from her view. "You're gracious, Madame, but no, not now." Still, he caressed her rounded shoulder, traced the thin scar that ran from behind her ear down her neck. A souvenir of the French Revolution, but, like many noblewomen who had lived through it, like his own Josephine, she didn't talk about that time.

"But everyone's on deck, sire. We could . . ." She fluttered her fingers.

"Not now." He pinched her earlobe and shut the door.

Cipriani's voice filled the confined space with the guttural Corsican tongue of their youth. "Little signora's getting aggressive, is she? Scared you'll find better amusements on the island?" His long, narrow nose pressed against the cabin's porthole. "This place, Master. *Mi pari assai malu!* Very bad! Devil's castle rising out of the sea. St. Helena—what, name of a Greek lass? Turk? Saint or whore, that sort's always bent on revenge."

"Fourth century, mother of Emperor Constantine," he murmured.

Cipriani chuckled. "As good as those encyclopedia fellows, aren't you?"

"She brought us Christianity, you pagan." He nudged his henchman from the porthole.

Beyond the glass, St. Helena's sheer cliffs, brown, barren, beachless, sliced into the sea with no more grace than a sharp-edged stone. Clouds hid the high points. Not a single tree in sight. If he'd been floating on a raft in the ocean, he'd have passed the monster by.

A crooked-toothed grin creased Cipriani's weathered face. "If your lady, St. Helena, was so blessed, why name a hellhole after her? No matter. You and me won't stick around long. Got to catch ourselves an Eaglet, eh?"

The Emperor's stomach lifted at the thought of his son. "First, we punch holes in this net the British have woven about us."

Cipriani's grin grew. "Love a day with plots in it. My sailor's a born smuggler. He'll get that snuffbox to your sainted mother, with its message snug inside. There's a wager for you."

The Emperor punched the Corsican's arm. "Bet against you? Not for any odds. How about the sailor Las Cases bribed?"

Cipriani rubbed his tuft of grizzled hair. "Look here, it's not only the courier that matters. My guess? Las Cases's flapping lips'll nick that deal. He's getting mighty chummy with that blackhearted Montholon, who's so eager to lend out his wife."

The Emperor frowned. "General Montholon's not black-hearted. He's just weak."

"So say you."

"And that should be enough for you to believe it." He patted Cipriani's leather cheek. "Time to go topside. No familiarities with me in front of the others."

THE HMS *NORTHUMBERLAND* ANCHORED under eight-knot winds in St. Helena's only bay. No dock—only a wharf for small craft. The ship's longboat rowed toward shore, crammed with British officers and jostling sailors.

The Emperor separated himself from his courtiers, who had gathered in the ship's bow to gawk. He spared a quick smile for Albine, who nodded happily.

Amidships, he extracted his spyglass from his jacket and steadied his elbows on the rail. Rocky mountainsides—240 meters high, maybe 250—opened into a steep V above paltry Jamestown. Cannons bristled on fortifications halfway up the hill and from two forts on the opposite mountaintops. He calculated the range of the artillery and reordered their placement until he remembered the cannons were not his. Let them stay where they were. They'd hem him in well enough from their weak positions.

Deep in the South Atlantic, 1,200 miles south of the equator, St. Helena was no Mediterranean Elba, from which he'd escaped his first exile. Still, a quiver of anticipation passed through him. As dismal a rock as it was, the island would supply news from Europe, a hot bath, a horse to ride, a woman who didn't smell like the stinking ship, and, above all, solid ground on which to plot his future.

The back of his neck prickled. He shifted his stance at the rail. Across the deck, Admiral Cockburn and Barry O'Meara, the ship's black-haired doctor, leaned on a portside cannon, observing him. No doubt the *Northumberland*'s head jailer was reconnoitering for weakness to report to London. But that doctor, a pleasant fellow, might prove useful. After all, the Irish bore grudges against the British king. The Emperor relaxed his stony face.

Returning to his spyglass, he skimmed along the wharf. A string of Black men, barefoot and naked to their waists, ferried bundles off a boat. Nearby, a white man lounged. The fellow held a whip. African slaves? But St. Helena wasn't some plantation colony where slavery was still allowed. For all their pushing for international bans on the human trade, these English were as hypocritical as the French. But he wasn't there to negotiate treaties.

He refocused on the longboat. As it passed a tidy schooner, reached shore, and unloaded, Las Cases and young Emmanuel Las Cases joined him at the rail. He frowned down the father's and son's conspiratorial grins.

Emmanuel pointed at the longboat. "That's our courier, the tall, red-haired sailor lifting the barrel."

The Emperor dropped his hand over Emmanuel's fingers. He raised his spyglass to watch a stout, mixed-blood sailor with a sack over his shoulder lose himself among the local crowd. Eh bien! Cipriani's sailor was on his way. His heart stretched toward his mother, toward his son. Perhaps both smugglers would get through. Small victories to turn the tide.

Faint cries came from a scuffle onshore. Emmanuel's sailor bolted from the brawl.

Shouts went up.

Gunshots cracked.

Father and son Las Cases flinched.

Their sailor took a bullet in his back and tumbled into the sea. The Emperor snapped his spyglass shut. "A pity, that."

Seeing tears on Emmanuel's cheeks, he kissed the boy's high forehead. He was a handsome lad and would be more so when his slight frame took on some heft—as long as he didn't turn out to be a dandy, forever twitching at his clothing, like his chubby father. He rotated the boy away from a British marine's hearing. "No crying, young man. If we surrender to emotion, we won't survive this exile."

Emmanuel wiped his cheeks. "But the sailor. It's my fault he's dead."

Las Cases hissed at his son. "Listen, would you? Our sire's wisdom is unparalleled."

The Emperor's fingers, squeezing the rail, whitened at the knuckles. The defeated had so little choice in their companions. Perhaps this exile would teach him tolerance. An amusing, if improbable, outcome. He chucked Emmanuel's chin. "You are what, sixteen? When not much older, I was leading troops under fire. You'll see worse in life, I promise you, than the death of this sailor—a man who, after all, betrayed his country for money."

Las Cases sniffed a scented handkerchief. "The fellow should've been more careful."

"No, no, Las Cases. Only a poor workman blames his tools for failure." He paused while Las Cases twitched his lace cuffs. The man was soft, unsuited to this exile. The Emperor tucked in his own well-rounded belly. Ah, well. Tolerance. "We skirmished, we failed, we move on."

Las Cases grabbed the rail as the ship rolled. "But we've lost your *Plutarch's Lives.*"

"And the messages inside—that's worse." Emmanuel sniffed. "General Montholon'll be disappointed."

Napoleon caught hold of Las Cases's lapel. "Montholon? You told him?"

Las Cases lowered his eyes. "I thought there could be no objection."

"Think again. When I trust you with a secret assignment, I mean it to be secret." The Emperor bared his teeth in a false smile. "I said show no emotion. Fear not. Sooner or later, I'll get word to my Eaglet that I haven't forgotten him. Tell that to Montholon."

ALONE IN HIS CRAMPED QUARTERS, the Emperor threw himself onto his camp bed. Despite the cologne-soaked rags Marchand had strewn about, the cabin stank as it had from the day he had entered it. A coffin of pine and pitch. He kicked the bulkhead. The red-haired sailor was dead, his beloved *Plutarch's Lives* lost, instead of carrying coded messages to the Eaglet. Eh bien, one must be nimble on the battlefield, make sacrifices to win.

But Montholon had known about Las Cases's sailor. Twice over the years he'd saved that man from disgrace—once for embezzlement, once for claiming false battle honors. A trained louse, as his mother said? Or a traitor. Yet when his entourage was so small, everyone had a use. He shook off the image of Albine's open thighs.

Still, in one month, two at most, when Cipriani's sailor fulfilled his task, his little black-gowned mother would open a snuffbox so familiar she didn't need working eyes to retrieve its secrets. When she learned the message inside, she'd leave Rome for the imperial court in Vienna, establish herself as the Eaglet's doting grandmother.

One day, she'd take the child for a carriage ride. They'd turn a corner. Blocking the path would be Cipriani and his men. Or he'd be standing there. Either way, the boy would grow up in Corsica. Or America. Someplace where they cared about more than cravats and waltz steps.

A soft knock interrupted the Emperor's musings.

Albine de Montholon.

He let her in. Before he could turn, Albine pressed herself against his back. Her arms stretched around his waist. He leaned his forehead against the door while her disembodied hands untied his pants and groped inside.

Ah! He had been right when he had forbidden Montholon to marry this woman. Thank God Montholon had disobeyed him. She was little better than a courtesan, but a welcome solution to an awkward need. Truth be told, he liked Albine. She was the only one on this journey who never complained.

The warmth of her body rubbing against his backside, her soft hands caressing his growing member, took over his senses. He clamped his lips to suppress a cry of pleasure.

"Now," he said, when at last he wiped himself, "we take care of you."

He lay on his back on the narrow camp bed. She straddled him, her bodice open to free her fleshy breasts, her skirts flowing over him. As was her habit, she was naked under her dress. He reached beneath her silks to give her the little pleasures she liked. She was still circling on his hand when he murmured, "Albine, I need you to do something."

She dropped her lashes and repositioned herself to take hold of him.

He smiled. "No, no, not that. I want you to watch your husband. Find out if he's working against me." He reached back under her skirt. "Or are you in league with him, my sweet?"

She rubbed her breasts on his chest and kissed him.

Afterward, she lay on his chest, satisfied, dozing. He nudged her. "Do you love him?"

She startled. "Who?"

"Charles, your husband. Do you love him? Does he love you?"

She pulled out of his arms. "You have no right to ask."

He tilted his head.

She bit her lip. "Your Majesty."

He drew her close and kissed the scar behind her ear. He liked this woman. He liked all forms of loyalty.

Albine

BACK IN OUR CABIN, MY NAILS dug into my palms. So foolish, so dangerous of Charles to make my Emperor suspect him.

I crossed my arms and squeezed, pretending Napoleon still held me. Before we'd shared a bed, I had thought he would be remote, noble, a marble statue, a romantic painting. Instead, I got warm flesh, a chuckle, a fart between the sheets. Human, yes, but a better species. He plundered kingdoms; I schemed about how to pay my milliner. He dashed off constitutions while I stole candlesticks. Yet we crossed our different bridges to reach the same pleasure island.

I wondered at the softness of his white hands, the lack of hair on his chest. And when I massaged his feet, to my delight, I spied the famous scar on his calf. He told me of the British spear in the Battle of Toulon when he was twenty-six (a story every Frenchman knew, but the Emperor reveled in its retelling).

"Bad luck," I said, my lips traveling the scar's faint ridge. His moan told me he liked that.

"No, no, good luck," he answered. "They didn't amputate the leg."

When I touched my own scar, he drew a line from ear to ear under my chin.

"Good luck," he said. "You had it, too, or you wouldn't be here. But, my poor Albine, yours taught you fear, while mine made me an optimist."

I shook myself. There I was, forty-three years old, on my third husband, countless men in between. Far too late to be enchanted. Not a time to fall in love.

The cabin door squeaked. Charles entered.

I whirled on him. "Fool, he suspects you."

He shoved his way to his latest cognac bottle. "Why would he?"

"Probably because of that sailor with the book. You should have told me before you turned informant."

"I don't answer to you." He raised that aristocratic nose. "You're not the only one with brains, though that's not the body part you employ, is it?"

I waved aside the insult. "If only you had waited till we were on land, where there will be more people to cast the blame on. He must have seen you talking to the admiral. Or that rat Cipriani overheard you."

"Nonsense, my dear wife—may I still call you that? I've made a point of talking to Admiral Cockburn only when the Emperor is at hand."

"Who, then? Who did you sell the information to? You said it was the admiral."

He leaned into my face till I tasted his sweet cognac breath. "Dr. O'Meara."

I laughed. "Clever, indeed. The Emperor's convinced that Irishman's on his side. And did you get paid today?"

Charles plunked gold pieces on our bunk. One, two, three.

"Nice." I helped myself to one. "But in the future, we work together."

I would have said more, but the lowering of another longboat drew Charles on deck to watch. I bit my new coin. How unambitious my husband was. Only three gold coins for Napoleon's hide? But Charles was right to stop Las Cases's sailor plot. If Napoleon was going to escape from St. Helena, it would be with help from the Montholons and no one else.

The ship lurched on its anchor, toppling me onto the bunk. The coin—my gold coin!—slipped from my hand and rolled. I scrambled like a spider on the cabin deck till at last my fingers curled around it. Minutes passed, I don't know how many, while I huddled in a corner, tracing the raised surface, moistening it with my breath, shining it against my skirt, my heart racing till the screams in my head quieted. The cabin was empty, I told myself. A cabin. Not a prison cell. No one to steal the coin. The stench, the peril, the hunger of my Revolutionary prison receded. The past faded. The present reformed.

I dug through my pockets. Half a cracker stolen from the galley yesterday at lunch. Only that? I pinched my arm in punishment. Once again, I'd let my stores of food run low. Still, I crammed the cracker into my mouth.

No need to shake, I told myself, no need to fear the morning roll call of those whose day it was to die. I clutched my thighs, anchoring myself to the present. But somewhere in the distance, a bell began to clang, clang, clang, clang, clang.

The morning bell. The guillotine list. The present collapsed in shards.

I fled. Fumbling in a dark passageway, I found a ladder and scrambled out of that hellhole of a prison, up, up, to where sunlight blinded me. Behind the glare, a hundred faces. A scream burned my throat. A man shook my arm. His body blocked the faces. His head blocked the sun. His voice dragged me back.

My sight cleared.

Francesco Cipriani.

I knew the present again.

The Corsican bent in a stiff half bow. "Better now, Madame Albine?"

I fumbled a curtsy. "I needed air."

He cracked a knuckle. "Get that way myself."

His kindness didn't fool me. That man recognized the terror in my flight. I might as well have been naked.

Chapter 5

Napoleon

THE EMPEROR WAS THE LAST of his entourage brought ashore. As British sailors rowed, moonlit water dripped from the longboat's oars. The bow's oil lamp shimmered on the black water. At the wharf, wood thumped against wood as waves knocked the boat about.

Two giant hands hoisted the Emperor to land.

The Emperor stared at the helpful dockhand. He was over two meters tall, a meter broad. Torchlight illuminated his pale, craggy face.

"Begging pardon, sir," the Hercules mumbled.

The Emperor bowed. "Merci—er, non. Thank you."

The man gaped. "I'll be damned."

The admiral spoke from the longboat. "Yes, you probably will be, considering you sound like a Yankee. Step aside."

The big man's mouth tightened into a surly frown.

The Emperor fastened his intense gaze on the ugly face. Slowly, the dockhand removed the stocking cap from his head and clutched it against his chest. From his height, the giant grinned down on him.

"Thank you." The Emperor allowed his eyes to smile. "My friend."

Hercules's grin stretched wider. He limped away, favoring his left leg.

Two sailors boosted the admiral off the longboat.

Cockburn stamped his boots. "Even an old salt like me is happy to be on land." He took the Emperor's arm, and they walked the wharf as though on an after-dinner stroll. At the end of a white wall stood a crudely made signpost. Its east-pointing arrow read AFRICA 1,244 MILES; a western one read BRAZIL 2,156 MILES. The north arrow proclaimed LONDON 5,124 MILES. On one pointing south, someone had painted a skull and crossbones alongside THIS WAY TO HELL.

Clouds billowed in, obscuring half the stars. Under the remaining light, the longboat receded across the bay toward the *Northumberland*'s masted silhouette. Shivers crawled up the Emperor's spine. His prison door had slammed shut.

HE SPENT THE NIGHT IN JAMESTOWN at Porteous House Inn, in quarters more cramped than the ship's. Alone in his narrow room, the Emperor unrolled the French newspaper the admiral had supplied. A Paris paper, his first since he had surrendered to the British three months earlier. He skimmed the articles. Blood rushed to his face.

He flung the paper against a wall. The admiral—bastard!—had circled the item.

Marie Louise. She'd gone too far. To live openly with that Austrian colonel. At least his own affairs had been—were—discreet.

Von Neipperg. That simpering courtier, whose eye patches matched his vests. He'd have the man shot, his body fed to pigs.

But he couldn't get to him. Or her. Damn them.

He paced the room, four strides from wall to wall.

A strumpet empress, cavorting like a widow while he was still alive. If he hadn't seen the Eaglet ripped from her bleeding body, he'd never have believed the woman was mother to his son. Thank God Marchand's mother was there to watch over the poor child.

No time to wait for sailors and snuffboxes to get to Madame Mère. Cipriani must return to Europe, kidnap the boy, hide out in the mountains of Corsica, raise the Eaglet to be a man.

He flung himself into a chair. Madame Mère and Marie Louise. Always, mothers and betrayal. He hung his head. A grief he and the Eaglet shared.

Tomorrow he'd work on Cipriani's voyage. Tonight . . . He dug through his trunk and pulled out the metal manuscript box. When his son was old enough, the Eaglet would read that a Bonaparte forges a mother's shame into cold steel.

CLISSON: THE EMPEROR'S NOVEL

Ajaccio, Corsica, 1779

Clisson peeked through a split in the wooden door. His father was dressed in a powdered wig, silver brocade coat, red high-heeled shoes with silver buckles. He tucked a tricorne hat under one arm. He didn't look like a Corsican.

Mamma had bound her hair in a scarf that matched her tiered peasant skirts. Clisson picked out where the bright fabric was missing ribbons. "Husband," she said, "you've grown too fine for your family. Even when you speak Corsican, you sound dainty, like the French."

His father answered with a threatening hand.

Mamma stamped her tiny feet. "And discussing philosophy? Is that what you call card playing? How much did you lose? You go too far with your fancy friends."

Father rubbed his long fingers. "You should be glad I have such friends. Ungrateful woman, they promise me a better position. We'll be rich."

Mamma's voice dropped to a whisper. "We're more likely to be branded as traitors to the Cause."

"The Cause? The Corsican Cause is dead." Father touched a handkerchief to his nose. "We, however, must live. I for one intend to live well."

"Then let me manage the new governor. We both know what he wants." Mamma brushed her body against Father.

Father tucked the handkerchief into the sleeve of his brocade coat. His hands explored Mamma's curves, unwound her scarf, and sank into her hair.

Clisson scampered down the hall, his father's library the destination. There, he thumbed through leather-bound books he wasn't allowed to touch. He couldn't read the ones in French or Latin, but they smelled the same as those in Italian. He liked their weight in his hands.

The stacks reached to the ceiling. He counted the number of books on three shelves, averaged to fifty-two, then counted the number of shelves and multiplied: 1,248, plus seventeen on the floor, four on the desk. Father would never miss one. Anyway, they all belonged to the family.

Heels clicked in the hall. He stuffed a book called *Plutarch* in his satchel and hid behind a drapery until the footsteps faded.

That week, Mamma and the maid, Camilla, sewed new black pants that buckled at Clisson's and his brother Joseph's knees. They transformed a tablecloth into white shirts for the boys. Mamma sacrificed her third-best skirt for their red waist sashes. A cousin provided shoes her own sons had outgrown.

The French governor sent a carriage for the long trip up the coast. Under the sunset, his mansion glowed pink. White balustrades, in stiff rows like soldiers' ranks, guarded the front. Inside, servants in emerald uniforms stood at attention. Clisson squeaked his heels across the marble floor.

In the garden, he and his brother sat on a stone bench while the perfumed man and Father talked French, Mamma smiling on. Clisson held his feet still, his face empty. He didn't lower his eyes, like meek Joseph. He riveted them on the man's wrinkled throat.

The Frenchman brought out bolts of silk, a box of white flour, red shoes for Mamma's feet. Father beamed as Mamma draped herself in lace. She claimed the old gentleman's arm. When they disappeared into the house, Father stayed in the garden, the Frenchman's wine red on his lips.

In the parlor after supper, the man kissed Joseph on the crown of his head. He said the gentle brother should be a priest or maybe a politician because he was anxious to please. "But this one, this Clisson, must be a soldier, or perhaps, with his arrogance, an innkeeper."

Father chuckled. "Without doubt, he belongs in the military, but how shall it be arranged, Governor? We Corsicans have no school for officers. His mother wouldn't be pleased if he were a common soldier."

"Is that what you wish for your son? A French military education?" The Frenchman fondled Clisson's mother's hand. "Well, then, so it shall be done, although the king may regret educating the rebel."

Father placed his hand over the man's and Mamma's. "Oh, no, not at all. Our Clisson's a proper Frenchman, born the very year France seized Corsica."

His parents and the governor laughed. They didn't know Clisson had learned enough French from the citadel soldiers to understand what they said.

That night when the sky was darkest, Clisson slid out of bed. He snaked on his stomach across the cold floor, careful not to wake his brother. Hesitating on the threshold, he studied the corridor until the blackness dissolved into chairs, tables, and portraits that lined the Frenchman's walls. As he tiptoed along the hall, he counted the doors until he reached his parents' bed-chamber. Bit by bit, cringing at the creaks, he eased their door until his head pushed through the opening. His snoring father sprawled on the mattress, an arm flung across his mother's belly.

Underneath Clisson's nervous feet, a floorboard squeaked. His mother jerked up, fear naked on her moonlit face. The man at her side stirred.

Clisson let out a cry. Not his father. A lecherous rooster, that wet-mouthed Frenchman, lay in the bed.

His mother had paid for his schooling.

Napoleon

THE EMPEROR TOUCHED A CANDLE to the admiral's newspaper. *Pooft!* Marie Louise's perfidy shot up in flame. No one in his entourage need know he knew. He had a certain dignity to maintain.

Near midnight, a noise awakened him. He tiptoed past the cot where Marchand snored. Peeking around the casement of the half-open window, he surveyed the garden.

Two British soldiers, shuffling through guard duty, disappeared around a corner. That was all the security he warranted? So, the English assumed the island's isolation could hold Napoleon Bonaparte in check. They would learn their mistake.

The tree by his window rustled.

He knelt beneath the window frame, waiting, listening. *Tap-tap* came from the tree. He *tap-tap*ped the window. The tree *tap-tap*ped. Not two meters away, Cipriani, dressed in black, hunched in the tree's crotch. The Corsican held up a black bag. The Emperor pushed the window fully open. Cipriani tossed his bundle.

The weight hit the Emperor's chest, and he stumbled backward. Inside he found a rope ladder, crafted from fishing net. Like when they were children in Corsica and sneaked out at night. He woke Marchand.

"But, sire," the valet said, "down is one thing, up quite another."

"Come, come. I'm not an invalid."

"But Dr. O'Meara says—"

"Doctors are fools. Help me untangle this thing. We'll secure it to the bedpost."

After the soldiers completed their next round through the garden, Marchand lowered the ladder. The Emperor scrambled down, leaping the last meter. Cipriani hurried him into a dark patch behind a boxwood hedge.

"Are we off?" he whispered to the Corsican. "You've found a way already?"

The Corsican's crooked teeth twinkled in the moonlight. "Hardly, Master. Even I'm not that clever, but give me time, give me time. Don't you want to stretch your legs?"

"Where to?"

"You'll see. Been scouting the island while the rest of you pottered about."

Four dark alleys led to the edge of the meager town. From there, the route meandered uphill through thigh-high brush. The tangy salt breeze, the musty soil, the spice of rich vegetation, Cipriani on the path before him: they all reminded the Emperor of his youth in Corsica. He sucked the flavors in and blew them out, clearing his lungs, clearing his head. He cursed the stitch in his side.

They came upon a hulk of a farmhouse, a goat and a cow staked in the yard. A horse whinnied at their approach. A voice called out. They lay low in a thicket as a man strode around his yard. A door slammed, and they were on their way again.

He tugged the Corsican's sleeve. "Dogs?"

"Cats. A ton of cats to catch the tons of rats. Watch your step here. Stay low. We'll take the road, then pick up a downhill path. Better for you than this uphill slog."

The road was lined in orange-trunked trees. The Emperor stopped short, holding his side, panting. "How much farther, man?"

"What? Can't handle a little midnight stroll?" Cipriani peered down the road. "Left here. If we turned right, we'd come upon the governor's mansion. Ah, here's the spot."

They dropped onto a grassy slope. A clearing lay ahead, sheltered on three sides with stone cliffs on which flowering vines draped like a woven tapestry. Nearby a brook gurgled, happy as a baby.

"Man-made grotto?" the Emperor asked.

"Nah, locals say the island herself created this hollow. They call it the Valley of the Geraniums. Spring water over there. Wandered here earlier. Thought you'd like it."

"I do. Reminds me of a cathedral. Let's taste the water." He took a step.

A huge Black arm knocked him off his feet.

Cipriani caught him. Together they scrambled backward.

A second Black man, taller and wider still, shoved them into the bare chest of the first. That man flung them into a third set of muscled arms. Out of the shadows appeared more men, their Black chests scarred, their faces painted ghostly white. One man was missing a left ear; one had the letter "R" branded on his forehead. Two wielded shovels. All had hands strong enough to crush a skull. Their mouths opened. A devil's chant filled the air.

"Shit, oh, shit," the Corsican said.

The human ring tightened around them, stamping, chanting, hissing, poking, swatting. The scars, the shovels, the eyes flashed white. The Emperor and Cipriani cringed against each other, their arms shields for their faces.

The Emperor tasted blood. He must have bitten his tongue. Afraid to spit, he swallowed. "Stilettos no use. Use your English. Negotiate."

The Corsican cleared his throat. "Look here, good fellows—"

Two of the men stepped apart. A stocky Black man with a red paper crown on his white hair entered the circle. He lifted the Emperor's chin, smiled, and murmured. The others dropped to their knees.

The Emperor's breath caught. "Franco, they know who I am. Tell him we're all prisoners together. You kneel, too." He bowed. "Good evening, Monsieur."

The leader pointed to himself. "Mahafaly."

The Emperor extended his hand. In the moonlight its whiteness shone, whether to his advantage or his disadvantage, he had no way to judge. "Good evening, Monsieur Mahafaly. I am the Emperor Napoleon."

Mahafaly combined their hands into a single fist and thrust it to the sky. His men muttered. He drew the Emperor's hand through his arm and guided him into the clearing while the others hustled Cipriani along behind them.

In a cove near the cascading spring, a dozen slaves appeared out of the shadows. They gathered around the naked corpse of an old Black man. Women dressed in colorful cloth formed a line to the water, filling, passing, emptying, passing, and refilling two copper cups. As the women poured, the men rotated the body. The man's back was flayed with crossed and layered stripes. They turned him over. The Emperor flinched. Scars covered his skin.

Mahafaly hovered his hands over the corpse while chanting in a language the Emperor couldn't fathom. It wasn't close to English, Egyptian, Greek, French, or any other he had heard. The others answered like a congregation at a solemn Mass. When the chanting stopped, Mahafaly placed his paper crown on the Emperor's head.

"Franco, God love you, as best you can, repeat what I say." The Emperor held his hands above the body and recited the only prayer his mother had managed to drum into his head. *"Ave Maria, gratia plena, Dominus tecum, benedicta tu . . ."*

He reached for the Corsican's hand. "Now, *o amicu*, we bow to the leader, then to the others. I give him back his crown. We walk away. Don't look back. Understand?"

The slave with the branded forehead escorted them out of the hollow, treading close, jabbing Cipriani's back.

"Keep going, Franco."

"Right-o. Ain't likely to stop with this fellow on my tail."

"But slowly, with dignity."

"Doing my best, considering I pissed myself half an hour ago."

At the edge of the road, they found themselves alone. The Emperor punched Cipriani's arm. "Shit, indeed. Got other sights to show me?"

"About as tight a box as we've been in, brother." The Corsican chewed on his knuckles. "What the hell was that, anyway?"

"No different than a Christian funeral. What hypocrites these British are, pushing to end international slave trade yet maintaining slaves where it suits their purposes."

"End slavery? They got hundreds here."

"Never pays to mistreat the people you rule. I should know after my disaster with the slaves of Saint-Domingue." The Emperor rubbed his jaw. "Speaking of Haiti . . ."

"What're you thinking, Master?"

The Emperor sniffed. "I'm thinking tonight you better change your stinking breeches. Tomorrow, find out how many slaves live here." He *tap-tap*ped Cipriani's chest.

Chapter 6

Albine

INDOLENT CHARLES SLEPT IN. Me, I yearned to walk, although the earth rolled beneath my feet as if the ship were still under them. I tottered down the inn's musty stairway, lurching between its banisters. In the dim entrance hall, a guard opened the door, and I emerged on the front steps. Sunshine cleared my head.

But the air! I almost spat it out. It bore the taste of the sea, all fish and salt and humidity, not an iota different from onboard ship. But oh, the joy of cobblestones, hard and unforgiving through the soles of my shoes. I never wanted to tread shipboard planks again.

I gathered my skirts and ran uphill on the main street, past cheery two-story buildings painted white, sky blue, and dark ocean. A tavern . . . another inn, not so nice as ours . . . a chandler shop with hemp ropes dangling in the window . . . a cheese-and-sausage store, and (I almost fell to my knees) a building calling itself an emporium. In its window, a bolt of cloth, a straw hat, a peacock feather, men's riding gloves. Solomon's Emporium: locked and dark inside. Pressing my face to the glass panes, I glimpsed a wall of apothecary jars. Dried hams, onions, garlic hanging from the ceiling. I knocked and knocked. "Solomon, open up. It's been so long since I've had anything new."

"Madame, may I help you?" a deep voice behind me asked.

Startled, I turned to encounter a blue-eyed English lieutenant (according to his stripes and with a rope of gold braid caught under an epaulette), slim bodied but with lovely power in the bulge of his muscles.

"English? Oh, no, I don't speak it." I dipped a curtsy to show off my breasts and the nicely turned ankle (so I've been told) that peeked below my raised hem.

My almost handsome officer switched to educated French. "Solomon's opens at nine o'clock, Madame. Did you arrive on the *Northumberland*?"

His precise uniform reminded me how stained my dress was, how my scalp itched for a wash. I grew shy. "Kind sir, I hoped to acquire some soap. You must know what a trial the voyage is."

He bowed. "What marvelous luck. I laid by some rose-scented soap to send to my sister. Much nicer than any you'll find here. You're at Porteous House? I'll have a servant deliver it." A gentle charm overflowed those blue eyes. "Your name, Madame?"

"Albine de Montholon. And really, you shouldn't."

"Lieutenant Basil Jackson. And really, I must."

Rose-scented soap? Marvelous luck, indeed. Nonetheless, as Lieutenant Jackson sauntered down the street, I paced in front of Solomon's Emporium till it opened.

Napoleon

THE EMPEROR AWOKE TO A RACKET in the street below. Throwing a boot across the room, he cursed the stomp of British hooves, the bark of British army orders, a British bugle's call. Too few guards at night, too many troops in daylight. What dolt ran this army? He snapped at poor Marchand for the lack of hot water. To his disgust, he vomited while the valet held the bowl. Land sickness, Marchand opined.

The valet barred the generals from the room until Bertrand, his jackboots polished, his tarnished sword at his side, barged through the man's defenses. Montholon trailed his fellow general with long, hesitant strides.

"Sire." Bertrand laid his gloved hand over the medals on his sturdy chest. "Without the proper invitation—and that invitation should come through me, your grand marshal—you must not ride with these British troops."

"Must not, Bertrand? *Must not?*" The Emperor pivoted on Montholon. "And you? Have *you* no orders for me?"

Montholon turned from the window. "I never question Your Majesty's judgment."

The Emperor searched the general's ferret features. "What do you see out there?" He plucked the curtain from Montholon's hand.

Across the square, Albine, her bodice squeezing familiar breasts into view, peered in a shop window. She had no money to spend, unless her husband had filched some from the common treasury.

"Where did she get—" The Emperor broke off.

A small Black boy burst from an alley. He sped past Albine and into the roadway as two mounted British soldiers rounded the uphill bend, in full gallop toward the wharf. And the child in between.

Albine hurled herself into the road.

For a split second, the boy and Albine disappeared behind thrashing hooves, a blur of horses, the scarlet uniforms of the men. The riders continued unchecked.

An oath escaping Montholon's lips turned to prayer.

Albine and the child stood entwined, safe on the walk. She shook the little one by the collar, swatted his bottom, hugged him, and sent him on his way. Out of her reach, the child bowed like a tiny gentleman and scurried uphill.

The Emperor released the breath he hadn't known he was holding.

A church bell clanged nine. The shop door opened. Albine vanished inside.

The Emperor patted Montholon's arm. "Good, brave woman," he muttered, before turning to General Bertrand. "Eh bien. You and Montholon refuse to join the escort. Me, I'll keep them waiting half an hour. That'll maintain our dignity. I must see this Longwood House where we're to be billeted." He stretched. "Mon Dieu, more than anything, I long to ride a horse." He gave his slight, sweet smile. "Though I shall avoid trampling civilians."

Dismissing the generals, he took out his writing box to fill the half hour. First, last night's slave gathering; now, Albine's saving a Black child. Destiny had a habit of appearing in unexpected places.

CLISSON: THE EMPEROR'S NOVEL

Ajaccio, Corsica, 1779

The next day at dawn, the family waited in the governor's grand entrance hall. Mamma wound and unwound the lace scarf around her ruffled hair while Father slapped silk gloves against his palm. While no one watched, Clisson bumped his brother off a bench. The old Frenchman sent his valet to bid them farewell. Father brushed a crystal vase to the marble floor. The majordomo called for the carriage.

As the coach rumbled home, no one spoke. When they paused along the road, Clisson slung his leather satchel across his chest and wandered inland toward the woods, to relieve himself, he said. Out of sight, he sprinted for the hills. At first, it simply felt good to run, his feet pulsing in new shoes, his arms wheeling free.

He heard his family's curses on the wind. "Clisson! Clisson!"

As the slope steepened, trees gave way to thicket. Dense juniper tripped him up; buckthorn ripped his skin. His new black pants tore at the knee. He crammed a stick in the pants' waist—now he wore a gun. A branch snared his sash; he pulled it free. He unknotted the red cloth from his waist and twisted it around his head. He was a lit fuse, and when his wick burned down, he'd explode. He squished berries to bloody his shirt. He was a wounded hero in the war. The Plutarch book bounced in his satchel.

Truth emerged, as stark as his island's granite peaks. His parents planned to sell him, as they had sold themselves. He, a true Corsican, born in revolution, destined to free the homeland.

"Let them turn traitor," he muttered against his knuckles. "I know who I am." He'd scour the maquis thickets, the landscape's refuge for Corsica's rebels. He'd find their camp. He'd join them.

As dusk cooled the air, Corsica's dark mountains drew Clisson upward. At last, he achieved what seemed the crest, but the high ground opened to a plain, great peaks spires on three sides. He shuffled forward in the night, sure the next mountains hid rebel friends.

The moon escaped a cloud bank.

Shivers crept along his spine. Across the plain, a horde of giants marched. Twenty—no, twenty-four—huge soldiers aligned in three straight ranks. Clisson dropped to his knees, cowering, watching the ramrod figures. Each wore a giant helmet, each carried a sword. A drum beat in his head.

"If I had a cannon, I'd tell these apparitions with one salvo," he whispered.

He crawled toward the Enemy. The massive warriors soared to three times his height. They didn't flinch at his approach. They held their swords and daggers low, shields at their sides. Together the soldiers melded into one fearsome battle monster yet became twenty-four men when picked apart.

He sprang to his feet and thrust his thin chest toward the twenty-four. "I am Clisson. Destiny sends me to fight for Corsica."

They stood in silent reply.

"I was born for war!" He blasted through their ranks, racing from one to another. His hand smacked each soldier, the stings reverberating to his shoulder.

The warriors didn't move. He'd turned them all to stone. Panic spurred his feet. He ran, afraid to look back. He slammed into a soft, thickset thing and screamed. A sheepskin-covered man enveloped Clisson, capturing his flailing arms, smothering his face, stroking his wild curls.

Clisson collapsed in tears.

He was only nine.

Napoleon

As Marchand helped him on with his boots, the Emperor twitched the man's earlobe. "You're my own dear Chand-Chand, nursemaid to me as your mother is to my boy. No need to blush. And here, give some coins to Madame Albine."

On the inn's steps, he shaded his eyes. Around him, paint on Jamestown's squat buildings peeled in air as humid as it had been onboard ship. Across the street in the entrance of Solomon's Emporium, a wizened, silver-bearded man bowed. A yarmulke topped his long hair.

And there, in a shadow behind the old fellow, lurked Albine. She blew a kiss. He raised his riding crop in acknowledgment. She had located a perfect ally. Jews the world over knew Emperor Napoleon had lifted Europe's ancient restrictions against their tribe. There was more to Albine than he realized.

A British soldier offered him the reins of a snorting white stallion. Admiral Cockburn leaned down from atop his own jittery mount. "He's called Bucephalus, after Alexander the Great's horse. I thought he would suit you."

The Emperor flashed the red-haired admiral his sweetest smile.

Uphill—for the island seemed either uphill or downhill, with very little flat—crowds had collected. British soldiers formed ranks to press the gawkers three deep against the buildings, clearing a passage on the road. Napoleon nodded at the turnout. He felt his best when on horseback in white knee breeches, with a few medals sprinkled across his green chasseur jacket, his sideways bicorne hat on his head. To these island dwellers in the South Atlantic, he had to be more exotic than a giraffe.

Admiral Cockburn maneuvered to his side. "The crowd's been warned to stay silent, Your Excellency, but a lot of people want a look at you."

"No doubt still more would show up for my execution." He tapped his horse's flanks.

Their horses haunch to haunch, they led the military parade. Despite the humidity, despite the enemy soldiers surrounding him, his chest expanded with his old exuberance. He turned to Cockburn. "Bertrand tells me you were involved in the burning of America's capital. As one who's been slandered with the burning of Moscow, I'm curious about your experience. In my case, I captured the Russian incendiaries and shot them."

The admiral stared ahead. "We had our orders. I hope to be remembered for more honorable tasks."

The Emperor softened his voice. "Most likely, you'll be remembered for escorting me."

The admiral spurred his horse.

Above Jamestown, a narrow road clung to the mountainside. After the first mile, the brown, arid hills opened to a verdant valley. At the base of a narrow waterfall spilling over a heart-shaped ridge, a pleasant estate lay tucked among manicured gardens. He filled his lungs with sweet, earthy air. Perhaps St. Helena's rough exterior hid a tender center.

Farther up the hill, they reached a crowded crossroads. A man, leading African slaves bent under heavy loads, cracked his whip to make way for the military parade. The admiral and the first two guards crossed through the intersection.

The Emperor raised one hand. The British troops behind him halted.

Six large Black men labored by. Three had bundles strapped to their backs with ropes that strained against their scarred chests. The others shouldered wooden barrels. They kept their gazes to the ground, except the last, who jutted his chin at the Emperor. A branded letter "R" stood out on that one's forehead. The overseer snapped a whip against the man's ankle.

When they'd passed, the Emperor motioned the troops forward.

Across the road, the red-faced admiral jerked his horse's head. "What, sir, do you think you're doing, giving orders to my troops? How dare you? The military doesn't stop for Africans."

The Emperor watched the slaves struggle off. "If not the men themselves, respect the burden they carry. But this place isn't some plantation colony. Why allow slavery here?"

The admiral shrugged. "Out of London's sight, out of London's mind."

With a finger flick, the Emperor restarted the military procession along the high, winding road. The wind picked up, and he clamped his bicorne more firmly on his head. Mist moved in and out. His thighs burned from weeks of inactivity on the *Northumberland*.

The admiral led them through a stone gateway marked LONGWOOD.

Beyond the gate lay an open plain. On two sides, the green field dropped into crevasses. Constant wind had forced some sparse pines to grow their branches all in one direction. In the middle of the flatland squatted a tumbledown farmhouse, part of its roof caved in. A few hundred yards beyond, a British regiment bivouacked beneath a triangular lookout peak.

The Emperor swallowed. "Longwood House?"

"Longwood House," Admiral Cockburn answered.

The Emperor's heart chilled as he trotted toward the dilapidated structure. In the yard, a rat scurried between the hooves of his horse, almost unseating him. Inside, his foot crashed through a rotten floor-board; the ceiling dripped with mold. Shutters rattled. The dining room's roof opened to the sky. Dust covered every surface.

The Emperor gripped Cockburn's shoulder. "I petitioned your government for sanctuary. What is this? A residence or a tomb?"

The admiral's rusty color deepened. "The place isn't ready, but you can't stay in Jamestown. Too close to the docks."

The Emperor stomped outside, his boots *squish-squish*ing in the boggy soil.

On the ride back, the weather cleared as they approached the estate under the heart-shaped waterfall. A signpost named it the Briars. At the sound of the hooves, a stooped Black gardener in a straw hat dropped his spade, snatched up his child, and trundled toward the main house. The little boy, a bit older than the Eaglet, peeped his cheery, round face over the slave's hunched shoulder and saluted.

Before he realized it, the Emperor saluted back. He reined in his horse. "Here, Admiral. I like this place. See if the owners will billet me while you repair that ramshackle farm."

A tall, well-dressed, mustached man stepped out of the house. The admiral called to him.

A pretty maiden with tangled curls, a dusty skirt hiked to her knees, burst from behind the man. She raced down the path, ducked under the nose of the admiral's skittish horse, and slid to a stop at the Emperor's stirrup. Peeking through chestnut lashes, she dropped into a curtsy. The slave child peered from behind her skirt.

"*Bienvenue à Sainte-Hélène*, Monsieur Bonaparte," she said. "*Je m'appelle* Betsy Balcombe."

He lifted his hat. "My dear, you arrive like an unexpected rose. And you speak French beautifully. Admiral, if they'll have me, I'll stay here until Longwood's ready."

Betsy clapped. "Yes, yes, stay in our summer pavilion. Oh, everyone'll be so jealous. Come, Tobyson!" She grabbed the little boy's hand and skipped toward the house. "Father!"

The Emperor surveyed the tumbling waterfall, the thriving garden, and, most of all, the cheerful girl pulling her father toward them. Too young for dalliance, but charming, fresh, full of life, like his beloved nieces. And this Briars, unlike Longwood's plain, was close to Jamestown and the port. His people—Albine—could come and go. Who knew what Cipriani's spy work might uncover?

Behind him, hooves sounded on the road rising out of Jamestown. Young Emmanuel Las Cases, hatless, his shirt half-buttoned, rode donkeyback up the hill. At the Briars' gate the boy swung off his mount, yelling, "Sire, sire, they arrested my father. They've taken him away."

The Emperor whirled on his escort.

The admiral stood in his stirrups. "I wouldn't worry. Provided the fellow knows nothing about a certain dead sailor."

Chapter 7

Albine

DO YOU THINK MY HUSBAND secured us a room in the Briars?
Of course not. We remained in Jamestown, marooned in musty
Porteous House, isolated from the Emperor. Charles excused his
lapse, saying he thought I'd be happier among the shops.

Only two days off the ship, but my first uphill trek to the Briars
killed my urge to walk. I arrived at the gate, hem soiled, curls snarled,
armpits wet. Across the lawn, under the cool shade of broad-leaved
trees, a gaggle of British ladies (most younger, some prettier, than I
felt) gawked at my dishevelment.

In the Emperor's one-room pavilion, valet Marchand acted
the general. At his barked commands, servants removed furniture
Napoleon didn't want, connected the iron rods of his camp bed,
draped the bed's green tent, shelved a hundred books. Within
moments, the Eaglet, Marie Louise, and divorced, deceased (always
valued) Josephine stared down from the bright green walls.

The Emperor kissed my hand, promised a tour of the nearby
waterfall, and suggested my visit would be welcome in a day or two.
Marchand marched me out. My dawdling husband arrived to have
the Emperor's door shut on his aquiline nose.

On the downhill trek, rain clouds rolled in from the gray ocean,
obscuring paltry Jamestown in the valley below. I slid on a pebbly
scree, landing on my bottom. My hands were scraped, my dress
ruined. I made no effort to get up.

Charles lifted me to my feet. "Why the sour mood, my girl?"

"Did you see the women?"

He paused in dusting my gown. "Well-bred British women. Nothing to worry you."

I shivered.

An hour later, in the quiet of our room, I interrupted his perusal of the latest newssheet. "One, I think, was the daughter of the house—the girl young Emmanuel raptured over. Sparkling little blonde? I tell you, Napoleon will eat that fresh virgin for dessert."

"And I tell *you*, you're the most vulgar woman I know." Charles retreated behind his paper.

The day had delivered too many uncertainties. Without planning to, I burst into tears.

Charles tucked his paper under an arm and stomped out.

Our chamber's silence, echoing the emptiness in my chest, quelled my sobs. Anyway, Napoleon wasn't going to deflower some British merchant's daughter without permission, which he was never going to get even if he wanted it. Besides, he wasn't that kind of man. He liked children for their innocence, women for his pleasure.

I hurried to the mirror, wondering if the kitchen could supply cucumber for swollen eyelids. Years ago, I'd sworn that when my looks faded, I'd end my days in a nunnery. A quiet life, chanting prayers, cultivating honey.

If only I believed in a merciful God.

But no, the Revolution had wiped me clean of faith. Yes, some aristos crawled out of prison more devout. Not this pretty cockroach. My cell was within screaming distance of the torture chamber, a thing you don't forget or forgive. More than twenty years ago. Five thousand miles distant. Even so, the dripping walls, the howls, the grope of desperate men bore down on me. My fingers dove to my pocket, scrambling for the touch of bread. I rode the moment through, almost pleasured in it, and emerged alive, once more on St. Helena.

Before long, Charles returned, replete with cognac and rumors. He settled himself on the bed, his back against the headboard, long legs stretched before him, ankles crossed. The humidity screwed his curls into ringlets. When we'd first become lovers, I'd anchored my fingers in that thick mat and held on for all I was worth.

He took a swig from the bottle. "They dragged the sailor's body out of the bay. He didn't have the damn book on him."

I chewed the inside of my cheek. "Could you have fingered the wrong sailor?"

"No, I had the right fellow. Las Cases is not smart enough to double-cross me."

"Could the book have gotten through some other way?" I went to the window. The large square church and the customs house obscured the docks.

"Forget about it. It's at the bottom of the bay." He lifted his cognac. "With any luck."

Me, I didn't rely on luck. Neither did the Emperor. Oh, he gabbed of its necessity but created his luck through action. I vowed to do the same.

At a rap on the door, Charles hid behind his paper. "You're on your feet. Answer it."

I opened the door a slit, then wider, to confront that sparkling blonde. The little virgin, thrusting forth a pink rose bouquet, curtsied as if I were the queen. The flowers mirrored her pretty cheeks, as young Emmanuel had attested (damn him). Fourteen, at most fifteen, she teetered between childhood and maturity, flaunting the charms of both.

"Chère Madame," she said in perfect French, "thank you for saving my dear Tobyson."

At that, a tiny, round-faced Black child, the one I'd dragged from horses' hooves, peeked from behind her. His size bespoke a five-year-old, yet his dark, full-lashed eyes weighed me with a reckoning beyond those years. He rushed forward to wrap his arms around my skirt. Rubbing his back, I soaked in the warmth only a child can bring to a woman's breast.

"And oh, yes, his father—our gardener—made a present for you." The girl tapped the boy's shoulder, and the child handed me a box of woven straw, small enough to fit inside his fist. I started to open it. The girl shook her head. "There's nothing inside. The box itself is the gift. On our island, Toby's famous for his weaving." She flashed pretty white teeth.

After they left, I remained in the doorway, clutching the straw box, sniffing my flowers.

"Can't you shut that door?" Charles demanded. "There's a draft."

"Give me some coins. I'm going to have a talk with the merchant Solomon." I plumped my bosom. It was the only thing I had over that British girl.

Napoleon

OUTSIDE THE WINDOW OF THE Briars summer pavilion, tropical plants mimicked a lush English garden. A pleasant place. Nonetheless—an oath escaped the Emperor's lips—a prison yard. He yanked the drapery shut.

His single, all-purpose room overflowed. Marchand fussed with linens on his camp bed. Cipriani played solitaire on a corner desk. At the round oak table that filled the center of the room, Montholon and Bertrand fiddled with paper on which they'd been recording his dictated memoirs.

His secretary, Las Cases, whose entrance had interrupted the dictation, trembled before him. The man was disheveled, whimpering, unhurt. His stench soured the tight space.

Las Cases's chin quivered. "I swear, sire. I didn't admit a thing."

"Then you did well." Mon Dieu, he hoped the fellow wouldn't cry. He tried to soften his face but found he didn't want to. "They didn't mention my *Plutarch's Lives*?"

"Not once. I insisted I talked to the sailor only to practice my English." Las Cases fingered his soiled cravat. "Six days. They wouldn't let me wash."

The Emperor scanned past Cipriani to settle on Marchand.

The valet gave a last tuck to the bedcover and approached Las Cases. "Good sir, six weeks on ship, then horrid custody. We'll borrow the Briars' cart, go to Jamestown, get you all cleaned up."

The Emperor patted Las Cases's shoulder. "Yes, yes, go with Marchand. We're the same size. Borrow one of my shirts. Then you and your son billet in the snug attic here. You're a brave fellow. I want you close."

Marchand herded Las Cases out the door.

"A brave fellow?" Montholon said. "That sniveler?"

The Emperor whirled on the general. "Yes, braver than you or I, for we're not afraid. He did his task despite great fear."

Marchand's raised voice penetrated the closed door. "Admiral, I must check if the Emperor is accepting visitors. Admiral, admiral, I insist."

The door swung open. Admiral Cockburn leaned against the doorjamb, *Plutarch's Lives* tucked between his arms and chest.

General Bertrand jumped up. "An outrage. You and I, sir, shall speak outside."

"Nonsense," the admiral said. "I'm in charge here."

"In charge? In my chambers?" The Emperor stepped forward. No one in the room, not the generals, not Cipriani, not the British admiral, could hear his pulse throb in his throat, though to him it thundered. "Is that my book?"

The admiral tossed the book onto the table, where it fell to pieces.

It took no effort for the Emperor to appear shocked; he was. He stroked the shredded spine, thumbed through the loose endpapers, reordered pages that had been sliced from the hinges. His steel eyes fixed on the admiral, he counted silently, slowly, to twenty, the old trick his mother employed to make him squirm when he was a boy.

Admiral Cockburn shifted his weight from foot to foot.

"You will explain," the Emperor whispered.

"Well, sir—" The admiral stopped, drew himself up, and looked down his nose. "We found that item in a crevice on the *Northumberland.*"

"Mon Dieu. Then this intrusion is an apology. You're forgiven." The Emperor juggled the book pieces between his palms. "Why did the thief rip apart my book?"

The admiral folded his arms. "My lieutenant did that. He felt obligated to search for messages. And rightly so."

The Emperor tilted his head. "Did he find any?"

"No, just your notes in the margins, and they are, frankly, illegible, even to we Englishmen who speak French."

General Bertrand frowned. "I trust the thief's been punished."

"Have no fear." The admiral glared at Las Cases, who cowered behind Marchand in the doorway. "The sailor had some notion of quitting His Majesty's service, a desire our marksman fulfilled permanently."

"Well done," Bertrand said. "As military men, we support discipline."

The Emperor glanced up from the broken book. "Proper sentiment, Bertrand. In the future, Admiral, I ask that your people treat my books with respect. This one belonged to my father."

Cockburn rubbed his rusty beard. "Did your father have many books? I thought Corsica in those days . . ."

The Emperor slapped his palm on the table. "British propaganda. Recall your sailors' disappointment on finding I was not a dwarf in an enormous hat. My father's library contained a thousand volumes. When I was nine and departing for French military academy, he presented me this book—now sadly ruined."

"*Plutarch's Lives of Great Men*? At nine years old?"

"Ah, you think my father prescient." He dropped the book pieces on the table. "Have you other business to discuss? If not . . ." He gestured to the door.

The admiral stepped farther into the room. "I do. A sloop arrived this morning with word a new governor—a proper person to manage your confinement—is expected in a few days. General Sir Hudson Lowe, by name."

"Hudson Lowe? Never heard of him." The Emperor frowned. "No doubt he'll have a letter from the regent reversing this exile."

The admiral clicked his heels. The door snapped shut behind him.

The Emperor kicked a chair.

Montholon examined the Emperor's scribbles in the broken book. A smile flitted over his lips. "Allow me to repair this, sire. A childhood memento, after all."

The Emperor gathered up the pieces. "Marchand'll handle it."

Montholon's smile faded. "You do have those you trust, don't you? Yet I—and Albine—will serve you well in this horrible place. You'll find Marchand and your Corsican minion here can't accomplish all you need."

Cipriani's head snapped up. "Minion? What Corsican minion?"

"Enough. You're all dismissed." The Emperor put a hand on Cipriani's arm. "Not you."

Marchand, ushering the generals and Las Cases out the door, paused. "Sire, the young lady's coming up the walk."

"Tell Miss Betsy to come back tomorrow. Go, Marchand. Tend to Las Cases." He turned to the Corsican. "I want to meet that merchant Solomon."

"Another midnight excursion?" Cipriani pressed his palm to the Emperor's chest. "Like old times, but risky, Master, risky. Pushing your luck and mine."

"You sound like my mother."

"As if you ever listened to that blessed lady."

The Emperor seized Cipriani's collar. He jerked him close. "You of all people know there's nothing 'blessed' about my mother."

Cipriani reared his head. "Touchy, are we? Those days—what you and me and her and your father were—gone and buried. Safe with me, anyhow." He raised his upper lip. "Back off."

"Forgive me." The Emperor, releasing him, smoothed Cipriani's crumpled collar. "Sometimes I forget who my friends are."

Cipriani caught his wrist. "We're square, brother, but don't go losing your temper with me. Can't say what that'll lead to."

"Come—you've put up with me for too many years to let me down now. What do you say? Tonight, eleven o'clock, at the waterfall? Bring him here." He patted Cipriani's cheek.

The door closed behind the Corsican. Now that everyone had left, he didn't like being alone. Yet the one-room pavilion with its emerald-painted walls had a touch of home. Josephine's bright Empire green, matching his camp-bed curtains. How she would have laughed to see that color fashionable on a British island half a world from Paris.

His glance wandered to the etching of the Eaglet on the mantel. His little son, who crawled into his lap, who smelled of milk porridge. His throat caught. The boy would soon learn his mother was an adulteress. Children always find out.

CLISSON: THE EMPEROR'S NOVEL

Ajaccio, Corsica, 1779

The shepherd led Clisson to his hut. He warmed mutton broth to soothe Clisson's throat, dry from running, raw from screaming.

"Is this your home?" Clisson asked, his arms around a lamb.

The shepherd nodded.

"The plain, too? Does that belong to you? And the mountains?"

The fire lit the shepherd's face. He was a young man, young enough to be a soldier, old enough to be a leader. The hair on his head and chin shone like black fleece. He tossed Clisson a blanket and drew one around himself. "What's your name? What're you doing here?"

"I'm Clisson from Ajaccio. I ran away."

"What do you want?"

"I wanted—"

"No, not what you wanted when you ran away. What do you want now?"

The fire's heat magnified Clisson's blush. "My Destiny is to be a soldier."

The shepherd drank from a flask. "So why not? What's stopping you?"

"My father—my parents. They want to send me to French military school."

"And?"

"But I'm Corsican." He dumped the lamb from his lap. "I can't serve the French king. I'm not a traitor, even if my parents are."

"Young man, Signor Clisson, all great military men use the Enemy to their advantage. Don't cavil at your future. Go to

France. You'll be more valuable to your homeland if you know the Enemy." He coaxed the fire into flame.

Clisson hung his head. "I am the Enemy. I turned your soldiers to stone."

The shepherd coughed behind his hand. "The paladini? Those stone knights of Charlemagne have stood on that plain for a thousand years. A greater feat would be to turn the statues into men."

Clisson's head snapped up. "I heard their drum."

"That drum was your heart."

"I know what I heard. I know what I saw."

The shepherd pulled at his beard. "My boy, the measure of your bravery was what you thought was happening. Come, young conqueror, you have conjured enough demons for one night. Tomorrow, we'll take a look at the ancient slabs in daylight. We'll read your future in the manner my mother taught me. And I'll give you a talisman, but you must go home."

In the morning, the warriors' stares were blank, their massive jaws weary, their carved weapons a burden for ancient limbs. An iron cross, mounted on a rock, jutted at an angle toward the ranks.

Clisson avoided its beam. "These statues are old men in retreat. I shouldn't have disturbed them."

Outside the hut, he held a lamb's head while the shepherd sliced its belly. Entrails spilled upon the ground; the animal's legs buckled. Clisson kissed its forehead. Why did everything important smell of blood?

The shepherd stabbed his knife among the entrails, bringing them to life. He pivoted on Clisson. "Who are you?"

Clisson cowered under the shepherd's knife. "What do you see?"

"Your destiny's not in Corsica. Go to France. Above all, leave me." He stalked away.

"But you promised a talisman to protect me," Clisson called to the man's back.

The shepherd stiffened. "You don't need one. The bullet's not cast that can kill you, but when your time comes? A fly can do you in. Now, on your way. This lamb says I'll be dead by spring."

During the journey home, Clisson divided long numbers in his head. A corporal in the citadel said he must know mathematics to excel at artillery. His clothes hung in tatters, but so what? His new school uniform might come with red pants and a plumed hat.

On the threshold of his home, his old nursemaid Camilla clutched him to her breast. His mother pointed down the hall. Camilla, straightening his hair, hustled him to his father's library.

Father, decked out as a traitor in French brocade, towered over his desk. Pain flitted across his drawn features. Mamma claimed if Father wanted to reach thirty-five, he must visit the witches for his stomach pains, but Father insisted on being modern. Clisson dug inside himself for emotion. No use—the tall man in the wig seemed a stranger.

Father sniffed his scented handkerchief. "You smell like a farm animal."

"Yes," said Clisson.

Father lowered his handkerchief. Clisson concentrated on a spot between his father's eyes. Father fiddled with a quill. "Clisson, there's nothing for you here. All winds now blow to France. There, you'll become an officer and make your fortune."

"Yes, Father."

"What? No argument?"

"Here or in France, I'll do my best for my country. For Corsica."

"Oh, don't judge us harshly." Father wrinkled his forehead. "When you're older, you'll understand philosophy and choices.

How you respond to distractions, principally women, power, and money, will determine what kind of man you'll become." He extended his ring to kiss.

Clisson marched from the room.

Chapter 8

Napoleon

ALONE WITH HIS THOUGHTS, the Emperor fingered the cover of his *Plutarch's Lives*. None of the great men in that book had grown up in a frivolous court like the Eaglet's golden cage in Austria.

A sheet of paper slid under the door, skimmed over the stone tiles, and settled out of reach. He squinted. His eyes had never been good and, at forty-six, weren't getting better. Whoever the unknown correspondent was, he had written a single word on the paper. *He* had written? Perhaps not. Perhaps *she* had written.

His paunch squeezed against his knee breeches as he stooped. The stationery was good-quality linen rag, nicely textured, although island moisture had tainted its scent with mold. On the top side, in pretty black script: *Une Lettre Secrète*. Ink showed through faintly from the other side. He flipped the paper over.

A paragraph, mostly in French, of neat, flowing letters:

> *Monsieur, my friends do not believe I have met you. They say you are an ogre with one huge eye. Would you write a note for me? In English. Something like "Dearest Betsy, I am enchanted to be your friend. Emperor Napoleon Bonaparte." Yours, Betsy Balcombe*

Why did that imp's French sound more authentic than his own? Perhaps he'd succumbed to that new disease Paris doctors wrote about: paranoia. It would cost little effort to find out. He wrote the note as instructed, taking pains to make the letters clear, the script readable, the English words spelled correctly. At the bottom, he signed his large "N" with a flourish. He folded the paper in tight fourths. His ear applied to the door, he pushed the note beneath it and poked the paper across the threshold.

A gasp. A rustle of muslin. Light footsteps darted away.

Eh bien, if his new friend could bypass guards so easily, she might prove useful. He didn't miss his golden crown. He missed the tools to get things done.

A FEW MINUTES BEFORE ELEVEN, the Emperor shrugged on his dark overcoat and wound a black scarf around his head. His heart pounded pleasantly. If a girl could evade these guards, he could. He clocked the British patrol's circuit: two minutes out of sight of the pavilion's door. Plenty of time to cross the yard to the waterfall path. No moon, but enough starlight to get him to Cipriani.

Now. Quick. Out the front door, across the lawn, and onto the path. A minute to spare before the patrol's return. Branches met above his head, cutting down the light, but he didn't fear a fall on the smooth path. Dirt muffled his footsteps. He reached the clearing.

No Cipriani.

The Emperor leaned against a tree. It hadn't rained. The waterfall trickled, sluicing the smooth rock face so gently, he could hear his heartbeat. Surely, he would hear Cipriani's if the man were nearby.

"*Shh*," said a voice near his ear.

"Son of a—"

Cipriani clapped a hand over the Emperor's mouth. "No insults to *my* mother."

He pried the Corsican's hand off his face. "Then don't surprise me. Ah, our guest."

A little man, whose starlit face appeared as wrinkled as a turkey's head, emerged from the shadows. Solomon bowed, his straggly beard almost touching the ground.

The Emperor extended his hand.

Solomon kissed it, lifted his lively eyes, and spoke in French. "Bless Your Majesty as a friend to my people. We're doubly bound, you and I, for, as a fellow Freemason, I'm your brother Joseph's sworn brother." The merchant rubbed his knuckles. "Though my business here is humble, I have friends around the world. How may we serve you?"

"I want my son," the Emperor said.

The old man stroked his beard. "Easier to get you off this island."

"Work on both fronts, shall we? See what you and your Freemason friends can come up with. *Shh* . . . what's that noise?"

The three men listened.

"Rats in the underbrush," said Cipriani. "Best keep our voices down."

The Emperor leaned toward Solomon. "Tell me, good sir, about the Africans on this island."

Solomon startled. "The slaves, Your Majesty? What can I say? With no native population, St. Helena needs manpower to survive." He grunted. "Our British friends have flexible morals. Somehow, it's illegal to transport new ones here, but the ones in place, their children, their children's children, and on and on? Slaves for eternity."

"'Tain't like in the Americas, though," the Corsican added. "Learned today the masters can't touch the women. Got laws against cutting off ears, branding, whipping too much, that kind of thing. The nasty scars and stuff we're seeing is remnants of the past."

Solomon's cheek twitched. "An abomination nonetheless."

"Well, not so good we're stuck here, neither," Cipriani said. "Enough conversation, old man. You wanted to meet your hero, and now you have. No sense getting caught where we shouldn't oughta be. You and I, we'll work together on the Emperor's orders."

Solomon faced the Emperor. His voice quavered, sounding older, feebler, hesitant. "Great sire, I'll aid you any way I can. My

thanks to Madame de Montholon for arranging our meeting."
Cipriani chuckled. "One blessed lady, ain't she?"

THE NEXT MORNING, THE EMPEROR awoke before dawn.

Outside his window came the sound of falling pebbles, a shovel
hitting stone. He drew on a dressing gown, pinched back a drapery,
and peeked out. An arm's length away, the Black gardener, Toby,
dug a drainage ditch. At the sight of the Emperor, the man stopped.
Slowly, he lifted his straw hat, revealing a shock of white hair.

Mahafaly, the leader of the slaves.

The Emperor fumbled to unlatch the window. Before he could
fling it open, a British guard marched around the corner, berating
the gardener, ordering him to move on. The Emperor hid behind
the drapery. When he looked again, no one was in sight. But Mahafaly. Right under his nose. A piece of luck to turn into a plan.

He rubbed his tongue around his mouth. Marchand hadn't left
brandy to wash his teeth, but the faithful valet would arrive soon.
Until then—he reached for the small brown pouch on a nearby
table—licorice would do.

He settled at the oak table, the etching of his son between his
hands. He sucked hard on the licorice. He'd always used his brain
like a cabinet to store memories, the good to savor, the bad to ignore
until needed. Time to peer into the long-locked drawer marked
Saint-Domingue.

Haiti, its rebel rulers called it.

For the hundred years before he'd come to power, France's
treasury had depended on that colony's sugarcane. He couldn't
have ended slavery there, no matter what the French Revolution
proclaimed. Given the choice, he would have freed the people grad-
ually without bankrupting France. It was not to be. Necessity had
triumphed over justice. As it often must.

So why did that slaughter of Blacks, whites, and mixed weigh on him? If God had wanted justice, He shouldn't have sent yellow fever to kill off half of the French troops he'd sent to restore order. If he'd gone to the island to manage the business himself, it might have turned out better, but a man can't be everywhere at once.

He kissed the etching of his son. "Slavery, my Eaglet? A sin that breeds more sin. And justice? Justice requires patience, power, and luck. Rare to have all three at the same time. I learned that long ago in school."

CLISSON: THE EMPEROR'S NOVEL

France, 1779

Clisson, vomiting over the side of the ship, missed the first glimpse of France. Wind gusted. Waves topped the bow. He couldn't keep his footing. His father, holding on to his collar, let him use his spyglass to distract from his heaving stomach, but the sight of sailors swaying in the masts sent Clisson to the ruil. "Definitely the army," said his father. "No navy for you, my boy."

As they headed inland in a stagecoach as big as a barge—the *Diligence*, his father insisted he call it—Clisson gaped. France had mountains higher, boulevards wider, buildings finer than those on Corsica. The stores brimmed with books, guns, copper pots, and silver plate, not empty shelves. Horses got enough to eat; some had ribbons in their manes. People in stiff clothes thronged the streets, speaking words he didn't know.

"Now you see," Father said. "We Corsicans overvalue our worth."

Clisson, forgetting the angry waves, longed for the smell of Corsica's salt water. His father grew paler every day, wheezed as he talked, cried out when the bounding coach thrust Clisson against him.

At last, the coachman yelled, "Brienne!" A thatched roof sheltered market stalls; a fine chateau, thirty-six windows on the front side, towered on a hill above. The school lay at the edge of town, at the foot of the chateau's long green lawn. They entered through black iron gates and followed a row of leafless trees to the low, L-shaped building.

The head abbé wore violet robes. The students had blue jackets with red pants, identical to the ones Mamma had sewn. When Clisson spoke in the French his Corsican tutor taught, the boys laughed. Even the head abbé chuckled.

Clisson, his face flushed, talked all the more loudly. Let everyone learn how a Corsican sounded.

Father, white around the lips, regained some color: a scarlet splotch on each cheek. He held his hand above Clisson's head. "Forget Corsica. Take advantage of your great luck, my son." Father clicked his heels. In a moment, he was gone.

"Farewell, Babbú." Clisson whispered the endearment he had never said to his father. He trailed other students to a barren classroom. The tallest man he had ever seen, in robes long enough to be draperies, handed him a book titled *L'Usage de l'Artillerie Nouvelle*. Clisson forgot his surroundings to devour its pages. His head was a great sack begging to be filled.

"This is what I want," he said, unaware he spoke out loud. "I was born for war."

A boy with polished nails giggled. "War? A Corsican, here on the king's charity? Why, conquering Corsica barely took a skirmish."

Clisson leapt with a roar, but the professor grabbed him by the waist. "Here, we read of war—we don't make it." He dropped Clisson into his seat and began to lecture.

Later, at the long wooden luncheon tables, students crowded

around the boy with polished nails—Loménie, son of the count who lived in the chateau. No one sat near Clisson; no one talked to him. It didn't matter. He chewed and chewed his roast chicken. His stomach churned when he tried to swallow. He spat the mangled meat onto his plate and, jumping off the bench, ran through the long corridor and up the stairs to his room. There, he hesitated at the threshold, about-faced, and marched to the lunchroom.

He had been born for war. He could survive this.

Seasons passed, and he grew into the larger uniforms his mother had packed. His third October, when new young boys arrived, older students set upon the weakest ones, stealing keepsakes from their rooms, exacting money and socks.

Clisson, outraged, demanded Justice. "And Order."

The head abbé brushed off his complaints. "The small always pay tribute to the strong. It's nature's way."

"Then let the People rise!" Clisson stormed down the hall to where the count's son, Loménie, was tallying his booty. Surprising the bigger boy, Clisson knocked him to the floor. It took three others to stop Clisson's pummeling fists. Still he snarled. "Give it back to the boys, you thieves, or walk these halls in fear of retribution."

The tall history professor bounded into the room. "What's this riot?" He closed the door to hide Loménie crying on a chair. "Clisson, there were better ways to get this done."

"No, Professor," Clisson said. "I asked first. When no Justice is forthcoming, a man has the right to make his own."

The professor grimaced. "Good luck with that."

Napoleon

IN THE QUIET OF THE BRIARS summer pavilion, a soft knock on the door made the Emperor jump. Annoyed at the interruption, he crossed the room to fling open the door.

Betsy's curls bobbed as she curtsied. Laughing, he dragged his fingers through the tangles, soft as his little boy's.

"Don't do that." Betsy retreated, colliding into the tiny slave boy who hid behind her. "I went to such trouble to arrange it for you."

He smiled. "Little elf, what are you doing here at such an hour? Is this boy your chaperone? Good day to you, young man."

"Don't be silly. You're too old for me to need a chaperone. Tobyson, wait on the stairs." She tilted her head. "Are you angry, Monsieur? You looked angry. Generals aren't in the habit of sleeping late, are they?"

He took her hand. "They are not. And your father? Does he know you're here?"

"Father's a gentleman. He doesn't rise early like generals and farmers do."

He chuckled. "A worthy salvo for a little girl. And those soldiers guarding me? What do they say to this intrusion on their prisoner?"

"They say a little girl can do no harm." She took back her hand.

"Obviously they don't know you."

She curtsied. "No, but I do think we should get to know each other."

He set his mouth into a severe line. "What do you want, Miss Betsy?"

"Must I have come for something in particular?" She met his stern gaze, dipped her eyes, and extracted his note from her pocket. "Oh, all right. You didn't sign it properly. Anyone could make an 'N.' Why didn't you write out 'Napoleon Bonaparte'?"

His imperial "N" couldn't satisfy a schoolgirl. So much for power. He was a sham, masquerading in a paper crown like the slave king. He turned to slam the door.

But in the yard beyond the pert girl, British sentries passed, saluted, and pivoted. They wanted to see him. That was why they had let the girl through. He stood straighter, lifted his chin, and looked them each in the eye. Here were men who didn't know him, who had never seen him, who only knew of him, yet his presence moved them. What a thing imagination was! Think where it had led him.

If he could protect his legacy and extend it through the Eaglet, then, for generations, these men's descendants would be told the story of how the Great Man himself had acknowledged them. He'd learn their names. They would be his forever. All over the world—Christian, Muslim, Jew, Black, white—soldiers were the same.

The morning was dawning, filtering gold through the girl's hair. Brisk air filled his lungs. If not an Emperor, if not free, he was still Napoleon. He grimaced. At least in imagination. That might be enough.

In the distance, Marchand trudged up the road from Jamestown. Behind the valet, Albine and her husband strolled, in conversation with O'Meara, the ship's handsome doctor. He had no patience for Montholon this morning, but he was glad to see Albine working on O'Meara. The good doctor was halfway on their side already.

Betsy tugged his sleeve. "Please, Monsieur, my paper. It's important."

"I'll sign your paper if you write me a poem—in French, with rhymes. Now go, before anyone else sees you."

"Friends?" she asked.

"Better than that. You may treat me like an uncle. Now go."

Betsy and her little slave raced down the walk. The Emperor wondered if that cheerful boy knew he wasn't free.

Chapter 9

⁓

Napoleon

Two weeks into the sojourn at the Briars, the afternoon air in the one-room pavilion tasted of spent passion. The Emperor lay passive, naked under the covers as Albine's small, strong hands massaged his feet. Efficiently, tenderly, she pressed and kissed, pressed and kissed, pressed and kissed. Warmth spread up his legs into his core. It filled his ears and fogged his mind.

He drifted in a sea of nothingness.

In the distance, a horizon. An island. He floated near, reached for it. The island cracked. A skeletal claw shot out and seized his throat.

He bolted upright.

Albine, in a thin cotton shift, perched on the foot of his bed. "Are you all right?"

"Yes. Yes, I'm fine." He rubbed his throat.

"Did I hurt you?"

"Of course not." He beckoned.

"Under the covers?"

"Yes, let me rub your feet for a change."

Her eyes widened. "Oh, no, sire."

"Why not?"

She lifted his hand to her cheek. "You're the one who carries the burdens."

To his surprise, her face was open, vulnerable, devoid of mockery. Almost wifely. "At least let me hold you, my dear. I must thank you for bringing Solomon into my orbit." He drew her in until she snuggled against his side. He kissed the crown of her head. She wore too much perfume, but he was growing fond of its cloying rose scent. They cuddled, legs entwined, in silence. The bed warmed.

Slowly, her soft body tensed against his. His muscles tightened. His chest hollowed out. She was going to ask for something. They all asked for something.

She spoke into his ribs. "I did what you ordered. I watched my husband."

He relaxed. "Ah, that. And?"

"I saw nothing. I swear Charles would never betray you."

He traced the scar from her shoulder to the nape of her neck. She flinched. He traced it again. "He doesn't spend time with the admiral's men?"

"No, no, of course not. He'd never conspire with your enemies, sire."

The Emperor waited.

Albine sucked her lower lip. "Does he hope to benefit from his devotion? Of course. Why should he not? We lost everything to follow you."

"And you had so much. Come, woman, I'm not a dunce. You had nothing in France but debts." He pinched her chin.

"Nothing?" She thrust his hand away. "You forget I left my son at school."

"Ah, something I understand. I apologize, my dear. Shall I send you home?" He tucked a loose strand of hair behind her ear.

"No, no." She pressed his knuckles to her lips. "I shouldn't have said—it's just, I keep thinking my Tristan's the same age you were when you were sent to France."

His gaze strayed to the desk that held his writing box. "Then don't fear for him. By that age, a boy knows who he is."

"But we'll go home soon, won't we, sire? Charles promises we will."

He swung his attention back to her. "Does he now? Let me know if he says how that's going to happen, will you? Come, we should get dressed."

The lines on her face deepened. Poor Albine. She was young and pretty only when she was making love.

"May we not be happy a little longer?" she asked.

"You're a sweet temptress." He rubbed his cheek against hers. "All right, for a bit. Your Tristan? Where is he at school?"

She sighed. "Switzerland."

"My nephew Louis-Napoleon's his age. They're bound to be friends one day. Here, stay under the covers. I'll read to you. But what you hear is our secret. And that means don't tell your husband."

CLISSON: THE EMPEROR'S NOVEL

Paris, France, 1786

Clisson pleaded to sit for the graduation tests one year early. He didn't care to be perfect or the best. Ugly victory outweighed a wait for total success. If he failed, the abbés warned, they wouldn't give him a second chance. Instead of attending the officers' academy in Paris, he'd get shipped home in disgrace.

When the scores were posted, he read the list from the bottom up to find his name more quickly. *Libartà!* Three names from last—he'd made the cut.

He raced to pack. The younger students assembled to watch him board the coach for Paris. He walked their ranks, here tapping a chest, there rubbing a head, tweaking an ear. From the coach steps, he gave a smart salute. As the coach turned a bend, he pulled *Plutarch's Lives* out of his satchel.

Paris! The *Diligence* entered the city through the St. Jacques gate. The clatter and the crowds, the horse dung in the streets. Masons covered in stone dust, emblems gracing carriage doors, dirty children and prostitutes half-dressed, bakers hawking bread . . . It went on and on, riches alternating with want. The coach could barely contain Clisson. He tapped a tailor's wife, whose massive back blocked his view. "Madame, you've been here before, while I have never seen it."

Her husband cleared a space for him. "Here, boy." He frowned at the woman. "Be generous, wife. Someday this youth will be a soldier spilling blood for France."

Clisson smiled shyly. "If I'm lucky, the blood will be someone else's."

Outside the window, the placid Seine flowed. A bridge spanned to an island in the river, where the sun reflected gold on a cathedral ten times larger than any he had seen. Its towering windows were stained with color.

"Notre Dame," the tailor said. "Wait until you see the glass from inside. That's the Conciergerie—don't get locked up there. Next, the Tuileries Palace, although mostly the king and queen now live at Versailles. And on this side of the river, the mint, where they make coins. Those low buildings? That's Les Invalides, the wounded soldiers' home. Now we're close to your school."

The tailor waved as the carriage left Clisson outside the academy. The domed school building went on and on. The dusty marching field in front covered more ground than his neighborhood in Corsica. He swallowed. The curriculum lasted three years. He'd give himself two years to finish it. By then he'd have turned eighteen.

Life had become a race.

Within a week, he was pacing the halls, his head thrust forward like a bull. These people weren't military; they played at army. Oh, the mathematics were hard enough, he liked the sword fighting, and Louis Monge, his artillery professor, knew his stuff. But five-course meals and dancing lessons? Born for quadrilles and pretty speeches? Those were what this king thought made a soldier? This luxury was ill spent, even if they turned out to be correct that sergeants did the work while officers played cards.

When his outrage outstripped his patience, he penned a letter:

> To Philippe Henri, Le Maréchal de Ségur, Minister of War:
>
> As a humble student of the École Militaire in Paris, I draw your notice to circumstances that reflect ill on the Nation, undermine the strength of the Army, and squander the gold of the realm. Here, in a place meant to familiarize the flower of youth with the exigencies of war, the students are wrapped in a softness better associated with a cradle. Shall cadets gorge on truffles while soldiers starve? Nay, instill the harsh joy of asceticism in those destined to lead. What better example than the education of the Spartan youth? Fewer servants, plainer meals, and harder beds will train your future officers for military campaigns. Act before a generation is lost to weaklings.
>
> Your obedient servant,
> Clisson, cadet

He liked the bit about the cradle. Concerned poor spelling might hurt his cause, he took the letter to Professor Monge for review. The old man wiped his spectacles. "You make a good point," he said. "But one better left unsaid."

"But if it's true—"

The professor held up his hand. "You plan to spend your life among the very fellows whom you chastise as weaklings. Yes, the army runs on discipline, but also on camaraderie. You'd do better to make a few friends if you intend to be a part of it."

Clisson bowed his head.

Professor Monge fingered the letter. "May I keep this?"

"Why, if I'm not to send it?"

The professor smiled. "Let us say I have a premonition."

Clisson returned to his room. After the spartan conditions in Brienne, he appreciated the extra space, the painted ceiling with its plaster leaf decorations, the heat of the faïence stove. To his relief, the supple new boots he wore came at no extra cost—little money was sent to him from home. Still, this luxury stuck in his throat. Stripping the extra blanket from his bed and rolling the carpet into the corner, he vowed to eat only one dessert a day.

His boots were blackened and polished, his red breeches fresh, his white vest spotless, his shirt crisp. With his hair caught back in a ribbon, he preened to see how his Roman profile resembled Mamma's. Camaraderie! He'd read about it existing in the army. He set his father's smile on his face and went to make some friends.

First, he sought out a certain mustached fellow with a youthful paunch. That one spoke with a strange accent. Foreigners should band together.

In the fencing studio, he came across the young man, lounging against a wall, awaiting his turn at foils. Clisson bowed, elegantly, he hoped. "May I introduce myself as a fellow foreign traveler to this French Gomorrah?"

The cadet grinned. "My father's French, but I grew up in England with my mother's family."

"Then you are the first Britisher I've met. How do *you* reconcile being schooled by your enemies?"

The young man's breath flowed over Clisson's face. "I find that insulting."

A grinning cadet wearing a gold signet ring pushed between them. "Speaking of enemies, have you met the new student who arrived yesterday?" He pointed to a slender, slick-haired youth with an outsized nose. "He's Genoese nobility."

"Genoese?" Clisson's voice rose.

A stout boy brushed the grinning cadet aside and offered his hand to Clisson. "My name's Des Mazis. Ignore my friend Berville here. He's a wealthy snob. I, like you, am a scholarship cadet. We thank our king for his generosity every day, do we not?"

"Genoese?" Clisson, his face crimson, was not listening to the stout boy. "Genoese, you say?" He seized two foils, popped off the tips, and stalked across the room. He tossed a blade to the Genoese with the aristocratic nose, who, with a start, caught it in a gloved hand. Without a word, Clisson saluted with his foil, whipped the steel through the air, and cried, "En garde!"

The Genoese moved into a relaxed opening stance. The foils touched. Clisson plunged beneath the other young man's guard.

Des Mazis rushed in. He looped his jacket over the foils before Clisson's naked point pierced its mark. "No tips!" Des Mazis yelled. "What the hell are you about?"

The foils clattered on the floor.

Clisson slammed stout Des Mazis into the wall. "You donkey, I almost had him!"

The white-faced Genoese cowered behind a line of cadets. "D-did I insult you? I'd swear I've never even seen you."

"Nor I you." Clisson bared his teeth. He kicked the foil at his feet. It spun across the floor. "But I am Corsican, sworn enemy to every Genoese."

"Genoese? I'm from fucking Pisa!"

Around the room, cadets hid their grins.

Clisson whirled to face Berville, the only one who dared to laugh.

"Forgive me," Berville said. "You seemed such a tiger. I swear I couldn't stop myself." He thrust out a hand. "God grant me always to be on your side in a fight. Friends?"

The last word struck a chord. Despite his fury, Clisson couldn't resist Berville's brimming charm, so reminiscent of his father, so unlike his own awkwardness. As he grasped Berville's hand, the handsome fellow wrapped his free arm around Clisson's shoulders. "Friends," they said in unison. Berville's pale blue eyes glinted into Clisson's gray.

Des Mazis barged up, rubbing his bruised hip. He clapped Clisson on a shoulder. "Join us for a glass of wine, Clisson. And, you, too, Whatever Your Name Is from Pisa."

Napoleon

ALBINE WAS COOING OVER THE story when the Emperor got out of bed to open a window. Yes, he would have to tell her to leave off the perfume. But not just then. He didn't want to spoil her joy in what he'd read to her.

She probably thought the rose scent reminded him of Josephine. Certainly, the two women had much in common. Both were clever, neither beautiful in the usual sense, but whereas Josephine had exuded elegance, Albine possessed not a drop. Poor, sweet Albine. Too late to his inner circle to satisfy her ambitions, but who was he to quibble with self-interest?

Albine

AFTER OUR LOVEMAKING, I WANDERED through the Briars gardens, admiring Mrs. Balcombe's roses, smelling the Emperor on my fingers, feeling his tug on my nipples. He married Josephine despite her sordid reputation. He could marry me. He could love me as (to my surprise) I loved him.

Down the hill from Napoleon's pavilion sat the handsome Briars house, where that sparkling blond Betsy girl lived. I turned my back on it to face the waterfall. The stream, spilling over a red rock ridge, fell twenty meters into a pond below. Years of flow had carved out a soft V, so that the ridge resembled a child's drawing of a red heart.

Napoleon lived in the shadow of a heart. That boded well for my future.

I trod a pebble path toward the lush English lawn.

Silly, selfish Marie Louise had performed her role, giving the Emperor an heir. But she'd fled at danger, stolen the Eaglet, then abandoned him—if rumor were true—to cavort with that Austrian von Neipperg. Time for her to make room for a new empress (me).

I settled on a shady spot in the grass. Other than the soothing patter of the waterfall, all was quiet. Within my reach, a vine grew small white flowers in profusion. Remembering the daisy chains I made as a child, I plucked a few of the bell-shaped blooms. My fingers, working from memory, needed no instruction to entwine their long stems. I fashioned a delicate circle, then unwound my braided hair.

No one was in sight. I slipped out of my pocket the hairbrush I'd taken from Napoleon's dresser. On the silver-plated back, garlands surrounded an imperial "N." I wanted to brush my hair, but no, better not to contaminate the bristles before preserving the Emperor's precious strands. The brush went back into my pocket.

I placed the flower crown on my head. (How I yearned for a mirror.)

Napoleon deserved a wiser woman than Marie Louise. I could be the comfort of his old age. Divorce, awkward on St. Helena, could wait until our return to Europe. Charles wouldn't mind if he got a lucrative position he could pilfer.

I plucked more flowers and started a necklace.

How proud my Tristan would look in a cadet uniform, presenting himself for the Emperor's inspection, side by side with Louis-N. The boys could attend school together, spend the holidays with Napoleon and me. Before long, we'd recover the Eaglet. I'd be his good stepmaman, kind and loving, unlike his faithless mother.

I tucked my hands to my hips and, seated on the grass, struck a pose, stretching my neck, presenting my best profile. Stepmother to a dynasty.

A long shadow darkened the lawn.

Charles jerked me to my feet. His face was full of laughter, his eyes mean, his breath brandy. "Playacting the empress, are we?" He ripped the crown from my head and kissed me hard on the mouth, only to fling me onto the grass. "You taste of sex, you moonstruck whore."

I scrambled on my knees out of his reach. "Careful, Charles. I could . . . Napoleon would—"

"You could do nothing. He would do nothing. You think the great Napoleon loves you?" He towered over me.

"How would you know? You're hardly in his confidence."

"Men talk, my girl. Want to know what he thinks of you?" Charles sneered as if he did know something.

Doubt arced through me. "What? What has he said?"

"He forbade me to marry you, that's what. Fined me, too, when I did it. You thought I lost that money at cards, you fool."

"No, it's not true." But my stomach knotted. It was too complicated to be a lie.

"Want to hear more? 'That stray cat. She'll cheat on you before the wedding luncheon's cold.'" Charles ground my crown beneath his boot. "So much for your romantic notions. He's using you as much as we're using him." He dragged me to my feet.

"No, no. That was years ago. You don't know how close we've become. He tells me things—"

"What things?" He shook me until my brain bounced against my skull.

I clawed at his hands. "Nothing. Nothing you—I mean, we— can use. I'd tell you if he did. I swear it."

"Nothing. That's what I thought." He stopped the shaking.

I sniffed back tears.

The flame went out of his eyes. His hands slid from my shoulders, down my arms, to grasp my hands. "Albine . . ."

I let my lips tremble.

He pulled me close. "I'm sorry, little love. Too much brandy. I didn't mean to hurt you. Forgive me?"

I cuddled in the comfort of his hug, my head against his chest, my arms around him. His ribs pressed into my breasts, his sparseness painful after Napoleon's padded depths. Yet, out of habit, I murmured, "Yes, of course I forgive you."

But, in that moment, five thousand miles from Paris, on a lawn under St. Helena's heart-shaped waterfall, something inside me stretched taut, snapped, and broke from Charles. Like the flower crown he'd ground beneath his feet, it was something that couldn't heal.

Napoleon

A WEEK LATER, A TALL SHIP under full sail arrived in Jamestown Bay at dusk. Two hours after, a soldier knocked on the pavilion door and handed Marchand a folded note.

The Emperor broke the seal.

General Bonaparte:

*I have arrived and shall interview you in your quarters
at nine in the morning.*

General Sir Hudson Lowe, Governor of St. Helena

"I think not." The paper fell to the floor. The Emperor clasped
his hands behind his back. He didn't want Marchand to see them
shake. "Write a note. I'm ill and unable to receive visitors. Tell this
Hudson Lowe he's to communicate with you tomorrow to determine when I am adequately recovered. Now, lock the door."

At four o'clock the next afternoon, he positioned himself at
the fireplace, his arm resting on the black mantel where his bicorne
stood. Marchand had brushed his clothing, hung two ribboned
medals on the green jacket of the Chasseurs of the Guard, and
shined his boots. Not the regalia of an emperor, but better. The new
governor, a military gentleman himself, would respect the power of
Napoleon's famous uniform.

Marchand shook his head.

"Ah, Marchand, you worry too much. Who knows?" He fondled the ribbons on his chest. "This governor could turn out to be
an ally, despite his insulting note."

"It's not that, sire. I don't want to upset you before the meeting,
but you insist on hearing news immediately."

"Yes? Say it, man."

Marchand took a deep breath. "I think Madame de Montholon
stole your best hairbrush."

The Emperor laughed.

"Sire, it's not funny."

He flushed, accepting the rebuke. "Do you have proof she was
the thief?"

"No, but no one else has access, and she's always asking for money." The valet frowned.

"Oh, don't be such a Puritan, Marchand. Tell Cipriani to recover the brush. Now, let me prepare for our new jailer." He turned his back on the valet.

MARCHAND, STATIONED OUTSIDE, knocked twice.

The Emperor deepened his voice. "Enter."

The door opened, and General Sir Hudson Lowe stood on the threshold, gnawing on his lower lip. His prominent forehead overhung a hawkish nose and a receding chin. In an unpleasant way, Lowe's long neck reminded him of his mother.

The lanky man spoke through his nose. "I should have liked to have seen you this morning when I informed you I would call. It was most imperative to write my initial report." He sniffed. "You do not appear ill to me."

The Emperor had been prepared to overlook yesterday's insulting message, but then he hadn't beheld its sender. Marchand closed the door, leaving him alone to face a man whose eyes shifted like a hyena in a trap.

With his blandest expression, he indicated a chair to his guest. "Have we met before? On the battlefield?"

"No," Sir Hudson said.

"Really? Why not?" He gestured again for the man to sit. "Everyone sent their best military men against me."

"I had other duties." Sir Hudson dusted the chair seat. "Indeed, we have much in common. I led the Corsican Rangers in the battle for Capri."

The Emperor snorted. "Traitors in service to the British." He stalked to the door, jerked it open, and told Marchand to bring coffee.

The governor pinched a bit of lint from his pants leg. "*Au contraire.* Brave soldiers fighting for our cause. But to the points at hand. Admiral Cockburn leaves tomorrow, and I have arrived with new orders. I have directed work on Longwood be expedited. As soon as possible, you will move from here to there."

The Emperor waited.

The governor's head bobbled. "Now, I understand that you've had free rein to move about with minimal escort. That must stop. I have here an outline of the territory around Longwood that will be at your disposal. With a military guard always, naturally."

"Do you have a wife?" the Emperor asked.

Sir Hudson wrinkled his forehead. "Why, yes."

The Emperor sat on the yellow sofa opposite his jailer. "And did she accompany you? Ah, Marchand, yes, I will have a cup. Please serve our guest first."

"Lady Lowe's with me, and my stepdaughter."

"Then since the lady accompanies you, and for her sake I am sorry to hear it, I suggest you gain her counsel on your manners."

Sir Hudson, red-faced, leapt to his feet.

The Emperor stood. His throat was tight, his diction precise. "This room is small, the island, not much larger. There is no space for error in our relationship. Do not presume upon my patience."

"Sir." The governor wiped his hand across his mouth. "You are my prisoner, sir."

"Ah, one more point on which we disagree. First, as a sovereign, I voluntarily sought asylum within your nation's mercy. Tradition and honor should have granted me hospitality, not captivity. Next, your government claims I'm a prisoner of war. Those wars are over, and, by international agreement, all prisoners are to be released. Your own nation's lawyers argue I'm confined illegally against long-held principles of habeas corpus. I grant your strength, but not your right to hold me. Do justice to my illustrious past or take your distasteful face from my sight."

A quiver passed up Sir Hudson's frame. "I, sir, am in charge and shall depart when I please."

"Certainly. Marchand, leave the door open so the flies may come and go." The Emperor picked up a book and began to read.

Chapter 10

Napoleon

WHILE CIPRIANI PEERED OUT THE pavilion window for intruders, the Emperor dictated to young Emmanuel. In his smallest script, the youth transcribed his monarch's complaints onto strips of muslin torn from Albine's underdress. Las Cases hung over his son's shoulder.

The Emperor, hands clasped behind his back, paced the perimeter of the green-painted room. "That martinet Lowe will be mortified. Yes, mortified to read his stupid words in a London paper. That's the thing—hit these British in their tender pride. They'll recall their bureaucratic rat to England."

Las Cases perked up. "And us as well?"

"Why not? What, Cipriani? What now?"

"The 'martinet' himself, Master. Marching up the walk."

"Mon Dieu, conceal those strips. Put out paper for dictation. Marchand, slow the governor down. No, Las Cases, hide the strips in my bedsheets."

Las Cases clutched the strips to his chest. "Sire, I can smuggle—"

"No, and that's an order. Pretend to scribble down dictation. Good boy, Emmanuel. Hand the other quill to your father. Cipriani, get on that stool, blacking my boots. A humble servant, remember?" He took a breath. "Las Cases, start writing. At Austerlitz—"

Marchand opened the door. His sloth-slow bow blocked Lowe's entry. "Sire, the governor's here. I regret he won't inform me of his business."

The Emperor slammed his palm on the table. "What? Without prior notice?"

Governor Lowe jostled past Marchand. "I shall see you whenever I deem it my duty to do so." He lifted a languid finger at Cipriani. "I'm here to deny the request for this Corsican fellow to leave the island."

Cipriani sprang to his feet.

The Emperor pressed on Cipriani's shoulder, returning him to the stool. "On what grounds? The man's a servant, not a prisoner."

"I beg to differ. He's a prisoner by association."

Cipriani slumped. "Wanted to see my sainted mother."

"Well, I won't have him roaming Europe, doing God knows what mischief. He stays where my people can watch him." Lowe craned his neck to read Las Cases's dictation paper.

The Emperor flipped it over. "Does your duty entail more than bringing despair to my servants?"

"Yes. Your move to Longwood is fixed for Thursday next. No more delay, I tell you." He sniffed. "This Briars place—unacceptable! People come and go, no fences, no guardhouse."

"And have I tried to escape?"

The governor shook a long, bony finger. "I know the tricks you pulled on Elba. You can't play cat-and-mouse games with me, sir. I've studied your past."

"While I have no interest in yours. Still, I shouldn't have been so impolitic as to classify you as 'a mouse.'" He inclined his head. "I bow to your self-knowledge."

"Sir—"

The Emperor thrust up his hand. "Sir, won't you leave before we harm our dignity?"

The governor's mouth squirmed.

The Emperor tilted his head toward the door.

Lowe squared his sloping shoulders. "For once, General Bonaparte, we agree."

As Marchand locked the door, Las Cases rushed to the camp bed.

The Emperor sank into a chair. "Las Cases, Las Cases, leave the smuggling to those who know how to accomplish it. And don't mention this message to Montholon."

Las Cases scratched his chin, looking like the squirrel Madame Mère had pegged him to be. The Emperor's jaw tightened. Madame Mère. Even if the smuggled snuff box got to her, Cipriani wouldn't be in Vienna to greet her.

But no, he'd not project despair. He cleared his face, beckoned to the Corsican, and made his voice crisp. "Quite the actor, my friend. On the bright side, I should have missed you if you had left. Now, wrap the strips in the package you devised."

Marchand peeked out the window. "The Balcombe girl, Master. Shall I shoo her off?"

"No, no, I need something to lighten my day." He concealed a wince at the ache in his side. "And, Cipriani, ask Solomon to impede progress on Longwood House. Run out of nails, vandalize the place, some such thing, so we don't move so soon."

In the doorway, Betsy peered around Marchand. "Monsieur?"

The Emperor shifted his shoulders, shrugging off a weight. "*Oui, ma petite*, is it time for our walk, or have you tracked down young Las Cases here?"

The blushes flooding Emmanuel's and Betsy's cheeks halted him midstep. He clasped his hands behind his back.

Cipriani slid into his grasp a pouch filled with the muslin strips.

IN A CORNER OF THE GARDEN, under the speckled shade of a gum tree, the Emperor leaned against a boulder. At his feet, Betsy sprawled on a horse blanket.

Nearby, Toby-Mahafaly unearthed sedge grass that encroached on her mother's roses. The slave's broadbrim straw hat lay on the ground. His face appeared no older than the Emperor's, but his hair was white and he stooped as if perpetually under burden. His son, Tobyson, a little older than the Eaglet, perhaps six, filled a bucket with weeds.

The Emperor nudged Betsy. "Like a soldier on parade, this gardener exhibits pride in his work. I want his history. Translate for me, including what's said between you."

When Betsy asked Toby to come talk, Tobyson followed, snuggling into her lap.

Toby frowned. "If you soil Miss Betsy's dress, she won't keep teaching you."

Betsy crinkled her nose at the child, who crinkled his in return. "Monsieur wants to know how you came to St. Helena."

"Tell him, 'Same as you, Your Majesty.'"

Betsy pointed a warning. "The admiral says he's not an emperor anymore. You must say 'Your Excellency' or 'Monsieur.'"

"That same admiral declares I'm property and not a man." Toby lifted his chin. "I'm a man nonetheless. And this good gentleman, he's a king, no matter what your people say."

"So tell him how you came to St. Helena, Old Toby."

"Tell him same as he did."

She translated, and the Emperor smiled. "I came on the wings of destiny and the anger of kings."

Toby nodded. "Much the same with me. Deceit and jealousy. Greed and destiny. The things in which men set their happiness and honor, their sorrow and their shame."

Betsy nodded. "Yes, but what actually happened?"

"As a boy, I was sent from my home to apprentice on a merchant ship. The navigator taught me all he knew. When I earned my freedom, I went to Madagascar, where I built a fine fleet of fishing boats."

Betsy sat up. "I never knew that."

"You never asked. One day I saw a dusky beauty dance at her sister's wedding. I wanted her as a wife. If I'd been satisfied with the two I already had, I'd be at home today. Though I treated her well, she betrayed me to slave traders. A man should know when he has enough."

"And this boy here?" the Emperor asked.

"I had one more wife, on St. Helena. She died giving me this fine son. He's more than enough for any man." He squinted. "They say you're a great soldier, that you fought these English. Is that true?"

Betsy reared her head. "Yes, but you're not allowed to ask."

The Emperor stood. "I am a soldier. You, my friend, are a navigator. A fortunate confluence." He nodded to Betsy. "Tell your father I want to buy this man's freedom."

Betsy clapped.

The Emperor bowed. "One way or another, Mahafaly."

The slave returned the bow. "For both of us."

Betsy searched the two men's faces. "You have a secret, don't you? How unfair."

"Never mind, missy." Toby lifted his son from her lap and returned to his weeds.

Betsy blew the Emperor a kiss. "You're so kind, Monsieur."

"Let's say instead, I recognize a blunder I made with slavery in France's colonies." The Emperor shredded a leaf, then another. "Under pressure, for good reason, any excuse you like, but a stain on my legacy nonetheless. Tell your father I want to set Toby free to rectify in a small way that disaster. He'll understand."

"I must say, I've never heard Old Toby talk like that."

He watched Betsy fold the blanket. "My little friend, you like secrets, don't you?"

She leaned close. "Excessively."

"And you go to Jamestown every day?"

"Almost."

"And if I had a small package I wanted delivered to Solomon?"

Betsy bobbed her pert curtsy. "I wouldn't tell a soul, not even Father."

They walked the path, hand in hand, Cipriani's packet tucked between their palms. At the pavilion, the Emperor disengaged his hand and she thrust her fist into her pocket. A risky tactic to depend on the girl, but battles had been won on slimmer odds. He hoped his Eaglet would be equally adventurous.

AT MIDNIGHT, WHILE THE GUARDS changed shifts, Cipriani boosted Albine over the windowsill into the Emperor's arms. She was fragrant like a peasant woman home from the field. Her loose hair streamed over her bare shoulders. The Emperor curved his hand around the nape of her neck. His passion rose at the dampness of her skin.

She tilted her face to his. Her small eyes shone with the piercing brightness he'd seen on Cipriani's face, on the faces of half a million soldiers risking everything to follow him. A chance for glory, a chance to feel alive.

He could taste desire on her breath. He opened his mouth and kissed her.

Albine

THE EMPEROR'S TONGUE CARESSED MINE. I fell into the abyss of his embrace. I wanted nothing else. Nothing but him. This great man could sweep me into the destiny he preached. He could give me a life I'd only glimpsed. We could do anything. Be everything. If he loved me.

Unless he caught Charles spying for the British.

He must have sensed me quake, for he raised his head. I clasped the face known around the world and guided his lips back to my own. Tonight was mine—ours—to savor. Caution belonged to tomorrow.

Footsteps crunched outside. The Emperor swung me into the shadows. A soldier's silhouette passed the window.

In the uncertain light, Napoleon resembled a young corporal, his unlined skin soft to my touch, his teeth as white as the moon, his worries tucked away. Once more, a man who didn't know defeat. He beamed a happiness I'd never seen from him before. I had given him that.

He pulled me close. "Brave girl. You should've followed the army into battle."

My lips brushed his ear. "I just did, my general."

He buried his laugh in my bosom.

"Is your pitcher full? I ought to wash. All the running—"

"No, I like you as you are." He led me to the bed.

Afterward, we shared a brandy while my Emperor—my now, my future—read out loud from *Clisson.*

Charles was wrong. Napoleon could love me.

CLISSON: THE EMPEROR'S NOVEL

Valence, France, 1788

An orange sun rose as eighteen-year-old Clisson cleaned his army boots on the inn steps. In the courtyard, weary passengers climbed into the *Diligence.* Ostlers roped luggage to its roof while its six gray horses danced in their cold traces. A dark-haired woman came out of the inn and gave Clisson a sleepy smile. She smoothed the skirt of her elegant traveling clothes. "Are you coming to Paris in the coach, Monsieur?"

He fixated upon a glossy curl caressing her left ear. The morning light tinted its chestnut deep red. He yearned to coil the tendril around his finger. "No, I'm coming *from* Paris. I go to join Le Fère regiment at Valence."

"What a shame," the young woman said. "I wouldn't have feared highwaymen with such a brave officer protecting me."

His stare strayed to her puppy-soft mouth. She had such little teeth for a tall woman. "What makes you think I'm brave?"

"Oh, your gray eyes, Monsieur. They slice through me like steel. Indeed, I'm a bit afraid."

His smile wavered. He reached for her slim hand. Blue veins adorned its delicate skin. "Mapped like butterfly wings," he murmured, as her fingers wrapped around his. "I should never hurt such a lovely thing."

She raised her hand to Clisson's lips. "I believe you. For all the fierceness in your eyes, you have a woman's mouth."

The coachman blew his horn.

She withdrew her hand and hid its loveliness in a glove. "Valence's garrison is but a day's ride from my aunt's home, where I live. We may meet again."

His heart soared, then plummeted. "But you're going to Paris."

"To fetch a friend. I return in a few weeks." She bestowed a fleeting smile and hurried to the coach.

His feet were rooted to the steps. What a clod not to have escorted her to the carriage. "How shall I find you?" he called after her.

"Visit the spa at Allès, near Champvert." As the coach rolled, she leaned out the window. "Eat breakfast, brave Monsieur. You're too skinny."

It was the longest conversation Clisson had had with a woman in nine years. He forgot to ask her name, which made it difficult to keep her in his head. "Rose" fit her elegance. *Rose of the Inn.* He rushed inside to find a mirror. Making do with a window that reflected, he hardened his arched upper lip into a manly line. A woman's mouth indeed.

She might be too tall, too old for him. How did one ask a lady's age?

Upstairs in the inn, he pounded on a chamber door. "Des Mazis, Berville! Awake! We are no longer lazy cadets."

Inside the room, someone heaved a boot against the door. Clisson pounded again. "Reveille!"

Large feet thumped across the floor. The door opened enough for Des Mazis's tousled head. "Must you always be doing? You'll wake the entire place."

Clisson grinned. "Reveille! The day moves on."

The door swung back. Des Mazis's sturdy form filled the opening. "We have three days before we report for duty. Come on, let's enjoy our first full day of freedom."

"Freedom, Des Mazis?" Clisson barged into the room. "You French know nothing of it, while I, a Corsican, can taste its rancid loss."

A second disheveled head, lean, square-jawed, with sleepy pale blue eyes, emerged from the bedcovers. "Now look what you've done, Des Mazis. You've set the fellow off again. Before long we'll be back to his 'born for war' shit. Not before I've eaten breakfast, I beg you, Clisson."

"Hurry, we must be on our way. I want to visit the Roman ruins at Vienne."

Berville bolted up in bed. "Roman ruins, you ass. All I want is a girl."

"What? Have you tired of your pillow?" Clisson asked. "Let me tell you, I, who rose early, have already kissed a woman."

Napoleon

"WHAT DO YOU THINK?" he asked.

Albine traced his jawline. "I think, above all, I like the knob on your chin."

He nibbled on her ear.

An hour later, when Cipriani *tap-tap*ped the window, he kissed her knuckles one by one. She swung her skirts over the sill and dropped to the ground. Cipriani grabbed her hand. Together they disappeared into the shadows.

He pressed his palm to the windowpane. A rush lifted his heart. He bit his lip. An old weakness. He'd become too enamored. Hadn't his father warned about women, power, and money—life's three distractions?

He paced off the room, each stride measuring exactly one meter. He'd won a bet or two with that trick back in his academy days. Never lost the knack, not as a general, not as an emperor, not during the first exile, on dull old Elba.

Four by five meters. Twenty meters square. Kicking off his red morocco slippers, he climbed on a chair and reached toward the ceiling to gauge its height. Three meters. His entire empire amounted to sixty cubic meters. On loan from an Englishman.

With so little room to maneuver, he couldn't afford to fall into a woman's trap.

When he moved to Longwood, he'd find someone else, a willing maid or neighbor girl who posed no risk of emotional ties. He leaned against an emerald wall. "Yet Albine's a woman in your mold, Josephine. Am I once again a fool?"

When the room didn't answer, he settled at his table and sketched two wigs he needed Cipriani to acquire.

Chapter 44

Napoleon

TWO BRITISH GUARDS TRAILED THE Emperor as he stomped down the garden path. In sixty battles, eighteen horses had been shot beneath him. At Wagram, a cannonball had grazed his boot. Years before at Toulon, an English pike had pierced his calf. That kind of death was acceptable. This caged life on St. Helena was not.

At the Briars signpost, he about-faced and marched back to the pavilion. There, Cipriani sprawled on a porch chair, a glass of wine in one hand.

The Emperor took the steps two at a time. "Rise when I approach," he barked.

The Corsican raised his glass. "To your sacred person."

"Get up, you lout." He kicked the Corsican's chair. "The guards are watching."

"Mi scusu!" The Corsican scrambled to his feet. "Appearances and all that. But sit with me *un pocu*. Been visiting Solomon."

The Emperor took the chair Cipriani vacated. "And so?"

"And so, the fellow's amazing. Got friends in every corner of the world. What's your pleasure? Escape to Brazil? Louisiana?"

"That simple, is it?" He knocked a chair out of Cipriani's reach.

"Ain't gonna let me sit, are you?" Cipriani glanced over his shoulder. Guards hovered a dozen steps away, frowning at the Corsican banter. "Damn sure those two don't understand us?"

"French, yes. Italian, maybe. Corsican, highly unlikely. Still, speak softly."

The Corsican mock-saluted. "Anyway, turns out Freemasons like Solomon—for all their humbug—got principles against slavery. Says your Governor Lowe don't like it much neither."

"We need to talk to Mahafaly."

"Got to find him first. Solomon never heard of a slave by that name."

"Once again, I must do your spy work." The Emperor raised his chin in the direction of a Black man tending a distant vegetable garden.

"What? That's Balcombe's slave, name of Toby. Old broken-down man's got a crown under his straw hat? Don't believe it."

"Much you know. He stands straight enough among his own people."

"I know this: I'm mighty set on getting off this dratted island. Open up, would you? What's the plan?"

"Ah, my plan." The Emperor concealed his mouth behind his hand. "A slave rebellion. Under cover of chaos, a few of us and a few of them sail to freedom."

Cipriani tipped an imaginary hat. "Now, that's the ticket. Can we trust Toby?"

"He's an honorable fellow."

"That right? Worth risking our necks on?"

"Look—not that I have to explain myself to you, but I need to do this."

"Harking back to the slave rebellion in Haiti, ain't you? Thousands butchered in that mess." Cipriani grinned. "I get it. Freeing this Toby fellow's gonna unlock Heaven's gates to you."

"Bah!" The Emperor, hiding the rare blush flooding his cheeks, dusted his boots with a handkerchief. "Who are you to lecture me, damn you? Remember my Black regiments? That wild mulatto General Dumas? What warriors. I tell you, if I'd gone to Haiti myself and formed an army of them, I could have ruled the whole Caribbean."

Cipriani rolled his eyes. "Yes, well, just saying, you got a history of trusting the wrong people. If it's all the same to you, I'll get Solomon working on his own plan. Right marvelous how he's delaying construction at Longwood House, eh?"

The Emperor nodded. "One more point to lighten that damn pessimism of yours: Toby's a trained navigator. We get ourselves a ship, a loyal crew, and he'll sail us wherever we want. Now, what're you grinning at?"

Cipriani locked his hands behind his head. "When my foot hits that blessed deck, I'll kiss your imperial ass for all to see. Reminds me: Solomon sent those wigs over in a tea crate. Left it inside for you."

The Emperor jumped to his feet. Devising plans, taking action, achieving results: that was the sort of leadership the Eaglet needed to understand. He hesitated at the pavilion's door. "What's Solomon's idea?"

Cipriani scratched his scalp. "Ever heard tell of a submarine?"

CLISSON: THE EMPEROR'S NOVEL

Valence, France, 1788

At Valence, garrison life became one long school day sans good meals. For three months, the newly graduated cadets served in the ranks, mounting guard, digging trenches, firing artillery with common soldiers. When the colonel wished, he promoted them up through the ranks to attend officer classes, supervise drills, construct batteries.

At the end of each grueling day, Clisson joined Berville and Des Mazis at the Three Pigeons Inn. The wine was harsh, the stew meat unrecognizable, but a good meal could be had on bread and cheese.

Berville tossed back his wine and coughed. "Even you, Clisson, must hate this boring garrison." He called to the serving girl to bring beer. "March, drill, study tactics. I thought when we finished school, we'd experience real life."

Clisson lifted his brows. "Perhaps you're not suited for the army after all."

"Not suited? You bastard. If we ever get to war, I'll show you who's the soldier."

"Can't you two eat dinner without a fight?" Des Mazis asked.

"No!" Clisson and Berville cried in unison. The three friends stared, broke into laughter, clinked their cups above their heads.

At night, alone in bed, he forgot his aching feet. Fantasies of the woman he met at the inn, his chestnut-haired Rose, vied with dreams of battle glory. They'd meet again at a dinner held in his honor following a victory stolen through his artillery cunning. She'd push through the throng to where he was being feted at the head table . . .

All conversation stopped at the unknown beauty's approach. "Excuse me," Rose said, her eyes melting into his. "We once met. I want to know you better." Her voice's music, her body's grace, spoke to his soul. Rose, who thought herself insensible to love, felt the fire of his passion. His devotion, the most ardent and pure that ever moved a man, smoldered throughout the day, to reignite each evening in her presence. Clisson no longer worried about other men, enemies, and war. He lived only for Rose.

Their hearts melded. They overcame all obstacles to be together always. All that was noble in love, tender in feeling, and innocent in sexuality flooded their souls. Oh, the exquisite touch of her hands.

Clisson awoke. With no Rose in his bed, he'd laid his own hands upon himself. Drumbeats penetrated his ears. A call to arms! He scrambled into his uniform.

The colonel issued emergency orders: at the king's command, protect a barge transporting scarce local wheat to Paris. Already, peasants, on behalf of their starving children, had torched the house of the merchant who sold the grain. The colonel rubbed his hands. "Yes, peasants go hungry here, but surely Paris must eat."

Des Mazis commanded the first watch, Berville the second.

At noon the next day, Clisson relieved a gaunt Berville at the granary beside the canal. The barge sat high in the water.

Clisson turned to Berville. "What? The boat's not loaded?"

"At dawn, we cut down the deputy mayor from a lamppost. Now the troops fear being strung up, too." Berville twisted his signet ring. "They refuse to split into groups fewer than five. After dusk, they won't patrol outside the warehouse."

Clisson slapped his gloves against one palm. "You allow this mutiny?"

"It's not that simple. Go ahead, you harangue them. See what it gets you. Personally, I have no desire to make my last stand over a load of wheat." Berville, protected by a dozen soldiers, marched off toward the garrison.

Inside the granary, muttering soldiers bunched together, heads low like cringing dogs. Sun rays shone through an opening in the rafters, lighting wheat dust in the air.

Clisson jumped on a crate. He waved his arms. "Soldiers, draw near. Stare duty in the face. You must not fear Death, my lads. No, defy Him and drive Him into the enemy ranks." He pumped an arm into the air.

A grizzled sergeant rubbed his thick mustache. "Nice words from a book, young lieutenant, but best used when you're facing Austrians across a battlefield. This is different. These are our own people. They want a full stomach or someone's head on a pike." He rested his rifle's stock on the ground and slouched against its barrel. "It's not our fault we're the ones in uniform."

"Hear, hear," a soldier said. Around the warehouse, others took up the cry.

Clisson raised a hand. "And, Sergeant Lyons, have you no pride in that uniform? Think you it was fashioned for parade? How came you by those stripes? I thought I'd heard a valiant story. Or am I mistaken?"

Sergeant Lyons's mustache twitched. He straightened his stout torso.

Clisson nodded. "This is a hard task, I admit, but Paris, too, must eat, or so our colonel says. We soldiers are but tools. Duty calls; we answer without recourse to politics." He pointed his finger along the ranks. "Or do you plan to hole up in this granary? Then I swear the rebels or I will see you burnt to a crisp inside this tinderbox. Fools, don't you know wheat dust ignites? Far safer to patrol outside."

Sergeant Lyons's eyes twinkled.

Clisson deepened his voice. "Now, out into the streets. This contingent on my left patrols the square tonight; those in the middle guard the barge on the canal. The rest protect the granary itself—from the outside, where it's safer. Sergeant, move 'em out."

The sergeant grinned at the troops. "This one's got his head on straight, not like those other lieutenants. He's right—it's more dangerous inside. Move out." Reluctantly, the soldiers fanned out into the street, shuffling their black-booted feet. Clisson strode among them, calling some by name. He repositioned the granary's defenses, set up a barricade before its doors. When he whistled a ballad, the sergeant took up the song in better tune.

At midnight, church bells clanged throughout the town. Rebels, brandishing kitchen knives, pikes, scythes, and hatchets, poured like grain into the square in front of the warehouse. Torchlight shimmered on their hard-set faces. Tonsured monks from the local abbey, widows in black bonnets, young girls with tricolor ribbons in their hair: all marched together, arms locked with boatmen, porters, bakers, farmers. A red kerchief encircled each rebel neck. Two hundred feet echoed on stone; a hundred voices reverberated around the square. "Our bread. Our bread stays here." The tallest rebel waved a red flag above their heads.

Clisson's chest swelled. His father had once marched thus. His uncle and his mother, too. Had their faces glowed in such passion the year he was born? He was Corsican, not French. Why not tip the scale the People's way? Didn't they deserve to eat? He clutched the granary key.

Sergeant Lyons barked a word. The troops spread out across the square, blocking the entrance to the granary. Twenty meters apart, the rebels and soldiers formed opposing lines. Both sides fidgeted in silence, broken by a baby's cry.

Clisson gulped, fingering the granary key, deciding yes, then no.

The tall rebel with the flag raised his eyes. From the church tower, bricks pelted the soldiers, bouncing on the cobblestones around Clisson, smashing soldiers' feet, knocking muskets from their hands, scattering their ranks. Sergeant Lyons, blood oozing from his scalp, collapsed.

Rebels surged as one toward the granary. Murder shone in the faces of the mob.

The soldiers rushed behind the barricade. Clisson sprang forward to drag the sergeant out of the fray. His back took a hit from a ricocheting rock. He crouched, his thin body a shield for the fallen sergeant. He yelled an order over his shoulder and ducked, covering his ears. Two cannons concealed behind the barricade exploded. Hot grapeshot, flying over him, blasted into the crowd. A dozen people—monks, women, farmers, the rebel with the flag—crumpled. Around him rose anguished cries from the rebels. Dismay echoed in the soldiers' ranks.

"Reload," Clisson cried.

Through the cannon smoke, the rebel mob stampeded in retreat, trampling the bodies of their comrades, slipping in the blood, tripping on their red flag, disappearing down narrow streets. The dead, the injured, the weak lay deserted, broken dolls on the cobblestones. Here and there, they moaned.

There was no need to fire a second time. Clisson waved to his men to stand down. Sergeant Lyons's eyes were closing. More than blood flowed from his head. Clisson held him, whispered in his ear, past the time when the man was surely gone.

Clouds blocked out the stars. No, not clouds—the shadows of his men, who had closed into tight ranks around him.

Napoleon

ALTHOUGH IT WAS MIDDAY, the pavilion's draperies were pinned shut. Candles lit the room.

The Emperor surveyed Las Cases's haircut. He took the comb from Marchand and fluffed his squirming secretary's forehead fringe. "Thinner than mine, don't you think?"

Cipriani laughed.

"Enough of that," said the Emperor. "But now that you have the color right, Marchand, if he keeps his distance, these British guards will never notice. Take a little more off here."

Las Cases flinched as the valet's scissors clipped his ear.

"Please, sir, you must stay still. Most of the time you'll wear one of the wigs that looks like your own hair." Marchand frowned. "Do you object to resembling the Emperor?"

"No, no, no, it's not that. Everyone admires our sire's chestnut hair—not a strand of gray at his age. And after all his reverses, too. Most admirable. But, sire, if they catch me with dyed hair under a wig, they'll know I'm impersonating you."

The Emperor patted Las Cases's shoulder. "You must take great care not to be caught."

Marchand extracted two brown wigs from the crate Cipriani had gotten from Solomon.

The Emperor fingered the thick sideburns. "How can you stand these furry mice on your face? I swear, Las Cases, you're as vain as the pope."

Las Cases rubbed his newly shaven cheeks. "I'll miss them."

Marchand murmured, "I'll glue the fake ones on you every morning until this charade has run its course."

Las Cases pressed the valet's hand.

"Stand. Let's have a look at you," the Emperor said. "Mon Dieu, my clothes fit you perfectly. Am I that fat? No, Cipriani, I don't advise you to answer. Now, we practice. Las Cases, put on my hat and take a stroll with Marchand around the garden. The guards must get used to this counterfeit Napoleon."

While Las Cases and Marchand ambled about the garden, Cipriani and the Emperor peeked around the draperies.

The Corsican pranced on his tiptoes. "What a dandy Las Cases is."

The Emperor growled. "It'll never work if he can't do better. Mon Dieu, here comes Betsy. Fetch them quick. We'll drill him in private."

Albine

JUST WHEN I WAS SURE the Emperor was within my grasp (and heart), he neglected me. Marchand bade me to be patient, not overwhelm the man with entreaties for his time. But why was he spending hours with Las Cases, I asked, and received no reply.

I was moping in bed when the maid brought good news. That very morning, the HMS *Camel* had delivered bonnets to Solomon's. I hurried to the emporium. New hats! Though they smelled of the goats that had traveled with them in the ship's hold, I bought two on credit. Solomon, for all his "dear, sweet madames," hustled me out before I could "purchase" more. I wore the straw with a poke front and blue ribbons. It was my son Tristan's tenth birthday.

At one o'clock, I strolled down Main Street to St. James Church, that awkward stone hulk with a crenellated tower better suited for a castle. While I awaited Charles, my fingers traced the swirls carved into the church's oak doors. What heights an English forest must reach to yield such massive wood.

In contrast, St. Helena's trees grew like scrub weeds—all except those transplants from India that stood at the top of Main Street. The Three Trees, as they were called, had a special aura, for in their shade the locals hawked their slaves.

The English oaks that made the church doors had an aura, too. Their mammoth trunks had survived kings and wars, plagues and science, drought and flood, to travel five thousand miles to witness a French emperor's humiliation. And my own desperation. I slapped the wood and got a stinging palm.

I jumped. Charles had sneaked up and pinched me. We'd barely spoken since he'd destroyed my flower crown, and he wanted to play games? Without apology, he swung open the door.

How drab—how British—it was inside. Dreary whitewashed walls. Starched cloth on the altar slab. No statues on pedestals. No worshippers, no incense, no sacred haze. I missed the Catholic Church. At least, immersed in its hocus-pocus, one could pretend to believe.

"Stop complaining," Charles said. "You're the one who insisted we go to church. Where'd you get that hat?"

"*Shh*, we're here to pray for Tristan." I tiptoed down the worn flagstones to scoot into a pew. Charles settled in next to me. "You go first," I told him. "Say your prayer out loud."

The roof *click-click*ed as its wooden trusses expanded in the midday heat. Charles rubbed his forehead. His jaw muscles flexed; his lips pursed in what I suspected was Revolutionary disgust. He sprang up.

I grabbed his sleeve. "You don't have to believe in God. Just make a wish for our son."

He shook off my grip but sat again. "All right, all right. I wish that Tristan studies hard, that he is one of the best students, but not *the* best, in his class." He flicked my nose, not unkindly. "No one likes the guy on top."

"That's a good one." I gave Charles a grin that belied the heaviness in my chest. "My turn. I wish that he makes friends—"

"Powerful friends," Charles interrupted.

I touched a finger to his lips. "Many friends. I hope when he finds love, that love lasts all his life."

Charles squeezed my thigh (as if he owned it). "I hope the lady's a charmer like Tristan's mother, but richer. In fact, less charm and more wealth would suit me fine."

I pushed his hand off my leg.

The sun, poking through the clouds, glared through the church's windows. In France, stained glass would have cast a joy of colors. In this Anglican place, the light passed through clear glass, illuminating thousands of imperfections in the air. That was their point. They wanted us to see life's disappointments. I unpinned a locket from inside the bosom of my dress.

Charles took it from me. "Thought you'd sold that." He released the catch to reveal a tiny portrait of our son. "You never liked it."

No, I didn't like the portrait and didn't look at it often. When I did, somehow I always expected to see something different, something better than the discontentment marring my child's face. But there it was, lying in Charles's palm, glaring up at me: Tristan's irksome dissatisfaction, captured in the wrinkle he squeezed between his brows. I didn't want my boy to be like me, always scraping the bottom of life's bowl, never finding a lick of happiness, but there he was.

"Your turn to make a wish," Charles said.

My thoughts hung like those motes in the air. *My Tristan, my beloved, I don't know how to fix your flaws. I cannot fix my own. I didn't mean to teach you unhappiness. Now I cannot hold you. I cannot reach you. You're on your own. You're on your own. You're on your own.* The refrain swirled in my head. All I could give voice to were sobs.

Charles held me until my flood abated. He dabbed my face with his handkerchief. "I wish," he said, giving me a gentle shake, "Tristan may grow as tall as I am, but broader and fatter, so he'll be a better lover."

I forced a watery chuckle. He was my only link to my son.

The tower bell pealed two o'clock. I winced at the clang.

Charles sat upright. "Now we get to business."

"What business?"

"You shall see what your clever husband has arranged." He took my arm.

A British officer—Basil Jackson, my almost handsome lieu-tenant—stood at the back of the church, leaning (disrespectfully) against the oak doors. Charles tucked me behind him, to hide my teary face, I guessed. All that crying. I had to look a fright. Worse, an old fright. I straightened my new hat and peeked around Charles.

Basil Jackson lifted his square chin toward a side door. Charles nodded. We three converged on the spot. The lieutenant unlocked the door with a large toothed key like the ones used in the Bastille. I hesitated, afraid of some trick leading to a dungeon, but the room proved to be a vestry, lit through smudged windows, filled with cassocks, stoles, and chasubles in colors for each season.

Lieutenant Jackson clicked his heels, perhaps to start the conver-sation, perhaps to display his perfect form (which the gesture did). Despite the jaunty bow under my chin, he didn't so much as glance at me. "General Montholon," he said, "the governor accepts your offer."

Charles's thin lips tightened as his eyebrows rose—his triumphal tic, which cost us dearly whenever he played cards.

"We burned your letter." Jackson clicked his heels a second time. "No more papers with my name or your signature on them. Record your observations in a diary, as if for yourself alone. Understood?"

"And the money?" Charles demanded through those tight lips.

"Banked in London, according to your instructions. Monthly deposits as long as you're useful. Nothing when you're not. For your safety, we'll make no payments on this island, though I'm authorized to pass you a few coins now and then."

My husband lost his stiffness. "Fair enough."

"I'm your conduit. When you wish to see me, tell the barkeep at Portcous House, 'Jackson.' He'll find me."

"Understood."

"Now, you two leave first." Lieutenant Jackson bowed over my hand. His tongue lingered on my skin, jolting my lower core. Perhaps, in my pretty new hat, I didn't look so bad.

Chapter 12

Napoleon

AFTER BRIEF AFTERNOON LOVEMAKING, the Emperor led Albine onto the pavilion's porch. A dozen meters away, Montholon, Bertrand, and Las Cases played cards in the shade of a canopy their host had constructed over the lawn. There, too, black-haired Dr. O'Meara chatted with Fanny Bertrand, his fellow Irishwoman, as she poured tea. All turned to stare at them.

A peal of laughter sounded. Betsy and young Emmanuel Las Cases emerged from a garden path. Betsy, seeing the Emperor with preening Albine, skidded to a stop. She would have fallen if Emmanuel hadn't held her hand.

The Emperor surveyed the field. Their outrage, anger, sadness, disappointment, and cynicism bit into him. Not a lick of compassion for the man stuffed inside his iconic uniform. Even Bertrand's battle-scarred chin jutted in rebuke, as if his emperor had transgressed some military regulation. These followers confined him to the heroic figure they imagined him to be. How dare they judge him?

Albine's grip on his arm tightened. She lifted her nose in the air. Marchand hurried around the corner. His eyes met his Master's.

The valet bowed. "Madame de Montholon, may I beg your advice on a personal matter?"

The Emperor disentangled from her clutch. He descended to the lawn alone. As he strolled toward the canopy, he waved at Betsy, who returned a faint smile. Dr. O'Meara fiddled with chess pieces. Fanny Bertrand contemplated her pretty hands. General Bertrand turned his back on Montholon, who laughed too loudly at something Las Cases said.

The Emperor swallowed the burn in his throat. He might lead these people, but not a one of them was his friend.

CLISSON: THE EMPEROR'S NOVEL

Valence, France, 1788

Clisson was scrubbing dried blood from his uniform when Berville and Des Mazis barged into his quarters. Berville pounded on the table. "You fired upon unarmed citizens? Bullets for starving women and children, grapeshot for farmers with scythes."

Clisson frowned. "The orders were to stop the mob."

"Not a mob—our fellow countrymen."

"Perhaps yours, Berville. You were born here. France is my country only as long as I choose to make it so."

"Careful," Des Mazis said. "Those are a traitor's words."

Berville threw himself on Clisson's bed. "You, who were educated on the king's bounty."

"My loyalty's not for sale, and get your boots off my blanket. God, you French are too turbulent, too inclined to rail. And loyalty? You're the ones saying I should have disobeyed orders."

"He panicked," Des Mazis said to Berville. "That's the only excuse."

"I didn't panic. They attacked the king's—*your king's*—granary. *Your* harmless citizens killed Sergeant Lyons with a rock. They carried knives and pikes." Clisson looked from Des Mazis to Berville. "*You* try staring down the throat of a mob. What would you do? Cut and run? In Plutarch, wives and children—"

"Plutarch?" Berville swept Clisson's books from a table. "Fool, how dare you give us one of your history lessons? This was real."

Clisson's face reddened. "You're the fool. History is written in the People's blood. You'll never be a soldier if you're afraid to shed it." He grabbed Berville by his lapels. "Pick up my books."

"Stand apart." Their colonel's bark from the doorway snapped the three lieutenants to attention. "Clisson did the task assigned. He pulled the injured sergeant out of the fray. While his bravery's lauded in the ranks, you two sit on your sullen asses. He'll be rewarded, but each of you must decide. Are you loyal to the king, or are you revolutionaries?"

All three looked at the floor.

"If you're sympathizers, you don't belong in my garrison. Report to me in the morning." The colonel's boots resounded on the stone as he strutted away.

Berville dropped his head into his hands. "Now we're in the soup. Look what you've done, Clisson."

"How is this my fault?"

"Stay calm, Berville," Des Mazis said. "We'll tell the colonel we were taking always perfect Clisson down a peg—anyone can understand that."

Clisson stormed out of his room. His friends—friends!—didn't understand. He was not one of them. He didn't fire on *his fellow countrymen*. The French had invaded his homeland. How often must he say it? He didn't ask to be French.

The next morning, the colonel quizzed Clisson on ordnance, tested his mathematics skills. His lips pursed, he listened to Clisson's idea to strengthen the garrison's fortifications with two well-placed redoubts. He promoted Clisson to first lieutenant and assigned him fifty men. He waved his hand. "The work may not be strictly necessary. Nonetheless, it's good practice." He picked up a document to read.

Clisson backed out the door. Some fine day, when justice found its balance, that colonel would regret his insulting dismissal. For now, Clisson accepted his promotion with pride.

He stayed up all night drawing plans for his redoubts. Construction quickly followed. At each dawn, he patrolled the works, correcting this, improving that, lecturing to all who had no choice but to listen. The sun baked the earth hard beneath the soldiers' shovels. The rations could not sustain hard labor. The ranks who had once admired him grumbled. His fellow officers, Berville and Des Mazis included, mocked him as "the colonel's genius."

At each accomplishment, the colonel assigned another task. The redoubts built, he sent Clisson on a sortie to clarify a conflict between two sets of maps.

Clisson, weary from the long day in the saddle, opened the door to his room. His mouth gaped. Ransacked! His books were strewn on the floor, his private papers trampled. Muddy boots had left prints on his second uniform. Someone had pissed on his mattress.

"Bastards!" Clisson tossed it out a window. The boot prints were identical to his; that pointed to fellow officers. If he told the colonel, they might feel some lashes or be cashiered.

Des Mazis? He would know who had done it, but had no guts to stop it.

Berville? Too smart to get caught but had probably instigated it.

Clisson wanted to pound his head against the wall. He was tired of serving with men who did not value him, who rewarded only mediocrity with friendship. They scorned his precision as priggishness, his dedication as bootlicking, his cool reserve as arrogance. So much for friendship in the army.

Still, these *comrades* needed to see he wasn't afraid. He'd find them at the inn.

At the Three Pigeons, Des Mazis and half a dozen junior officers crowded around Berville, swilling wine, feeling up the serving girl. Conversation stopped when they saw him on the threshold.

Clisson tossed precious coins on the bar. "A round of wine for my friends."

Des Mazis offered a hand. "Thanks, Clisson. Just back from the sortie?"

He pushed Des Mazis aside. "Returned an hour ago. Had some cleaning to do."

No one met his eyes, except Berville, who smirked.

The servant girl topped off each cup around the silent table.

Clisson lofted his drink. "To comrades in arms who watch each other's backs."

Everyone raised his cup, except Des Mazis, who looked about to cry. As the others gulped their drinks, Clisson stood. He poured his wine onto the table and upended the pitcher. While the wine rolled into their laps, the officers, including Berville, stayed seated.

"My apologies," said Clisson. "I never drink with pigs."

If only Rose of the Inn had been there to see his triumph.

Napoleon

THE EMPEROR LAID HIS HEAD on his arms on the table. It wore him out, this pretending to be well.

"Master." Marchand's gentle hand rested on his shoulder.

The Emperor raised his head. "I didn't know you were here."

"So I gather. We'll have Dr. O'Meara visit tomorrow. He can be trusted."

Albine

FOB ME OFF ON MARCHAND, Your Imperial Highness? You think I didn't notice? Didn't sense you stiffen at those haughty faces? Didn't feel your contempt when you removed my polluted hand from your sacred arm (moments after you gloried to my touch)? I could have told you, if you'd bothered to ask, I was a woman experienced with scorn.

And Marchand made me as cross as a camel with his foolish questions about lavender oil and cucumber paste. I stamped a foot. "Stop it, do you hear? I know what happened on that porch." But, truth was, I didn't know why Napoleon's love for me had dwindled into a sordid, passionless affair. I glanced at the path to the pavilion.

Marchand shook my elbow. "No, Madame, don't go there."

He was right, of course. Time to withdraw from the scene. Luckily, at the Briars gate, the old slave (the one Napoleon had befriended, though I couldn't imagine why) had hitched a pony to a cart. I'd go back to town. I'd buy something. Or, better yet—a naughty grin lifted my spirits—*sell* something to recover my self-respect.

I hurried down the garden stairs. The old man grunted (politely, I must admit), nodded that he was bound for Jamestown, and helped me onto the wooden bench seat. I demanded to know what we waited for, but the man had no language. His gestures made no sense. He ignored mine.

When I'd almost melted in the sun, Tobyson, the child I'd saved, appeared out of nowhere. His father directed him into the cart behind us. Instead, the boy climbed up next to me, blinking a question with his thick lashes. I pulled him close, and the cart trundled off, bouncing along ruts and over rocks. By the time we reached Jamestown, two things were clear: the little boy spoke French, and I'd spared my feet only to bruise my backside.

Porteous House was empty, all my compatriots being at the Briars. In my bedchamber, I transformed a pillow into the Emperor and wagged my finger in his face. *How dare you take my hand from your arm, as though I were a kitchen maid? My family lost all they had in the Revolution, but they were aristocrats. Unlike you Bonapartes, the spawn of imaginary Italian nobles. Ha! Carnival barkers or rag pickers, more likely. In the old days, my father wouldn't have invited yours to dinner, much less let you touch his daughter.*

But the pillow returned the same scorching look Napoleon had given me on the Briars porch. Not hate. Worse: distaste. Blood pulsed in my cheeks. I'd seen that on other men's faces, though none so illustrious as his. It heralded the beginning of the end. One more affair dumped on the trash heap of my love life. I buried my face in the pillow.

Determined to spread my shame around, I retrieved Napoleon's hairbrush, ran its stolen bristles through my hair, and set off to find a buyer. On Jamestown's Main Street, I surveyed the prospects. No, not Solomon. He'd apply payment to my store account. (Never pay old debts with fresh coin, as my father, a *true* aristocrat, used to say.)

Up the street, to the left of the Three Trees, a cheese-and-sausage monger tended a tiny store. I popped my head inside. The cramped space stank of overripe curd, bluish cheese, and blood sausage. Ten minutes in that place, and the Emperor's brush would stink, too. Thankfully, our English–French divide proved no barrier to commerce. Before I was out the door, the brush lay in the shop window under dangling sausage links.

Armed with coins to jangle, cheese to munch, and dried sausage for emergencies, I wandered toward the quay. The two brown hills that formed Jamestown's valley towered above me like prison walls. In front of me, the docks opened to the world beyond. But there, the steel ocean formed a wall, hemming me into St. Helena, the perfect prison cell.

Already I missed the precious brush, but Napoleon had made it plain: he didn't want me. Without him, I was no use to Charles.

Worse, my failure sentenced Tristan to the prison of poverty. My son's future, my future, my present: everything was blank.

At the church, I threw my weight against the oak doors to bang them open. The church's profound plainness seemed an affront to God, who'd given humankind roses, camembert, and sex. I kicked off my shoes. The cool flagstones were delicious against my bare soles, the disrespect, a balm to my pride.

I padded into the pew where Charles and I made wishes for Tristan. In front of me, a prayer book lay on a narrow ledge. I opened it to read a prayer, but in this church (unlike the sausage store), the English language formed a barrier. The words were as incomprehensible to me as my French had been to the old slave Toby.

I ripped a page, then another, from the prayer book and dropped them near my naked toes. As I chose a third, I saw that the first two sheets had vanished. I felt around with my foot. No paper. Surely, those drab walls housed no miracles. I tore another page and watched it fall.

A small Black hand crept from beneath my pew. I slammed my foot on the paper. The hand withdrew without its prize. I waited.

Tobyson rolled over the back of my pew, landing next to me. His round face was grave, yet forgiving, as he removed the book from my grasp and stored it out of reach. "I sneak in here, Madame, when I'm sad," he whispered in his lovely French. "Are you sad?"

I nodded.

"If we sit long enough, you'll feel better. I promise." He hummed soft melodies.

I soaked in the comfort of his music, of his warm hand in mine. My anger dissolved into a fitful peace. Perhaps happiness wasn't always built on quicksand that devoured it. Perhaps this child knew—was—the secret to finding solid ground.

But as I examined Tobyson's sweet face and he examined mine, his mouth froze. He snatched away his hand and scrambled under the pew in front of us, and under the next, and the next, until he burst into the aisle and raced out the side door.

I covered my face. What ugliness had he seen in me to frighten him so?

From behind, a hand grasped my shoulder. Fingers traced my prison scar. My heart *thump-thump-thump*ed in my stomach. It was worse not to know. I turned.

Basil Jackson smiled down on me. He lifted my chin.

We kissed.

Chapter 13

Napoleon

THE EMPEROR WINCED AT DR. O'MEARA'S palpating his stomach. "It's the worst on the left. Do you feel the hard spot?"

"Your father dead at thirty-five, Your Majesty?" The young doctor helped him to sit up. "You're lucky to be alive at fifty. Over time, the condition inevitably progresses."

So, the stomach trouble that had hastened his father's death, the abdominal pains that had sapped his own energy from Eylau to Moscow to Waterloo, had followed him to St. Helena. Time, that unrelenting master, was almost through with him. His fingers clung to the earthbound solidness of his camp bed. His poor Eaglet, left alone.

The doctor reverted to a lighter tone. "My immediate concern is the swelling in your legs. Indeed, I don't like this nausea and fatigue, or the color of your skin. Likely all from hepatitis, which is rampant on the island."

Ah, something useful. He perked up. "Will our illustrious governor believe you?"

O'Meara shrugged. "When I recommend your return to England, he rants he'll not trust an Irish doctor. Claims we're all revolutionaries."

"Are you?"

The doctor colored. "At any rate, I've written directly to the Admiralty in London."

"A brave maneuver." The Emperor placed his hand over the doctor's. "You may not have the power to cure me, but you could rid me of this maggot governor."

The doctor fiddled with the latch on his bag. "Sire? Although many in Ireland would have welcomed you, would have helped you invade England—members of my own family—we must put past dreams aside. I'm a loyal officer in the British navy."

"But?" The Emperor moved his hand to the doctor's shoulder.

"But I feel compelled to warn you there are those on this island, not English, but French—members of your own entourage—whom you shouldn't trust. The other day, I saw names on a paper on the governor's desk."

Two guards tromped past the window.

O'Meara picked up his bag.

"Montholon?" the Emperor mouthed.

The doctor nodded.

"General or wife?"

He raised his eyes to Napoleon's. "Indeed, I didn't think to distinguish between the two."

As the doctor was closing the door behind him, Betsy stuck her head in. "Monsieur? *Permettez-moi?* It's most important."

"Perhaps later, my dear—" The Emperor broke off. Betsy's eyes were too bright. With remorse? Fear? Ah, well, he could use a diversion. "All right. We'll take a short walk, and you'll tell me what's 'most important.' What's in that unladylike portfolio? State secrets?"

She held her finger to her lips.

They followed the path toward the waterfall, ducking under dripping fern tree branches, muddying their shoes in the boggy soil. He sidestepped a low spiderweb. Two British soldiers trailed them, the first cursing as he barged into the web. At the edge of a clearing, Betsy lifted an imperious hand to keep the soldiers at a distance. She led the Emperor to a stone bench, flounced down, and dropped her face into her hands.

She peeked between her fingers. "Cher Monsieur!"

He tucked a wild curl behind her ear. "Are you in despair or playacting, *mon enfant*?"

Betsy cast him a resentful glare.

"Tell me your troubles, child. I know a little about despair." He reached for her hands.

Her knuckles whitened around the leather portfolio.

"Did you indeed steal state secrets?" He pried her fingers off the case. When he opened it, he turned on her. "How dare you?"

The girl's brashness vanished. Though she trembled, she confronted his fury as unblinkingly as his bravest soldier awaiting punishment.

His face softened. He pinched her chin.

Her lips quavered. "I-I didn't know the papers were important when I stole them from your writing box this morning. But they are, aren't they, Monsieur? I'm so sorry. It was meant to be a silly revenge because you cheated me at cards."

"Did you read it?"

"Some. Your handwriting's atrocious." Her face brightened. She touched his arm. "Will you read it to me? Is it true? Are you Clisson?"

He regarded that hand, resting on his sleeve. How he missed his nieces. Prison walls had indeed shut off his person from the world. He laid his soft white hand over Betsy's firm, youthful one. "When I started this, I was trying to forget a woman. No, not a woman—an idea. The idea of a perfect woman."

She clapped. "That's what I thought. It's a love story, though it starts with war."

"I'm a soldier, Betsy. In my life, everything starts and ends with war. But while this story's a novel, I cobbled it together from events and ideas that have been important to me." He ruffled through the limp pages. "I've carried the manuscript with me for twenty years. A few weeks ago, I started writing again. I should have been distressed if you hadn't returned it."

She hung her head. "I meant only to tease, Monsieur." She looked up, her eyes sharp with curiosity. "Why didn't you finish it when you were young?"

"The spark extinguished itself. The French say, 'A boy becomes a man when the young poet within him dies.' I went to war. The poet inside me was swallowed up."

"Maybe when a man grows old, the poet gets reborn. Like I once saw a new tree growing out of an old stump."

He pulled her earlobe. "You're impertinent to call an emperor an old stump."

She whispered, "Let's finish it together."

"I don't know, little chick." He shook his head. "It's more than a love story. I'm telling truths about my life in a roundabout way the Eaglet might understand when he's older. A story to inspire him. And to explain about my life and his."

"But I know all about novels. I've read dozens of them. Let's work on it together. I want to get into the love story."

"My girl, love's not as simple as you think. Did you get far into the manuscript?"

She shook her head.

"Let me read to you about the reality of love," he said.

* * *

CLISSON: THE EMPEROR'S NOVEL

Part II: On Destiny Delayed
Valence, France, 1789

Clisson never again ate with the junior officers at the Three Pigeons Inn. After all, no one wanted to discuss philosophy, Corsica's injustices, or military strategy. Plus, the colonel, blind to the rift within the ranks, banned political discussions as incendiary, now that revolution was rife on the French streets.

"Close a mouth, close a mind," the colonel said. "Better not to talk politics."

Clisson passed evenings in his room, studying tactics, philosophy, history. He read Corneille, Racine, and, although he didn't admire him much, dry old Voltaire. Rousseau, a romantic foreigner trying to be French, spoke to his ardent soul.

He ended each day writing the fantasy that held his heart in a pincer.

Rose and Clisson married. They retired to a secluded, simple life, having forgotten the world and the world having forgotten them. Content in the company of each other, they farmed their food and ventured forth only to buy necessities and give alms to the poor. Each night, Clisson rejoiced in the weight of Rose's head on his shoulder.

But when the sun woke him, Rose's head was not on his shoulder. His chest felt as hollow as if someone had removed his heart. He checked for a scar. The woman he'd never known, the warmth of a body he never embraced—their loss was no less painful for having been imaginary.

Eating less so he could spend on books and save for his leave, Clisson lost weight, neglected to cut his lank hair. His cheekbones protruded; dark circles ringed his eyes. Only his uniform, hanging loose on his lean bones, stayed pristine.

Berville had been right. Garrison life dulled the soul.

As Clisson dreamed of visiting Champvert to find Rose, winter turned to spring. He applied again for leave. "Unsettled times," the colonel said. "You're needed here. But Champvert? I've family there. When the time comes, ask me for a letter of introduction."

Clisson redoubled his efforts to gain the colonel's respect. While he directed troops to fill in a marsh, other officers played cards. The colonel napped as Clisson positioned artillery, drilled the battalion, lectured troops on defense.

One gray day, he received a package. In the box, he found Father's spyglass and a letter. He held Mamma's gardenia-scented paper between his thumb and forefinger and, under a somber French sky, read silently:

Dearest Son, Pride and Support of My Life,

Your father died last Tuesday. His pain seared like a hot stiletto in his side, yet he bravely smothered his cries. The neighbors complained only a little. In his last moments, he knocked your brother Joseph to the floor and called for Clisson's valiant sword to save him. Upon those words, his soul took flight, rising Heavenward, no doubt, for, while some complain of his business dealings, his openhandedness to his friends surely commends him to our Savior. No one knows better than I how much the man gave away. Now my poor husband, in his best silver brocade, shares a grave with your namesake under the church's floor. The butcher sent a roast lamb, and your Pozzo di Borgo cousins provided wine for the funeral. I ate and drank none, fearing poison, but the funeral guests suffered no ill. All would be lost, except the governor has been so generous. He brought ells of black silk and a black mantilla so my appearance could do your father's memory justice. Your brother says I am a pretty blackbird now.

Without your father, I cannot maintain the house. The political temperature here is such that your brother leaves to finish his law studies in Pisa, while I have moved down the coast. The governor's a veritable guardian angel. Judge not your mother, for she is a grieving widow.

About the marsh you said you were draining: keep your feet dry. You know how you catch cold.

Your dearest Mamma

PS: The spyglass is a token to remember your father by.

A token to remember Father by? How about treachery? A canker in the stomach? Clisson tasted blood from biting his tongue. "Babbú, Babbú, you sent me into exile from my home. You made me French. I do not forgive you." He looked down to reread the letter. It was crumpled in his fist.

Napoleon

As THEY STROLLED TOWARD THE HOUSE, British guards in their wake, Betsy nuzzled the Emperor's ear. "When I go back to England, I'll smuggle your manuscript to the Eaglet."

He shook his head. "You don't comprehend the danger that entails. Run along, my dear."

Entering his pavilion, the Emperor found he was not alone. He shut the door to conceal his intruder from the guards. The slave child Tobyson, wearing soiled gardener clothes and the Emperor's bicorne, balanced on a chair. The mirror above the mantel reflected his horror at being caught. The too-large hat tipped over one eye.

Forcing a frown, the Emperor strode forward. Solemnly, he straightened the hat and, with his handkerchief, wiped the child's dirt-smeared nose. He kissed the boy on each cheek. "Go forth, my son. Conquer the world."

Tobyson broke out his accustomed grin. He puffed his chest. "Na-po-le-on!"

"Yes, quite a pair, we two, pretending to be emperors." He rested his head against the boy.

Tobyson patted the Emperor's cheek.

Voices sounded outside. Tobyson jammed the bicorne on the Emperor's head.

"Yes, no more playtime." The Emperor lifted the boy down from the chair. "*Vraiment*, you don't want that hat's weight on your soul." He waved the child to the door.

Tobyson bowed General Montholon in before running out.

"Sit, Charles." The Emperor pointed to the oak table. He poured two glasses of wine and handed one to Montholon. "To what do I owe this pleasure?"

Montholon's long fingers massaged his glass. "I've been approached—bribed, actually—to spy on you for the governor. I thought you'd like to know."

"Fascinating." The Emperor relaxed into the chair across from his general. "Why you?"

"I don't know."

"Don't know?" He leaned forward. "No idea?"

"I'm reporting it, aren't I? Why are you suspicious?"

"I ask myself the same question." The Emperor held his wineglass to the sunlight. "A very nice wine. Solomon imports it from Cape Town. Do you like it?"

"No."

"Why not?"

"Too sweet."

The Emperor put down his glass. "And yet you drink it. What did they offer you?"

"Money."

"That's all?"

Montholon hesitated. "A lot of money. Ten thousand pounds sterling in a London bank when we return to Europe."

"We?"

"Albine and me."

"Ah." The Emperor admired his glass. He rolled the stem between his fingers. "And I?"

"You're to stay here."

He looked up. "Forever, Charles?"

"Didn't ask."

The stem of the Emperor's glass snapped. The wineglass's bowl spiraled over the tabletop and shattered on the tile floor.

Montholon flinched.

"For God's sake, man, find out. Meanwhile, here are your orders. I'm not well. Convince them to return me to Europe for medical care. Otherwise, my death will be on their heads, and those heads will roll. It's my liver. Their own Dr. O'Meara will substantiate it."

Montholon nodded.

"Also find out all you can about Hudson Lowe. He can't be much of a general if none of us have heard of him. Discover some weakness we can use. British people love gossip. Give them some of ours, and get theirs in return."

Montholon edged his chair from the table.

"Sit. Do they know about my relationship with Albine?"

Montholon crossed his arms on his chest.

"I take it that means yes. That's why they chose you?"

"They didn't say so."

The Emperor softened his voice. "You know how I feel about half-truths."

Montholon shrugged. "That fellow Jackson—the governor's man—threw it in my face. He's lucky to be alive. I didn't hurt him much but thought it best if they got I was resentful."

"Are you?"

Charles wiped a knuckle across his mouth. "No."

"You proposed this situation, not I." The Emperor gripped Montholon's wrist. "If you've changed your mind—or Albine has— say so. I take no man's wife against his or her wishes."

Montholon shook off the Emperor's hand. "Are we through?"

"Repeat what you're going to tell them."

"That you're ill, sicker than you look. Maybe dying. That Bertrand's a pompous prig living under his wife's thumb. That you let dirty slave boys hang around you. That Cipriani—"

The Emperor raised a finger. "Not Cipriani. The rest is good. Keep your lies close to the truth. But you know how to do that. And take the money. Otherwise, they'll be suspicious."

"That was always my plan, sire." He tossed off his wine, straightened his long frame, and headed for the door.

"Charles!"

Montholon turned.

The Emperor held out his hand to shake. "Don't tell Albine about this British offer."

"No, of course not."

Alone again, the Emperor wiped his palm on his handkerchief. Cunning fellow, that Montholon. Hard to figure which side he was double-crossing. Best to keep in mind what Madame Mère always said: when you're top of the heap, everyone beneath you has a dagger pointed up.

Chapter 14

Napoleon

ON NAPOLEON'S LAST MORNING AT the Briars, William Balcombe stood on the porch, under the glare of a clearing sky, contemplating his boots. "Won't be possible to free Toby, Your Majesty."

The Emperor raised his brows. The forbidden "Your Majesty" from this British subject?

Balcombe pulled his thick mustache. "Governor's dead set against having more freedmen on the island. Not long before you arrived, a local white woman gave birth to a Black child."

"Hardly my fault, Balcombe."

"No, sire, but, needless to say, it created a great deal of ill will toward our free Blacks." Balcombe shook his head. "To keep peace, Sir Hudson's forcing all Blacks—freedman and slave alike—to attend church thrice a week."

"Save their souls? Yes. Free them? No. This governor's a petty pope." The Emperor shielded his eyes to gaze across the distant ocean into a past where popes buckled under his will.

"Well, truth is, I'm pleased to keep old Toby. He sends his gratitude, by the way." A grin appeared under Balcombe's mustache. "'The good gentleman,' he calls you. He suggested, and I agreed, that if you like, you can take little Tobyson to Longwood as a page."

"Tell Mr. Toby I shall take care of his son." The Emperor smiled. "As he would mine."

"You won't be sorry, sire. The child's smart as a whip." Balcombe bowed. "It's been an honor to host Your Majesty. Hope my saucy daughter didn't give you too much trouble."

While Marchand finished packing, the Emperor strolled the Briars garden with tearful Betsy. She paused by a large boulder under a gum tree. "Our favorite place to sit. How forlorn it seems now. Father says, if you'll allow it, I may come to Longwood to give lessons to Tobyson."

"My dear, come as often as you like. You're an indispensable companion."

She threw her arms around him.

He kissed the top of her head. "I can't imagine when I'll be as close to someone again."

"Why, when you have your Eaglet," she said, straightening the bicorne she had knocked askew. Arm in arm, they strolled to the Briars' gate. There, Generals Montholon and Bertrand waited on horseback. Tobyson bounced on the seat next to Mr. Balcombe's coachman, who drove the luggage wagon.

Two dozen British soldiers swung onto their mounts.

As the Emperor raised a foot to his stirrup, Toby approached, holding out a wide-brim straw hat identical to his own. The Emperor grasped the man's hand. Taking the hat, he removed his bicorne and placed the straw on his head.

"Sire, your dignity!" General Bertrand protested.

"Silence, Bertrand. This straw's worth more than gold." The Emperor inclined his head to Toby. "No price can be placed on a slave's labor freely given." He wore the straw until the Briars had dropped from sight.

As they approached Longwood's stone gates, the Emperor halted the procession. He took out his spyglass to survey the windswept plain. The house's roof appeared repaired. Effort had been made on a flower garden. Emerald-green latticework adorned the front porch. Still dismal, but better than expected.

A movement caught his eye. Sir Hudson Lowe paced behind those green screens. Albine peeked out the doorway. She and Lowe exchanged something. Paper? Money? Albine disappeared. First a thief, now a traitor. What a fool to let her get close to him. He snapped his spyglass shut.

The British lieutenant in charge of the escort reached for the Emperor's horse's reins.

The Emperor jerked the horse away.

Bertrand trotted up. "What's the problem, Lieutenant? Give His Majesty a moment."

The Emperor motioned Montholon up from the rear. "That dratted governor's on the porch. I want a diversion to put him in his place. What do you say to switching to my bicorne? You gallop wildly to the house while I employ that side door."

"If I must." Montholon slumped in his saddle. "I suppose they won't shoot me if they think I'm you."

They maneuvered their horses to align Montholon's with the lieutenant's. At the Emperor's signal, Montholon crouched over his horse's neck, clapped on the bicorne, and dug in his spurs. Most of the guards, with the lieutenant and sergeant in the lead, careened after him.

General Bertrand pursed his lips at the Emperor.

"For our dignity, Bertrand. We're nothing if our jailer always has the upper hand." He showed his face to the remaining soldiers. "You. Good men. *Après moi.*" He wheeled his horse and led the diminished escort through the garden to a side door.

Dismounting, he handed his reins to a waiting servant. He paused. It was the same craggy-faced Hercules who'd lifted him off the *Northumberland*'s longboat and set him on St. Helena's shore. The huge man pulled off his knit cap and grinned.

The Emperor entered a small room that already held his camp bed. Through an adjacent passage, he spied a large copper bathtub—a luxury in store. With five guards and Bertrand in tow, he trooped through the house and flung wide the front door.

Across the plain, between the clouds, he spied a patch of ocean. Somewhere out there were France, Austria, and his son. Three steps below him in the yard, the governor shrieked orders at Montholon and the red-faced lieutenant to find Napoleon.

"Governor!" he called. "Did you wish to see me?"

Sir Hudson whirled. Head rammed forward, fists clenched, he stomped up the steps. The Emperor held his ground. If the fellow hit him, one or both of them might be returned to Europe. He lowered his chin to protect his teeth.

General Bertrand moved between them.

"Bertrand, Bertrand, better if he had assaulted me." The Emperor sighed. "But really, I should not use my renown as a shield. Talk to him. I'll wait inside until he's recovered."

An hour later, the Emperor received the governor in Longwood's shabby reception room. He placed his coffee cup on a scratched table, saying, "Put this farce behind us, shall we?"

Sir Hudson, still stiff with anger, strode about the room. "I shall not put this day behind us until I've had a satisfactory explanation." He picked a clock off the mantel, flipped it over, and slammed it back on the ledge. "General Montholon shall meet me at my offices tomorrow."

The Emperor lifted his cup in mock salute. "Just don't clap him in irons. No benefit can come from enlarging a minor incident."

"Minor? You destroyed Sir Neil Campbell's reputation when you gave him the slip on Elba. I shall not have that happen to me, do you hear? Like it or not, our lives are intertwined."

"So you have said. Thus far, however, your experiences have narrowed your vision, while mine have taught me to think on a grand scale. Now, divulge the purpose of your visit."

Sir Hudson hovered over him. "I'm establishing guard positions outside every window."

The Emperor gripped the arms of his chair. "Outside every window?"

"At all times. Furthermore, all communication to leave this island from any member of your party, including you, is to be submitted unsealed for my perusal and approval. Henceforth, all incoming correspondence travels that same channel." The governor reached inside his jacket. "I bring you the first such letter. From your mother."

The Emperor beckoned Tobyson, who was curled in a corner. "Get Monsieur Marchand."

The page scampered from the room.

The Emperor kept his voice soft. "Sir Hudson, I'm not an empty symbol of the past. When it becomes the fashion once again to do me justice, you shall regret your role here."

Lowe held out the letter. "You're wrong to ascribe malice to my actions."

The Emperor forced a chuckle. "Oh, I never ascribe to malice what's adequately explained by incompetence. Ah, Marchand, you arrive." He turned back to the governor. "You read this private letter from my mother?"

"Yes." The letter fluttered in Sir Hudson's hand. He seemed unable to draw it back.

The Emperor pinched the paper between two fingertips and tossed it into the fireplace. "Marchand, show this person out."

As soon as the door latched behind the governor, the valet grabbed the fireplace tongs. In a corner of the fireplace, the letter smoldered. Marchand reached into the burning coals.

The Emperor pulled him back. "No, no. The letter's not worth scorching yourself."

A silhouette of a British guard passed outside the window.

The Emperor collapsed into his chair. His mouth was dry, his chest empty. Mold already splotched the newly painted walls. "Look at me, Marchand. A great throne whittled down to this common chair."

"Sire, take heart." Marchand tamped the charred paper. "Look, I saved your mother's letter. At least the middle part. So clever to toss it into the corner."

The Emperor sat up. "What does it say?"

"Something about your sister Pauline. I can make out 'disgrace' and 'husband.'"

"Pauline and scandal? That's not news. What else?"

Marchand squinted. "*Happy here in Rome . . . Do not like . . . weather*—I think, I'm sure, the word is 'weather'—*in Vienna. Your uncle and I . . .* Sorry, sire, I can't make out the words. *A clairvoyant foretells heart*—maybe 'health'—*would suffer in Austria. No use . . .* The words below might be 'snuff box,' something about angels. Maybe Africa? The rest is burned."

The Emperor rose. He leaned his forehead against a wall. His skin didn't touch the mold, but he smelled it growing all around him. Even if he and Cipriani could gather together a rescue squad, his mother wouldn't be in Austria to provide access to the Eaglet. Neither of the sailors' messages had meant a damn. His blessed, cursed mother.

CLISSON: THE EMPEROR'S NOVEL

Valence, France, 1789

France was bankrupt. In the interval of peace with its European neighbors, there was no money to pay soldiers. Orders came to close the garrison.

"You wanted leave," his colonel said to Clisson. "Now you have it. Too bad about the pay. Take this letter to my family in Champvert. They'll let you stay with them."

Clisson grinned for the first time in weeks.

The colonel waved his gratitude aside. "My brother-in-law is a parvenu, a successful silk trader who settled in the countryside to establish his only child, a daughter your age. The old fellow's eccentric, but, coming from Corsica, you won't be offended."

Clisson's body went rigid. "Excuse me, sir?"

"I mean the LeGrands won't delve into your pedigree, nor you into theirs. Despite his fortune, they're simple people, Lieutenant."

Clisson, swallowing his pride, rushed to pack.

As the garrison disbanded, the officers forgot their quarrels. Des Mazis and Berville clasped Clisson's hand, punched his arm, and claimed they'd meet again. Des Mazis was to return to his parents in Lyons; Berville would stay in Valence on the garrison's skeleton staff.

When Clisson mounted, Berville muttered, loudly enough for Clisson to hear, "Hey, Monsieur Born for War, let's see how you fare in peace."

As Clisson's grip tightened on his riding crop, Des Mazis slapped the horse's haunch to send him on his way.

Only two hours of light remained in the day. To save money, Clisson forewent an inn to bivouac next to a creek. Once he'd cared for his horse, he settled down to bread and wine he'd stuffed in his old satchel. Behind him, leaves rustled, a branch cracked. He whirled to his feet and met the startled stare of a squirrel.

The last time he had been alone in woods, he had encountered a Corsican shepherd. As the night grew dark, no amount of army training prevented his scanning the shadows for spirit creatures, a lurking squad of stone soldiers, or the wandering souls his cannon plowed down in the square.

But this was sane France, not Corsica, where magic lived. Stars peeped out. Venus's bright point hung above. In that celestial light, dull tree trunks gleamed. He lay on his blanket to contemplate the sky.

What was up there?

He had no God. His mother's candles before plaster idols mocked intelligence. His father's worship of ideas had corrupted the man's flesh and led to treachery.

Ten years, Clisson had struggled to become a soldier. To what end? To face the hungry peasant's scythe? To uphold a cannibal king who fed upon the People? Was there ever a king who did not deserve to be deposed? But the Revolution that wanted to tear down the throne promised only disorder.

France's newest philosophers, like his father, worshipped the rational mind. But what rational God created this aimless fool named Clisson? Why would that God strip him of home, friends, and hope? If he found Rose, chances were, reality would yield another disappointment.

If war offered no glory, if comrades mocked and strangers scorned, if mothers traded their cunts for lace, how could a young man thrive? There was no point in going on. He could end life with a pistol shot, but did a man have the right to die by his own hand? Perhaps if his death harmed no one and if life was an evil for him. But when was life pure evil? When it offered nothing but suffering and sorrow. Yet since suffering and sorrow changed moment to moment, there was no time in life when a man had the right to kill himself.

In truth, there must be no man who hadn't wanted to kill himself but would have regretted it a few days later. Indeed, the man who kills himself on Monday would want to live by Saturday. Yet, once done, suicide couldn't be undone.

Clisson sat up. There he went, playing word games, engaging in pointless argument on an unanswerable subject. How like his father.

At daybreak, everything was fresh. Bluebirds sang in the trees, frogs grunted on the bank, grasses swayed in the meadow beyond the woods. A healthy piss confirmed he was alive. Usually, it took a lot of brandy for him to be such a pigeonhead as he had been last night.

Midmorning, his horse pitched a shoe. Walking the road, he came across a wagon in a ditch and helped push it out.

The farmer gave him a ride to the next town, where the man's brother was the blacksmith. That evening, in a drafty hovel, he feasted on warm bread and good cheese with the blacksmith and the farmer, discussing politics and revolution. He felt as close to the earth as he had as a child. Still, these were the kind of people he had opened fire on. He understood them, loved them, but with detachment.

Napoleon

LATE THAT NIGHT, ALBINE DOZED at his side. Her little mouth pouted. When he stroked her hair, she snuggled against his hip. He should have turned her over to Cipriani, but he didn't want her to be hurt. He got up and dressed.

In the candlelight, she looked innocent. She wasn't. He leaned over the bed, breathed her rose perfume, and touched two fingers to her throat. Springing awake, she cowered in a corner of the camp bed, clutching a blanket to her breasts. Her eyes darted. When they landed on him, her panic ebbed.

Albine

IT WAS NAPOLEON WHO TOUCHED ME. I was safe. I was with him. I lowered the blanket to display my breasts. "Forgive me. I didn't mean to fall asleep. Do you want . . . ?"

His mouth curled. "God, no. Cover yourself."

I reached for his hand. Why was he dressed?

He pulled back. "Do not touch me."

I covered my panic with sweetness. "Something's the matter, dearest sire?"

The steel in his eyes (how he resembled his mother with that cold stare) showed he'd already passed judgment. I was guilty, and he knew it. He detected my frantic glance toward the door. Too late, I remembered he'd locked it. "Sire—"

He cut me off. "Cipriani's outside that door. Marchand guards the other. Besides, where would you go? To Hudson Lowe?"

I couldn't meet that steel stare. "Why are you scaring me?"

He cupped my chin in his hand. His palm was soft, his grip firm, his tone ice. "Are you spying for Hudson Lowe?"

"Of course not, sire." If only I could touch him. I reached.

"I said don't touch me." He shook my chin.

That hand, that once caressing hand. I reached again.

"I told you no." He shook my chin harder, enough to blur my vision. "The truth, Albine. Are you spying for Hudson Lowe?"

"No, no, I love you. I would never—"

"One more chance."

I shielded my nakedness with my hands.

He let go of my chin. I pulled the blankets over me. Thunder pounded behind my forehead. A crust of bread. A cracker. Maybe I could seek shelter in the past.

His voice jerked me into the present.

"I had hoped you would cooperate." He pulled a set of garden shears from under the bed.

I bolted up. "I'll scream. The guards—"

"If you scream, you'll prove you're a traitor." He rested the wicked shears on his thigh. "Let's start again. Before I arrived at Longwood House today, Hudson Lowe handed you something on the porch. What was it?"

"You're mistaken."

"Don't lie, my girl."

"What can you mean?"

"I saw you through my spyglass," that icy voice said.

The air went out of me. "You must understand . . ." My voice came out too shrill to be believed. I began over. "We lost everything, everything, when we followed you to this horrible place."

"You've used that line before. Try something new."

I eyed the shears. What would this cost me? A finger? I hid my hands behind my back. "Sire, have mercy on my weakness. I can't sleep. I steal bread, hide it under my pillow. I can't stop myself. I'm so afraid of being poor."

"So, it was money?"

"Twenty pounds . . . to send to my son. I swear I gave nothing in return."

"The governor doesn't pay twenty pounds for nothing. Besides, you told me your child's school was paid for two years." He raised the shears. The cold blade rested against my nose.

Dear God, not my nose. "Charles made me—"

Napoleon winced and gripped his side. He laid the shears on the bed.

I longed to smooth the pain, the defeat, from his face. Forgetting my danger, I threw back the blanket. "Charles doesn't know. I'm to get more when I report."

"Report what?"

"How you feel, what you eat. Anything. The governor's desperate to know the smallest detail. I could see no harm." He didn't shake me off when I caressed his arm. "Yes, I lie, I steal, but I'm no worse than many others. The Revolution—my first husband—I was on the street. It's a poor excuse, I know, but after a woman's been hungry, used her body to survive, she needs to have things—money, food—hidden away." I held out my hands. "If these hands have ever given you pleasure, forgive me, sire. I know you understand. Your Josephine—she was the same."

"My Josephine!" He caught his breath. "My Josephine—who's not for you to judge."

A direct hit on a tender spot. "No, sire, I didn't mean that." I lowered my lashes to hide my hope. "But if she were here now, she would understand. Please, oh, please, don't tell my husband. He'll kill me."

"What? For getting caught?"

"How can you say such things? Charles is devoted to you. Why else would he allow this liaison we've had?" I leaned toward him, hands in prayer. "And now he won't touch me. Think of all I've lost. My son left behind, same as yours. Twenty pounds is so little. Forgive me. You've forgiven so many for so much more. And I love you."

His face softened. I lifted his hand to my cheek.

Besides, you rejected me first, you bastard. But I didn't have the courage (or foolishness) to say those words.

Chapter 15

⟨⟩⟨ ⟩

Napoleon

THE EMPEROR HADN'T THOUGHT A replacement for Albine would prove difficult to find. Cipriani combed the docks. Marchand approached servant girls with tact. After a third attempt in two weeks, at midnight the Emperor opened his bedroom door a slit.

The valet emerged from the shadows.

The Emperor shook his head.

"I'll send her home," Marchand whispered.

The girl smelled too much of cows, manure, and sour milk. At least her closeness to the earth was healthful. The one before had been a whore, part Chinese, part African, who practiced her arts for sailors in Jamestown. That one's skin had been tawny, her eyes almond. She writhed her torso like a snake. In choosing her, Cipriani had been half-correct: the Emperor was attracted to the exotic. On the other hand, he didn't like whores and hadn't used them since his cadet days in Paris, thirty years ago. The Jamestown one enjoyed her work. An important trait for a whore, a soldier, or a king.

Yet, while her hands upon him had been pleasurable, he hadn't wanted to enter her. Who had been there first didn't matter. Who had been there last did. Probably some dirty British sailor. He made her wash twice. In the end, there'd been no pleasure in touching her, as young and firm as her breasts had been. Nice to look at across the room, he told Marchand, but try something else.

So the valet chose the dairyman's daughter. The father was eager; the girl, no less. Some local man had spoiled her already. But she smelled so much of cows.

Which brought him back to Albine. She was familiar, clean, French, endearing. Her touch softened the misfortune of St. Helena life. She would be hard to resist.

WHEN BETSY CAME TO LONGWOOD, she tumbled cushions Marchand arranged in military symmetry. Her laughter echoed through the gloomy halls. The earnest page Tobyson reverted into a giggling child, the gardener Hercules clipped flowers to please her, and the cook made cakes.

After an hour of tutoring Tobyson, she read *Clisson* aloud to the Emperor. When she wasn't looking, he held up his palms to her, as though to warm himself. The sunny optimism of her youth reinfused him with hope.

CLISSON: THE EMPEROR'S NOVEL

Champvert, France, 1789

At last, Champvert!

As Clisson trotted his horse down a shady lane, the prospect opened to a trim lawn. A stone path led to a charming manor house, its mansard roof black slate, its fanciful towers lending medieval pretension to construction still underway. Bushes pruned into animal shapes dotted the lawn. Here nested a horse-size bird; there, a man-size squirrel munched a nut. Rounded bushes formed a sinuous caterpillar.

Clisson clutched his introduction letter. That this family

lived near Champvert, where Rose could be found, propelled him up the steps. Before he could lift the brass fleur-de-lis, a white-wigged butler swung open the door. The butler rubbed his nose.

Clisson sniffed. So he smelled of horse. How could he not?

In the entrance hall, more animals abounded, these stuffed. Avoiding a snarling bear, Clisson banged his head against a tusk. The butler plodded across the high-ceilinged space, his heels clicking on chessboard marble squares. Clisson tiptoed in his wake, sidestepped a peacock in frozen strut, evaded a panther's pounce, and, with relief, passed through glass doors into the rear gardens. There, amid towering cypress, tiered fountains trickled purple water. Twenty well-dressed guests reclining on blankets picnicked on the lawn. Servants glided among the groups, presenting silver trays of fruit, bowls of cream, and sweet cakes plentiful enough to satisfy a brigade.

Clisson, the taste of the blacksmith's bread lingering in his mouth, waved off a pastry tray. When the revolution came, as it had to, these spoiled bourgeois would have to choose: perish with the *aristos* they emulated or share their spoils with the humble rest. Clisson nodded. He'd welcome that day.

The butler paused at the nearest blanket, where middle-aged women in country dress fluttered ivory fans.

"Madame," the butler said in a funereal tone, "we have an unexpected guest."

A chubby lady, head to toe in purple ruffles, peered up. Like the butler, she rubbed her nose. Two footmen hoisted her to her feet. Too much purple, too much rouge, too much bosom—like the house, too much of everything. If this was his colonel's sister, he'd do his damnedest to avoid the niece. He breathed in a cloud of lavender and sneezed.

The lady inspected him with the authority of her brother's rank. "Bless you, my dear. May God fulfill your wish."

These French. In Corsica, they said a sneeze let in the devil.

"Excuse the dirt from my travels, and accept greetings from your brother, my colonel." He mangled the formal bow they'd taught in officers' school. "Your brother believed it would be convenient for me to spend part of my leave in your kind company. I carry a letter on his behalf, dear Madame LeGrand." With what he hoped passed for a flourish, he handed her his colonel's note.

"Mon Dieu," the lady uttered, as she broke the seal on the letter. "Hmm, well, yes, of course, I see."

Clisson knotted his fingers behind his back. Around him, the guests, chewing sweet cakes, turned up their noses at his scuffed boots. These people were no better than he was, yet most were plump where he was lean. His hostess's ugly picnic dress undoubtedly cost more than his horse. Tucking a strand of lank hair behind his ear, he tamped down the urge to stalk away.

The fat lady folded the paper. Her features took on the softness of a doe. "You are most welcome to our home."

Faced with kindness, he chucked his sneer.

Madame LeGrand brightened. "Let me present my husband."

Her lips moved, her words blurred. Behind her, among a group of young women on a blanket, lounged Rose of the Inn. The landscape spun. She was here. She was right there on that blanket. She was real.

"Yes, yes, thank you." Clisson pumped his hostess's pudgy hand. "I . . . I see someone I know."

The purple-ruffled lady's words floated after him. "How like my brother to send such a surprise. And how strangely the young man speaks. Whatever will we do with him?"

Throughout the months since Clisson had encountered Rose, his life had passed in a daze. Three long strides catapulted him into a new universe, vibrant with her flesh. If he extended his trembling finger, he could trace the part in her chestnut curls. He stopped midreach.

Tiny gold shoes peeked from under her melon-colored dress. He'd have kissed its hem if all these strangers would have vanished, leaving him alone with Rose. He hovered, gazing down upon the women on the blanket.

The young girls chatting in the group fell silent one by one, until Rose's voice alone sparkled through the air. A girl with a big-eyed kitten face tittered. Rose turned to see what had caught her friend's attention.

Clisson's skin prickled the length of his legs and through his core as Rose confronted his mud-splattered boots, made a path up his quivering body, paused at his mouth, and pierced his moist eyes. Behind his back, he wiped his palms on his pants. He should have stopped at an inn to wash.

The goddess rolled her eyes around to her friends. "Who is he?" she mouthed.

Panic rose in his chest; she'd forgotten him. "Mam'selle," his voice squeaked. He cleared his throat. "Mam'selle, we met some months back. On the road to Paris?"

She cocked her head, like a peacock, like a queen.

He aimed his tone for yet a deeper note. "In March. The eighteenth, at eight in the morning."

Two girls collapsed, giggling in each other's arms. Across his cheeks spread warmth, but absent anger, like when the convent girls of Corsica had teased him. Surely that was the last time he had felt so young.

Rose's brows arched. How he'd like to plant kisses beneath their curves. "Ah, yes, I remember your accent. And your mouth." Her face brightened. "You were en route to your regiment, and I was off to fetch Eugénie here."

He followed her hand to where it pointed at the girl with kitten eyes and a button nose. His curt nod dismissed this friend, this Eugénie. She was porcelain next to his crystal goddess. His attention snapped back to Rose.

"I have waited forever to see you. Will you stroll with me?" For the first time in his life, pains like his father's attacked his stomach.

"Another conquest for Amélie," one of the girls on the blanket said. "To the torture chamber with the prisoner!"

"You must go, Amélie," another said. "It is our patriotic duty to support the army."

The one named Eugénie frowned. "Hush."

Amélie. She was called Amélie. The name alone was poetry. Amélie Rose.

He reached down a thin hand, thankful he had pared his nails. Accepting it, Amélie floated to her feet in a whirl of summer muslin and orange-blossom water. She stood half a head taller than he did. He'd forgotten that. At the inn, he might have been on a stair.

Her friends simpered, except the one named Eugénie, whose thick lashes veiled solemn scrutiny. He shrugged off the other women's mockery, but the cross kitten's censure irritated.

His Rose, his Amélie, laid her hand upon his arm. His ardor soared. He tried to meld their eyes. Hers turned away in surprise. They were hazel, wider and more brilliant than in his dreams, the whites so white, the brown specked with malachite and gold. And how could he have compared that vibrant flesh to crystal? A peach, an apricot, a newborn foal—anything alive and yielding, anything but lifeless glass.

"Still so thin." She touched his uniform sleeve. "Didn't you follow my advice to eat breakfast?"

She remembered him. If only Berville could have seen him, at last in the throes of life.

Napoleon

BETSY PUT DOWN THE PAGE and sighed. "I'm so glad Clisson found his Rose. And that earlier part where he's figuring out the world? I wonder the same things."

The Emperor blew his nose. "Yes, my dear, we all try to figure out our destiny, but even I, who did so much, strayed from my path." He fiddled with his bag of licorice. "I tell the true history to my generals, who write it down for posterity. Someday you'll read it."

"I'd rather read this story we're writing."

He tugged a lock of her hair. "It's nonsense. But the best kind of nonsense. Like the Corsican stories my mother told me. I fear we stray from my message to the Eaglet."

"Oh, no, Monsieur. Who but the Eaglet's father should teach him about women?"

"All right, my charmer, but I warn you, that kind of story rarely turns out well. Ah, Las Cases, Marchand, you're on time."

His secretary stood in the doorway, kneading his fingers.

"I have work to do, my dear." He pinched Betsy's cheek. "Come back soon."

"Next time, I'll bring some of Mother's fortifying broth. You look tired, Monsieur." She curtsied to Las Cases and Marchand.

As soon as she was gone, the Emperor lost his smile. "Come with me into the bedroom, Las Cases. Strip down and remove your wig. Dress in the clothing on my camp bed."

"But, sire, that is your dressing gown."

"No questions. I want your clothes immediately. Marchand, help me with my wig." The Emperor went into the closet to change, emerging in Las Cases's clothes.

Albine rapped on the chamber door.

"Las Cases, sit on the bed," he said. "I want Albine to get a good look at us."

At the door, the Emperor—disguised as Las Cases—bowed to Albine. She brushed past him, giving his false Las Cases no more than a glance. Las Cases himself, dressed as the Emperor, sat on the camp bed, dabbing his cheeks.

She hurried forward, hands outstretched. "Sire, what's wrong?"

Napoleon shut the door, saying in his own voice, "Albine."

She whirled from one man to the other.

Las Cases, in the Emperor's dressing gown, his hair combed and dyed to resemble Napoleon's, lowered his handkerchief.

The Emperor read shock, anticipation, and what he took for shrewd calculation flit across her face. And he had thought Las Cases the weak link in his scheme. He'd keep a sharp watch on his lady friend.

Albine gave a brisk nod. "Indeed, it may work, if no one gets close. What's my role?"

"Good girl." He put a caressing hand on her arm. "When Marchand and I leave, strip down to your shift. Then you two get on the bed. We're going to leave a drapery partway open. Put on a good show for the guards, will you, my dear? I'll return in an hour."

Albine

WHEN NAPOLEON SENT FOR ME, my female parts pulsed. I was so happy, so certain, so eager to begin again. My almost handsome British lieutenant meant nothing next to him. True, Las Cases's opening the bedroom door gave me pause, but I supposed he wouldn't stay. I brushed past him.

Las Cases bolted the door, with himself inside. Marchand stepped from the bed to reveal the weeping Emperor. Behind me, Napoleon spoke my name from his Las Cases disguise.

I steadied myself on a chair back. Not lover, not empress-to-be. A mere puppet on the Emperor's grand stage. He might as well have sliced my heart with his garden shears.

Marchand set the draperies awry to provide the guards with a view. While I curtsied on the threshold, Napoleon (dressed à la Las Cases) and Marchand bowed their exit. I secured the door. The real Las Cases (à la Napoleon) snuggled beneath the sheets.

Napoleon demanded a show, did he?

I strolled about the little bedchamber, crossing before the window, discarding my overdress, loosening my shift to free my bosom. I preened half-naked in the splash of sunlight. Before long, three guards gathered behind a bush, jostling over a spyglass. I cupped my breasts to serve up nipples for "the Emperor's" gluttony. Oh, I pranced, I twirled, I strutted until Las Cases panted. Mounted on a chair, I swished my skirts to expose bare legs, and—if the guards watched carefully—something more. In brief, I did all I could to raise Napoleon (and lower myself) in the British Army's esteem. I did it in white-hot anger, I did it till my juices ran, and, damn it all, I did it till I reveled in it.

Anything was preferable to joining Las Cases on that bed, though in the end I did that, too. We tussled awkwardly till I found (no surprise) my show had aroused him. "We're playacting, you fat bastard," I hissed, scratching flesh from his backside.

Chapter 16

Napoleon

THE SUN SPARKLED ON THE afternoon's raindrops as Las Cases ambled onto Longwood House's porch. He had permission to visit Jamestown, so Hercules had saddled the gray mare. Las Cases twitched his cuffs. Hercules took a close look at him, huffed, and handed over the reins.

Las Cases trotted past the guardhouse, his airy wave receiving a smart salute. Beyond Longwood's gates, the mare broke into a gallop. Under the brown Las Cases wig, the Emperor grinned. Clisson's youthful blood surged in his veins again. At the crossroads to Jamestown, he veered onto a rocky uphill path.

Around a bend, Toby-Mahafaly waited.

The Emperor kicked off a stirrup, offering it and his hand. Toby stuck his sandaled foot into the stirrup, grasped the hand, and swung up, landing behind the saddle. He gave a deep laugh and touched the wild sideburn Marchand had pasted to the Emperor's cheek.

As the Emperor coaxed the horse up the rough path toward Diana's Peak, the highest point on St. Helena, the view beneath them opened to St. Helena's lush valleys and desiccated plains, and the surrounding vast ocean. Giant tree ferns dripped the morning's rain on their shoulders and heads. They were halfway to the peak when Cipriani and the slave with the branded forehead blocked the path. Toby-Mahafaly swung off the horse.

Cipriani caught the mare's bridle and murmured up to Napoleon, "This fellow's Randall, Toby's lieutenant. Far as I can tell, got no use for white men."

The Emperor dismounted and shook Randall's large, callused hand. The man was a forbidding figure, although not as tall or as broad as Hercules. His hair and brows curled into an untidy mess, a touch of gray among the tangles. His nose had been broken in several places. He jerked his hand from Napoleon's and edged away.

As Cipriani tied up the mare, Toby and Randall cleared brush from the entrance to a hidden cave. Inside, a shelf chipped in the wall held an oilskin sack stuffed with blankets and food. Cipriani clapped at Randall's cowhide pouch of wine and his wooden cups.

Toby held out his arms in invitation.

The Emperor sat cross-legged on a blanket and helped himself to a chunk of cheese.

Toby raised a wooden cup. "I know what ship to take. Hudson Lowe's two-mast schooner, the HMS *St. Helena*."

The Emperor smiled. "Commandeer the governor's own ship? Excellent."

"I've had my eye on it for months." Toby used a stick to draw an outline of the ship in the dirt. "She's fast, easy to sail, anchored near the wharf."

"How many on board at night?" Cipriani asked. "They armed?"

Toby considered the Corsican. "Usually two sailors. Knives at the waist, probably pistols on board, but they don't wear them. We could station a fishing boat nearby to row out to her."

Randall stuck the cheese knife in the ground near Cipriani's knees. "You set that up. They whip us Blacks for getting near a fishing boat."

Cipriani glared at Randall. "Thought there was laws against whipping."

Randall glared back. "Against whipping too much. Ten or a hundred lashes, you're still a slave, aren't you?"

The Emperor wiped the cheese knife and handed it back to Randall. He silently counted to twenty to clear the air before addressing Toby. "And where shall we sail this ship?"

"A thousand miles to the nearest coast of Africa, reprovision there, then skirt around the Horn to my home in Madagascar. From there, my people'll get you wherever you want."

The Emperor closed his eyes. His bedroom in the Tuileries, the Eaglet asleep down the hall, Josephine's boudoir, the year of 1804 . . . No, these people couldn't take him back to wherever he wanted. Still, a future beckoned. "May I ask why you've hesitated doing this on your own?"

"With or without you, we'll make our escape." Toby grimaced. "Truth is, we fear those cannons overlooking the bay. They say you know all about big guns."

Cipriani bared his teeth at Randall. "None better."

"So, how do we get shut of them?" Randall muttered.

"My thoughts exactly." The Emperor unfolded a map he had sketched of St. Helena's cannon positions. "This is what I remember from the day we landed." He ran his finger over the map. "Here are the weaknesses: a close-in blind spot and a narrow passage their land-based cannon can't hit. Beyond this arc, we're safe. I recommend spiking some of the cannon to give ourselves more room to maneuver."

Randall rubbed his branded forehead. "What's spiking?"

Cipriani leaned in. "Ah, fix 'em so they can't fire. Isn't hard. Just need clay and wood spikes. Getting access, that's the trick. Can you arrange that, man?"

Randall shoved his face into the Corsican's. "Inside their forts? Trying to get us killed?"

Toby pulled Randall back. "Patience, brother. Listen to what they have to say."

The Emperor tapped his map. "Not the forts—the smaller installations, here and here."

Randall sat back on his heels. "Need a few days to look them over."

· Toby nodded approval. "Now, since you arrived, sire, patrol ships circle the island. There's an inlet on St. Helena's far side. My people can set a fire there to distract them."

"Excellent, sir," said the Emperor.

Randall jumped to his feet. "This is the plan? A few of us on that little ship? Mahafaly, we running away?"

Toby gripped Randall's arm.

Randall wrenched free. "Thought your great general was going to lead us into battle."

Cipriani moved to rise, but the Emperor pinched his sleeve. The Corsican sank down.

Toby said to Randall, "We'll talk later, you and I."

"Yes, talk it over." The Emperor looked from Toby to Randall. "Decide who's joining in, but your lives—our lives—depend on choosing wisely."

"I know my people." Toby nodded to Randall. "I know who to trust."

Randall stared at his knuckles.

The Emperor clasped Toby's shoulder. "We rely on you, sir. There's much left to decide—provisions, weapons, training, timing—but I must return to Longwood."

"Yes, we have to get back, too. Sire, Randall's right. Only a few of us can go. The *St. Helena* carries twenty-four people at most. How many do you propose to bring?"

"For our part, Cipriani, me, your son, perhaps two more, perhaps a woman. That leaves space for eighteen of your people. Fair enough?"

"More than fair." He fondled the woven blanket they sat on. "I don't like to ask, but we will need money for provisions and to compensate those left behind."

"Yes, I thought of that." He held out a pouch. "Twenty gold Napoleons, but you must be careful. They may only be spent or exchanged for coin at Solomon's. Anyone caught with these will be questioned, perhaps hanged."

"Understood."

"Then we'll plan training next, timing last." He rose and saluted Toby. "To freedom."

"To freedom." Toby returned the salute. "Take your man on the horse. Better if I walk with Randall."

On the ride downhill, Cipriani was silent while the Emperor managed the horse on the treacherous trail. When the path flattened, they halted on a ridge from which they could see Jamestown harbor. The Emperor pulled his spyglass from his jacket. "Want a look at our schooner?"

"Not especially."

The Emperor passed the spyglass over his shoulder.

Cipriani took a quick look and handed back the monocular. "Don't like that Randall."

The Emperor scanned the bay through the spyglass. "Franco, sometimes I wonder how you survived so long as a spy."

"What the hell's that mean?"

The Emperor twisted in the saddle. "You'll learn more from Randall if you conceal your thoughts. Make him a friend. Find out if we can trust him."

Cipriani gave a shout of laughter.

"What?" the Emperor asked.

"Aw, thinking on how that scrubby Napoleon boy I knew in Corsica is schooling me." Cipriani swung off the horse. "I'll get myself home from here without your help." He rubbed his chin. "Take that any way you please."

Albine

I BADE THE LAS CASES EMPEROR—under threat of scratching out his eyes—to stay put behind the camp-bed curtains. (To my surprise, he obeyed.) Tired of the lecherous guards, I threw up my hands in pretend dismay, jerked the drapery shut, and got dressed. But how to pass the time until Napoleon's return? I lit a candle and, knowing where the Emperor hid his keys, found the *Clisson* novel in his locked desk.

CLISSON: THE EMPEROR'S NOVEL

Champvert, France, July 1789

Clisson glanced around the estate's lawn, unsure of where to take Amélie Rose. He had to get the woman alone.

Eugénie scrambled to her feet. At any rate, the short girl's vitality compensated for her gracelessness. "Amélie," she said, "your aunt would wish me to accompany you." Despite her rich alto voice, her words rankled.

A man—a buck in a perfumed profusion of silk and bows— approached. The lilac apparition extended a leg, removed his tricorne hat from his powdered wig, and bowed. "Quite proper, Eugénie," the Fop said. "We may be on the verge of revolution, sweet cousin Amélie, but society's proprieties still hold." His eyes traveled over Clisson. "No matter what class one hails from "

Sweet cousin? Amélie's kinsman? Ah, well. If not, he'd have run the lilac'd ass through. A hand clutching his arm recalled the lady herself. Her rapier glare at the Fop eased Clisson's anger. Like his mother's pinpoint fury, this woman's eyes skewered her quarry. The Fop retreated, twitching his cuffs.

Amélie's pressure on Clisson's arm led their steps to a winding path, which plane-tree branches overarched in mimicry of Notre Dame's grand vaults. Flower incense swamped the sun-speckled enclosure. In the dim light, the lady's hazel eyes glowed amber, her chestnut hair glistened almost black.

Eugénie scampered at their heels, talking, talking. Clisson cared not of what.

Amélie's musical voice interrupted. "Your name, Monsieur?"

He swore she must have perfect pitch. He could listen all day to her recite the alphabet. "Clisson."

From behind, Eugénie thumped his back as if he were a mule. "Where are you from? I don't recognize your accent."

"Corsica, miss," he said over one shoulder.

She thumped again. "How came you to my father's house?"

At that, he turned. His colonel's niece. The poor girl, whose youthful form verged on matronly, was doomed to take after her purple-clad mother. He laid his hand over where Amélie's rested on his arm. "Do you live here, too? I can't believe my luck. Destiny has directed this."

Amélie's lashes fluttered. "Then Destiny, Monsieur Clisson, shoots off its mark like a drunken Cupid. This is Mademoiselle Eugénie's home, not mine. At present, I live three miles distant at my aunt's. You just spoke with her son, my cousin."

"The Fop?"

"As you so rudely put it, the Fop. Now, we must rejoin the others. I don't wish to be a spectacle, wandering off with a stranger."

"I assure you, Mademoiselle Amélie, we're not strangers." Clisson had a speech forming in his mind, but his goddess dropped his arm to seize a blossom-laden stalk.

"Look, Eugénie, your mother's tuberoses are in bloom."

His head whirled as the friends chattered about scents and flowers. He swore he'd forgo Heaven to stretch that moment into eternity. Emerging from the shaded path with a girl on each of his arms, Clisson strutted, drunk with luck.

His host, a square-shaped man with a wide jaw, accosted them. "There you are, Lieutenant. My wife insists I show you to your room, where you'll find a warm bath."

Clisson blushed. So he did need one.

Monsieur LeGrand clapped his shoulder. "My brother-in-law's letter says you're a bit of a hero. No doubt the ladies'll pester you for details."

Amélie's head perked up. "I didn't know, Monsieur. I'll show more respect."

"Artillery, eh?" Monsieur LeGrand said. "And a mathematician? He was right to send you our way, regardless of how my wife complains."

"Father!" Eugénie said. "Your manners."

"Come, come, girl. He's your uncle's lieutenant—almost family. No need to stand on ceremony." He elbowed the girls aside to claim Clisson's arm. "I'm an amateur scientist myself. I must keep busy, since my wife insisted I give up trade to become respectable." He leaned his chin into Clisson's face. "You'll want to inspect my laboratory when you tire of the pretty ladies. Weather and electricity are my specialties. I could use your help on a few calculations."

His host's words washed over him. That Fop would have known how to make an adroit escape, but Clisson couldn't devise any polite tactics to avoid this unwelcome diversion. He surrendered.

Albine

OH, CLISSON'S "FOP" (MODELED AFTER LAS CASES) could have made a cat laugh. How I longed to believe I was Amélie. Alas, I could read no more. From behind the camp-bed curtain, Las Cases protested his confinement. I had half a moment to stuff *Clisson* into the writing box before he emerged, resplendent in the Emperor's dressing gown.

Within minutes, the Emperor himself returned. With a distracted thanks, Napoleon dismissed me and Las Cases. Miffed, I meandered into Longwood's garden. As always, trade winds blew. Our daily scourge, they brought dust, rain, clouds, humidity, and sun—drenching and desiccating within a single hour. Their howling never ceased. They knotted such tangles into my hair, I considered cutting it.

I hadn't gone far before Tobyson ran up to offer me a straw bonnet. Marchand had procured the boy a miniature uniform, complete with black boots, white breeches, and a green jacket. I wondered at the valet's temerity—I'd be afraid to mock the Emperor with a little copy.

When I took the proffered hat, Tobyson squinted. "Madame, you're unhappy again," he said, and led me off to admire a canary's nest with three brown-freckled eggs, which he and Hercules were protecting from stray cats. The thought rose that saving Tobyson from those galloping hooves might be the best thing I had ever done.

But as I remembered my performance with Las Cases, hot shame waxed through me. Once again, I'd wallowed in a wanton role. Years earlier, I'd known a lady, Madame de C. (no need to divulge her name). We shared a prison cell. The morning they summoned her for the guillotine, she thrust her hand between my legs and whispered, "If you can't have love, lust will do."

Charles. Napoleon. Basil Jackson, next in line. Yet that almost handsome lieutenant held the promise of something deeper. Hadn't they all started that way?

Leaving Tobyson, I skirted the stone wall that marked Longwood's border. My favorite bench lay ahead, hidden among windswept pines whose branches pointed toward the ocean. In that privacy, I'd devise a plan to deflect my life's downhill trajectory. Somehow, others managed to succeed. Look at Fanny Bertrand, with her devoted husband (not that I wanted a lapdog).

French voices floated from the grove. Two men sat on my bench, their backs to me. That toad Las Cases, in talk with someone quieter, less fluent. Please, let it not be my lieutenant.

I crept closer.

No, not Basil, but Dr. O'Meara, whose loyalties skittered around the globe, based on his audience. I hid behind a tree.

"I swear the lady's got the sweetest bottom, color of a peach." Las Cases lowered his pitch (as men do when they brag). "And when she rubs it on you, well, I tell you, it beats those whores in Palais-Royal."

I bit the inside of my cheek to keep from crying out.

O'Meara answered, "But the Emperor? Aren't you afraid?"

"No, no, he's tired of the gal. Got his eyes on that Balcombe filly."

Longwood's wind pounded in my ears, drowning O'Meara's response.

"Her father trades in Black men," Las Cases said. "For a price, he'll sell his girl."

(O'Meara's softer words were lost again.)

"I'll lay you odds he takes the Balcombe girl with him to Europe." Las Cases thumped the doctor's shoulder. He gave a shout of laughter. "He'll leave Albine to St. Helena's sailors."

That bastard! I stole closer, the path loose rock beneath my feet. I grasped a hefty stone. Another clinked into its place.

At the sound, the men jerked around.

I stood in plain sight, my arm cocked to throw.

They jumped to their feet.

But for my heaving chest, we might have been three red-faced figures captured in a painting. My temples throbbed as rage vied with dread that Las Cases was right. I was destined to live out my days as a sailors' whore.

British manners unfroze the scene. Dr. O'Meara bowed like a lord, separated from Las Cases, and strode away.

That left two French people face-to-face, one with a hefty rock. I edged closer.

Las Cases edged away. He managed an apologetic shrug. "Madame, the Emperor—"

"The Emperor, you worm, demands loyalty. Cross me again, he—and Cipriani—will hear of your treachery." I hurled my rock.

Chapter 17

Napoleon

BETSY JOINED THE EMPEROR IN the shade of the garden trellis. Nearby, Hercules tilled a vegetable garden. Betsy blew him a kiss.

"Don't flirt with the gardener while we're working." The Emperor cleared his throat and read, "'Clisson was born for war.'"

"Why must it start with war, Monsieur?"

"Because, my girl, *I* was born into civil war. Rebellion flowed from my mother's breast. This hero must be the same. And the first line of a novel is as important as its last."

Betsy pulled a ribbon from her pocket and restrained her mass of wavy curls. She thumbed through the manuscript. "More people might enjoy it if it started with love."

"More women, perhaps. Although they, of all people, know that's not how life begins. We claw our way out of our screaming mother's womb, or else a man slices her belly and rips us from her. Either way, we're bloodied at the start."

"Bah! Those are not words you should say to a little girl."

"No, but I said them to you." He leaned back. "At your age, miss, I had been living away from my family for five years."

Betsy sighed. "Like dear Clisson. Weren't you lonely?"

"So lonely that to this day I don't know what loneliness means. It became completely normal for me." He absorbed the sadness on her face. "A man—especially a leader—learns to walk through life alone. You do well to remind me."

CLISSON: THE EMPEROR'S NOVEL

Champvert, France, July 1789

The picnic guests stayed for dinner, although to Clisson it seemed they had just finished lunch. Having changed their country clothes for brocades, they gathered in the tapestried dining room around a candelabra-laden table. As Eugénie introduced him, Clisson kissed ladies' hands but ignored their names.

At dinner, Amélie sat between newly washed Clisson and the scented Fop, who bore the title of count—one more reason for a Corsican republican to slit the man's throat. The fellow's nails were polished like those of that pesky boy count Clisson had fought with long ago in school.

Eugénie sat on Clisson's right. Amid the platters and the wine, the brocade and powdered hair, Clisson, in sober uniform, brooded before picking up the wrong fork. Eugénie stopped his hand, indicating the smaller one. He shot her a grateful smile, at which she beamed. She was prettier than he had thought.

Over dessert, the Fop babbled about Prince So-and-So, Versailles, and his pilgrimage in Paris to the church of Saint Eustache to visit his family tomb.

If only they had interred him there.

Clisson leaned across Amélie to confront the man. "And what do you think of the abattoirs in Saint Eustache's square? I've read it's the latest Parisian controversy."

"Pray, sir, what have I to do with butchers?" the Fop asked.

Clisson sat taller in his chair, smiling at the rapt company. "Sir, their stalls surround the church you describe so minutely. Surely, one so observant noticed the slaughterhouses that imbue that lovely edifice with their stench. And how the offal in the gutters attracts rats."

Eugénie gasped. Her father barked across the table. "Come, come, Lieutenant. There's nothing wrong with commerce. The populace must have meat."

"I apologize, kind host. I thought the gentleman wished to present the complete picture of his family's sacred burial place."

Amélie's hand stalled the Fop midleap to his feet.

The Fop dropped into his chair. "As you wish, chère Amélie." He glared at Clisson. "Monsieur, your inexperience of polite company offends the ladies. Allow me to offer lessons in decorum."

Clisson half rose, but Amélie laid her other hand on his sleeve. "Nonsense," she said, looking pointedly at each of the men. Syllables dripped off her tongue. "No one is offended." Clisson sat.

Amélie addressed the bemused company. "Surprisingly, our sweet Eugénie delights in the Gothic, although I admit I could have gone all day without the rats."

"Enough, enough. You'll give me nightmares," one of the young women tittered.

"So let's talk not of abattoirs, necessary though they be," Amélie said, with a graceful head tilt at Monsieur LeGrand, "but rather of our midnight picnic plans. I'm eager to hear more of this ruined abbey of Saint Felix. It truly lies in a sequestered vale? How romantic."

"I cannot comprehend how you didn't get there last summer." Eugénie paused. Color stained her cheeks. "So, so sorry, chère Amélie. You were in mourning then."

Amélie directed a brittle smile at her friend. "No matter. You always mean well."

Around the table, people restarted conversations. Clisson could think of nothing to say. Amélie must have lost her parents. That must be why she lived with her aunt. After dinner, he'd verify the facts with Eugénie.

"My dear girl, how can you care for ancient ruins when we have a military hero in our midst?" Monsieur LeGrand asked.

Eugénie tried to catch his eye, but her father charged on. "Your colonel brags of your accomplishments, Monsieur Clisson. And that stiff-necked aristo, he's not an easy man."

"Now, now," murmured Madame LeGrand.

"Trifling affairs, I assure you." Clisson bowed his head.

"Well, your modesty commends you. But I avow, my brother-in-law sees you as an up-and-upper, scaling the ranks, as long as there's action on the field. Which he, the bloodthirsty bastard—excuse me, ladies—hopes for. He writes you single-handedly saved a sergeant from a mob. Our dear Amélie will want to hear the details. She's had a passion for the military since her young husband died in battle."

The room swayed beneath Clisson. Amélie's husband. His pounding heart hammered the air from his lungs. His Amélie Rose: a widow. So much for the joy of mutual discovery. Must he be the callow youth to an experienced mistress?

"Clisson?"

Clisson didn't hear his host's question. The tapestries on the walls swirled. He hazarded a random answer. "I only did my duty, good sir—nothing beyond the usual."

Nods approved his modesty; the Fop's tight lips showed Clisson the advantage he had gained. Eugénie gazed at him, her countenance shining like the younger boys' at Brienne. But he didn't wish to brag of facing down farmers' pitchforks and firing upon their wives. Especially since the sergeant had died. He asked about the weather.

Amélie brimmed with approval. He yearned to taste her soft mouth. If one couldn't be the first, then one should be the last upon that sacred ground. He struggled to focus on his host's interminable speeches while reordering his own dreams.

After dinner, his hostess led the guests into a pink-painted salon to play cards. Amélie, the center of attention, pealed laughter when she lost her bets. Her eyes outshone the chandeliers. Clisson avoided the tables. He couldn't afford even the lowest stakes.

Eugénie sat alone in a corner. Her mother shrieked at the turn of each card. Her square-faced father wandered the room, dispensing advice.

Clisson sat by the daughter. At her side, he wouldn't stick out as awkward. "Don't you like to play?" He selected a sweet biscuit from a silver plate.

Eugénie pouted. "I may as well confess, since you're bound to hear. My father, to nip my love of cards in the bud, bids me to refrain. He fears I've inherited his own father's love of gambling."

He blinked. "Have you such a passion?"

"Oh, yes. Winning's so exciting. Last month I collected more than my whole dress allowance. That's when Father said enough is enough." Her expression darkened at Clisson's raised brows.

He forced a smile.

"I see you don't understand," she said, "but truly a woman can crave as much excitement as a soldier."

His smile grew genuine. "And here, I thought you a kitten, when you're a tiger."

Her forehead was too high, her mouth too small, her haunting eyes strangely prominent in their deep-set sockets, but she projected a fetching, confiding manner he liked. At least she hadn't inherited her father's chin or her mother's shriek.

"Tell me," he started, but Amélie's laughter diverted all attention.

Across the room, the Fop slid a bracelet from his goddess's wrist. "I claim my winnings," he proclaimed, with a flourish Clisson planned to practice.

Clisson stuffed a dessert biscuit in his mouth.

"Tread carefully, Monsieur Clisson," Eugénie whispered. "Those cousins have an understanding."

The biscuit turned to soot on his tongue.

If only he could get Amélie alone, but no. Fawning men and worshipping women thronged her. Clisson drifted among the company. One conversation roiled around a local scandal; in an alcove, the Fop and two friends bantered about cravats. All very French, like smothering good sausage under cream.

Near midnight, moonlight poured through an open drapery. How its light would dance in Amélie's hair, a worthy counterpart to the morning sun, which had reddened her stray ringlet at the inn. He went to lure her to the window but found her readying to leave. "Stay a bit," he begged. "I'll have my horse saddled. I'll escort you home."

Amélie looked down demurely. "No, my cousin accompanies me."

The moonlight haloed her carriage as it disappeared down the tree-lined road. Clisson's world was empty again.

Napoleon

BETSY TUGGED THE EMPEROR'S SLEEVE. "Monsieur, you're not paying attention to my romantic additions."

"I heard every word, but tell me, dear, what do you know about our gardener, Hercules, over there?" He locked the metal manuscript box. "I bump into him everywhere: saddling horses, gardening, painting this trellis, blushing when you throw him kisses."

She made a face at him. "I know he loves that you call him Hercules."

The Emperor watched the big fellow heft a barrel. "What else?"

"Well, you've heard about the horrible British press gangs? Oh, of course you have. Anyway, he was working on an American merchant ship when the British navy kidnapped him and made him work on one of our ships. They dumped him on St. Helena when he broke his leg. That's why he limps."

"Ah, a disgruntled American sailor," the Emperor said.

"Actually, Tobyson says he was a second mate. But that's like a sailor, isn't it?"

"Even better, my useful friend." He tweaked her nose.

Albine

To ASSUAGE MY DESPAIR ABOUT the future, I begged Sergeant Kitts for permission to go to Jamestown. (After dreary Longwood, a visit to that dismal town constituted a seashore holiday.) The afternoon was cool, and Jamestown's deep valley blocked the odious winds. At the emporium, Solomon bundled my purchases in bright cloth tied with blue ribbon, which he assured me was free of charge. I added a frivolous lace sun umbrella to my unpaid account.

A word to the Porteous House barkeep brought Basil Jackson to the church, where that precise lieutenant ushered me into the vestry. This time he kissed my hand with respect, asking, "Are you here on your husband's behalf?"

My stomach plummeted. Had I misread his intentions? I said nothing.

He caressed my cheek, as tender as a new mother. "We're far from home, both of us, aren't we? I know a pleasant perch above the sea where we won't be seen."

Tucking my hand inside his arm, Basil led me out a back door to a footpath behind the church. St. Helena's giant ferns formed a canopy, shielding us from view of the fort on the hill. He took great care to steady me on loose stones, lifted me over a stream, and held my waist as we traversed a ledge to reach a cave overlooking an inlet where waves frothed over rocks. Gulls *gaw-gaw*ed, and a swallow-tailed black bird soared. I unfurled my dainty umbrella to cast flattering shade on my complexion.

Basil laid his jacket on the ground for us to sit upon. He pointed out breeching dolphins and spotted whales skimming the sea. He told me of his home in England, his schooling, and his brother. As sun warmed our hearts, we laughed companionably (although afterward, I couldn't recall over what). He asked about my son. "What's his name? How's he doing?"

"Tristan, and I don't know." I knotted my fingers. "I haven't received a letter since we left France."

He made a little *tsk*. "The governor holds back quite a few, you know."

I looked up. "Is it possible . . . Do you think he might have ones from Tristan?"

Basil smiled, his eyes alight.

"Can you check? I'd be so grateful."

He rubbed his square jaw. "Governor Lowe's a strange, reticent man, my dear lady. He trusts no one." He hesitated. "If I could gain his confidence . . ."

We both stared out to sea.

Basil pressed my hand. "So far, your husband—forgive me, I don't like to speak of him—provides trivial information. When I relay it to Sir Hudson, he curses and bans me from his office. If I had something significant . . . but I don't like to ask. Tell me more about Tristan. Do you think he writes often?"

"I'm sure he does. And my sister, too, who lives in Paris. I write to them every week." I clutched my stomach as fresh worry came over me. "Do *they* get *my* letters? Can you find out?"

"My dear, if I were caught sleuthing, Hudson Lowe would send me to England in irons."

"No, we can't have that. But what can we do?"

"Let me think." He rose to pace around our little nook. The

waves broke relentlessly on the shore, wearing down the rocks, wearing down the years left to me. Basil helped me to my feet. He brushed off my dress. "We must go. It's getting late."

I brushed his jacket and straightened its gold braid before we hurried off.

At the stream, he lifted me to carry me across, paused, and returned me to my feet. His hands played at my waist. "I shouldn't tell you this. The governor's in a fury. He caught wind of British subjects smuggling French messages to England. If I could be more useful to him, he'd be more open with me. Then I could help you."

I wanted to believe that earnest, almost handsome man. Most of all, I yearned for a letter from Tristan, for paper my son had touched, for his words to echo in my head.

That day, I didn't betray a Frenchman, although I was tempted. No, that day, I betrayed an enemy to France, an Englishman (an Irishman counts the same) against whom I held a grudge. I told Basil that Dr. O'Meara had written to the Admiralty on the Emperor's behalf.

I did it for my son.

SOLOMON, HOPING FOR A GLIMPSE of the Emperor, drove me home to Longwood in his donkey cart. To his disappointment, the guard forbade him on the grounds. Carrying my bundle, I took a shortcut to the nearest side door. Too late, I saw Cipriani lounged against it.

He flicked his stiletto open. He flicked it shut. He flicked it open. Guilt dried my mouth.

"I ain't interested in small talk neither," the Corsican said. "Got a simple message, my lady—as some people call ya." His blade caught the sun. He squinted at it, then at me. "Breathe a hint of the Master's and Las Cases's masquerade to them Brits? You'll find yourself at Hell's gate, blood dripping from that pretty throat of yours."

Chapter 18

Napoleon

Cipriani, returning from Jamestown in the afternoon rain, laid a damp packet on the Emperor's desk. "Mixed blessings today, Master. Solomon's got no stomach for your slave rebellion." He shook his wet hat.

The Emperor shot out of his chair. "Must you drip all over me? Unless Solomon's got some other scheme—"

"Told you he does."

"Ah, yes, the submarine. Bah! Next you'll have me escaping in one of Da Vinci's flying machines."

"Don't know about those." Cipriani scratched his nose. "Stick with the submarine for now, eh? Solomon's got connections to a man in London who's building one. They bring it here, we sneak on board, and *presto*—we show up in South America."

"Ride a submarine two thousand miles to Brazil? Are you mad?"

"Thought you understood these things. It's just a little closed-up boat. Like a banana skin with no fruit inside, Solomon says. Holds five people: you, me, the captain, and two crewmen who propel it. Skims beneath the surface with air pipes sticking above the waves. We ride a few hours till we find the real ship waiting out of sight of the island."

"Travel a few hours in that death trap?" The Emperor clasped his hands behind his back. "Who's the man in London? Not Thomas Johnson, I hope?"

Cipriani whistled. "How'd you know that?"

The Emperor poked the Corsican's chest. "You forget who I am."

Cipriani grinned. "Only when you let me."

The Emperor laughed. "Yes, well, back eight years ago, an American inventor, name of Fulton, proposed using a submarine to blow up the British fleet. He worked with this Johnson fellow who thought an underwater fleet would be useful to his smuggling trade."

Cipriani rubbed his hands together. "The smuggling thing's a fine idea. Anyway, Johnson's the man."

"Too bad. Not sure I'd trust him with my horse, much less my life. Still, Fulton's machine worked. I should have tried it, but you can't do everything, and our dismal navy . . . No point in reminiscing." The Emperor reached for his etching of the Eaglet. "Solomon can get a submarine here?"

"So he says. Didn't pursue it. Thought you'd be against it."

"Tell him to arrange it. If we can't get something going with Toby-Mahafaly, we'll be eager to board it. What else?"

"Got that Hercules fellow set to join us. Mighty eager, he is, as you predicted."

The Emperor nodded. "And the bad side of this report?"

"Well, the Masonic lodge in Vienna ain't keen on springing the Eaglet from that palace. Might help if you were there to give 'em guts, but not going to act on their own."

The Emperor returned the etching to the table. "Those damn Freemasons always were more talk than action. My brother Joseph fit in perfectly."

"No argument there. On the other hand, you'll like this." He extracted a journal from his damp packet.

"News from London? Eh bien, that's something." The Emperor grasped Cipriani's arm. "Mon Dieu, you really are skin and bone."

"I keep telling you this damn island don't agree with me." The Corsican shook off the Emperor's hand. "You want the journal or not? Judging by what I read, you'll be amused. Governor Lowe won't be." Cipriani cracked his knuckles. "Get Lady Fanny to translate. Sergeant Kitts's expecting me for a little card game."

"Let him win. Last thing we need is a new sergeant instilling discipline around here."

Cipriani grimaced. "Not so easy to lose to Kitts."

"Consider it a challenge. I'll fund your losses. Go."

The Emperor gulped a glass of port, but the wine didn't drown the acid burning in his throat. He sent Marchand to fetch Fanny Bertrand.

When gentle Fanny read the article in London's *Morning Post* that described Sir Hudson's first visit, ending with *Marchand, leave the door open so the flies may come and go*, she hooted like a barmaid.

Her soft eyes shone. "Oh, there's more. *The Duke of Wellington, who knows Sir Hudson intimately, is reported to have said that Britain could surely find a better guardian for the world's greatest man than a pettifogging bureaucrat with no manners.* Oh, sire, I can't translate 'pettifogging,' but if we have the Duke of Wellington on our side, our exile has to end."

"And yet Marchand and I were the only ones to hear those words spoken." The Emperor's rare grin faded. "We shall suffer for this minor victory."

TWO HOURS LATER, MARCHAND RUSHED into the Emperor's quarters. "Your Majesty, Dr. O'Meara is riding up—he's under military escort."

The Emperor flinched. An unforeseen casualty. "So we move from skirmishes to war. Let us see Lowe's first move."

He was sitting at his writing desk when Marchand brought O'Meara in. The British guards stood in the doorway, hats under their arms, faces curious. The doctor's black hair was disheveled. He plucked at his clothes.

The Emperor willed the man to be strong. He kept his own face neutral, his voice indifferent. If his friendliness with the doctor were reported, it would taint O'Meara, perhaps brand him as a traitor. Far better the doctor return to England to plead for their release.

"Your Maj—" O'Meara took a deep breath. "General Bonaparte, I cannot continue to perform medical duties for you. The governor and I have . . . agreed . . . it's best if I return to England." He clicked his heels. "I wish you good health as . . . as a doctor, I would wish for any man."

The Emperor inclined his head and retired to his bedroom.

There, Cipriani emerged from the shadows. "Not so bad, I'm thinking. Can't deny a second doc's reports of your illness, can they? Then, when—er, if—this slave thing collapses, we get home on sick leave."

The Emperor leaned his back against a wall. "A fine man, O'Meara. I hope they don't do him harm." His eyes drooped closed. "Lowe's not stupid. He's banished an ally of mine as punishment for that article. I guarantee that's not the end of the matter." He kicked off his slippers. His feet didn't look swollen. Perhaps his hourglass had not yet run out.

CLISSON: THE EMPEROR'S NOVEL

Champvert, France, July 1789

All night Clisson lay awake, remapping his dreams.

When morning came, he rang for paper and pen. In the struggle to transform his scrawl into evenly slanted letters, he produced something like Berville's aristocratic script.

Dear Amélie,

I have learned of your sacrifice for our fatherland. Your young hopes were plucked when yet a frail bloom. War and man's incomparable passion for destruction are to blame. Let your suffering turn my own path from violence to construction of a better world. For me, to love you alone, to make you happy, to do nothing which would contradict your wishes, this is my Destiny and the meaning of my life. With your help, I, who was born for war, can renounce glory to become a vicar of peace.

Clisson

He scratched out the last line. It sounded good within his head, but he had no desire to be a priest. He tried *I yearn to stand in your fallen hero's stead.* But was he ready to be married? He had no means to support a wife. Perhaps Amélie had her own fortune. That would solve a multitude of problems.

To love in person was so startling, it left little time to reason. His past had been solitary, and lately his whole being taken up with a single thought: finding Rose. He craved exercise—commotion—to cool his passions.

At all costs, he had to avoid Eugénie's father, who could talk an eagle blind. He peeked out his door. All clear. At the stairs, he ducked behind a stuffed bear, while nearby Monsieur LeGrand issued orders to the butler. When the two men left, Clisson ran out the front door, across the lawn, and down the lane.

Not a mile from the house, an open carriage rolled toward him. Amélie Rose. No foppish cousin. No talkative Eugénie. He couldn't believe his luck. He waved for the coachman to stop.

Amélie, in a dress the color of her cheeks, smiled brightly. "Why, Monsieur Clisson, where are you off to?"

He attempted a variation on the Fop's bow. "My passions, Madame, run deep this morning. You, above all others, may imagine why I need exercise."

She pouted a pretty frown, without diminishing the warmth

in her face. "Then it's not wise to deprive you of it. Do you have a destination?"

"I did. Although I thought it unattainable, I have this minute reached it." He thought the extemporaneous phrase witty. "What's your destination?"

"I'm on my way to visit Eugénie."

"May I accompany you?"

"If you can safely dispense with exercise." She indicated the bench seat alongside her. He vaulted into her carriage as the coachman's reins slapped the horses.

"Are you enjoying the company at the LeGrand house?" she asked. "As a soldier, you must be used to more physical exertion than you find in that atmosphere."

"Yes," he said. "I need action. Action and lots of exercise. You smile at my bluntness."

"Let us say, it is an unusual trait in polite society."

"And frowned upon?"

"Did I frown, Monsieur Clisson?"

"No." His memory had been correct. In the sun, her dark curls were lit with red.

She stared at the road ahead. "Pray, continue to be blunt."

Hope ballooned in his chest. He could tell her anything; from his dreams, he knew her intimately. "To answer your question, I am grateful for the hospitality, especially since I found you among the guests, but I'm unaccustomed to the small talk, the gentle taunts and wordplays, that are habitual to polite society. Why, just a few days ago, I spent an after noon in a blacksmith's hovel. There, among the uneducated, I discussed freedom, equality—things that matter. Am I wrong to despise gallants who debate cravats while the country starves?"

"So that's why you appear so unyielding. You despise us." Nestled in her lap, her hands trembled.

"No, no, not you—not ever you, dear lady. I would kneel at your feet were we not in a carriage. You must forgive my impetuous tongue. I'm a rude soldier, used to harsh garrison conversation."

They rode in silence, each immersed in thought. He had no greater ambition than to sit next to her, listening to the horses clop. If only he could have stretched the mile into ten. And the ten into a hundred.

The carriage was halfway back to the LeGrand estate when Amélie cried out, "Jean-Paul Coachman, stop!"

Napoleon

THE NEXT MORNING, AS MARCHAND and the Emperor strolled the garden, angry voices erupted from Longwood's reception room. The valet paused to listen. "Governor Lowe."

The Emperor nodded. "Arguing with Bertrand."

Marchand hurried to open the door.

Hudson Lowe stood in the center of the shabby reception room, with two British soldiers at his back. General Bertrand— within arm's distance—clutched his sword hilt. Nearby, Fanny Bertrand huddled in a chair, wringing a lace handkerchief, while Las Cases cringed on the velvet sofa. In a far corner, Albine clung to her smirking husband.

The Emperor bellowed, "Stand apart."

The guards snapped to attention. Sir Hudson Lowe's high color deepened. He thrust a finger toward the doorway. As the guards tromped out, he wheeled on the Emperor. "Do not give orders to my soldiers, sir."

The Emperor crossed his arms. "I spoke to you, sir, not them. Now, what's this tumult?"

Fanny hurried to her husband's side. "It's about me, sire. I went in to Jamestown. The shopkeepers refused to sell a thing. They waved a proclamation from this . . . this *monster*, saying no one is allowed to sell to us. Oh, sire, I couldn't even buy a bit of thread!"

The Emperor turned on Sir Hudson. "What's this nonsense?"

"Nonsense?" The governor snorted. "Necessary precautions, *General* Bonaparte. I intend to stop your message smuggling. If Madame Bertrand wishes to purchase goods, she may inform my office. The merchant will send the items to us, and, after inspection, a soldier will deliver them."

Fanny lifted her tearstained face. "I should like to see Lady Lowe live under such conditions!"

"You will leave my wife out of this."

Bertrand's battle-scarred chin twitched. "You will not speak to *my* wife in that manner."

The Emperor slammed his bicorne on a table. "Sir Hudson, are you prepared to rescind these ridiculous orders?"

Hudson Lowe raised his chin. "Are you prepared to swear on your honor that no messages have been smuggled off this island?"

The Emperor relaxed his shoulders. He chuckled. "So, you've received copies of the London *Morning Post*, as have I. The truth, Sir Hudson, has a way of rising to the surface. The more you suppress it, the greater its insistence to be heard. I've told you before: the world is watching. How shall it react to the news that this gentlewoman may not shop for her household?"

"The world, sir, will say I'm doing my duty."

"The world, sir, will say—has said—you're a 'pettifogging bureaucrat.' Now, you may not like it when the British press tells the world I called you a 'fly,' but if you plan to have an apoplexy, do it elsewhere. I have important work to do with my memoirs."

Sir Hudson pulled himself up. "Your memoirs? Important work? Let me tell you, you've been a mere distraction, nothing more. After Waterloo—"

"You dare to mention Waterloo?" The Emperor gave a soft laugh. "You, whom Wellington dismissed from his post on the eve of that great engagement? You couldn't even run a supply depot to Sir Arthur's satisfaction."

"Slander!" Sir Hudson cried. "I was sent on a diplomatic mission to Genoa."

"Sent from the site of battle and replaced by an officer two ranks below yours. You see, I *do* know your past. Small wonder Wellington scoffs at your ability to manage my exile."

"You know nothing of it," Sir Hudson muttered.

"And Waterloo? Waterloo's not my legacy." The Emperor shifted his voice into the full-throated pride he had almost forgotten. "When I came to power, sir, revolutionary excess had France in chaos. I dragged my country back from the brink. I not only saved the revolution but spread its modernity throughout Europe. Merit over birthright, Sir Hudson—that's the system your kings and queens, your lords and ladies, your archbishops and popes fear." He lowered his voice. "That is my legacy."

Sir Hudson sniffed. "Merit over birthright? This from a man who reinstated slavery in Haiti?"

The Emperor glared. "This from a man who presides over St. Helena's slavery today?"

Sir Hudson flushed. "Well, my fine emperor, I'll show you that won't be my legacy."

"I doubt you have the courage."

"As for your legacy, monarchs have returned to their God-given thrones, nobility and clergy to their inherited rights. What you built has been destroyed." He snapped his fingers. "*Poof!* Aside from those who died in your name, it's as if you never were."

In the mirror across the room, the Emperor confronted a white face—his own. His eyes flicked to Lowe, who quaked before him. His hand clutched an imaginary stiletto. A single slice at the man's pulsing jugular. Blood would splatter.

General Bertrand disengaged himself from his wife's clutches.

"No, Bertrand." The Emperor's voice was cold. "Leave him to me."

Lowe inched toward the door. "Such arguments are beneath my position."

"Yes," said the Emperor, "but the subject matter is above you. Go, before I sink to your level. Go, before—"

Sir Hudson thrust a folded paper into the Emperor's hand and fled.

The Emperor threw his bicorne at the closing door. "*Merde.* Pardon, Fanny."

Bertrand clicked his heels. "Sire, I request the loan of your dueling pistols."

Fanny seized her husband's arm. "Oh, no, no, Henri."

The Emperor turned to the mirror. He watched their affection play out behind the reflection of his white, solitary face. He swallowed hard before speaking. "No, no, indeed. We should lose both you and my pistols, regardless of the outcome."

Las Cases piped up from the sofa. "Who smuggled the message to the London press? Betsy's father?"

"That, my secretary, is confidential."

"But I have safe channels—"

"Las Cases, I've warned you not to engage in espionage." He turned on the Montholons. "Did you two enjoy the spectacle?"

Montholon lifted a shoulder. "Aside from Lady Fanny's distress, yes. Particularly the part about Lowe's missing the Battle of Waterloo, since I supplied you with the information. Timely, wasn't it?"

"As you say." The Emperor jammed into his pocket the note Hudson Lowe had thrust upon him. "Now, all of you, leave me."

Albine dropped him a shy curtsy, offering a peek at her breasts.

Chapter 19

Napoleon

ALONE IN HIS MUSTY CHAMBERS, the Emperor wondered if Albine had admired his prowess battling the governor. Most likely, the insults flung and received diminished him. Yet the woman made a point of displaying her allures. Ah, well, it shouldn't matter.

He wiped the day's dust off his writing box. Rats and dust: the twin banes of Longwood House. He'd settle into work and forget them.

CLISSON: THE EMPEROR'S NOVEL

Champvert, France, July 1789

Clisson helped Amélie descend the carriage. Once her feet touched the ground, she laid a finger on his lips. "Like you, I must walk. Do not speak. I wish to think."

The sun flitted among snowy clouds, speckling the road through the trees. On the dusty surface, his steps sounded like muffled drums; Amélie's slippers were silent. The carriage followed in their wake.

She slowed her steps. "May I ask your indulgence? I have no one to talk to."

Clisson's pulse raced. "It seems to me there are always too *many* people, rather than too *few*, surrounding you. Last evening, I couldn't break through the crush."

"Oh, LeGrands and their ceaseless parties. But I shouldn't complain. My aunt—she is not well and doesn't go into society. I'm grateful Eugénie's family embraces me."

"And yet?"

"And yet they talk only of the trivial, never, God forbid, the difficult, unless it be Monsieur LeGrand's mathematics. I discern you, however, have a serious nature."

He dared to take her hand. It lay like a prize in his. "I feared you mistook my bluntness for vulgarity. I admit I scorn society's games and coquetry. But what do you wish? Is there a dragon I might slay for you? Or, in your honor, could I skewer a Fop?"

"Pray, be serious. You must promise not to be shocked." She hesitated, seemingly teetering on an edge, ready to draw back. Her words came as a punch. "I should like to know what war feels like, what it means to kill and to die."

He stopped midstep. Amélie maintained her pace. He regained his stride, afraid to lose the hand he held.

A tear hovered in her lashes. "I couldn't be with my husband in his last moments. We'd planned to marry since we were eight. Until he joined the army, we shared everything. Everyone thinks it's better if I forget. I shall not. Not ever."

The conversation didn't coincide with his dreams, but Amélie fascinated him all the more. "My dear—"

Again, she put a finger to his lips. "I must finish. Is killing a man in battle like shooting an animal? Like watching a deer die? No one will talk to me of it. The most they say is that he lost a leg and bled to death. I think that might be the quietest way to die, except for drowning. I thought you would know."

Sergeant Lyons; Giovanni, the butcher's son; the people he had mowed down in the square—all crowded into his brain. He trembled, unable to speak. His mind stumbled to concoct an answer. He was relieved she didn't wait.

"I often imagine the aftermath of a battle," she said, a touch of sunlight on her nose. "Is it as horrible as I think? Men moaning for their wives and mothers, doctors sawing limbs, blood seeping into snow? That is why you must stay away from me. I want no more soldiers in my life."

"No, my—"

"You must think me as Gothic as Eugénie—speaking of whom, here she arrives, ending our tête-à-tête."

He'd have done anything to forestall Eugénie's approach, including bowl her down with cannon fire, but the relentless girl cantered toward them on a feisty gray, a groom shadowing her. Her horse, shying at Amélie's carriage, bucked. When the groom grabbed her bridle, Eugénie whacked his wrist with her crop.

Amélie shrank against Clisson. "What was her father thinking to buy her that stallion? And look, her new riding dress matches the horse. So much money."

The gray reared, wild-eyed, its hooves flailing. Eugénie's eyes sparked willfully beneath her gray-plumed hat.

"Miss, I beg you," the groom said. "Your father will have my head if you come to harm."

"Her? What about us?" Amélie whispered.

Clisson wrapped his arm around her. Her heart beat against his ribs.

"Oh, fine." Eugénie pouted at her groom. "Take him home. I'd rather walk with my friends." She slid down from the frothing horse. On her boots, silver spurs tinkled.

She kissed Amélie's cheeks. "Dearest, I hope I didn't frighten you. You always take the lead, don't you? Except when it comes to horses. I see you admire the Brunswick jacket on my new riding habit—all the rage, I assure you, although we French don't often take our fashions from the English." She hung on Clisson's other arm. "Where have you two been?"

Amélie answered the girl's rapid-fire chatter. When the barrage was directed at Clisson, he returned a syllable or two. Yesterday, shy; today, aggressive—this little woman, this Eugénie, whose head barely reached his shoulder, upended all tranquility.

Amélie's inquiry confounded him. Aside from his skirmish with the mob, for him the army consisted of marching drills, building fortifications, besting fellow officers at debate. In books, no one talked of a battle's aftermath, except in Homer, and he never cared for those Greeks who lost sight of their goals. But, to his shame, he—who was born for war—couldn't tell Amélie what combat was like.

Eugénie pinched his arm. "Monsieur Clisson, what makes you so distracted?"

Afraid his voice might quaver, he managed a smile.

When they reached the manor house, Monsieur LeGrand paced the front steps. "My Eugénie, don't tell me Gray Man's too much for your horsemanship?"

"Father! Of course not. I wanted to walk with my friends."

"Well, run along now." Her father took Clisson's arm. "I want our guest to see my laboratory."

In LeGrand's tower, amid pots and tubes, formulas and calculations, Clisson barely heeded his host's inquisition. Afterward, he realized he'd said too much. Rash words about his family's olive grove, summer house, winery, mulberry trees raised on a grant from the king: all convinced Monsieur LeGrand that he hosted a propertied Corsican noble. The man couldn't conceive what a meager existence that meant on an island where goods were bartered and few coins exchanged. Clisson had nothing to offer a wife.

Napoleon

AS HE STORED HIS WRITING BOX, Napoleon remembered the paper Hudson Lowe had thrust upon him. He pulled it from his pocket. The governor had clipped a journal announcement and supplied a French translation.

The Emperor held it under candlelight.

Marie Louise, former Empress of the French, now Duchess of Parma, has given birth to a healthy girl. Her name is Albertine von Neipperg.

The paper fell from his hands. A cuckolded husband. Better to have died in battle. Better to have been shot full of holes and left hanging from a tree than to bear this final insult. His empty arms hugged his chest. He was not an emperor. He was nothing.

Albine

AS ARRANGED, SERGEANT KITTS drilled three soldiers outside Longwood's gate while I stole into his guardhouse. Basil caught me so tightly in his arms, the locket with Tristan's portrait bit into my breast.

Charles's bony form made lovemaking uncomfortable. The Emperor's plumpness transformed it into duty. Basil, with his sturdy chest, was a man to steady my erratic life. A man to erase worry before it etched my face.

An Englishman. It would never work. Still, I raised my lips invitingly.

He put me from him. "Sit," he commanded.

I sat on a stool, disappointment chilling me.

The guardhouse—a tall wooden box with slits for windows— had a table but no second chair. Basil crouched, hands on his thighs, face level with mine. When he'd shaved that morning, he'd missed some bristles. I reached to touch them.

He brushed my arm aside. "You tricked me. That's how you return my kindness?"

I thrust a hand into my skirt pocket. "But my information worked. The governor sent the doctor away."

"Lower your voice. Do you want to cause more trouble?"

My fist closed around my crust of bread. "I told the truth."

"Yes, just enough truth to get me in a hobble." He rubbed his brow. "My girl, O'Meara's treachery was stale news, information someone else—no doubt your husband—had already revealed to Hudson Lowe, though not through me."

"But you're the only conduit Charles has. I thought if he'd already passed the information on, you would know it." In my pocket, the crust crumbled between my fingers.

He rose from his crouch. "I trusted you."

"We trusted each other. Was Sir Hudson angry?" I peeked at him through my lashes. "Does that mean you don't have a letter from Tristan for me?"

"I thought Frenchwomen were subtle." He shook his head. "You're nothing but a pretty child displaying your desires for all to see."

"I'm not a child."

"But I'm not complaining, my adorable girl. I like the child in you. No, no letters today." He raised me to my feet. "When the governor doesn't trust me, it's too risky to get them. I told you, I could face court martial."

No one called me "girl," much less "adorable," anymore. He took my hand before I could brush the crumbs from it. I pulled it from his grasp and rubbed it on his shoulder, whisking the morsels away. "Risks for me, too. If Napoleon knew I helped you, I'd be dead before morning."

"How's this? France's Emperor, a common murderer?"

"Oh, no. Others do his work." Cipriani's leather face loomed before me. The ache between my legs hardened into a warning. As much as I yearned for a letter, as much as Basil tempted me, the game was too dangerous. I shivered.

Basil looked down on me. Were those the eyes of a puppy or a fox? It didn't matter. Safer to stay a loyal Frenchwoman. Let Charles work alone to damn his soul (and earn us gold). I caressed the bristles Basil had neglected on his chin. "It's too risky for both of us, my dear. It's better . . . we should say goodbye."

"Goodbye? No, not goodbye. Dearest, that, too, would be like death to me." Again, he held me in his arms. "Don't you feel the bond between us? We could be happy, you and I. We could make a home, peacefully, in the countryside in Europe." He stroked my hair. "Give me one more name. I'll get you a letter. Then you must never spy again."

Napoleon

WHEN HERCULES BROUGHT NEWS THAT Toby was ready to meet, the Emperor retired to his bedroom to hide his qualms from the others. If the enterprise went awry, they'd lock him in a prison cell. He'd never see the Eaglet again. He retrieved his poison vial from Marchand.

That night, as Marchand wrapped a black scarf around the Emperor's face, Cipriani cracked his knuckles. "Ain't you ready? Got to get outta here afore the moon comes up."

"Stop that endless cracking, will you?" The Emperor loosened the scarf. "Do you want to smother me, Marchand? Why are you hanging on me, Tobyson?"

Tobyson released the Emperor's sleeve. "Let me come. Please, Master."

"I told you no."

"But my father'll be there." The boy's eyes filled with tears. "And if you get lost, I can lead you home. I'm old enough."

"You're also old enough to follow orders." The Emperor took his hand. "Your mission—a very important one—is to comfort Marchand. He's shaking like one of Cook's custards."

Marchand put his arm around the boy.

"See?" the Emperor said. "He needs you. Give me Hercules's stocking cap."

As Marchand stuffed a folded cloth inside the Emperor's jacket, he patted the valet's cheek. "Eh bien, my friend. Stay alert for our return."

The Corsican, a wooden box tucked under one arm, flowed down the dark hall like a shadow. The Emperor followed, conscious of his footsteps' echo. They passed into the garden. Silhouettes of familiar trees, the chairs and table where he lunched, the pergola Hercules had built, all loomed in the darkness like enemies poised to attack. Night air sent a shiver down his back.

Ahead, two patrolling soldiers crossed the path. Cipriani flung out an arm, pinning him to Longwood's wall. He held his breath.

One soldier jostled the other. "Bastard, I tell you, and I'll swear till I die, you're a card cheat."

The other shoved back. "Weren't me, I swear. 'Twas that devilish gardener."

"What's he got to do with it? You're the one what's won my money."

The soldiers moved on. Cipriani crept forward in a crouch. The Emperor followed suit, his thighs screaming. At the gardener's shed, Hercules drew them inside. The gardener removed planks from the shed's back wall. The three of them slipped through the slots and the adjacent fence onto Longwood's open plain.

Hercules led them along a back route to the Valley of the Geraniums. Cipriani always moved like a cat, but the limping gardener's sure-footedness came as a surprise. Although the man clutched a bulky package, his huge moccasins landed like velvet on the dirt. At the entrance of the grotto, the big man whistled.

Two Black men half-hidden in the darkness waved them in. The grotto, walled on three sides and open to the starry sky, teemed with people. Women, some with children on their backs, arranged sacks of provisions. The men guarded pathways into the grotto. In the center, Toby and Randall conferred in angry voices. At their feet, a rustic blanket displayed rows of knives.

The Emperor frowned. Twenty people in all: five women, nine strangely quiet children. That would make ten children when the rarely silent Tobyson was added. Including Cipriani, Hercules, and him, there'd be nine men to sail the ship and fight off the British or an occasional pirate. Longer odds than he'd expected. He unwrapped the scarf from his face.

Toby-Mahafaly and Randall broke off their argument. Absent his crown, Toby's white hair shone in the moonlight, setting him apart from and above his followers. He led them to the spring, where a tall woman served cool water in wooden cups. "This is Sylvie. She speaks for the women."

"Do not use my slave name. I am Miora." She offered a cup to the Emperor.

He bowed low. Her almond eyes recalled East Africans he'd seen in Egypt.

He and Toby sat on boulders while the others gathered around, men seated in the nearest semicircle, women and children behind. Randall stood to the side, holding a torch that flickered light across the faces. The smell of its burning pitch filled the air, reminding the Emperor how much he disliked ships.

Toby pointed to the provisions. "Rice, dry beans, meat jerky, coffee, sugar. For now, we'll store it in the cave on Diana's Peak."

"Excellent, excellent." The Emperor smiled at the women. "No doubt it was difficult to gather without detection."

"Enough we won't starve, not enough to be missed." Toby hesitated. "Water's the problem. Even if we had barrels, they'd be too heavy to transport to the cave and down to the ship. We'll have to collect rain during the voyage."

Hercules spoke. "Can't count on that. I tell you, water's more important than food. To start with, everyone can sling a couple of full pouches on their bodies. Should be a few barrels stashed on board already. Let me see what else I can do."

Randall bent forward, his branded "R" like a stamp of white man's flesh in the torchlight. "You French gonna bring more gold? Buy us supplies in Africa?"

Cipriani, translating the question, added in an undertone, "That what this all about, Master? Take our gold, toss our bodies overboard?"

"Have faith," the Emperor said. "Tell him yes. And compliment the knives."

Toby nodded. "One for each man and woman, a few for older children."

The Emperor turned to Hercules. "Show Monsieur Toby what you made."

The big man unwrapped his bundle. He held up a rough wooden model of the governor's schooner, fitted with spars, wire rigging, and rice-paper sails.

A broad smile spread across Toby's face. "Ah, the HMS *St. Helena*. A perfect training vessel. Let me see it."

"In a moment. Cipriani, show him what you have."

The Corsican opened the wooden box to reveal the Emperor's dueling pistols. The crowd murmured. The Emperor lifted a hand. "We use these pistols for defense only. We don't intend to kill anyone."

"Then what's the point of knives and guns?" Randall cried.

"Here, here," several men called out.

The Emperor forced himself to examine Randall beyond the horrific "R" burned in his forehead. The broken nose came as no surprise on such an aggressive fellow, but his unyielding mouth gave the Emperor pause. For the first time, he questioned Toby's judgment. The Emperor's jaw tightened. "The point is, we'll have ourselves a clean, bloodless exit."

Randall shook his torch. "I'd rather take a few of the bastards out for good. Teach 'em a lesson for all they done to us."

"No," Toby said. "It's the escape, not revenge, that matters. Now, we have much to do before this night's over. Hercules and I will explain his model ship and its sails to my men and, I think, a couple of strong women. The children and the rest of the women will go to Diana's Peak to hide our supplies."

Miora raised her long fingers. "Mahafaly, remember."

Toby sighed. "We carry the customs of our homelands with us, good sire. The women demand we ask the island permission to leave. They want you to join us in this ceremony."

In the Emperor's mind flashed an image of his mother on her knees in the humble cathedral on Corsica. He made the sign of the cross. "Yes, we all carry our customs with us."

Miora draped her scarf over her hair. "Everyone, join hands. You, too, Randall."

The Emperor, grasping Toby's hand and Cipriani's, thought them fitting links to his future and his past. He conjured up the Eaglet's cherub face while the women chanted their farewell. When they finished, he asked Toby if he could speak.

Toby folded his arms. "But don't forget. They remain my people."

The Emperor bowed to Toby so all could see. He faced the seated crowd. "My friends, we embark on a great venture to obtain that which is most precious in this universe: our freedom, our children's freedom, and the wealth and happiness that come with freedom."

His lips twitched as Cipriani, translating his words to English, delivered them in a mimicry of his grandiose tone. Hard to tell whether his Corsican friend was mocking or respecting him. No matter—the effect on his audience was the same.

"Friends, I have a son. My enemies hold him in slavery far from St. Helena. I seek my own freedom to gain his, much as you seek your children's freedom. This voyage binds our families. My son is your son, and yours are mine. Surely, the gods have brought Mahafaly and me together as brothers to lead you.

"I was born on an island like this one. My homeland was captive to conquerors who stole our riches and restrained our bodies in chains like those you bear. My people rose in rebellion to gain freedom. That is what you and I do now." He raised his hands to the starlit sky. "A powerful destiny is behind our quest. You ask how I know? Let me show you.

"The people of my island are white men like me, yet, for reasons not revealed until this moment, this is the rebel flag my people fought under. This is the rebel flag I was born under. This shall be our flag."

He shook out the cloth Marchand had sewn for him: the Corsican Moor's head flag. On a stark white background lay the profile of a young Black soldier.

Mahafaly's followers jumped up, stamped their feet, and cheered.

His heart swelled at their cries, at his own words, at the prospect of action, at a future with his child, only to deflate when Cipriani rolled his eyes at him.

Later, when he and the Corsican crept out of Hercules's shed, he stumbled over an empty flowerpot. It clattered like a peddler's cart across the patio. The Corsican slammed him into the shadows against Longwood House's wall.

From around the corner, a British guard shouted, "Who goes there?" Four soldiers rushed by, bayonets at the ready, screaming, "Halt, halt!"

A toad leapt out of the kitchen doorway. Tobyson leapt in its wake. "Hallo! Hallo! Just me! No, no, oh, please, don't step on him." He barreled into one of the guards. His round, innocent face crinkled into a grin. "Nighttime's the best time to catch frogs, don't you think?" He popped another out of his jacket and chased it down a garden path.

While the laughing guards trailed Tobyson, the Emperor and Cipriani stole inside the kitchen door.

Chapter 20

Napoleon

THE EMPEROR AWOKE LATE, HIS doubts banished, his old exuberance restored. A few details to resolve, training for his crew, a date set, and, as Cipriani liked to say, *presto*—they'd be off. Meanwhile, he'd work on the story for the Eaglet.

CLISSON: THE EMPEROR'S NOVEL

Champvert, France, July 1789

The sky had turned as hard and gray as metal. Leaves hung still. The birds were silent. Last night, Monsieur LeGrand had insisted his barometers were dropping precipitously, indicating a violent storm. Clisson reined in his horse to hold up a wet finger. No wind. LeGrand should forget predicting weather and return to hawking silk.

As Clisson crested a hill, Amélie's aunt's property undulated below in a verdant valley that a placid stream traversed. Oaks bordered green patchwork fields. Cypress shielded the manor house. A mill stood on the riverbank; a vineyard crept up a slope; cows roamed an enclosure. All this belonged to the Fop.

Clisson owned nothing. Even his boots belonged to the army. He had planned to knock on the door. Now, he wasn't sure.

In the distance, a woman strolled across a field toward a wood. Clisson pulled his father's spyglass from inside his jacket. Amélie Rose.

He urged his horse to canter, keeping a bead on where she entered the wood. When he arrived, she'd disappeared. He tied his reins to a branch and stepped between the trees.

The air was cool, musky scented. Sunlight slanted through branches. Shadows hazed the way. He listened. Not far away, water gurgled. The rustle of Amélie's unseen footsteps floated to his ears. He followed stealthily, snatching glimpses of her bright clothing.

Her empty shoes lay unattended. Amélie, her back to him, straddled a tree trunk fallen across the stream. Her skirt was bunched above her knees; her bare legs dangled naked feet in the water. Her chestnut hair hung like a mantle about her shoulders. She leaned back to stretch out on the log, providing him with a view of rounded breasts spilling out of her bodice. She lay still, legs spread, vulnerable.

"Oh, Clisson," she said.

He opened his mouth. *Wait.* She didn't know he was there. Perspiration gathered on his upper lip.

She pressed her palms on her breasts. "Oh, Clisson."

He took the last steps quickly, his boots filling with cold creek water. He gently laid a hand over her mouth and kissed the nipple peeking from her bodice. She came to life, sinking teeth into his flesh. Her fingers grabbed his hair. He seized her wrists and brought his face close to hers.

"You are mine," he said. "I am yours."

Fear fled her face. Indignation took its place. She swung her leg to dismount the log. "Don't touch me."

He caught her ankle and kissed the arch of her foot. It was cold, wet, and delicious.

She sucked in her breath. "If you are a gentleman—any kind of a gentleman—you will leave."

"I promise not to touch you. But leave? No, we have plans to make."

"There are no plans for us."

"But I love you and you love me. Why else would you call my name? I shall never forget the taste of your beautiful foot."

"Swear you'll never mention that again. Swear it."

"Swearing doesn't change what happened."

"I'm marrying the count." She waved a sapphire-and-diamond ring in his face. "Out of my way, or I'll have him horsewhip you for manhandling his wife."

"His wife!"

"We're to be married in three months."

"But why did you call my name? I heard you. I did."

She flushed. "Because I'm a fool. But not such a fool as to cast my lot with you. Tell me, now that you have seen this estate, what do you have to offer?"

He turned away. His poverty exceeded that of the blacksmith who had shoed his horse, yet he considered that man little more than a peasant. His voice shrank to a child's plea. "You cannot be so crass. Do you care only for riches?"

"I married for love once, only to be saddled with widowhood and debt. I won't marry a second soldier who will die on the battlefield." The hardness in her face collapsed. "With this revolution coming, I must have security. Only wealth can buy it." She pushed his chest. "Now go, you naive boy. You're not the sort of man I'd marry."

He sloshed out of the creek and stalked to his horse. His cold, wet feet added to Amélie's insults. He jammed his heels into his horse's flanks. The animal bolted. Clisson sat tall in the saddle, swaying, divoting the count's fields, hoping Amélie witnessed his wild gallop.

As he topped the hill, he reined to a walk, his anger spent. What kind of woman spread her legs in a wood and called a lover's name? He might understand if he had followed Berville's lead with the Paris prostitutes, but, no, he'd spent what little money he had on books. He knew no more than a farm boy who watched sheep cavort. Why stay pure when the woman you desired had tasted what you hadn't?

Out of his confusion, triumph sprang. She had touched her breasts. She had called his name. If he'd waited, he might have seen more. Clisson smiled at his bulging crotch. For the first time in his life, he had awakened a woman's passion. By the time he arrived at the LeGrand mansion, he was half convinced the meeting had gone well.

Napoleon

BETSY ARRIVED AT NOON, BRINGING sunshine in her wake. The Emperor and she sat outside in the warmth, reading about Clisson and Amélie's encounter with Eugénie. He held back the chapter about the meeting in the wood.

She pulled a small envelope from her reticule. "I almost forgot. Here, from Solomon."

"Betsy." The Emperor's hand closed over hers. "You mustn't bring me any more messages. It's too risky."

The mischief on her face flattened. She stared over his shoulder. He turned.

Montholon stood in the shade of the trellis. "Am I interrupting?"

"Not at all, sir." Betsy shook out her skirt. "I must be going home before the rains start again. I'll leave Monsieur to your good company." She kissed the Emperor on both cheeks. "Might I have a bit of licorice before I go?"

He gave her his bonbon pouch. Her little hand slipped the envelope inside. She winked, dropped a candy in her mouth, and pranced away.

The Emperor frowned at Montholon. "And you complain Cipriani lurks in the shadows." He went inside, calling for Marchand. The valet closed the bedroom door after them. "Are you unwell, sire? Your color—"

"No, no." The Emperor emptied the licorice pouch onto the bed. "A message, Marchand. See, the writing is small. You must read it to me."

Marchand squinted at the envelope. *"Philippe Welle, botanist from Austrian court, arrived St. Helena today. Message for Marchand."* The valet dropped the note. "For me?"

"Keep your voice down. Cipriani's not the only one who listens at the keyholes." He scrutinized the paper. "There's more. Read it all. Quick, man."

"Gathering specimens for Austrian Emperor's collection. Former master gardener at Schönbrunn Palace." Marchand's face lit up. "Then the message comes from my mother. Oh, Master, the man must have seen the Eaglet."

"Yes, yes, is there more?"

"A tiny line at the bottom: *Pony from Uncle Pascal.*" Marchand clapped. "On my tenth birthday. Who besides my mother would know?"

"Maybe your mother, maybe espionage." The Emperor held the envelope up to the sunlight. "But the Austrian court! This could represent a diplomatic breakthrough. Small wonder if my father-in-law—if I can still call Emperor Francis that—has changed his mind over this absurd exile."

Marchand let out a lengthy breath. "What a relief to call off your entanglement with those slaves."

The Emperor gave a half smile. "We shall see. Open the envelope."

Inside they found a note in Marchand's mother's hand: *You will find enclosed a lock of my hair. Your Maman Marchand.*

The Emperor crumpled the note. "I don't understand. Why not send this through official channels?" He shook the packet. A blond curl, too delicate to have come from Marchand's gray-haired mother, fell onto his palm. His mouth quivered around a prayer. He brought the Eaglet's curl to his face and breathed in. He couldn't smell the child, but he could remember. He could remember every molecule of him.

THE NEXT MORNING, SUN SHONE through the fog. The Emperor, feeling energetic, had Marchand rouse Las Cases and fetch General Bertrand. The clock had not struck seven when the three rode out from Longwood House, four British guards trotting behind.

God, he hated that windblown climate, with its rains and fog darkening the sky three times a day. British newspapers described St. Helena as temperate, healthful. Maybe for Englishmen, who liked rain punctuated with sunshine to transform the mud to dust. Too wet, too dry, all in the same day. Healthful? Perhaps for mold.

"Did Your Majesty say something?" Las Cases asked.

Had he said something aloud? He must take more pains in front of his entourage.

The path dropped below the ridgeline, out of view of Longwood House. A pheasant burst from the brush. Las Cases's horse shied, nearly unseating him. Las Cases flushed and straightened his ruffled sleeves. Bertrand laughed, spurred his own mount, then reined the animal in a mincing dance.

These two men disliked each other more every day. Neither of them got along with Montholon. Fanny Bertrand barely spoke to Albine de Montholon; everyone talked down to Marchand and despised Cipriani. He had to keep them focused on him, or in this island's small universe they would consume each other.

He turned to Las Cases. "Eighteen horses."

"Your Majesty?"

"That's how many horses I had shot from under me in battle."

Las Cases's blush faded. "Eighteen! Can I get a list? Do you remember each time, place, and name of the horse? How I should like to add that to your memoirs. A miracle, truly a God-sent miracle, you survived."

The Emperor looked into the distant ocean. "Luck."

Bertrand sniffed. "I was there much of the time. Once, I threw myself at great risk—"

"Yes, and I thank you for it. Quite often, considering I don't remember the incident." The Emperor pushed his mount between the other two horses. "Single file on this narrow track?"

Their hooves thudded on hard soil, the hillside ascending on their right, the sun behind them, the land on the left descending into valleys that folded in upon each other. Diana's Peak rose at the Emperor's back. Before him, the ocean stretched like a great steel plain. When they reemerged on the ridge, wind pummeled them.

The triangle of Flagstaff Hill, with its steep paths leading to the British lookout, lay ahead. What was the point of going up? To view more ocean? To look down desolate cliffs no army could scale? If all went well with his escape, they'd never worry him again.

His stomach hurt, as it often did. Either his stomach or his feet, or both.

He was ready for his coffee.

"We're out of the governor's limits, sire," Bertrand said. "The guards are nervous."

The Emperor swung his horse east. Dead Wood Plain offered a straight line to Longwood, but in between a British regiment bivouacked. Those soldiers were his jailers. On his left calf, the scar twitched. His lucky scar, the only wound he'd received in all his sixty battles—that British soldier's pike at Toulon when he was twenty-four. Damn surgeons had wanted to amputate his leg. If he'd been unconscious, those saw-mad doctors would have done it. There would have been no empire for a one-legged man.

He was lucky, always lucky. Until he was not.

"Sire?" Bertrand asked.

They were in the open. The encampment stirred. A bugle sounded to arms.

The Emperor tucked in his stomach. "I want a look at these enemy soldiers."

"Is it safe?" Las Cases asked.

Bertrand moved to lead the way.

The Emperor flung out his arm.

The general fell behind.

The field before them came alive. A second bugle sounded, then another. As they approached, shouts rose. He could pick out English phrases. "Boncy! Boncy! Boncy's come to visit!"

He reined his horse to a stop fifty meters away.

In the camp, arms were thrust into jackets and hats slammed on heads. Hundreds of boots pounded the earth. If the camp had been a boat, it would have capsized as its inhabitants rushed to one side of the perimeter. Soldiers flooded the road.

Las Cases's horse pawed the ground, but the Emperor kept his mount's hooves quiet. He knew how to hold a horse still. He waited.

As with a wave passing over the soldiers, the pushing, the shoving, the talking ceased. Three hundred men organized into an army. Within moments, they stretched two deep along the path, guns at salute, faces resolutely ahead. Boot tips and noses pointed in perfect lines. Two sergeants walked to the head of their soldiers. First one, then the other, brought his hand to salute. Only the sound of muffled hooves and the call of a distant bird broke the morning air.

The Emperor walked his horse forward, pausing to acknowledge a trim figure here and there. He moved his lips to mouth, *Excellent!* He rode the length, cantered back, and beckoned to his two companions to follow him in a second review. At the end of the ranks, he saluted, wheeled, and galloped toward Longwood.

His horse's hooves thundered; the wind blasted his lungs. Blinding sun shone through the clouds. Las Cases, Bertrand, and the British guard galloped in his wake. If only he had a flag to wave. He formed his lips around the shout "Hoorah!" and dug his heels into his horse's flanks.

In the distance, Sir Hudson Lowe's carriage crossed the opposite ridge. His impromptu review had been seen. The 53rd regiment would suffer, but the Emperor would not forget. Soldiers—British, French, Mohammadan—always gave him his due, politics aside. Those London cartoonists could portray him any way they liked. Every soldier he'd ever met respected him.

Only a fool denied his destiny.

He was born for war.

In front of Longwood House, Betsy's pony chomped on his grass. The girl was waving madly. "Oh, Monsieur, we're leaving. Governor Lowe's sending us away!"

He slid from his frothing horse. "What do you mean, my child?"

"Into exile *off* the island! Governor Lowe blames Father for the London rumors of your illness and who knows what else. He says we must pay."

He seized her shaking hands. "When?"

"Now—today. Mother's in hysterics, and Father curses you for losing him his position. He says to tell my friend the Emperor I shall not have a dowry and may never marry. Can that be true?" She buried her face in his chest. "Did I cause this by smuggling your messages?"

He pushed her to arm's length. "So, he sends you as collector, does he? Did you come to see if I have diamonds to give out?"

"Oh, no, Monsieur." Her chin quivered. "But if I'm not to see you again, I ask one thing."

"What is that?"

"A lock of your hair, and I shall give you one of mine. Oh, and here. The licorice I had Father order for your birthday."

He took her in his arms. "Betsy, you are the first to give while asking so little. I shall miss you dearly, child."

She pulled out of his hug. "But, Monsieur, you must promise two things. First, you will finish your novel. Second, you'll keep teaching Tobyson to be a gentleman. Toby travels with us to Australia, but Father says Tobyson belongs to you and I mustn't complain." She brushed tears from her cheeks. "You'll have to find someone else to take your book to England. They'll search our things."

He brushed a hand across his eyes. "Yes, yes, my dear, I promise to finish *Clisson*. But what's this? You're taking Toby?"

"He's already been loaded on the ship with the luggage. Monsieur, they put him in chains. I cried and cried, but they wouldn't take the irons off him."

"No, no, no. Child, you must watch over him on the voyage. Make sure he has food and water. Do you hear me?"

She tilted her head. "Yes, oh, yes, of course I will."

"And tell him I never thought to meet a leader of his stature on St. Helena. And that I'll take good care of Tobyson. And when he's sad, call him Monsieur Mahafaly." He pressed her hands. "One day, you'll know what it meant to me to speak with you as an equal." He took out his handkerchief and wiped her cheeks.

"As a friend, cher Monsieur."

"As a friend, my unexpected rose." He tweaked her nose.

"Now I shall never get to read how Clisson gets along with Amélie and Eugénie."

"Who knows? Perhaps someday you will. Grow well, and tell the world I'm not an ogre. Stay a moment." He went inside and returned with scissors to cut a bit of each of their hair. He closed her fingers over a knot of torn cloth. "A diamond. Sew it inside your clothes. One more secret not to tell your papa." He tossed her up onto her pony.

Before she could put her heels to the animal's sides, the Emperor hurried indoors. He sat in his bedroom, sipping coffee, letting Tobyson's tears express his own sorrow.

An hour later, the governor arrived to arrest Las Cases and his son. Their quarters were ransacked and their clothing shredded, as the governor's men searched for contraband. The Emperor paced in his room while General Bertrand maintained an outraged front in face of the assault. The Montholons hid out of sight.

Afternoon rain beat against the windows. The Emperor, his *Clisson* manuscript in his lap, stared into the blazing fireplace. "Today is worse than the day I abdicated," he told Marchand. "Go. You need to rest."

Cipriani slouched against the doorframe. "Now what?"

The Emperor fingered the soft pages. "No plan without Toby."

"Thought as much. I'll see about the damn submarine." He kicked a table leg and left.

The Emperor stirred the fire. How much did Sir Hudson Lowe pay his informants? Montholon or Albine, most likely. It didn't matter. Over the years, he'd grown accustomed to living amid traitors. A small price for power.

He clutched the manuscript to his chest and inhaled. He couldn't smell Betsy on it. She wasn't old enough for perfume. One more beloved child he'd never see grow up. His battle-scarred calf convulsed.

Chapter 24

Albine

DODGING THE GUARDS, I SNEAKED into our quarters. My dresses, hairbrushes, jars of creams lay scattered on the floor. Our cots were tipped over. "Mon Dieu, did the British search our room, too?"

Charles turned. He thrust Tristan's letter in my face as though it were a pistol. "What else are you hiding? What else, damn you?"

I reached into my pocket.

He grabbed my wrist. My skirt ripped in our scuffle. A precious crust spilled on the floor. He pinned me to the wall. "Strip. Everything off." He bared his teeth and growled.

I would have laughed if I hadn't been so scared. I tore a nail fumbling with a button. My knees wobbled. I don't know why I shook like that. There was nothing for Charles to find. I handed him each article of clothing for inspection.

Naked, shivering, I gathered a nightgown from the floor.

He ripped it from me. "First, we talk."

I rushed for the door.

He beat me to it. "Escaping naked? With British soldiers scouring the place?" His eyes narrowed. "What have you been up to, my pet?"

"Charles, I beg you, let me dress. I'll tell you everything. What you're doing—it's like prison." I went down on my knees. (Forgive my weakness. I should have screamed, argued, threatened to expose him to Napoleon. But the kneeling worked.)

"Oh, get some clothes on." He traced the furrows in my forehead, erasing them, ebbing my fear. "And, mon Dieu, stop groveling."

I dressed slowly, considering and discarding ideas. I straightened the room, hung up garments, returned books to their shelves. When all was neat, we sat on our cots, facing each other.

"Before I tell you anything," I said, "give me the letter from my son."

"*Our* son." He flung it at me. "You didn't think I had a right to see it?"

I tucked it into the bosom of my dress. "I planned to show it to you."

Charles felt under his cot for the brandy bottle. "I'm supposed to believe that, you little liar? When?"

I reared my head. "When you had earned it."

"Enough sparring." He bit the cork and spat it out. "Who gave you Tristan's letter? What did you do to get it?"

I plunged into the safest lie I knew. "Dr. O'Meara gave it to me."

Napoleon

IN THE DARK OF THE NIGHT, the Emperor awoke. His hand sought the stiletto under his pillow.

Tobyson knelt at his bedside. "Master, outside the window."

"Shh, my son. A visitor can mean opportunity."

Tobyson crawled onto the mattress. The Emperor rubbed his cheek against the child's. "You aren't hiding in the safest place."

Tobyson sniffed. "I'm protecting you."

"Good boy. But sometimes the bravest choice is to run from danger. You return to fight when you're stronger." He hugged Tobyson. "See my bicorne? Protect it, not me. If someone bad comes in, grab it, race from the room, and raise the alarm."

"But who will protect you?"

"My old friend Signore Stiletto." He showed Tobyson the knife. "Best for me to confront danger head-on while you bring in the reserves. Go. Open the window. Then hide."

Tobyson saluted. He unlatched the window, opened it partway, and scurried to the bicorne. He retreated into a corner.

Outside, a British guard patrolled, moonlight on his bayonet.

Two hands gripped the windowsill.

The Emperor clutched the stiletto between his teeth. He reached under the camp bed and eased out a loaded dueling pistol.

Above the sill, a forehead appeared, the letter "R" burnt upon it. The Emperor hid his pistol. "Quick, Lieutenant T. Help him in."

Tobyson ran to open the window. Randall pulled himself over the sill.

The Emperor placed his knife on a night table within easy reach. "Tobyson, translate. Randall, you couldn't have found a less dramatic way to communicate?"

Randall crouched next to the camp bed. "Tell me what day you and Toby set for the escape."

"Ah, sorry, my friend. Without Toby's navigational skills, we'll never reach Africa."

"That big American, he's a sailor. He can do it."

"No, the plan's no longer operational. I have no desire—and my guess is, neither do your people—to die lost at sea."

Randall slammed his fist on the mattress. "Then why not rebellion? We steal guns. We take over—spike—their cannons. You lead us."

"No."

Randall bounded to his feet. Tobyson's voice quivered with his translation. "Goddamn you, I will not die a slave."

The Emperor squeezed the boy's hand. "Get down, Randall. They'll shoot you."

"Death means nothing to me. If you won't do anything, by your God and mine, I will." He thrust open the window, rolled out, and sprinted across the garden in full moonlight.

The night's crisp air poured through the open window as Randall's silhouette raced through the flowerbeds toward the stone wall that imprisoned Longwood House. The Emperor hugged Tobyson against his chest. "He can make it, he can make it, he's almost there," he whispered to the child. "Over the wall, Randall, over the wall. Mon Dieu, he's going to make it. He's at the wall."

A guard shouted, shattering the night. Another answered.

A shot exploded.

As Randall fell, so, too, for Napoleon, did the decades fall away. Though he murmured comforts in Tobyson's ear, for him, it was not Longwood's garden outside the window. It was a Paris street where before the Church of Saint Roche he had ordered cannon fire upon rioting French Royalists, civilians in their midst. He'd ridden that blast—and many others—into his illustrious future. Surely, a single musket shot on a South Atlantic island could not bring down his curtain.

He reached for his stiletto. It was gone.

WHEN NEITHER TOBYSON NOR THE Emperor could fall asleep, Tobyson brought the writing box to the camp bed and lit a candle so the Emperor could work. The youngster crawled up on the mattress, turned his face from the light, and slept at the Emperor's side.

CLISSON: THE EMPEROR'S NOVEL

Champvert, France, July 1789

Before supper, Clisson joined a gathering in an alcove near the candelabra'd dinner table. As the company milled about, awaiting other guests, the Fop, reading from a friend's letter, brought news of trouble in Paris. The Bastille prison had been stormed. King Louis was a prisoner in his palace.

"The bourgeois will rise." Monsieur LeGrand rapped his knuckles on the table. "As the Jacobins whisper, *le pain se lève.* This augurs well for business in the long run. As for the short term, that's why I invested with the Swedes."

"Careful, sir," the Fop said. "You speak treason. The old ways must prevail."

Clisson shouldered his way into the conversation. "Perhaps your perfume is too aristocratic for you to discern which way the wind blows."

"Bravo, Clisson." His host raised his wineglass. "Yet let us tread lightly. In these uncertain times, news, like wind, shifts before it settles."

"Ah, I have still more news." The Fop shook out a folded bulletin. "This interesting paper reports on troubles near your garrison, my fine Lieutenant. The locals, it appears, consider your military prowess more cowardly than brave."

Clisson snatched the journal. He read of troops cowering behind barricades, grapeshot slaughtering civilians, two mothers and their infants dead. A lieutenant identified as "Cl—" bore the blame for an army run amok. Berville's accusations echoed throughout, sharpening the sting.

"Slander!" Clisson thrust the journal into the fire. "To denounce duty, to equate the rule of law with iniquity."

The Fop laughed. "Burn away. Noxious truth, my boy, is a harder weed to kill."

"You shall not spread lies about my honor, sir. And I am not your boy."

The butler announced the remaining dinner guests who flowed into the room. Madame LeGrand bustled to greet the local priest, the family doctor, two widowed sisters, and a half dozen others. In the polite shuffle, Amélie sequestered the Fop in a corner.

Endless conversation ensued. Peasants starved, Paris rose in revolt, yet all talk centered on a moonlight picnic at a ruined church.

Madame LeGrand fussed over the table seating until Eugénie sat at Clisson's side, Amélie out of his reach. He endured soup, fish, and roast mutton. He waved off sweets, and, murmuring about a headache, fled the room.

Above all, he sought unpeopled air. In the garden, the moon lit his way to a fountain. In French villages, children lifted empty buckets from dusty wells; in this house, as at Versailles, steam power forced lilac-tinted water uphill. Still, he had no sympathy for the starving when they transformed into mobs. Revolution would succeed only if some great power stepped in to redistribute life's unequal lots.

But his path was war, not politics. The orders that decided the Revolution would not emanate from him. A colonel's epaulettes on his shoulders would satisfy his ambition. On that rank's pay, he could support a wife. He could support Amélie.

A soft step sounded. Turning, he found her next to him. Her hair, her skin, her mouth exceeded all dreams.

Her cold voice staved off his touch. "I see you've invaded my favorite spot. I love this fountain."

"Why?" he asked.

"Do you really want to know? I'll match your bluntness. My husband first kissed me here. Does that spoil everything for you?"

He swallowed, hurt, unsure. "Do you want it to?"

"Yes."

"Why?"

She bent close. "My cousin claims you, like all of Corsica, are poor. Is that true?"

"Yes." His head swam in her orange-blossom perfume. "Tell me, does he have reason to campaign against me? Does he fear I have a chance with you?"

"Have you anything beyond your lieutenant's pay?"

"Yes."

"What?"

"My love for you, and the will to succeed where others fail."
He reached for her hands.

She retreated, hiding them behind her back. "My cousin's
right. You're an adventurer. I won't risk my happiness on another
impoverished soldier." She threaded her fingers through her
hair. "Clisson, you don't understand. I'm trapped, do you hear?
My family disowned me for marrying my husband. His death
left me in debt. Only my aunt pities me. Her son wishes to marry
me, I know not why—perhaps as a respectable ornament so he
can follow his own inclinations. What choice do I have? I have
no wish to be a governess teaching watercolors to spoiled brats."

"The choice is clear." He opened his arms. "Take me."

"Just like that? No, you see the world in black and white. I
tell you, it's dull gray."

"And yet I think you love me a little—enough to make our
lives a paradise. I love you, Amélie. Be brave. Throw in your
lot with mine."

"That is a rash offer to a woman you barely know. You should
think it through." Amélie moved closer.

He could taste her sweet breath. "No, I never hesitate. That's
what gives me an advantage over others." As he leaned to kiss
her, a hand gripped his shoulder.

"I think not," the Fop said. "My boy."

Clisson whirled, swinging a punch. The Fop stepped out of
range. Clisson tripped against the fountain wall.

"Stop," Amélie snapped.

"My honor . . . ," Clisson said.

"No, I tell you." Amélie thrust her palm against his chest.
"He has the right. We are engaged. Truly, Clisson, before you
make things worse, leave us."

Eugénie's dry voice came from behind him. "In fact, every-one should come inside before I have to fetch my mother."

Clisson's fists fell.

The Fop lifted Amélie's hand to his lips. "Give our excuses, Eugénie. My fiancée and I intend to stroll the garden. Monsieur Clisson, always a joy to see you."

"You will pay dearly for that moment of pleasure," Clisson said.

Amélie, clinging to the Fop, motioned Clisson away.

Eugénie pulled his arm. "Forget honor—look to your pride." She led him, Amélie's words thundering in his dull mind, into the house. In the chessboard entrance hall, he broke Eugénie's hold and fled up the stairs to his room.

Ricocheting around the bedchamber, he bundled his gear. If he started immediately, he could bivouac in the woods before the moon went down. He'd return to that first village and learn to be a blacksmith. No, he'd desert the army and head for Corsica. Or join the Pasha's army. Halfway through folding shirts, he wadded one in a ball and tossed it in a corner. He threw himself upon the bed. He could shoot that Fop or die in a duel, but what was the use? Either way, he'd lose Amélie.

His Amélie Rose. She'd be sorry one day.

All acclaimed his victory. They sang his praises in the streets and pasted his portrait on their walls. Amélie, her gown in tatters, begged for a minute of his time. Did the Great Man remember her? she asked.

Remember her? How could he forget?

Chapter 22

Albine

I SHOOK CHARLES AWAKE. "Outside the window. Someone's there."

"The guards," he mumbled, his voice thick with the evening's brandy.

"No, no, not the guards. Someone else is in the garden."

"Probably Cipriani back from tomcatting some girl. Go to sleep, would you?" But at the musket shot, he sprang up and crept to the window. "Mon Dieu, the guards are dragging a body. They're laughing. Can't be one of us."

I glanced at the clock in the bookcase. Two in the morning. A perfect time to corner half-sober Charles. "Do you think Napoleon has someone new smuggling his messages?"

Charles reached for his bottle. "For God's sake, Albine, not now."

"I mean, since you got rid of Las Cases and Balcombe."

He downed a swig. "Didn't inform on Las Cases. Silly fellow must have gotten caught on his own. Go to sleep, I say."

Damn, but that made my stomach ache. I'd been certain Charles had already ratted on Las Cases before I betrayed him to Basil. It had earned me a letter from Tristan (plus Basil's gratitude, which counted for something). I stretched across the empty space between our cots and shook Charles's shoulder. "But Balcombe? What harm was he doing, sneaking Napoleon a newspaper or two?"

My husband sniffed. "Wasn't Balcombe I turned in. Was his daughter."

A breeze fluttered our curtains. Charles's hair, more silver every week, glistened between the dancing shadows. I once loved those curls, once admired that man. Then, our heads had shared a pillow. We'd whispered dreams of riches, of honors for our children, of grandchildren who'd carry on our legacy. I withdrew my hand from his shoulder and wiped each finger clean on my sheet. "A little girl. How petty, Charles."

He belched. "Damn it, I did it for you. Eliminated your rival, like you wanted. Much thanks I get. But I swear I didn't turn in Las Cases. Did you?"

The lie slid out as if my tongue were ice. "No. Of course not."

"Wasn't smart if you did. Was saving him for later. If I'm to get paid, have to come up with something for the British every month." Charles snuggled under his blanket. "Enough. I'm going to sleep. And for all I care, you can sleep or you can go to hell."

I drifted asleep on a cot as lonely as a raft at sea, but inside my pillow Tristan's letter crinkled, a sound more satisfying than the crunch of bread.

Napoleon

A DISTANT CANNON SOUNDED THREE volleys. Another answered. Amid shouts from the guards, a carriage thundered up to Longwood. A crash at the front door brought the Emperor to his feet. Tobyson had helped him into a robe before a kick broke his chamber door from its frame.

Sir Hudson Lowe barged in. His shirt half tucked into his breeches, his vest buttoned askew, his hair standing in a tuft, he could have been a harmless drunk, except he waved the Emperor's stiletto, its blade extended, in the air.

British soldiers followed on the governor's heels. Behind them, Marchand and Cipriani piled in. Tobyson raised his little fists.

Sir Hudson slid to a stop. "But you're here."

"The question is, why are you?" The Emperor held out his hand. "Give me my knife, Sir Hudson."

Lowe waved the stiletto. "By God, you admit it?"

"Admit what? Where did you find my knife? Why the musket shots in the garden? Explain yourself." The Emperor confronted the crowd in his doorway. "And the rest of you may leave."

Cipriani, grinning, drew Marchand away. The British guards edged into the hall.

Sir Hudson's mouth worked. "The guards shot dead a slave—a troublemaker with a brand on his forehead—trespassing in the garden. He had your stiletto. How can that be?"

"What a fuss over a common thief. My knife—it was my mother's, you know—disappeared a few days ago. We assumed someone stole it. What would I have to do with some slave?"

The governor's watery eyes rested on Tobyson. "You own that one, don't you?"

"In a manner, he owns me." The Emperor motioned Tobyson to his corner. "I've heard you disapprove of slavery, Sir Hudson."

"Always have, I assure you. A great evil. A veritable sin against Christianity."

"Ah," the Emperor drawled. "We are in agreement on something."

Lowe started. "But you reinstated it in Saint-Domingue. I thought so badly of you."

"Yes, a disgrace that diminishes my legacy. Let us say, France's urgent needs came before my principles. But here, in your remote fiefdom, you have the power to do better. In your place, I'd set things right. Perhaps you'd like me to draw up a plan so you wouldn't need to shoot Africans in my garden."

Sir Hudson snorted. "Don't think I'm going to let you run this island like you did Elba."

"But a plan with my name on it, presented in London to Parliament—"

"Oh, go to sleep. I don't need your help." Sir Hudson tossed the stiletto on the bed and stormed out.

The Emperor carried his knife to the washbasin, where he wiped the blade with a damp towel. Sensing Tobyson at his side, he said, "Perhaps we can squeeze good out of tragedy."

IN THE MORNING, WHILE HERCULES repaired Napoleon's door, Tobyson and Albine played a game of catch in the garden. The Emperor pressed his palms to his windowpane. He yearned to feel their laughter.

CLISSON: THE EMPEROR'S NOVEL

Champvert, France, July 1789

As sunlight penetrated the curtains, Clisson, still dressed, stumbled out of bed and picked up his pen.

Dear Amélie,

I awake full of you. Last evening, you inflicted a terrible wound. Your lips say you are affianced to the Fop, while your eyes promise love to me.

What is this talk of debts? I love you. Must you have great wealth as well? How could a sentiment so low have been conceived in so pure a soul as yours? I am surprised by it, no less than at the impulse that, on my awakening, over- came me: that of throwing myself, unwillingly but without rancor, at your feet.

Let us say I am guilty of weakness. Let us utter the weakness's true name: love. Give me an hour to convince you of our future.

I send you three kisses: one on your heart, one on your mouth, one on your eyes. Do not return any to me. The thought alone boils my blood.

Your Faithful Clisson

He opened his door to search for a servant to deliver his letter.

Eugénie yawned on a chair across the hall. A grin broke across her face. "A letter? I guessed that's what you'd do. If only I could have made a bet."

"Pardon, Mam'selle? You overstep our acquaintance."

"My poor Clisson, you are in a bad state, aren't you? I meant it as a compliment. Step with me into the garden. In five minutes, I can solve all your problems."

He stuffed the letter in his jacket. "Oh, all right. Not that I admit to any problem."

Eugénie led him down back stairs into an arbor overlooking unkempt, spindly woods. "This is my favorite spot," she said, settling on a stone bench. "No purple fountains, no pruned animals, just nature running wild. If only I can prevent my parents from fixing it up."

He sat beside her. "Mademoiselle Eugénie, you always surprise."

She chuckled. "Which you, Monsieur Clisson, do not. I mean that in a nice way. You did intend to leave?"

"Yes, but . . ." He met her sympathetic eyes. "I may as well tell you. I wrote a letter to Amélie, begging one more conversation. If, after that, she . . . It doesn't bear thinking of, but if she's intent on marrying that Fop, well, then, I'm on my way. I know not where."

"No," Eugénie said. "I absolutely forbid it. You may not go."

His lips twitched, lightening his pain. "Why not?"

"Why, you will miss the midnight picnic and, more important, opportunities to change Amélie's mind. I know her well. She can be diverted from this marriage. She doesn't even like the man."

"Then why is she marrying him?"

Eugénie leaned in, her breath warm on his ear. "She's a mercenary flirt."

Clisson recoiled.

Eugénie frowned. "You should have seen her in Paris. She thinks I can't appreciate being poor and having to make do with last year's dresses, but she—"

"You think this *gossip* solves my problems? Why would I stay if what you say is true?"

Eugénie ticked off her fingers. "First, you don't believe me. Second, if I am right, you should stay to punish her. Third—"

"Punish her? I don't want to punish her. I love her."

"Well, she should never have trifled with a man who expects honor in every part of his life. If, on the other hand, she's not trifling, if she really is unhappy, then it's your duty to save her. Don't you see? You can't leave until you know. If you run away, uncertainty will haunt you."

He slumped. "Eugénie, where do you get your logic?"

"From Maman. Papa's a dreamer—like you."

"Me? I'm a man of action."

She chuckled. "Time will tell. Now, give me the letter. I'll have a servant deliver it, if you promise you'll stay through the picnic."

Clisson kissed Eugénie's hand to seal his vow. With a lighter step, he retreated to his room to unpack.

After breakfast, he met Eugénie on the lawn. She had changed her dress to one of white muslin, frilled about her ample breasts, ending in a flounce above her ankle. She handed him a stringed racquet. "Come play a game of tennis."

"Play a game." He savored the words. He hadn't touched a ball since Brienne. He looked around with regret. "I should be making plans."

"Oh, have a little fun." She dragged him, protesting, into a barnlike building where a net was strung from wall to wall. "Have you played?"

"Of course not."

"Time you learned. It's the game of kings. That's why Father built this court. I'll be your teacher. Go over there." She batted him the ball.

He forgot his racquet and caught the flying ball, dropping it when it stung his hand. He glared at her laughter.

She waved her racquet. "Clisson, use the racquet to hit the ball."

He glanced around—no one could see them. He tossed the ball into the air, as he had seen her do. But when he hit it over the net, she hit it back and he missed it. They tried another volley. Soon he was returning every ball. "It's like artillery," he said. "Geometry and judging distance."

When she missed one of his shots, she beamed. "I'm such a good teacher."

"No, you're not. I'm a good learner." He stretched over the net to kiss her cheek. "Thank you. I'm not used to having fun."

Her eyes blazed.

As they strolled to the house, a servant met them. He handed Eugénie the letter Clisson had sent to Amélie. Unopened. There was a note for Eugénie, but nothing for Clisson.

She opened hers and read to herself.

Clisson craned his neck. "What does it say?"

"She sent her engagement announcement to the news journals."

As he stormed off, her voice trailed him. "Remember, you promised to stay for the picnic. Besides, it's useless to run away."

He pivoted to face her. "I have never in my life done anything useless." Anyway, Eugénie was wrong: the only way to survive this love was to flee it.

Chapter 23

Napoleon

ON HIS RETURN FROM JAMESTOWN, Cipriani plopped into a chair and rested his feet on another. "Slave thing's not over yet, Master. Ran into one of the governor's gardeners. That blockhead Lowe spent the night wandering the halls, talking to you."

"Get your dirty feet off my furniture," the Emperor said.

"Right, right. Anyway, this morning, Lowe calls together Plantation House's slaves and announces he's buying their freedom—with his own money, no less. Now he's got a big meeting with the other slaveholders."

"I hope he gives me some credit."

"Slim chance of that." He grinned at Napoleon. "Making up for your past sins, ain't you? Damn me if you ain't got Lowe smoothing your way into Heaven. Never thought you'd pull that one off."

The Emperor put down his pen. "What? You doubted me?"

"You doubted yourself." The Corsican's grin melted. "But tell me, brother, how's this getting us home?"

Blood warmed the Emperor's face. "We'll get back to that. Have faith."

The Corsican cracked his knuckles. "Faith? Bah! Rather get a submarine."

"That ought to keep you busy." The Emperor returned to his manuscript. But when Cipriani left, he laid down his pen. He wasn't one step closer to his son. Escaping with slaves had been a romantic notion. He needed a real plan.

CLISSON: THE EMPEROR'S NOVEL

Champvert, France, July 1789

As Clisson joined the garden luncheon table, the air hung thick, without a breeze. The trees were empty of birds. In the stables, Gray Man bit Eugénie's groom, breaking his finger. Madame LeGrand complained of an aching head.

Monsieur LeGrand cautioned against the midnight picnic. "This weather is uncertain. My barometer's plunging like I have never seen."

"You and your science," Madame LeGrand said. "Look at the sky. Trust what you see, not silly glass tubes."

"My dear, you don't understand."

"Let the children enjoy themselves." Madame LeGrand tottered from her chair.

Eugénie pouted. "Besides, we must go tonight. Clisson says he's leaving soon."

Monsieur LeGrand crossed his arms. "Well, I advise against riding that wild gray."

"Now, why did you buy the animal for her, if not to ride it?" Madame LeGrand said from the doorway. "The outing can't be ruined because you're nervous, my dear husband."

At dusk, a dozen young people gathered on the manor's lawn. A footman loaded the chaperones' carriage with blankets, wine, and food. The last to arrive were Amélie and her Fop, who drove a sleek open carriage. Their horses must have been worth five years of Clisson's army pay.

Monsieur LeGrand turned to Clisson. "That's everyone. I feel better since Madame Fontaine has Monsieur Tours with her.

He knows how to manage young people. And you, Clisson, you'll keep my girl safe? Her groom can't go with that broken finger."

"You may count on me, Monsieur LeGrand."

Just then, Gray Man shied at the bush shaped like a squirrel. Eugénie, eyes sparking at her stallion's bucking, led the party at a trot.

Clisson took up the rear. Ahead of him, Eugénie rode alongside a young man, exchanging pleasantries. A fortune hunter, no doubt. In the open carriage, Amélie hung on the Fop's arm, laughed at his banter, gazed at his face as though she couldn't see enough of it. When another young man claimed her attention, she flirted with him as well. Her gestures were overlarge, as if she were onstage.

So much for constancy in a woman who claimed devotion to her dead love. More like the merry widow on the prowl. Eugénie had hit the mark. His Rose was a mercenary flirt. He must have caught Madame LeGrand's headache. His teeth throbbed; his chest felt bound in rope. He'd had enough leisure. Tomorrow he'd return to the garrison and beg for work at half pay.

Amélie smiled brightly at some witticism from her Fop. Was the woman never serious? He trotted past Amélie's carriage and edged his horse between Eugénie and the young man riding at her side.

The road rose into a hilly countryside. At the crest of a steep incline, a valley opened beneath them. Nestled on a low plain stood the ruined monastery. The side walls had three tiers of arches that stained glass had once filled; a single grand arch occupied an end wall. The other end had holes for a round window like Notre Dame's great rose. Monks' chants had reverberated within this space, now roofless, still sacred.

Night closed in as the party wound down the hill. In uncertain light, they turned their horses over to the grooms. A servant ignited torches for them to carry.

To reach the church ruin, they walked a field of tilted gravestones. Torch flames tossed shadows across their faces, across the stones. Two of the young women held hands and giggled.

Eugénie took Clisson's hand. "How many do you think there are?"

"A couple hundred, easily."

"Two hundred ghosts?"

He bounced their joined hands against her little nose. "Two hundred gravestones, silly."

They entered the church through a threshold that had once held doors, which the Fop, with an elaborate bow, pretended to open. Stone walls rose around them; sky pressed in where windows had once filled arches. Here and there, a vaulted column remained in place. With a grass floor and the starred sky for a ceiling, it beat out Notre Dame's dinginess. Clisson had never been anywhere so romantic.

Neither had the women. One was already letting a young man kiss her neck.

Clisson glanced around. "Where are those chaperones?"

Eugénie laughed shakily. "I wonder why Maman allowed it. Monsieur Tours is Papa's solicitor. Madame Fontaine's been on the catch for him forever. She'll pay no heed to the rest of us."

Two servants stretched blankets on the ground and spread out picnic food. Clisson and Eugénie found a place among her friends, while Amélie and the Fop perched on a broken column rolled against one wall. The stars shone full bright.

Clisson pointed. "That brightest one's Venus."

Beyond the church, their horses snorted; one issued a long neigh.

"The loudest one is Gray Man," Eugénie said.

Clisson nodded. "Horses can smell ghosts."

The young women's eager shudders gratified him. Amélie turned his way.

He crossed his outstretched legs. "We Corsicans know a thing or two of ghosts."

"You've seen them?" Eugénie asked.

He lowered his voice. "In Corsica, they walk every night. There are women there, the *voceri*, who commune daily with the dead. It's their job to send souls to Heaven. Let me tell you a story."

The Fop smothered a yawn.

Clisson waited a moment, then began. "My mother's uncle was a bishop, a cultured man, educated against superstition. His reality was the church and its teachings. Anything beyond that, he considered heresy. Firm about right and wrong, he denounced the local practice of vendetta."

"Vendetta?" one of the women asked.

"The Corsican custom of murdering those who insult us." Clisson scowled.

The girl cuddled closer to her friend.

"But that's another story." Clisson waved his hand. "At my great-uncle's deathbed, I asked him what he saw ahead. Didn't a believer go to Heaven joyously? 'Dear Uncle,' I begged, 'cure me of my heritage of superstition.' My soul writhed, because on my way to see him I witnessed a procession of ghostlike figures parading to his house. Foolishly, I ran toward them. They disappeared like mist.

"At first my uncle wouldn't speak. I begged him to save my soul. His eyes, yellow as egg yolk, stared into eternity. 'My dear nephew,' he finally whispered, 'do not ask me to choose. I am Christian baptized but Corsican born. I must admit what I have seen. Let a merciful God be my judge.' Those words brought him strength.

"'In my youth,' he said, 'before I took my vows, I was a wild boy, beautiful and pursued by women. I had the bad luck to fall in love with a widow. She was what we Corsicans know as a *mazzera*, a dream-walker who lives a normal life in the light but at night becomes a hunter of men's souls.'"

Eugénie laid her hand on Clisson's arm. "Do such things exist?"

"Where it's civilized, I don't know." Clisson smiled down into her face. "But in Corsica and sacred places like this abbey that have sheltered a thousand years of saints and sinners, the old ways prevail. Look around you. Don't you feel a difference in the weight of the air? Is the darkness here the same as the darkness that surrounds your bed at home?"

As Clisson spoke, the stars disappeared behind clouds. The wind picked up. Eugénie drew to his side.

Amélie's sharp voice broke the silence. "And your uncle?"

"Ah, my uncle." Clisson didn't look at Amélie. In a show of gathering courage, he moved his head from side to side. "'I was weak,' my uncle said. 'I gave that woman what she wanted.' At that, my uncle ripped open his nightshirt to lay bare a jagged scar upon his chest. 'Beware,' he uttered. 'Clisson, beware. Hungry spirits hang around your soul.' His eyes rolled back till I could no longer see his pupils. His cheeks grew hollow as if, when his breath left his lungs, a force sucked his chest inward. His nose grew sharp. His eyes sank into their sockets.

"Without looking, I reached for the blanket to cover his face. I snatched my hand away. It came back warm, wet, dripping red. Blood oozed from the scar on his chest. 'Heaven save me!' I cried. The voceri women, waiting in the anteroom to sing his soul to Heaven, rushed in. A dozen hands pressed on his chest to stop the red flow. A dozen hands dripped with my uncle's blood.

"In fear, the women raised their faces Heavenward to chant their mourning song. Not a sound issued from their mouths. As long as their hands touched my uncle's chest, they were struck mute.

"The doctor arrived at last. He tried to stanch the blood. He turned on me. 'What did you do?' he cried.

"'I? Why, nothing.'

"'But his heart,' the doctor said. 'It's gone.'"

Clisson's audience sat frozen. He hid his face in his hands to conceal his grin.

Eugénie gripped his arm. Amélie's harsh laugh cracked the spell. "What a bugbear you are, Clisson. Eugénie will sleep with her mother for a week."

One of the men snickered.

"It's not true? Not even in Corsica?" Eugénie turned on her friend. "How would *you* know?"

"I know spirits don't rip out your heart," Amélie said.

Clisson rose to face her. "And yet love can rip a heart from a chest. It doesn't take a ghost. Love itself is enough to destroy a heart, a life."

"But can it happen like in the story?" Eugénie rose, too. She stamped her foot.

"I can't answer for the barbaric island that spawned our Clisson," Amélie said. "But here, no. And love has nothing to do with it."

Albine

I WORE MY OLDEST, STURDIEST pair of shoes, knowing how rough the path was between Jamestown Church and the cave overlooking the cove. It was a fine, sunny day, but rain the day before had left behind slick mud. I gathered my skirts in one hand and used the other to grab hold of branches to keep from falling.

The large boulders were in sight when Basil caught up with me, full of apologies for being late and for the state of the path.

I laid my hand on his cheek. "No, my friend. Muddy shoes, a dirty hem, mean nothing. Consider how far we've traveled to find one another."

He kissed my fingers, before turning away. "Waterloo."

"You were at the battle?"

He nodded. "Strange, isn't it, for those bloody days to lead to you? I couriered messages, saw friends maimed, killed. I survived unscathed, but others suffered for us to meet here."

"No, Basil, how can you sully what's growing between us? Napoleon, Wellington, Bathurst, your government and mine, they're to blame for the wars, not us." I silently cursed his unlucky thoughts.

"Forgive me. A soldier doesn't forget." He smoothed my forehead. "You at least are innocent. Come, this path's perilous. Let's go only as far as those boulders."

We settled in some shade. Basil basked in his melancholy, his smiles forced and fleeting. I dreaded that a goodbye was coming.

He reached inside his jacket. A letter from Tristan, but he didn't offer it to me. I guessed I'd have to earn it. I juggled people's lives in my head: Hercules, Solomon, Charles. No, I couldn't. Maybe Toby. He was out of their reach. I'd tell Basil how Napoleon had made him a friend. But he was little Tobyson's father. They might punish the child instead. I couldn't risk it.

I'd overheard talk about Freemasons in Vienna. If only I knew details.

I touched the bread in my pocket. My underarms began to sweat.

Basil crumpled the letter in his tight fist. (I think he forgot it as he rambled on to other things.) "Before Waterloo," he said, "I worked for Sir Hudson in the quartermaster service. He requested me for this assignment. Quite an honor, I thought, but it's a miserable existence. When he praises me, other officers laugh. They claim I'm as punctilious as Sir Hudson himself."

I hadn't known. I hadn't considered his life beyond my orbit. And all I could think about was how he was crushing my letter. Best to flatter a man with hurt feelings. "Perhaps you are as disciplined as Sir Hudson, but, I swear, much, much more handsome."

Again, that fleeting smile. "Yes, discipline—that's the thing. Somehow I can reconcile stealing these letters, because they do in fact belong to you. Sir Hudson's been too busy with his slavery project to notice me pilfering his office." He opened his fist.

My fingers ached to grab the letter. A muscle twitched in Basil's jaw. He had more to say. I kept my hands in my lap. (When a man needs to talk, a woman needs to listen.)

"I think I love you," he said.

Discipline flew out the window.

Chapter 24

Albine

THAT NIGHT, AS I LAY ON my cot with Charles snoring nearby,
I closed my eyes, not to sleep but to relive Basil's words. When he
told me he loved me, my life started afresh. But, at his next words,
my toes (curled tight when our lips connected) splayed out flat.

For, as we sat on those boulders following our bout of kissing,
he added, "We can be together as soon as you give them up."

"But you said you don't want me to spy," I protested, a wary
knot in my chest.

"So I did. And I mean it. I can't put you in danger, my precious."
He kissed my nose. "More than that, I don't want a wife who's a
traitor to her country."

A wife? When had I agreed to that? My hand dove in my
pocket for a touch of bread. "What do you mean, 'as soon as I give
them up'? Give up whom?"

He jerked his head (impatiently for such a polite man). "Perhaps my French is not clear. I mean your husband and Napoleon
Bonaparte, of course. You can't be someone else's lover if you're
going to be my wife."

I swear I didn't nod agreement. For certain, I didn't say a word.
Somehow he took my acquiescence for granted. I lowered my lashes
and contemplated this masterful new man.

"It will be awkward until we leave St. Helena," he went on. "But
Sir Hudson's allotting me a small house. When you're ready to make
a public break, we'll move there. Perfectly safe, too. We won't allow
the French near it."

How about a Corsican? Acid burned my throat. Compared with what Cipriani would do to me, Randall's shooting would be sweet death. As Basil rattled on about the charming cottage we'd have in the Cotswolds (wherever that might be), I marveled how these naive British could have beaten my Napoleon.

For now, he'd rented a room, Basil informed me, in a house the other side of Longwood's stone wall. It had a private door. He'd arrange a pass for me with Sergeant Kitts.

I fussed with the medals on his chest. "I need to break off my liaisons carefully. We French practice a certain civility, you know. It will take time."

"Certainly, it's delicate. I understand." Basil stood. "But, Albine, until you've cut your ties with all other men, until you can be faithful to me, we must maintain a chaste relationship. I shall do no more than kiss your lips." He gave me the merest peck. "You see, I've thought everything through."

He'd transformed me from a loose woman into a blushing English bride. British officers were such snobbish prudes. While stationed on St. Helena, they might "marry" a local girl whose dusky shade was far from native English, but once issued orders to go home? Oh, how quickly they deserted the exotic for home-brewed girls.

But we French presented a subtler problem, not of skin but of *esprit*. For us (even before the Revolution), passion was too wild to be caged. And what was fidelity, if not a cage?

The leopard can't change its spots, I thought, recalling the Bible quote. Yet changing spots was exactly what Basil asked of me. Couldn't his English spots change instead? Peering into this British soldier's square face, I found a constancy that couldn't be translated into French.

SEVERAL NIGHTS LATER, I LAY ALERT, waiting. Soon, Charles snored, an empty brandy bottle by his bed. Before dinner, I had alerted Sergeant Kitts that I intended to visit Basil late that night.

If I encountered a guard, I was to say, "By Saint George." I gathered my courage, wrapped a black shawl over my nightdress, and eased my way into the dark hall.

I counted my steps.

At number six, an arm seized my waist. A hand stopped my mouth. Someone lifted me as if I were a child. I tried to discern my attacker's scent. I hoped it was Charles. I couldn't tell. The hand across my mouth covered my nostrils.

We moved quickly down the hall to Cook's storage closet. Jars of pickled vegetables and jams lined the shelves. Garlic dangled from the ceiling. My captor kicked the door shut.

"Not a sound," he said in my ear. "One twist will break your neck, no one any wiser."

Cipriani.

He set me on my feet.

I was afraid to turn around.

He chuckled. "What? Ain't interested in seeing my pretty face?"

I filled my voice with relief. "Franco, thank God it's you! Oh, how dare you scare me?"

He stiffened. "Where you off to? Let's hear it, my fine girl."

Darkness, cloaking our expressions, gave me courage. "I don't have to tell you."

"Right-o. How about I escort you to your husband? We'll let him do the questioning, what say you?"

"I say the Emperor will be furious." I poked his chest. "What say *you*, my fine friend?"

He guffawed. "I say you got more balls than the British army. How about we test this tale of yours, eh?" He grabbed my arm. "Silence, now. Don't want to wake the household, particularly that nasty husband of yours."

"But where are we going?" I hissed.

Cipriani gave a crooked smile. "You and me, we're on a visit to my old friend Napoleon."

Napoleon

TAP, TAP, SCRATCH, SCRATCH.

The Emperor laid his *Clisson* manuscript on the blanket.

Tap, tap, scratch, scratch.

Past midnight. Why was Cipriani scratching to come in?

No sense in waking Tobyson. The Emperor got out of bed. As soon as he cracked open the bedroom door, rose perfume assailed him. A familiar scent, yes, but not in recent weeks.

He swung the door open.

Albine shook Cipriani's grasp off her arm. She melted into a court curtsy such as he'd last seen in the palace at Fontainebleau. As her forehead touched his knee, he wondered that she could maintain her balance. The lady was practiced at so many arts.

Leaving her in the awkward position, he jerked his chin toward the corner where Tobyson slept. "Carry the boy to Marchand," he said to Cipriani. "Try not to wake him."

Cipriani curled his lip. "Not expecting us, were you?"

"Well, not you," the Emperor said evenly. "Take the boy and get out of here."

He led Albine to the bed. Was she a traitor? Did it matter? She was warm and comfortable, adept at fulfilling his needs, joyous at fulfillment of her own. For the first time in his life, the weight of inexorable aging shook him. He took her face between his palms and kissed her lovingly. He needed her and hoped, almost prayed, she needed him. He hadn't realized that with age, the weaknesses of youth returned.

AFTERWARD, AS SHE CARESSED THE knob on his chin, she told him she had come to say goodbye. Goodbye as a lover, but, she hoped, greetings as a friend.

"May I take the place in your heart Betsy Balcombe filled? May I help you with your *Clisson* novel? May we share laughter in the afternoons?" she asked.

CLISSON: THE EMPEROR'S NOVEL

Near Champvert, France, July 1789

The Fop held out his hand. "It's raining. Amélie, let's get home."

Madame Fontaine, with Monsieur Tours in tow, bustled over. "My dears, it seems Eugénie's father was right about the weather. We've had the horses saddled."

As servants carted off blankets and food, the young people hurried toward the horses. Amélie and her Fop picked their way through the graveyard and climbed into their carriage. Clisson remained behind, alone in the moon shadows. The picnickers mounted horses, and the party filed off. The voices waned, the carriages rolled out of sight, the horses' *clop* faded. Still, Clisson didn't budge.

Storm clouds, swept in a swift current, rushed across the moon. Wind swayed the trees. A stone a mason had laid lovingly eight hundred years before tumbled from a parapet. What a joy to see—to feel!—the whole monastery, all these tons of stone, crashing down upon his head.

A hand touched his. Eugénie. Gray Man and his own horse were tied nearby.

"Don't you want to leave?" she asked.

"I want to see this place alone. Go with the others."

"I came back for you. Papa said you'd look after me."

Clisson sighed. "Then we'll catch up to them."

"We can leave in a moment. We ride faster than they do." Eugénie wandered among the arches. "How beautiful this place is. How can it be that among ruins surrounded by a graveyard, I should feel so alive?" She pulled the pins from her hair so that it streamed below her shoulders. The swirling wind whipped it into a halo around her head. She twirled in a circle, her arms outstretched.

Lightning flashed.

Clisson, riveted at the ecstasy on Eugénie's face, reached for her.

Thunder cracked. Gray Man screamed, pulling free the reins Eugénie had tied loosely. As Clisson leapt for the bridle, the stallion wheeled and galloped off. Clisson held his own horse's head against his chest, quieting him.

Dense raindrops began to pelt. Eugénie, standing in the center of the roofless church, grinned. Her dress was drenched, her hair clinging to her shoulders. Clisson shook his head at her.

Lightning illuminated the sky. A sudden gust almost knocked Eugénie off her feet. Hail the size of tennis balls ricocheted against the abbey walls and bounced off the ground. Eugénie cowered.

"Shelter!" Clisson pointed. "Over there!"

Eugénie, hands over her head, ran for the solitary nook where a fragment of roof had survived. Clisson urged his horse into the space. Hail battered slate above their heads; ice balls blanketed grass where they had lounged with their friends.

Eugénie's teeth chattered. "Is it safe?"

Clisson eyed the roof. "It's lasted this long. We'll wedge ourselves between the wall and the horse." He pulled an army blanket roll from behind his saddle and wrapped it around them. Eugénie shivered in the circle of his arms, her head against his chest. Despite the rain, the wind, the hail pounding on the roof, she slept till dawn. Clisson dozed, supporting her, leaning against his placid horse.

When Eugénie woke, her sleepy eyes were as gray as the fleeing clouds. He tweaked her little nose. She laid her head on his chest.

"This isn't what your father had in mind when he said 'look after you,'" he said.

She came alive. "Oh, they must be frantic with worry. We must hurry!"

She mounted behind him, straddling the horse, her arms around his waist. They cantered through wheat fields the storm had beaten flat. Everywhere, great oaks lay cracked open on the ground. Swaths of young trees were flattened reeds. A barn smoldered from a lightning strike.

"Worse devastation than war," Clisson said. Eugénie's breasts rubbed against his back. He slowed the horse so the ride would last.

When they reached the manor house, the front yard teemed with servants, grooms, and horses. Eugénie's injured groom, dashing amid the topiary, was trying to catch Gray Man's loose reins, while the butler and Madame LeGrand bundled Monsieur LeGrand into a sporting carriage.

Eugénie swung herself off Clisson's horse and ran for her father.

Madame LeGrand collapsed on the steps.

They gathered in the big salon. Monsieur LeGrand strutted about, planting his big feet with a certainty that matched his words. "A night alone together. You must marry. Call me bourgeois, young man, but this would be a better world with more bourgeois morals." He took his daughter's hand. "We'll marry you two in the village church tomorrow. Civil requirements take too long, and the priest owes me a great favor—an interesting story, but I ought not explain it. I rely upon your honor, Clisson."

Clisson swallowed hard, swept like last night's clouds into an inevitable current. Monsieur LeGrand insisted again: no, no, he did not question Clisson's honor, but his daughter's reputation was at stake. Clisson searched Eugénie's blissful face, surprised he was happy to be trapped. He clasped Monsieur LeGrand's outstretched hand.

"Yes," he answered.

Eugénie beamed.

Madame LeGrand had regrets; she wanted an elaborate wedding. She clung to her daughter. "Dearest, I had such plans. Ah, well, we really must have a talk." She hustled Eugénie away for a hot bath.

Clisson retired to his room. Hours later, the butler, bearing luncheon on a tray, woke him. He pulled on his clothes and, with shaking knees, tracked Monsieur LeGrand to his laboratory, where he confessed his family's poor estate.

The big man chuckled. "I have more than enough money for all of us. You'll live here, in the gatehouse, until I can build you a home. Truth is, I'm glad you're poor. I feared you'd take my chick to Corsica. Just don't tell her or her mother."

The next morning, the incense-laden village church reminded Clisson he must write to his own mother. Candle flames cast shadows on the crucifix. Madame LeGrand had filled the place with pink flowers and laid pink silk on the floor. Eugénie wore a pink ball dress that turned her skin sallow, but as the priest recited the words, her complexion blossomed. Clisson smiled at her upturned, rapturous face. Yes, he could love this woman.

Napoleon

THAT AFTERNOON, AT THE SOUND of women singing and metal clanging, Tobyson rushed in from the garden. He dragged the Emperor to his feet. "Come quick, Master. It's Black women, lots of them, dressed in pretty colors, and they're singing, and dancing, and banging on pots. You come, too, Monsieur Marchand."

The Emperor and Marchand followed the page onto Longwood's porch, where Montholon and Cipriani already watched the parade's approach.

"What're they saying, boy? 'Tain't English," the Corsican said.

Tobyson pounded the women's beat on the porch railing. "'Freedom for the children, freedom for the children.' Do you think that means me? Are my people coming to get me?"

The Emperor patted the boy's back. "Go see what you can find out."

Tobyson raced across the lawn.

Cipriani shaded his eyes. "That's Miora, ain't it, Master? The tall one leading the rest?"

Montholon stared. "What does the Emperor know of these women?"

Cipriani shrugged.

Tobyson scampered back, a paper flapping in his hand. "A declaration from the governor. Want me to read it to you? The women say slavery's going to end." But when Tobyson squinted at the governor's words, his face puckered. "*Any child born to a slave woman on Christmas Day of this year or any time thereafter shall be born a free person. The woman's slaveholder shall be responsible for the child's education and maintenance and shall have such labor as may reasonably be given until the child shall attain the age of sixteen. Thereafter, such person shall be free, with all the rights and duties of a citizen of St. Helena.* But what about me?"

Cipriani whistled. "Freeing newborns at age sixteen? Weren't worth the trouble."

"What trouble?" Montholon asked.

The Emperor took Tobyson's hand. "*Shh*. Watch the parade. We'll talk of this inside."

As the women passed Longwood House, singing and beating their pots, Miora separated herself from the parade and approached the fence.

The Emperor descended the porch steps. He stood across the lawn from her and bowed.

Miora clapped her hands above her head and danced on. She at least seemed satisfied.

A dark place in the Emperor's heart brightened. He hadn't written a constitution or won a battle against all odds or replenished France's treasury. His actions hadn't advanced his own purposes the slightest jot, but maybe, in a small way, he'd tilted a scale toward justice. It wasn't all he had hoped, but Toby might have approved. The Eaglet would be proud, Josephine amused.

He strode inside, his people trailing in his wake. At his chamber door, he stopped Montholon.

Montholon stiffened. "I can be trusted, sire."

The Emperor forced a smile. "I know that, but the child won't appreciate an audience." He closed the door.

Tobyson curled in a blanket in his favorite corner. Marchand crouched at the boy's side. Cipriani sprawled in a chair.

The Emperor beckoned the Corsican. "Freedom for the unborn while the rest stay enslaved? That was the best Lowe could do? The man has the imagination of a snail."

Cipriani scowled. "I'll scout out how this dashed proclamation's being accepted."

"Yes, go." The Emperor took his chair. "Tobyson, come here."

The child wiped his sleeve across his nose. His other hand clutched the declaration. He dragged his feet to where the Emperor sat.

The Emperor rested his hands on the boy's shoulders. "My estimable young man, your father gave you into my care. I didn't buy you, nor do I own you. It's my hope that one day you'll travel to Europe with us and choose your own future. Would you like that?"

A smile trembled on Tobyson's lips.

"But right now, your legal status is unclear. If I ask Sir Hudson to declare your freedom, you might be taken from us."

Tobyson rocked from foot to foot. "I don't want to be sold."

"What do you say we make our own declaration? Starting now, Marchand will pay you servant's wages. But if you wish to leave my service, you may do so." The Emperor lifted Tobyson's chin. "You are a free man, my son, and always were."

Chapter 25

Napoleon

AS THE WEEKS WENT ON, the Emperor's energy, that monumental force that had propelled him from the sewers of Corsica to the thrones of Europe, vanished. While Cipriani dreamed of escape on a submarine, the Emperor hid in his *Clisson* book, stroking the manuscript's soft pages, reading with Albine, and adding chapters.

Although he ate little, his weight increased until he avoided his own puffy face in the mirror. When Marchand called him to his bath, he sank to his neck in the hot tub water, his fingers closing around a roll of his belly. Heavy, pliant, muscleless flesh. Like a woman's, like Marie Louise's. Yes, like the Eaglet's mother's breasts. Not like Josephine's. His first wife's breasts had been small, wily creatures. When he and she were young—he stared at his loose belly, so ugly when magnified under the water—those lively breasts had given joy.

He wondered who might be stroking Albine's joyful breasts. Marchand said she'd been seen with a British lieutenant. A Frenchwoman's passion couldn't be suppressed, and Albine was French through and through. Ah, well, she might not want to be his lover, but she excelled as a collaborator on *Clisson*. He stared at the mold-pocked ceiling, instead of himself.

CLISSON: THE EMPEROR'S NOVEL

Champvert, France, July 1789

Clisson and Eugénie had a sleepless night of bliss in a room softened with quilts, silk sheets, and damask pillows. At dawn, he awoke to find her, in her nightgown, kneeling at a window, weeping. He took her in his arms and carried her back to bed.

"My beloved, my wife, did I hurt you?"

"No, not that." She smiled through her tears.

"I'm glad," he said. "For I did think you were enjoying it."

She blushed.

He opened the bodice of her nightgown and kissed her breast. "So, tell me, why the tears? Do you not love me? Yesterday you swore to."

"Oh, you know I do." Her hand brushed through his hair, with the motherly touch his mother lacked. "Indeed, I've loved you since I first saw you, but you . . . You love Amélie. You told me you did."

"I was mistaken. I only thought I loved her." He cleared his throat, pretending to himself his rising anger was remorse. "Why must you be so worried when I'm just becoming happy?"

"Tell me how it's possible. Please, I must know."

He tried to kiss her.

"No," she said. "First, I want to know exactly how you feel about Amélie and me."

He laid his head down on the pillow and stared at the ceiling. "So, you want a pretty speech, do you?"

Eugénie pouted. "Pretty *and* true."

"You shall have it." He closed his eyes. "Amélie is like . . . like a piece of French music that is agreeable to hear because one is familiar with it and can follow its melody. It pleases everyone, and everyone admires it, because it is so easy to see its beauty. You, Eugénie, are like the song of a nightingale or a piece by Paësiello, who pleases only sensitive souls, whose melody transports and impassions those ardent enough to appreciate its depth." Clisson opened his eyes. Eugénie's face hung over his. He tried to snatch a kiss, but her palms against his shoulders held him flat.

"Go on," she said.

Confronting the faith in her sweet face, he selected his words. "So while Amélie may rule in the public drawing room, you enslave in private. You inspire a passion worthy of heroes. I hope I can be one for you."

She threw her arms around his neck. "I swear if you stop loving me, I'll die. Now we must get dressed. Maman planned a luncheon for all my friends."

Clisson slumped. "Couldn't you ask your father to send us somewhere alone on a trip? Maybe to the coast?"

"To Corsica!" Eugénie cried. "I'll wait until he's in a good mood."

Albine

BASIL'S ROOM HAD THE APPEAL of army barracks. His mattress wore its linens as neatly as the man wore his uniform. I guessed the straw palette was hard, like his muscles, but he wouldn't let me share it. We were in our Chaste Period, a sacred era inviolate to sex.

We played chess. I let him beat me. (Though Charles had taught me a trick or two, I never used them on Basil.)

I ironed his shirt. He had to buy another.

I made a meal only once. Chicken à la Marengo (Napoleon's favorite)—a simple enough dish—emerged a charred, salt-laden mess. Basil ate it stoically. I swore my mouth would never heal. After that, I bribed Longwood's cook to provide me with baskets of cold collations.

If only we could have employed that mattress. There, I would have displayed talents extraordinaire. Instead, Basil began English language lessons.

I wasn't born or bred middle class or English. Yet Basil was a worthy man, steady as a church. I wanted to love him. I wanted more of my son's letters, and Basil even sent funds to his school, something Charles wouldn't consider. And every day my mirror reminded me to fear my future.

One afternoon when Charles had permission to go to Jamestown, I arrived unexpectedly at Basil's door. He'd given me a key for such opportunities. My poor lieutenant was asleep, his square jaw bristling whiskers, his soiled uniform crumpled on the floor. He'd been on duty for a thirty-six-hour shift. I nestled under the covers.

Basil startled awake, proclaiming in a voice remarkably like Sir Hudson's, "Discipline! If we can maintain it for these months, if I can break you of your habits, we will succeed a lifetime." He shoved me off the bed. "I want to—must—love you. Don't tempt me, Albine."

Must love? Break me? What, like a wild filly? And discipline? You'd have thought he was fulfilling a duty. I picked myself off the floor and, rubbing my behind (on which I'd landed), strode to the window that looked toward Longwood House.

While I contemplated this unfamiliar sort of love, turning it this way and that to find its hazards and its charms, the governor's carriage barreled up to Longwood's green latticed porch. My curiosity aroused, I said, "Basil, quick. Something's happening across the way."

He came up behind me. I leaned against his body and felt his passion rise. What pleasure might be in store if I could "break" this man.

On Napoleon's porch, Bertrand and Sir Hudson played their parts as if they were onstage, waving their arms, shouting their lines. British soldiers milled about. Marchand and Tobyson came out on cue.

From the governor's coach, on the side facing us but hidden from the house, Charles climbed out. Only Basil and I could see him as he flitted down a garden path, turned, and strolled back up it, as though just arriving on the scene.

"Hurry," Basil said, "get back before you're missed."

Napoleon

THE VALET RAPPED ON THE DOOR. "Sire, the store ship *Baring* has arrived."

The Emperor shifted in the tub. Dust on the water's surface swirled around his knees. "What's that to me? Bring more hot water."

Marchand poked his head into the room. "The ship brought a marble bust of your son."

He burst out of the water.

But when the Emperor joined his entourage in the reception hall, Sir Hudson Lowe's upper lip rose above his horsey teeth in an expression that was pure English. "We'll let you look at the statue in our presence. Then we have to smash it."

"Smash a bust of my son? Have you no human feelings?" The Emperor winced at the shooting pain in his side. "No, Marchand, I won't sit. Let this executioner finish his assignment."

Sir Hudson wrinkled his brow. "How else can I be sure there's nothing inside? I am but doing my duty."

"Yes, as a hangman does his." The Emperor dropped into the chair Albine urged upon him. "How dare you make me haggle for an image of my son?"

"How dare you call me a hangman?" Sir Hudson loomed over the Emperor. "Besides, Corsicans view haggling as a religion. You should relish the opportunity."

General Bertrand pushed between them. "How dare you?"

The governor tossed his head, for all the world like Betsy used to do.

The Emperor swallowed a laugh, despite his anger. "Fall back, Bertrand. The insult's meaningless." He crossed his arms behind his head and smiled into the governor's face. "Coming as it does from a 'stupid man wanting in education and judgment.'"

Sir Hudson flushed. "You can't—"

"Yes, the Duke of Wellington's words. Do I have them exact?" He glanced over the governor's shoulder at Montholon, who winked.

The governor lifted his chin. "That same man declared you're not a gentleman."

The Emperor chuckled. "And by that, he meant he didn't like who my parents were. Neither did I. You ignorant man, that was the point of the French Revolution. The pivot from circumstances of a man's birth to his merit."

"Merit, sir, is born and bred in aristocracy."

"And yet Wellington—England's greatest general—thought you lacked it." The Emperor, concealing the effort it cost him, pushed himself out of his chair and onto his feet. "Too bad! I might have won at Waterloo if he'd kept you as his quartermaster."

"Enough! This conversation has nothing to do with the bust of your son."

"Indeed it does. Wellington and I are military men, the best of our generation. Is that what rankles? That we both hold you in contempt? Tobyson, give me your shoulder." With the page's support, the Emperor crossed to the mantel.

"If you want to drag up the past, well, then let's do so," Lowe sputtered. "At least in the matter of slavery, I've upheld my principles, whereas you did evil. You stole your precious Revolution's liberty from Haiti's slaves. In this house, you acknowledged that action sullied—"

"Sir Hudson, are you such scum as to reveal our private discussion? Perhaps you'd like me to publicize how you spent the rest of that evening?"

"You can't know . . ." Sir Hudson gripped his collar.

"You walked the halls of your residence, talking to me. As, apparently, you often do."

"You, sir, will never see that bust of your son." Sir Hudson stalked to the door.

"Stop him."

Bertrand blocked the exit.

"Come to agreement on this bust, or I swear you'll read every petty threat you've ever made in the London papers," the Emperor said.

"Ha! You can't. I've cut off all your smuggling."

"I can and I will." A smile curled his lips.

Bertrand drew the governor aside. "Be prudent, sir. We knew nothing in advance of this gift or the gunnery officer who delivered it."

The governor twisted a corner of his sleeve. He glanced over his shoulder, as if afraid the Emperor were about to pounce.

Montholon joined them. "I, too, attest we had no knowledge of this statue."

Doubt spread on Sir Hudson's sharp features. His eyes slid from Bertrand to Montholon. "Maybe I believe you. We'll see. After I've interrogated the fellow who carried it here."

Montholon took Sir Hudson's arm. "I'll escort you out."

As the door closed behind them, the Emperor dropped into a chair. "Thus," he said, "we make the jailer wear the prisoner's chains."

Bertrand shook his head. "But your dignity, sire. Let me handle this fool for you."

"Yes, you shall do so from here forward. I forgave all those who betrayed me: Bernadotte, Talleyrand, Fouché, Ney, even my own brothers. I forgave them all, when I could have executed them with a lift of a finger. But I will not forgive this Hudson Lowe." He scanned the room. "Oh, I'll humble myself to get a remembrance of my son. After that, don't let Lowe near me. I swear I'll rip him apart with my bare hands."

Tobyson shrank against Albine's skirt.

Cipriani peered around a doorjamb. "Bravo! Still a Corsican."

Bertrand bent to the Emperor. "I tell you, that man skulks like a rat."

The Emperor, pushing Bertrand aside, grasped his compatriot's hand. "Well said, Cipriani. One more battle, eh? Nothing we can't handle." The Emperor rubbed his jaw. "Leave me, all of you. I want to think."

When the others had filed out, Cipriani strode to the fireplace. The Emperor joined him there. "Time for a new strategy."

"Been waiting for you to come to that. Many more weeks on this damn island, and I'll be going the way of Randall. I ain't joking." Cipriani *tap-tap*ped the mirror. "What'd you have in mind? Something better than a submarine?"

"Perhaps." The Emperor *tap-tap*ped back. "I had a book. No, don't laugh."

"You've had ten thousand books." Cipriani's grin faded. "What's special about this one?"

"I bought it in Marseilles, when I was distraught over my first love affair." The Emperor pulled the Corsican closer. "It's about poison."

Cipriani *tap-tap*ped the mirror. His smile matched the Emperor's. "Damn me, I like that. Who we going to poison, Master?"

The Emperor *tap-tap*ped. "Me."

Chapter 26

Napoleon

SWALLOW A BIT OF ARSENIC EVERY DAY. Enough to sicken him but not to kill him. His extremities would swell. He'd develop a hacking cough, headaches, stomach pains, and, in time, convulsions. So many symptoms, no doctor on St. Helena would be able to diagnose the cause. Afraid his death in exile would make his prisoner a martyr, Hudson Lowe would transport him to England for medical treatment. They'd reunite him with his son.

If the plot didn't work, he'd taper off the rat poison and, *presto*, he'd be cured.

But stomach pains.

Convulsions.

Ah, well. All for the Eaglet.

He was through using other people's bodies as weapons. He'd use his own. As long as he never had to explain what he'd done. Not to his son, not to his mother, not to history. Only Cipriani would know.

The Corsican waxed ecstatic. "Bravo. What a plan. We'll squirrel away a barrel of Solomon's Cape Town wine. Lace it with arsenic. Better than a leaky submarine, that's for sure."

The Emperor shoved him away. "You're not contemplating convulsions."

"Softly, Master, softly." Cipriani rubbed his nose. "If you have second thoughts, we stop the poison. Two weeks later, you're as good as new."

"If that book was right."

"What? Afraid?" The Corsican tugged the Emperor's lapel.

"Hands off, do you hear? When have I shied from danger?"

"So I'm not to touch the Emperor's sacred person, eh? *Mi scusu!*" Cipriani spat on his palms. "What I meant is, this situation's different. Like being eaten from within."

"All right, let neither of us take offense." The Emperor tapped Cipriani's chest. "But the rat poison may permanently damage my health. What good would that do the Eaglet?" The Emperor lifted the etching of his son from its shelf.

"Well, you think on it. This arsenic's the best idea you've had since 1812."

The Emperor glanced up. "Good thing I trust you, old friend, or I'd have you killed."

Cipriani's harsh face broke into a wrinkled grin. "Likewise."

Five days later, on a rainy afternoon when the Emperor's hope had waned, General Bertrand presented him with the small marble bust of the Eaglet. The Emperor kissed the general on both cheeks. "I don't know what it took to wrest this statue from our jailer, but if I had a kingdom to assign, it would be yours." He rooted through a box for one of his medals and looped its ribbon around Bertrand's neck.

He kissed the statue's little marble nose. "It's very like him as a baby," he told Marchand. He looked down, encountering his protruding belly, rather than his toes. "How the years have gone by. I wish they'd made a statue as he is now. Eight years old! He must have thick hair like his mother's, maybe curls like his cousin Louis-N. How can a father not know?"

After Marchand wiped the dining room mantel free of dust, the Emperor placed the statue on the ledge and settled in a chair opposite it. For a long while, he sat talking to his Eaglet, fingering the envelope that held the boy's hair.

In the morning, he started the poison.

Day after day, his condition worsened. The coughing fits became so frequent that Marchand wept. His skin, always pale, turned ghostly white. His legs swelled, his feet didn't fit in his boots, his gums bled. His stomach ballooned until he couldn't close his breeches. He lay upon his camp bed in a dressing gown, drifting in and out of sleep.

Marchand and Bertrand whispered in the doorway.

The Emperor dangled his arm over the edge of the bed. A warm little hand grabbed hold. Tobyson's round face came into view.

The boy tucked the covers under the Emperor's chin. "Yes, dear Master?"

"Tell them not to talk about me. Tell them . . ." He paused for breath. "Talk to me."

But when Marchand and Bertrand stood above his bed, their voices merged. The room grew gray, then swirling white. He floated off on a cloud, dreaming of a son who smelled of porridge. He dreamed of Betsy's bright chatter. He dreamed of Corsica. He dreamed of the man he once was. He dreamed of Clisson.

CLISSON: THE EMPEROR'S NOVEL

Champvert, France, July 1789

Midday heat, oppressive even for July, foretold another storm. Nonetheless, the dining room filled with clinking champagne glasses, heaping platters of food, and blushing maidens who whispered questions in Eugénie's ear. Clisson's back was clapped so often, he thought it would show a bruise.

When a fidgeting Amélie, the Fop at her side, extended her hand, Clisson raised it to his lips. His eyes met the Fop's.

Madame LeGrand beamed.

"We shall be neighbors now," Clisson said. "And friends."

Amélie snatched her hand away. She turned to Madame LeGrand. "I'm sorry, but we must leave. I took a cold in that terrible storm." Her eyes were indeed red.

"Lieutenant Berville!" the butler announced.

Berville, wearing his uniform with the natural grace Clisson envied, swept in. He faced Clisson, suppressed a grin, saluted, and clicked his heels. In his hand he held a sealed paper. "Lieutenant Clisson, your orders!"

Clisson, rolling his eyes at Berville's dramatics, accepted the paper. Eugénie peeked around his shoulder while he read.

Berville bowed to Madame LeGrand. "Your guest must leave. We are called to war."

"No!" Eugénie lunged at Berville. Clisson caught her around the waist. She struggled free and ran to Amélie. All color had fled Amélie's face. Above the sobbing Eugénie, her stricken eyes met Clisson's.

Clisson wet his lips. He forced them to move. "My apologies, Berville. This woman is my wife."

"Really?" Berville, his blue eyes gleaming, looked from Amélie to Eugénie. "Which one? Congratulations, my friend, but we must leave within the hour."

Common sense wouldn't calm Eugénie, nor wisdom comfort her distress. Clisson begged her not to waste their few minutes together in hysterics. "Think of our beautiful night at the abbey. If lightning, thunder, and torrential rain melded us together, what can tear our love apart?"

"But war will change you. I know it will." She wiped her red nose on her sleeve.

"Your husband will never stop loving you. I'll return." He kissed the tip of each of her fingers.

Eugénie pressed her fingers to her breast. "Now that I know love, how can I live without it?"

"Eugénie, don't put me through this anguish. You married a soldier. Accept that war has always been my Destiny. Now I have a wonderful reason to survive. Be brave. We must say adieu."

He led her to the terrace where Berville and the family waited. Amélie and her Fop had stayed to wish him well. The Fop's mouth was harsh-set. On second glance, he looked envious.

Clisson's horse was saddled, his few possessions stowed on its back. Monsieur LeGrand strapped his personal *nécessaire* to the rig. Clisson accepted the box of toothbrushes, razors, and clippers with gratitude.

Monsieur LeGrand gripped his arm. "Return safely, my boy." The old man winked. "I'll see what I can do to buy you a discharge."

Berville's eyes seemed stuck on Eugénie's sweet face. He kissed her hand and turned to her mother. "You two are much too lovely to be related to my colonel." He kissed the mother's hand, too.

Madame LeGrand nudged her husband. "Now, that's my idea of a gentleman."

Eugénie accepted Clisson's kiss, her arms limp at her sides.

"Adieu," he whispered. "I love you."

As they cantered down the stone path to the main road, Berville frowned. "Someday you must explain to me what happened there."

"What's there to explain? I got married."

"Yes, but why did you marry the little one, when clearly the gorgeous Amazon's in love with you? If it had been anyone else, I'd have said it was for the family's money."

"Berville, I'll thank you to remember I am *not* anyone else." Clisson raised his riding crop. "And that's my wife of whom you speak."

Berville, chuckling, tugged his horse out of range of the crop. "I forgot you have no sense of humor. And a wife? Maybe these bourgeois country folk don't know the regulations, but you should. An officer may not marry without the king's permission. Under the law, your marriage is a sham. We'll see how our precious colonel appreciates your ruining his niece."

Before Clisson could reply, Berville dug his spurs into his horse's flanks. As his friend galloped off, Clisson lifted his hand to smell Eugénie. His lips closed around a finger. Things had progressed too far for his colonel to object.

Late the next afternoon, Clisson and Berville dismounted in the deserted garrison courtyard.

"What ho?" Berville's call brought Des Mazis, quill in hand, barreling out of the colonel's office.

Des Mazis clapped them each on a shoulder. "Now we can get on the road."

"What? Has the regiment taken off?" Berville asked.

"Marched out hours after you left," Des Mazis replied. "I remained behind for you stragglers. It's what you've been waiting for, Clisson. We're off to war."

Berville huffed. "Except our Clisson's done an about-face. Turns out he's born for love, not for war."

"Enough, Berville." Clisson turned to Des Mazis. "He means I've gotten married, but don't think that's stripped the fight out of me. Can we catch up with the colonel?"

"Ah, the colonel," Des Mazis said. "He's been transferred to the south, replaced with some general named Barras. Nice enough fellow, if a little gruff. But married, Clisson?" Des Mazis whistled. "All I did on leave was visit my mother."

The following morning, as they left the garrison, Clisson posted a letter:

Dearest Eugénie:

I am consumed with imagining how you spend each moment. If I think you are happy, I am forlorn that you have forgotten me. If I imagine you lonely, my grief grows all the greater for your sorrow. Are you riding Gray Man? Does he buck and rear under you? I am so jealous. My imagination chases you down the flowered trails, into your boudoir, into your bath.

Be not too happy, my love, but a bit sad. Let my absence always be in your thoughts.

Your husband,
Clisson

Napoleon

THE EMPEROR AWOKE. IT WAS MORNING. He wasn't sure what day, but his head was clear. Cipriani dozed in a chair by the bed. The Emperor felt for something to throw at his friend. Finding nothing within reach, he pinched the man's pants leg. The Corsican jumped.

The Emperor's lips cracked as he tried a smile. His voice came out gravelly. "You haven't assassinated me yet, old friend."

Cipriani fell to his knees. "Forgive me. I gave you too much. Worse, the governor refuses to let you travel in this condition."

The Emperor stroked Cipriani's head. "We'll get the dose right next time. Onward together, Franco."

Albine

I WAS DUSTING THE BOOKS in our shelf-lined quarters when I told Charles I wanted to nurse Napoleon. "Does Marchand think his hands gentler than mine? And that tin soldier Bertrand, allowing his own wife to visit, keeping me out. How can you let it happen?"

Charles dealt a game of solitaire.

"I'd think you'd want me in there with Napoleon." I clapped two books together to dislodge the dust. (Practice for being Basil's middle-class wife.) "Don't you need information to sell?"

"Damn you, keep your voice down," Charles hissed.

"Sorry, sorry. But who knows how much time Napoleon has left?" (*Clap, clap,* a few more books. I closed my eyes against the dust.) "If he's going to die, I can at least make him comfortable. Won't you talk to Bertrand?"

He turned a few cards. "Bertrand doesn't do what I say."

"Then you offer to watch over Napoleon. You can let me in." I smiled over my shoulder.

"I have no desire to be a nursemaid, even to Napoleon." He reshuffled.

I stopped my cleaning. "Charles, they won't let you, will they? Do you think Napoleon told them about your deal with the British?"

"No, kind of thing he'd hold to himself. He likes to dole out his tactics so no one knows too much." He snorted. "Besides, the money would tempt others to sell out, too."

"Maybe Bertrand thinks you'll get drunk and fall asleep." Charles was engrossed in his cards. I kept my back to him, dusting the books. "Are you still working through Basil Jackson?"

Before I realized the danger, Charles had long fingers around my neck. He squeezed enough that I knew what was possible. "Don't play a double game with me, girl. You've been seen with Jackson. I know it. Napoleon knows it." He bit my ear and released me.

I stifled a cough. As air—and shame—filled my lungs, I clapped two books together, letting the dust land where fate took it. I had to see the Emperor. It might be the last time.

AT MIDNIGHT, BERTRAND'S SHIFT ENDED. His footsteps receded down the hall. Marchand's shift began at five. Till then, they left Tobyson on watch. I slipped into the dark room, where a single candle flickered.

Tobyson was on me in an instant, pushing me to the door. "No, no, it took forever for him to get to sleep. Please, chère Madame."

The Emperor flung the camp-bed draperies open. His stiletto flashed, but, seeing me, he clicked the knife shut.

I matched my voice to Tobyson's whisper, just loud enough for grinning Napoleon to hear. "Silly boy, I've got the medicine he needs."

"Lieutenant Tobyson," the Emperor called. "Let the lady be."

"But, Master—"

"Not another word. Take your blankets and sleep on the dining room rug."

"Monsieur Marchand says I'm not to leave."

"Tobyson, come here." The Emperor drew the boy close. "Good soldiers do not question their general's orders." He raised his hand in salute. "And tell no one."

Still, the child dragged his feet. He gathered his blankets and, with a resentful look at me, tromped out.

The Emperor lit a second candle. "What have we here, my girl?"

His skin, usually white marble, had a dusty translucence. The knob on his chin had sharpened, its dimple a deep valley in a sharp cliff, as though St. Helena Island were imprinting her features onto him.

I crossed to his camp bed. My hair flowed about my face. (This was not the time for a Marie Louise chignon. Besides, the loose style looked younger.) At his bedside, within reach of his eager hands, I untied my nightdress.

I gave him what he needed.

Chapter 27

Napoleon

THE NIGHT WITH ALBINE PUSHED death away. He brought her back into his life as a friend but resumed the arsenic treatments. To limit damage to his precarious health, he alternated months, one on arsenic, the next off. The respites restored his strength, if only temporarily. He hoped the sick times eroded Sir Hudson's resolution to keep him on St. Helena.

Before dinner, Cipriani delivered his special wine. Under the Corsican's scrutiny, he forced his hand to tip the glass, his throat to accept the bitter liquid, his stomach to receive it. At night he dreamed of drowning.

As the month passed, his legs swelled. Marchand rubbed them to improve the circulation. The valet's frown lines deepened. "I was convinced you were better, dear Master."

"One doesn't outrun destiny, my friend." He laid his palm over the etching of the Eaglet. "The future lies with my son. I must finish his book. Tell Albine I need her help."

Marchand pursed his lips.

Napoleon pursed his at Marchand. "Do as I say. If the British won't transfer me to Europe when I'm in this condition, well, then I'll die on this forsaken rock. But I won't make it easy on them." *And with the arsenic, it will be my choice, on my terms*, he thought.

But the poison, the only positive step—if one could call it that—to end his exile, didn't convince Hudson Lowe that his condition required a return to Europe. After thirty days, the Emperor stopped the doses. The swelling in his legs receded. Marchand regained his optimism until another thirty days passed and the Emperor's legs swelled again, much worse.

IN A RARE SHOW OF UNITY, Bertrand and Montholon entered his chamber shoulder to shoulder. The Emperor shifted in his chair, easing the constant pressure near his liver. He laid down his pen and indicated that they should sit.

Montholon bowed. "No, sire. We shall stand. What we have to say about Cipriani won't take long."

Bertrand, one hand on his sword hilt, moved forward. "The man is everywhere he should not be, doing things he should not do. Last week, I caught him in conversation with Hudson Lowe's carriage driver. Yesterday, he played at dice with Sergeant Kitts. Montholon discovered him in the pantry, scooping rat poison. Madame Albine swears she saw him coming out of their room. You give him unwarranted—and we think unwise—access to your person and to the household at large." He clicked his heels. "The man is untrustworthy."

The Emperor folded his arms. "And you, Montholon? Do you agree with this—this character assassination of my old friend?"

Montholon rubbed his chin. "We don't mean to question your judgment   "

"Then don't. I've known Cipriani since I was a child. Do not interfere with him. He is in effect my minister of secret police. When you find him in places you think unusual, assume he's acting on my behalf."

Montholon tilted his head. "Entering my room?"

"Was anything missing? Disturbed? No? Then there's no call for concern. Now, I want to return to my writing." He picked up a quill.

Bertrand paused at the door. "If he's spying on your behalf, Your Majesty, you might trust us—your generals—with the information he gathers."

The Emperor didn't raise his hand from the paper until the door closed behind them. "Tobyson."

The page popped out from behind a curtain.

The Emperor hugged the boy. "That was a lesson in how difficult it is to tell traitors from friends."

Tobyson's face puckered. "But, sire, I don't see how you do tell the difference."

The Emperor touched a fingertip to Tobyson's nose. "That, my son, is the lesson. Once you're a leader, you can't trust anyone."

CLISSON: THE EMPEROR'S NOVEL

France's Northeast Border, 1790

Clisson, Des Mazis, and Berville joined their regiment at the northeast border.

All France was in turmoil—everyone speculated on the spread of *la panique*. Prices rose. Royalists hung from lampposts. Some said it was a conspiracy of the Revolutionaries. Some claimed the Royalists brought it on themselves. The Church's property was seized; aristocrats were on the run. Wealthy bourgeois, like Monsieur LeGrand, trod a narrow line. As power beckoned with an open hand, the anger of the mob held them back from seizing too much for themselves.

The Austrians, sensing weakness, seeing France's Austrian-born queen besieged, moved to take advantage. Generals, even intrepid Barras, dared not issue orders, for fear of the representatives of the People. In turn, these local citizens' committees feared power shifts in Paris. Each military decision was put to a motion and passed only by acclamation. No individual bore blame. No one person merited praise. Among the officers, only Clisson led his squadron on sorties. Even so, he spent hours on a cot in the semidarkness of the officers' tent, listening to Berville complain.

Berville tossed the news journal to the ground. "I'm as revolutionary as anyone, not even against elimination of inherited titles, but I don't like the way that citizens' committee glares at me."

Clisson, stretched out on his cot, contemplated the letter he was composing. He crossed out a word. "I told you: remove your damn signet ring before someone cuts off your finger."

"Right, *Captain* Clisson. I should follow your advice. I should bow before your new rank. Maybe if they hadn't assigned me a bunch of cowardly dotards, I'd get promoted, too." He threw his pillow at Clisson.

Clisson batted it away. "I had the luck to come upon that skirmish."

Berville had to hunch his back to stand in the low tent, yet he paced. "You always have the luck, don't you? First, you're noble enough to attend the king's military school. Then you're bourgeois enough to marry a rich tradesman's daughter. Now, you're enough of a commoner for the soldiers to take you for an equal. You're a chameleon if God ever made one."

"And you are an aristo with a lackey's soul," Clisson answered. "That should serve you well in this People's Revolution. Sit down before you rip the tarpaulin."

Des Mazis ducked under the tent opening. "At each other's throats again? My God, don't we have enough conflict with the enemy? What's going on, Berville?"

"Oh, I was telling Clisson here that he's a lizard. Don't worry about my opinion, Captain Clisson. Continue writing to your rich wife."

"I may be a lizard, and you, Berville, may be an aristo—although in this great time of revolution, I'd not boast about

it—but the truth is, you're an excellent officer and we're brothers."
Clisson offered Berville his hand.

"Mon Dieu!" Berville ignored the gesture. "Can't you see I'm
bored? You get all the adventures, Clisson. When do 7 get to experience life?" He pushed past Des Mazis to storm out of the tent.

Clisson retreated into his letter.

Dearest Eugénie,

*You have read what lies in my soul. The immaculate sweet-
ness that characterizes you, the happy candor that belongs
to you, inspires me with devotion. The grace of your person,
the charm of your character, conquered me. A stranger to
tender passions, 7 must be wary of thinking of you too often,
lest my ardor interfere with my duties.*

*You have an inclination to music. Acquire a piano and
a good teacher. Music is the soul of love, the sweetness
of life, a consolation for suffering, and the companion of
innocence. Your voice will grow perfect, and your talents
will give pleasure to your husband when he returns.*

*You will find enclosed the book list 7 forgot to send with my
last letter. 7 have included those 7 consider most useful and
agreeable for you to read.*

Think of me when you wash. 7 kiss you there and there.

Clisson

Satisfied, he folded the paper and went to find a messenger
to transport it. Outside the tent, he tripped over a discarded
cooking pot. A dozen lounging soldiers laughed. The breeze

shifted. He wrinkled his nose at the stench of the latrines, or was that from the garbage heap? He stepped around a woodpile dumped between two tents. The chaos annoyed him. He'd have been glad to impose order, but the generals and the committee wouldn't allow him to enforce discipline.

It was one thing to be a republican; it was quite another to accept the inefficiency of the mob.

Every day he penned another letter to Eugénie. Hers to him must have gone astray. He received less than one per week.

Albine

OUR LAST NIGHT OF LOVEMAKING, the Emperor gave me a diamond. "Not to buy your body," he said, "but because, my friend, you're among the few people in my life who sees me as I am."

A lonely man, I thought, but didn't say it. That would have hurt his pride. I returned to my room, aware—farewell, chastity—I had failed Basil.

Yet was my action wrong? God says a loyal subject must serve the ruler as best he or she can. Thus, a man who loses his leg to win the king's battle receives honors, pension, and a medal. Being a woman blocked that glorious path from me. I had but one currency to offer. I couldn't hoard it from the great Napoleon. My companionship (let's call it that) restored his health, his spirits, and his drive. I rescued him from as great a battle as Waterloo.

Though he handed me a diamond, I gave my love freely.

For several weeks, I avoided Basil. His call for discipline, celibacy, and honesty wore me out. I despaired of being the woman he wanted to love. So, instead, after he left for his duties, I'd deliver one of Cook's food baskets to his room. Some might say, despite my love for Napoleon, I planted one foot in each camp. Yes, a woman must.

Charles, who hadn't touched me in months, liked to watch me dress. Most mornings he lay in bed, his head supported on a crooked arm, while I did my hair and put on my clothes. I took precautions to divert his attention, but he noticed nonetheless.

"Mon Dieu!" he cried. He spun me around, poking my belly, pinching my breasts. "By God, you're pregnant. Who's the father?"

"Not you," I said. "You spill your seed into a towel."

He reared to slap me.

I stopped his hand. "I wouldn't. A greater man than you, Monsieur Aristocrat de Montholon, has a stake in this body."

Napoleon

ON A BRIGHT MORNING IN early spring, the Emperor worked at his writing desk. Marchand's knock preceded General Montholon's brusque entry. At the Emperor's nod, Tobyson laid aside his book and left.

Montholon slammed the door behind the boy. "My wife's pregnant."

"My felicitations, Charles." Unlikely the baby was his. After all, he was fifty, ill, and poisoned. He didn't know if Albine still had relations with her husband, but Cipriani reported her visits to the British lieutenant's quarters. Poor Montholon—he'd never know for sure.

Every man's dilemma.

The Emperor pointed to a chair. "Please sit, Charles. Truly, congratulations."

Montholon remained standing. "No, sire, congratulations go to you."

"It's been weeks since I've been with the lady. If it's not yours, you must look elsewhere."

"She says it's yours."

"Yes, my fellow, that's what she would say."

The general stared at his boots. "She must return to Europe."

"As you wish. You as well?" He wondered if the pregnancy had been planned.

Montholon lifted his chin. "Not unless you want me to. I do have skills Bertrand lacks."

The Emperor's lips twitched. "True. It shall be as you choose."

Montholon crossed his arms. "Albine requires a means to live. We gave up everything to follow you."

"Yes, yes, that familiar refrain." The Emperor sighed. "The British will search her luggage, so she can't take much with her. However, my Madame Mère has plenty of resources to take care of your wife. You, too, if you go."

Montholon nodded. "I'll stay, but Albine leaves as soon as Lowe approves her travel."

The Emperor picked up his pen. "Just be sure she doesn't take any property of mine with her. Cipriani reports she hasn't broken that old habit of hers."

"Cipriani! Tell that bastard to keep his opinions to himself." Montholon stomped out.

The Emperor shuffled his papers. There had been that one time. Well, two. The last six weeks ago? No, the child wasn't his. Montholon would have to claim the unlucky infant.

Tobyson tiptoed into the room and curled at the Emperor's feet.

"Are you here to chase rats from my toes?" the Emperor asked.

Tobyson scrunched his eyes and lifted his small fists. "I'll throw them out the window."

"Good boy. I could have used your services a few moments ago."

Chapter 28

Albine

HOW I WISHED BASIL WOULD scream at me. Instead, this man who confronted death at Waterloo cried into a handkerchief that bore an iron scorch as testament to my incompetence.

I went down on my knees. (I cried, too. How could I not?) "I was afraid to tell you."

"To read it in a dispatch. Cruel, how cruel." His nose ran as much as his eyes. "First the deed, then the lie. Twice betrayed."

Understand, if you please, I'd never experienced constancy like Basil's. How was I to know a rock felt pain? I tried a lie to salve his misery. "But, Basil, I couldn't deny my husband. He was so drunk. I woke up. He was on top of me. All the discipline in the world couldn't have stopped it."

"I'd kill him if that were true."

"No, no," I stuttered. "I'd lose you as well." The room tightened around me. I reached into my pocket, forgetting there wasn't any bread. I'd been trying to break my habit. I swallowed my panic. "We'll raise the child as Tristan's sibling, then have another, just for us."

"Thrice betrayed, Albine," Basil said.

I couldn't look at him.

He lifted my chin. "It's Napoleon's baby. Your husband reported the truth to Hudson Lowe."

"He lied," I said. "He concocted that story because he thought you'd pay him more. Then you'd send me away, someplace where Napoleon can't raise the child in his image. In one shot, he'd get paid and be rid of me."

Basil threw a book across the room. "Leave me."

"Charles was drunk. He doesn't remember—"

"You have no constancy. You never will. Get out," he whispered. He whispered it a second time. The third time, his voice rose to a shout. "Get out! You lie, you lie, you lie, till I don't know what to believe. Get out, get out!"

"But, Basil—"

"Get out, do you hear? While you dole out your lies, tell Napoleon the baby's mine, why don't you? Oh, Albine, there's not a whit of truth in you." He kissed me till it hurt, but then, as suddenly, he bellowed in my face, "Run, damn you! Get out! Get out!"

NAPOLEON. CHARLES. BASIL. I LOST ALL THREE.

Marchand cleared a storage room, and I moved there alone. Charles remained in our old, book-lined space. Napoleon no longer welcomed me in his chambers or at his table. Every morning and at dusk, I did sentry duty at my single window, hoping for a glimpse of Basil, as he came and went from his quarters. He brought me no more letters from Tristan.

I was without a man.

Oh, not entirely. Hercules clipped flowers to brighten my chamber, and Marchand smuggled pretty trifles from Solomon's Emporium. Best of all, Tobyson tutored me in English while I improved his French. The sweet boy played a clever game of backgammon, too. My life became my room, Longwood's garden, and my swelling belly.

I was too old for pregnancy to render me beautiful. My skin developed splotches, my feet overflowed shoes, my heavy breasts drooped. I abandoned rose perfume. Yet I loved this person within me. Where once I would have yearned for a boy to continue Napoleon's dynasty, as I crocheted tiny hats, I craved a girl.

I was learning constancy.

Napoleon

SUMMER APPROACHED. GENERAL BERTRAND designed an outdoor birdcage as tall as a man. Cooing pigeons nested on its three levels, but the Emperor opened the cage doors, saying, "Let the birds come and go. We have enough prisoners on this island."

A new water pipe leading from the cistern on Diana's Peak allowed an extension of the garden. Marchand purchased two full-grown lemon trees, and volunteers from the 53rd Regiment transplanted them. Hercules threaded vines through an arched trellis to create shade.

The Emperor said nothing. He didn't want Longwood to feel like home.

When Marchand related his Master's persistent ills, the doctors prescribed a two-week course of mercury pills. The Emperor shook his finger at the valet. "You took mercury when you were sick, and it loosened your teeth." He pushed the pills away.

Marchand gathered them up. "I know you can't venture far enough to ride a horse, sire, but won't you enjoy the new garden?"

The Emperor opened a book.

Tobyson whispered in his ear. "Let's water the plants. I'll man the pump."

The Emperor wrapped an arm around the boy's waist. "Would you do that for me?"

Tobyson's smile spread. "Oh, yes, Master, and Hercules will help. Please come outside. Watering's so much fun." He took the Emperor's hand. "Wear the hat my father gave you."

The Emperor, with Toby's straw hat on his head and Tobyson's small hand in his, inspected the improvements. His spirits lightened. "The lemon trees smell like Corsica. Marchand, you're a genius. I needed a project. We'll all take up gardening."

For a few days, while good weather held, the Emperor rose early and supervised new plantings. He picked green beans, although his stomach was too frail to eat them. It ached when he was on the arsenic treatment and when he was not.

In the garden, under the lemon trees, Albine de Montholon let out the seams of a dress. Despite her silks, with her swollen breasts and darkened complexion, she looked like a peasant. It suited her.

The Emperor joined Montholon on a bench. "What news? The next ship for your wife?"

Montholon jiggled a handful of stones. He tossed one at Hercules's prized lilies. "That ass Hudson Lowe hasn't decided. At this rate, the baby'll be born on St. Helena." He sniffed at the Emperor's straw hat. "And grow up to see his Imperial Majesty dressed like a garden slave."

The Emperor stopped Montholon's hand midthrow. "The man who made this hat gardened with pride."

Montholon threw his stone. "He, like I, gardened under duress."

The Emperor narrowed his eyes.

"Don't bother. I'm onto that old staring trick you pull. No one else is in earshot, so I'll tell you: I'm returning to Europe with my wife." Montholon spat out the last word.

"Tobyson!" the Emperor called.

The boy dropped the stick he was poking into the birdcage and hurried over.

"Tell Marchand that Montholon needs more trunks. He's going to Europe with Albine."

Tobyson's dimples puckered. "Yes, sire."

"And give me your shoulder. I wish to go indoors, where the air is less vile." As he limped away, Montholon's voice followed.

"You should have died in battle. It would have been better for the rest of us."

The Emperor flinched. He hoped it hadn't shown. "One more word, and we'll never speak again."

Montholon stood. His gaze, hesitating on his wife, returned to Napoleon. He bowed.

Alone in his bedroom, the Emperor exchanged the straw hat for his bicorne. He stared into the mirror. Betsy, Toby, and Las Cases were gone. Albine leaving. Charles, too. Every day, Fanny Bertrand bent her husband's ear: *Take me home, Henri, before I'm an old lady!*

His feet were swollen, his breath short. He couldn't separate the arsenic symptoms from the stomach cancer he had inherited from his father. No matter. "We cross the bridge once more," he whispered to his puffy face in the mirror. "All for the Eaglet."

CLISSON: THE EMPEROR'S NOVEL

France's Northeast Border, 1791

Across the border from Clisson's regiment, the Austrian army's campfires grew more numerous each night. The French considered retreating.

Clisson spread a map on his commanding officer's table. "But, General Barras, if we place our batteries here to dominate their position, they'll withdraw before the battle's begun."

The general reviewed Clisson's plan. "I'll see what the committee says."

For a week, Clisson waited. He hiked the hills, scouting through his spyglass, gathering intelligence. Another squadron of Austrians ranged along the border. After days of drenching rain, the committee agreed to his plan.

But the cannon wheels sank in the mud. Horses stumbled under the artillery's weight; one had to be shot. Soldiers took over the hauling. Their shredded palms turned the ropes red. Clisson, racing from effort to effort, sank up to his knees. Mud oozed over his boot tops, stained his pants and vest. He could taste its grit. When the Austrians charged, the cannons were but halfway up the knolls, too low to shoot.

Frenchmen died on the field below, cut down one by one. Despair raged in Clisson's chest. Two more hours, and he could have saved them. He snatched his hat from his head and trampled it in the mud.

His fit ended as suddenly as it had begun. He took out his spyglass to observe the field. He knew what to do. He dashed through the muck, barged into headquarters, and seized the map. "Send in that platoon they haven't seen. Move this infantry square to their left flank, where they least expect it. Now, as their center starts to turn—and it will—charge from the right with the cavalry."

Barras gave the orders. Clisson pulled out his spyglass to watch the movements unfold. The French forces buckled at the Austrian center. "Stay, you fools! Don't retreat!" he yelled. They couldn't hear him. He vaulted onto the general's horse and rode among the soldiers' ranks, oblivious to shot whizzing by.

"Follow me!" he cried.

Against all odds, the French soldiers did.

Chapter 29

Napoleon

THE EMPEROR HID BEHIND HIS bedroom door, flinching at screams from Albine's quarters. Tobyson's patter signaled hot towels from the kitchen. The cook trudged along, delivering sustaining broth. But what role did the coachman play? No doubt monitoring the progress. Cipriani had camped out in the stables, taking wagers on the exact moment the infant's head would break through.

Where was the damn doctor?

Giving birth was a woman's war to wage. How it took him back to that horrible, wonderful day the Eaglet had been born.

At the Tuileries, there'd been no privacy for Marie Louise. Law, politics, and tradition demanded a dozen witnesses for a future emperor's birth. Around the bed where Marie Louise moaned, noble attendants in court clothes gorged on chocolates. In one corner, scribes prepared proclamations. In another, priests burned incense. All ceremony to prevent the secret swap of a frail royal girl for a lusty peasant boy.

Marie Louise struggled on and on, blood everywhere but in her parchment cheeks. The Emperor—stoic witness to battlefield carnage—vomited behind a screen. He loved his pristine wife then. Surely she loved him, too. If not, how could she bear it?

Finally, when it seemed she would be torn apart, he'd ordered the doctor to save her and let his dynasty die. "For God's sake, use the forceps. Help the poor woman."

His courtiers shrank back in shock.

But at that moment, his perfect Eaglet burst onto the scene. Marie Louise forgotten, his attention fixed on the whimpering babe, on examining fingers, on listening to the heartbeat, on feeling the tongue behind the lips. His heart would never be the same.

His ignored wife, half-dead with exhaustion, never forgave him or the Eaglet. He wondered how she felt about the two illegitimate children she'd had with von Neipperg.

Ah—at last, the doctor's heavy boots tramped through Longwood's corridor. His calm British voice banished Montholon, Marchand, and little Tobyson from Albine's chamber. How scared yet curious Tobyson must have been.

Poor, sweet Albine. She would have been a better woman if she'd lived under better circumstances. The Revolution had ruined her, as it had corrupted his dear Josephine. Alchemists should forget changing lead to gold. They should transmute fear to courage, treachery to loyalty, debauchery to innocence. And God should force a man to suffer his wife's birthing pain.

He retreated to his writing desk.

CLISSON: THE EMPEROR'S NOVEL

Part III: On Destiny Claimed
France's Northeast Border, 1791

Austrians, their forces turned by Clisson's charge, trampled through their campsites in retreat. On the battlefield, smoke hung in the air, scorching Clisson's lungs. Around him, the wounded begged for water. General Barras, neat and clean, rode up on a spotless horse.

"If we'd positioned the artillery earlier, fewer men would have died. And fewer would have been maimed," Clisson told him.

The general took off his glove to grasp Clisson's filthy hand. "Thankfully, this government doesn't demand a tally of soldiers' legs and arms. Well done, *Major.*"

Clisson found his way to the field hospital, searching for one of his sergeants. He had thought when he was eight that the sight of Giovanni's torture had hardened him, but the ditch where they buried limbs turned his stomach inside out. Amélie's first husband's leg stole into his mind. Had they buried it with him or separately?

If Amélie had asked him that day what war was like, he would have said, most of all, it stank. Latrines that smelled like latrines; meat that did not smell like meat. Officers who did not bathe; soldiers who wouldn't if they could. Blood and guts on your shirt, from a man or a horse.

The dead man he never knew who lost a leg, an ideal woman who never really existed: they haunted him still. Amélie. Amélie Rose. Would every battlefield bring her to mind? He tromped to his tent to write to his wife.

Dear Eugénie,

You do not know what we face in battle. Ah, the Sacrifice and the Glory, when life means so little, yet so much. The smoke will never leave my nostrils. Yet the French soldier marches willingly into the fire for his children's future. This revolution has freed them. They need only a great leader to bring the world to its knees before their valor.

I myself rely upon luck. Luck and Destiny. Truly, I believe what a Corsican shepherd foretold: no bullet has been cast with the power to bring me down.

I hope Amélie's companionship will not lead you astray. Did her husband flee to England, as I have heard? These émigrés have absconded with so much of our country's wealth.

Embrace your mother, thank your father. I will buy new boots because of his generosity.

Your loving husband,
Clisson

Albine

I NAMED HER JOSÉPHINE NAPOLÉONE.

She was perfect. A princess. A queen. An empress. I almost drowned in love. For two days, I kept her to myself. She took to nursing, but my milk was slow. Cook brought in a niece to supply what I could not. Jealous, I snatched Joséphine from the woman's teat. I'd been so proud when I gave birth to Tristan. But this! This beautiful new being was Napoleon's daughter.

On the third day, I told Marchand the Emperor could visit at noon. Charles and I set up the chamber. Heavy draperies blocked the sun. A single candle alleviated the darkness. When the door opened, a breeze jittered its flame, casting mysterious shadows. I lay under bedcovers, a still mound, my back to the door, my Joséphine hidden in my arms.

The smell of baby was sure to draw Napoleon in.

He hesitated on my threshold. (The man's instincts were legend.)

When I didn't hear him move, I spoke his name.

He took the step. "Ah, my dear girl, how are you?"

I rolled to face him. Even in candlelight, I looked worn, older, in need of cucumber paste, but fresh motherhood added more than it took. My mirror reflected a Madonna. More than that: a euphoric empress, a triumphal queen.

I peeled back the coverlet to reveal Joséphine. Her round, pink face. The shock of black hair, her eyes squeezed shut. And, beneath the nondescript nose, a heart-shaped mouth with a cleft knob on a pointed chin.

That imprint of his own face should have slammed a cannonball into his chest, but Napoleon grinned. He rushed into the fray, his arms outstretched. His words tumbled over each other. "We must make plans . . . I didn't know . . . didn't think she could be mine. Oh, God, let me hold her." He chuckled at my hesitation. "Come, give the girl to me. I'm an old hand at this sort of thing." He reached for Joséphine.

Charles stepped out of the shadows.

Napoleon

THE EMPEROR SWEPT HIS OUTSTRETCHED hands behind his back. He crushed his fingers together. They were quite a pair, those Montholons, transforming an infant into a trap. No way to tell where the husband ended and the wife began. He watched Albine's face tighten as she looked from Charles to him. Calculating and triumphant until, encountering his rage, her expression melted into dismay.

"Congratulations, Charles," the Emperor said, pleased at his measured tone. "Your daughter's lovely." He offered a hand to shake.

Montholon ignored it.

The Emperor pivoted. Though it rent his heart, he retreated from his little Joséphine.

HE FORBADE MARCHAND TO MENTION the child or the Montholons. But in the following days, when his valet (and Tobyson, too) smelled of sweet baby, envy rooted in the Emperor's heart. He strained to hear her cries. Within a week, he begged Marchand to bring Joséphine to him.

Little Joséphine gurgled when he held her. He'd taken off his jacket so he could feel her warmth on his chest. He filled his nose, his mouth, his lungs, soaking in the baby scent, craving, remembering. Something was missing. The chamomile, he decided. They probably didn't have any on St. Helena. He hummed Joséphine a tune dredged up from his past and whispered stories of his Eaglet. He rocked her while she slept. If he'd been a sculptor, he'd have carved her image to join the Eaglet's bust on the mantelpiece. Instead, he chiseled it into his memory.

Marchand rested his hand on the Emperor's shoulder. His voice grave, he said, "Lowe granted Albine permission to leave for Europe."

He clutched the infant. "When?"

"As soon as she is able."

AS TIME GREW SHORT, MARCHAND urged the Emperor to see Albine before she left. "Sire, it would cost you nothing and mean so much."

The Emperor hid behind a gruff reply. "As you wish. Albine only. Not Charles."

So Marchand formed a cradle on the camp bed where the swaddled infant could safely lie. The valet took the precious bundle from Albine, propped up the blanket barriers, and kissed Joséphine's forehead. Shooing Tobyson before him, he left.

Albine, her blouse loose over a maternal belly, sank in a deep curtsy. "No, no," he said. "You'll injure yourself."

"First, forgive me, Your Majesty." She hung her head. "I reverted to my tricks. You know it's so. I have no . . . no discipline."

"You were in a weakened state." He caressed her curls. "Old faults lie near to the surface, my dear."

"When I saw Joséphine, ambition overtook me. I swear, sire, it was for my—our—daughter. Can you understand?"

From a nearby shelf, the etching of the Eaglet stared at him. She knew he'd look at it, of course. Still, he answered, "I understand."

"I beg you to blame me, not Charles." She laid her wet cheek on his hand and wept.

French girls learned to cry, French boys to resist the tears. Yet, as he always asked himself when granting pardons to family, friends, and enemies, who was he to judge self-interest?

CHARLES, IN A RARE SHOW OF DELICACY, sequestered himself, leaving Napoleon, Albine, and Joséphine three weeks together, eating, laughing, reading—almost a family. While Tobyson and Marchand minded the baby, Albine copied out the *Clisson* manuscript in her sloping script. When the British searched her luggage, she was to say she had written it.

On the last evening, the Emperor joined Albine in the garden. The sun was on the horizon. The clouds raced west, revealing evening stars. The nearer scenery, Albine's eyes, were stormy. He gave her his handkerchief; she blew her nose into it. That prosaic blast of air and the tiny hiccup that followed moved him more than a poem.

He steadied his voice. "You won't forget the words to say to my mother?"

"Chestnuts in the cellar." Albine sniffed.

"She'll be generous to you and little Joséphine Napoléone. Above all, convince her to move to Vienna to be close to the Eaglet. She must be there to free him. Do not fail me."

"I'll do my best, sire." She twisted the handkerchief into a knot.

"And tell Madame Mère she must send my manuscript to my sister Pauline. I'll smuggle her the rest when it's finished."

"Pauline never liked me," Albine whispered. "And your mother wasn't kind."

The hollowness in her voice broke his resolve to be severe. He lifted her chin. "You leave a hole in my heart, Albine. I won't forget you."

"Nor I you." Her laugh broke on a sob. "I'll see you in our daughter's face."

He kissed her knuckles. "No doubt those singular features will win over my mother."

They sat, in the comfort of old companionship, gazing at the stars popping out in the dusky sky.

He sighed. "I wish I could do more for you, my dear."

She touched the cleft knob on his chin. "But you can."

His jaw hardened. Always some new demand.

She pointed. "Do you see that star? The one above the old gum tree? I should like to have it in memory of our times together."

His sight blurred. He couldn't tell which star she meant. "No, I already granted that one to Marchand. You may have the larger, brighter one to the left. It's the best my poor empire has to offer. Share it with little Joséphine." He met her shining eyes. She was a tainted woman, a liar, a thief. No matter. He would miss her desperately.

Chapter 30

Albine

THE NEXT MORNING, SOLOMON DISPATCHED his one-horse
calèche to Longwood House. In pelting rain, the driver and Hercules
strapped on my trunk. The carriage took off for Porteous House Inn,
where we'd await documents to board the HMS *Lady Campbell*. As
we passed the guardhouse, I stuck my head into the rain to catch a
final glimpse of Longwood.

My heart tore. The Emperor's bedroom window framed his
silhouette.

In Jamestown, dear Solomon filled my chamber with mementos,
dried food, and trifles for Joséphine. When I teased I'd never kissed
a man with such a fine, bristly beard, he retorted he'd never known
a lady who wore his hats so well. But to the gold Napoleon coins I
offered to pay my account, he replied, "Dear Madame, no, no, no."

I laid them on his counter. "The Emperor gave them to me
expressly to pay you."

"All the more reason for you to keep them." He bustled off to
help a customer.

In the end, I forced the coins upon him, only to find them
redeposited in my pocket.

From the emporium, I returned to Porteous House to retrieve
Joséphine from a watchful maid. As I strolled toward the ocean, the
baby drew stares. (More rumors than Napoleon realized seeped out
of Longwood House.) I squared my shoulders.

I wanted Joséphine to see St. James Church. Someday she'd
hear the story of St. Helena, and I could tell her she'd been inside

its church. For luck, I rubbed her little hand across the carved oak door. Pushing it open, I peeked inside.

Whitewashed walls, creaking beams, starched cloth on the altar (I cringed, newly appreciating what skill it took to iron). No people.

We slid into the pew I'd shared with Charles. And Tobyson. And Basil. I chatted with Joséphine about her half brother. I practiced explanations of Charles, Napoleon, and Basil. Failing at those, I scattered dust motes in the sunbeams.

When I turned to leave, I cringed against another St. Helena wound. Basil wasn't leaning against the church's doors. He hadn't come to say goodbye.

One last lesson in constancy.

THE FOLLOWING DAY, TO MY DELIGHT, when it came time to transport my trunk, Hercules and Tobyson appeared. The craggy face of a big American and the sweet, knowing eyes of a small African—they were the last and kindest sight of my St. Helena friends. Hercules (who four years before had lifted me from my arrival skiff) lowered me from the island's shore. I reached up to brush Tobyson's fingertips.

British sailors rowed Joséphine and me to the HMS *Lady Campbell*.

At noon, sailors winched in the anchor. Others set the sails. The ship swung to sea. I climbed to the aft deck with Joséphine in my arms to watch the island disappear.

As our sails billowed, a uniformed man rushed under Jamestown's white stone arch and onto the wharf. Waving his arms as we sailed away was Lieutenant Basil Jackson.

Napoleon

WITHOUT ALBINE'S SPICE, THE ENTOURAGE settled into a quieter life. In time, even Marchand reminisced less about little Joséphine Napoléone. "You predicted well, Your Majesty," the valet said, as he guided a fresh shirt over the Emperor's head. "General Montholon seems more content since Albine left. Tobyson, stop playing with the Master's medals."

The Emperor stuck his hands outside the shirt cuffs. "Yes—"

Hellish shrieks came from the hall. The bedroom door flew open. Montholon and Bertrand flung a screaming Cipriani at the Emperor's feet. The Corsican writhed, clutching his throat. His face contorted, his mouth foamed, his wild eyes rolled.

Tobyson cringed in Marchand's arms.

"Franco!" The Emperor sank to the floor. He cupped his friend's ashen face. "Mon Dieu, what's happened?"

Cipriani gripped the Emperor's leg. "Poison."

Montholon slouched against the doorjamb. "Rat poison, to be exact. I hope we've killed the traitor."

Bertrand held out a small sack. "Sire, we caught him dumping arsenic in your wine. That's why you've been so sick. Charles, pick up the culprit. Let's finish him off."

Montholon wrenched Cipriani's arm. The Corsican shrieked. Montholon dragged him to his feet. Cipriani's arm dangled at his side.

"Oh, stop whining." Montholon pulled back Cipriani's head. "Pour in the rest, Bertrand."

Cipriani squirmed loose. His good arm stretched toward the Emperor. "Brother—"

The Emperor clasped his hands behind his back. His gaze slid from the Corsican's plea to the confusion on Marchand's face. They'd never understand his poisoning himself. A woman's ploy. Europe would laugh. The Eaglet would be ashamed.

Bertrand locked the bedroom door. "Let's do it, Montholon."

Cipriani's legs buckled. "Tell them, *o amicu*. They don't believe me." He coughed up on the floor. "He knew. I tell you, he knew."

Bertrand raised the arsenic bag. "Right—of course he did. Eat the rest, you coward."

Cipriani shielded his mouth. "Speak, brother. For God's sake, someone have mercy."

Tobyson reached out a hand. Marchand snatched it back.

The Emperor opened his mouth. Shame stopped his words.

"You deny me?" the Corsican howled. "For what, brother? For what?"

For what? The Emperor focused. For the prestige that held this petty court together? For the son he'd never see? For the little dignity he had left? By God, no. He was better than that.

He knocked the sack from Bertrand's hand. "Let him go. Let him go, I say. Quick, Marchand. Get that emetic the doctor left. If he throws up right away, we can save him. Tobyson, run for Hercules. Marchand needs his help. Not now, Montholon. I'll explain later. Here, Marchand, help me get him to the bath."

Marchand didn't move. His arms held Tobyson in place.

"Marchand?" the Emperor said. "That's an order."

The valet looked at the floor, his face pitted stone.

"Marchand, I tell you, I did it to myself. Cipriani didn't poison me. I did it. Let the boy go. We must help Cipriani while we still can. Don't die, don't die, Franco. Please, Marchand."

Tobyson shook Marchand. "Monsieur, Monsieur."

The valet flushed. He helped the Emperor drag the Corsican into the bathroom. They draped him over the edge of the tub and rinsed the arsenic from his blistering mouth.

"I'm sorry," the Emperor whispered to his valet.

Marchand gave him a look as raw as a lover's. "I would have talked you out of it."

"That's why I didn't tell you." His stomach twisted at his shame.

Tobyson scampered in. Hercules followed, filling the small room.

Between them, the valet and the gardener reset Cipriani's dislocated shoulder, poured emetic down his throat, and rinsed his mouth clean of arsenic after every vomit. Tobyson fetched towels and water.

The Emperor pressed himself into a corner. When it came time to clean the Corsican's bowels, he fled. It was easier to confront his generals.

Bertrand stood at the fireplace, rehearsing a speech. The general broke off, frowned, and began again. "Sire, although Montholon and I may bicker, we are united in devotion. We would not have let you follow this disastrous course. The swelling in your legs, the daylight hours you sleep! Thank God we discovered this before it was too late."

The Emperor interrupted. "Yes, yes, the two of you once stopped me from dying in battle. After these years on St. Helena, I won't thank you for that. But you think this poisoning was the suicide of a desperate man? No, it was a careful tactic, designed to end our exile. Has it gone awry? Admittedly. That damned governor won't act, no matter how sick I get."

"You might have told us," Montholon said.

"Yes, I might have, if past reversals hadn't destroyed my trust."

Bertrand's hand flew to where his sword hilt should have been. "In us, Your Majesty? That is an intolerable insult."

"No, Bertrand, not in you."

"In me." Montholon came forward. "You believed Cipriani was your friend, but he was not. Not if he helped in this wild scheme. Sometimes I may not seem . . . do not behave as if I were, but, on my honor, Your Majesty, I am your friend."

To the Emperor's relief, Marchand came in, his long face somber. "Hercules and Tobyson are with Cipriani. If he makes it through the night, he should recover."

The Emperor clapped him on the shoulder. "Thank God and your efforts, my friend. Now, shall we settle this affair? I've devised a tale to our advantage, one that none of us must breach. Not now, not after my death, do you hear? Cipriani shall die tonight of a fever. No, Marchand, he won't really die, God willing. We must put it out that he has one of those contagious fevers prevalent on this hellish island. And in the morning Hercules will throw his corrupted body into the sea."

Montholon spoke over his knuckles. "So the Corsican disappears? What then?"

"Then? He'll hide in Hercules's hut until he's well enough to move to a safe contact on the island. At first opportunity, he'll stow away for Europe."

"That is more than the blackguard deserves," Bertrand said.

"Who's the contact?" Montholon asked.

"As much as I may trust you, that's a secret I'm not free to divulge." He struggled onto his painful feet. "Onward, yes? Together, yes?"

Afterward, alone in his room, his hands shook. He dropped into a chair and crammed them under his thighs. Order had been pulled out of chaos, the generals satisfied, Marchand pacified. Trivial accomplishments. Cipriani on the mend. That was more important.

But his hesitation, his primal urge to save himself, seared his soul. All his life, he'd been exposed to traitors. Their insidious infection had corrupted his own loyalty.

He yearned for a hot bath to cleanse the shame from his pores.

For the comfort of Albine's arms. No, not for her. She, too, was a traitor.

For his son. He tucked the etching of the Eaglet under his arm. He'd spend the night watching over Cipriani. He'd read to his old friend what he'd written about old times.

CLISSON: THE EMPEROR'S NOVEL

France's Northeast Border, 1791

One victory was not enough to end the invasion. Austrian rein-
forcements massed along the border. The French troops made
ready for battle.

Outside their tent, Major Clisson clasped hands with Lieutenants Berville and Des Mazis. Des Mazis forced a grin. "I'll
come out of this fight a captain," he said. "If not, send me home
to be a farmer."

They rushed into the battle fire. Smoke clouded the air.
By afternoon the fighting was too dense for bullets, much less
artillery. Uniforms all looked the same. Blue and red and white
and blood. Faces grimaced, showing teeth. Mouths cried in
anguish, felt or feared. Swords slashed, clanged against one
another, sliced through flesh like the butcher's cleaver.

Des Mazis pushed forward, swinging his saber. Through
battle grit, he grinned at Clisson. He'd lost his hat, his hair was
scorched, his cheek bled.

From Clisson's left, a sword swooped down, death gleaming
on its edge.

Horror flooded Clisson's chest.

Des Mazis lunged in. His neck buckled under the blade.
He tumbled into Clisson's arms, his blood spurting on Clisson's
face. "Go," Des Mazis rasped. "Forward."

The Austrian soldier, yelling through missing teeth, came at
Clisson. Berville jumped into the breach. He rammed his sword
into the man's chest. The Austrian crumbled to the ground. Des
Mazis's body slipped from Clisson's hold.

Clisson met Berville's eyes. Hate shone from the face of the friend who had saved his life. Berville roared away, his knife slicing the nearest Austrian.

Clisson stared down on lifeless Des Mazis.

Pain erupted. From his leg, a bloody fountain sprayed. Bone gleamed white between open mounds of flesh. An Austrian bayonet stuck in his thigh. It looked like someone else's leg. Clisson collapsed onto Des Mazis.

When he awoke, Clisson lay on a table. Screams filled his ears. Some of them were his. He struggled to rise, but his arms were bound, his chest strapped to the table. A doctor held a bloody saw.

Clisson screamed. Berville appeared. "Stop them, stop them," Clisson begged. "Berville, don't let them amputate, don't let them cut me. Get me out of here."

Berville raised his bloody bayonet. Clisson shrank against the table. Berville cut the straps and swooped Clisson into his arms.

"He'll die," the doctor hollered. "Bring him here the moment that damn leg stinks."

Clisson fainted from searing pain.

Clisson woke with a scream. His leg was aflame.

Berville poured something on it. "Yell all you like," he said. "I agree. It's a crying waste of good brandy."

General Barras leaned over. "It's gone to a good cause: cleansing your wound. Wrap the leg tightly, Berville. The cut doesn't look all that bad. You'll do, my boy."

Clisson gulped, bit his lip, and nodded.

"Get well so that you may be useful to your nation. Take care of him, Berville." The general ducked out of the tent.

Berville emptied the brandy bottle into his own mouth.

Napoleon

IN THE MORNING, THE CORSICAN still hypersalivated. His throat was raw, his mouth blistered. "So, I'm to die," he croaked. "And reappear."

The Emperor kissed him on both cheeks. "Rome first, Austria next, then Corsica. Get my mother's help. Teach my Eaglet what I cannot." His gaze wandered. "Close call yesterday."

Cipriani lay back on the pillow. "Worth it if it gets me off this damn island."

Hercules wrapped the Corsican in a sheet. In the garden, Marchand burned the mattress. The guards tied kerchiefs over their faces to protect against the infected smoke. They kept their distance when Hercules hobbled off, the lifeless body slung over a shoulder.

Within an hour, Hudson Lowe pounded on Longwood's door. As Bertrand answered it, Napoleon eavesdropped from the hall.

"What? What? That shifty Corsican's dead? What right have you to dispose of his body before we've examined it?"

"Have you had this fever?" Bertrand asked. "Do you think it wise to be here?"

The Emperor strolled into the reception room. He pulled up short at the sight of the governor, leaning on a chair back. "Sir Hudson, brave of you to come. But I wouldn't touch anything. Yesterday, poor Cipriani played solitaire at that very spot."

Sir Hudson yanked his hands off the chair. "I don't believe a word of this faradiddle. Unless I have proof—"

"Marchand!" the Emperor called.

The valet appeared, wiping his hands on an apron.

"Show the governor my bath."

"But, sire, the mess."

"Exactly. The governor desires to see, perhaps to smell, the mess, as you put it." He turned to the governor. "I don't advise you to get close to my valet. He nursed the patient."

"Pooh," said the governor. He followed Marchand down the hall.

Bertrand and Napoleon waited.

The governor bolted past them and out the front door. His carriage drove off at a gallop.

The Emperor sighed. "If everything were so easy, Bertrand, we'd long ago have been back in France. Why am I so weary? Perhaps I have that fever Cipriani caught."

Bertrand bowed. "You jest, sire."

"Do I, Bertrand? Yet it would be a miracle if he hadn't infected me."

Chapter 34

Albine

FROM THE HOUR ST. HELENA's dark cliffs disappeared from view, Joséphine refused to suckle. In calm seas and in rough, below deck in our cramped cabin or topside in the breeze, swaddled or unswaddled, rocked or still, if awake, she cried. If asleep, she moaned. Since she refused my breast, I dipped a finger in my milk. I tried a milk-soaked cloth. A sailor milked the ship's goat to tempt her. She refused it all.

The captain—a family man with a brood of his own—suggested brandy. Joséphine spat it up. He thought a man's touch might soothe her. When he cooed, Joséphine shrieked. I implored him to return the ship to St. Helena.

"Madame, we have orders," he said. "My crew wouldn't change course if I were dying."

Dying? Until he said the word, I hadn't thought it. The endless gray sea became a prison. I made my way to the ship's galley, where I stuffed my pockets with crackers.

I hoped Joséphine had only the colic. Or distress at the change of environment. She didn't have a fever or a rash. She was a hardy infant, I told myself. She would adjust.

At last, she sucked, but like a beggar afraid to take too much. Afterward, she slept more (to the relief of the crew). Though her cries persisted, they sounded less inconsolable. Day by day, she became increasingly frail, until I feared she'd crumple in my hands. Her skin acquired a gray undercast. Her tiny Napoleonic chin grew as pointed as a stick.

I damned myself for leaving St. Helena. Worry (then panic) became my new constancy.

After five weeks at sea, Tenerife's volcano loomed in the distance. I rejoiced. My plan was to disembark on this, the largest of the Canary Islands, find a doctor, and stay there a year or more, until Joséphine grew strong enough to travel. If I ran out of money, I'd take in wash. I'd sell my diamond, my body, my soul to feed her.

"No, Madame." The captain stroked his beard. "Orders, you know. I'm to deliver you from St. Helena to Portsmouth. No land in between."

"But my baby—"

"No, Madame. They'd bust me to a sailor." He walked away (but not unkindly) to oversee the dropping of the anchor. We stayed a week in the shadow of the volcano while the ship was provisioned and the crew granted shore leave. I prayed over my gaunt baby till my knees bled on the rough pine deck.

Courtesy of the captain, the last longboat to return from Tenerife brought a ewe. From the first, Joséphine took to sheep's milk. Although her weight didn't increase, it stabilized. She smiled again. So did I. So did the captain.

But oh, the storms we weathered. Through wind, wave, lightning, and thunder, I huddled in our cabin, crawling out in search of food, which I promptly vomited up. Two weeks later, as England came into view, the winds died, becalming us, stretching out our interminable voyage.

At last, we docked at Portsmouth. I barely had the strength to dress. My trunk was lowered to the wharf, my crying baby swaddled heart to heart against my chest. I kissed the captain, doled out coins to the crew, and in feeble triumph placed my foot on England's stable ground.

On the wharf, a swarm of soldiers snapped to attention. From their midst, an officer in a smartly tailored uniform stepped forward. My knees buckled.

Lieutenant Basil Jackson.

Napoleon

AT LONGWOOD, EVERY AFTERNOON the winds came, carrying dust. Even without Cipriani's arsenic-laced wine, the Emperor's legs remained swollen, his feet sore, and his stomach distended. Though Solomon sent carts packed with lamb, chickens, fragrant cheeses, sweet wine, and fancy cakes, the Emperor consumed little. He watched others savor what he couldn't. He wished Betsy were there to enjoy the cakes.

When he found Marchand stuffing paper between the window jambs, he shuffled up behind him. "What is this nonsense?"

The valet jumped like a thief. "To keep out the dust, Your Majesty."

"With precious paper?" The Emperor pulled it from the casement. "Come, man, what's the use? The dust will make its way around the door."

Marchand lowered his chin.

"Ah, try to smile. I like you better when you're cheerful." The Emperor patted his arm. "Did the traps catch any rats today? I don't want a bitten finger like poor Hercules."

"No, sire, that's why the boy sleeps on your floor."

"To be bitten instead of me?"

Marchand bowed. "It would be an honor for Tobyson."

"I doubt he'd think so. Well, yes, he would, but not until he was much older and I was long dead. Then he'd tell the story over an ale at the tavern until his friends were sick of it. He'd show the scar and brag he'd saved the French empire from being consumed by rats. Yet that is what is happening, my friend. The rats of London and their minion rat, Hudson Lowe, are consuming me day by dusty day. Light the fire. Everything is damp."

The Emperor lay on the couch with a book. He'd read *Young Werther* again. It was short, and he'd always loved its romance. He didn't want to fall asleep over Tacitus or get riled up over *Le*

Moniteur's latest analysis of Waterloo. Yesterday he had done both. He had no energy to write the end of his book.

Hours later, he awoke, spitting dust that had gathered in his open mouth. Sir Hudson Lowe's voice came from the hall. Marchand slipped in, offering the Emperor his green uniform jacket. "In case you have to meet him."

The Emperor waved him off. "I vowed not to."

They listened as the argument grew angrier. Bertrand's protests followed Sir Hudson Lowe's demands. "No, you'll not enter. Your guards' reports are proof he's here."

Sir Hudson's voice cracked. "How do I know it's not some impostor you have in there?"

"You have my word, sir."

"Your word? Why, you'd say anything for him."

"No, sir. I'm a man of honor, but I'll protect his dignity with my life."

"Bravo, Bertrand," the Emperor said. "My privacy is my last possession. Without it, I'm nothing. Yes, I'd better put on the jacket. And load my dueling pistols."

Marchand's hands shook.

"What? Afraid?" The Emperor clasped the valet's shoulder. "My friend, you of all of us will go to Heaven."

Bertrand knocked on the door. "Sire, Lowe threatens to get soldiers from the Fifty-Third to break down your door."

"Come in, come in." The Emperor embraced Bertrand. "You, my general, deserve another medal."

Bertrand's jaw tightened. "The man wants to break us into little pieces, to destroy the memory of who we were."

The Emperor touched the scar on Bertrand's chin. "Prepared to see this to the end?"

"Yes. If our time has come, let it be. The enemy returns. No, wait. Not the enemy. It's Montholon, with your page and gardener."

Charles carried his bare sword. He dropped to one knee. "At your service, sire."

The Emperor laid his hand on Montholon's bowed head. He saluted Tobyson and Hercules. "Soldiers, listen. We shall strive to avoid your sacrifice. Hercules, out of sight unless you're needed. The British won't take kindly to your switching sides. Marchand, to the front door. When Sir Hudson returns, tell him I'm armed. If they break down my door, they must shoot me. If they take away my pistols, I'll fight them hand to hand. If they kill me and my valiant protectors, we'll die in glory while he and the Fifty-Third shall forever besmirch their honor. If that message doesn't convince him I'm here, nothing will. Tobyson will translate so the soldiers understand what's said."

Tobyson stood as tall as he was able.

The Emperor smiled. "You'll speak loud and clear, won't you, brave child?"

The boy saluted.

The Emperor locked his door. He positioned a chair in the center of the room. He put on his bicorne, nodded to himself in the mirror, and picked up his loaded pistols. His stomach felt better than it had in months, although the old wound on his calf twitched. He regretted not having written that last chapter for his son.

Muffled voices came through the door. He couldn't make out what was happening without leaving his chair. Better to remain at his post.

Twenty-five years earlier, at Arcole, he'd picked up a tattered battle flag and led French troops onto a bridge. Soldiers had died around him, some to save his life. Musket fire, cannonballs, grape-shot—all had flown past him in battle after battle. In Jaffa, he'd comforted plague-stricken soldiers when no one else would touch them. At times, a third of his army died of disease while he himself stayed strong. But the Corsican shepherd's prediction had come true. Hudson Lowe was the fly who could do him in. He pointed a pistol at the door.

As his mother liked to say, God owed him nothing.

Still, this tawdry finale tasted sour, stank of defeat.

Outside the door, his little army cheered.

So. He'd made it across the bridge again.

He put aside his pistols and opened his door.

Sir Hudson Lowe, standing on the other side, raised a naked sword.

The Emperor recoiled.

Tobyson barreled in, stripping the weapon from the governor's hand. The steel clattered onto the floor.

Lowe flung the little boy against a wall. "I'll have you whipped."

The Emperor stalked forward. "You're not whipping anyone, Lowe. You're a worm to that boy's lion."

Lowe held his ground. "I, sir, am a gentleman. That boy—"

"Once again with the 'gentleman' rubbish. Who cares who your father or great-grandfather was?" The Emperor knelt at Tobyson's side. "In the French army, this boy would be a general, whereas you'd be drummed from the ranks. Are you all right, son?" The Emperor helped Tobyson to his feet. "Where are your soldiers, Lowe? Why did you attack me with that sword?"

"I wasn't attacking. I was saluting—for all the good it did." The governor scrambled to retrieve his weapon.

Tobyson saluted the Emperor. "Sir! The colonel from the Fifty-Third told the governor that 'they would guard General Bonaparte, they would pursue him if he escaped, and they would protect his person from intruders, but without orders from a more senior authority, they declined to attack him.'" He clicked his heels. "Sir!"

"Bravo!" The Emperor clapped the child on his shoulder.

"We were all laughing, Master," Tobyson said. "That's when the governor pushed past us into the house."

The Emperor surveyed the governor. "You had the courage to attack alone? You do surprise me, Lowe. But now you have seen me for the last time. We shall never speak again. Show him out, Bertrand."

Bertrand escorted him to the door. On the lawn, the British guard mingled in disarray. Bertrand, responding to the governor's silent plea, stepped onto the porch. The soldiers snapped to attention. As the governor came out, Bertrand bowed. The governor returned his bow and descended the steps, barking orders to his troops as Bertrand strolled inside.

The Emperor nodded approval. "Magnanimous, Bertrand. If not the man, respect the military order. In my life, I have seen thousands die. Many were dear friends. Many left this earth calling my name." He examined Bertrand, Marchand, Montholon, Tobyson, and Hercules, who had reappeared from his hiding place. "Gentlemen, I am through with that."

CLISSON: THE EMPEROR'S NOVEL

France's Northeast Border, 1791

In three days, Clisson's fever was gone. The Austrians had retreated. Clisson, although weak, could change his wound's dressing himself. He gritted his teeth against the pain. Alexander the Great, too, had had a blow to the thigh, but Plutarch said it hurt him not. Clisson would be no less of a man.

Berville, questioned about his pedigree by the citizens' committee, filled his knapsack. "General Barras says to make myself scarce. And no, I don't need to hide out at your wife's."

"But you must go to her," Clisson said. "Eugénie will never believe I'm not dying."

"Mon Dieu." Berville let his knapsack fall. "Can you talk about anything other than that woman? You have no idea how much I miss Des Mazis."

Clisson fell silent.

Berville bustled around the tent, gathering more gear. Now and then he glanced at Clisson's hangdog eyes. "All right," he finally said. "I'll go to Champvert and reassure your precious love that her hero lives."

"Hoorah!" Clisson grinned. "I swear you won't regret it. Besides, with the Revolution going on, you're not safe in Paris. Let me finish this letter."

Dear Eugénie,

I send this by Berville's hand so you will know, though wounded, I survive intact. When our friend Des Mazis lost his life protecting me, Berville guarded me from further danger.

You feared what war would do to me. Indeed, I will not change, yet how can a man forget what he has seen, what his nostrils have smelled, what his mouth has tasted, what pain has racked his soul?

I honor Berville as you would my brother, for such he truly is. Treat him tenderly, love him for his valor. He, like Des Mazis, saved my life.

Dreams of you speed my recovery.
Adieu, my tender love.
Clisson

Clisson and Berville clasped hands. Suddenly, they were in each other's arms.

"Swift journey," Clisson whispered over a knot in his throat. The tent flap closed behind Berville.

Clisson, under a tarpaulin that held three cots, stood alone, as empty as the tent. He limped to Des Mazis's corner and pulled his dead friend's knapsack from underneath the bed. Upending it, he shook out the contents. A clean shirt, some underthings, extra uniform pants. Letters from his mother. A folded page torn from a book: *Plutarch's Lives*. His own, judging by the margin notes in Clisson's messy hand. The text was Julius Caesar. Where the chapter ended, ten-year-old Clisson had scribbled, *I will conquer more than you.* Below Clisson's childish scrawl, an older Des Mazis had penned, *Let me tag along.*

How long ago had Des Mazis written that note? When had he, in embarrassment, ripped out the page? When had Des Mazis become more acolyte than friend?

Death was the final right of every soul. Why had it not come to him on the battlefield, as it had to Des Mazis? A man of more courage than talent, his friend had gone to his end willingly, sentencing Clisson to live.

No more would Des Mazis's gentle patience make peace between him and Berville. Des Mazis had shown himself a man at the end, for which Clisson's chest swelled in gratitude. Yet to have lived small, like Des Mazis, without glory, without issue, without leaving a trace, was to have not lived at all.

Chapter 32

Albine

As Basil half carried me across the wharf, Joséphine's cries gave voice to my internal scream. When my weak knees wouldn't lift me, he boosted me into the coach. Soldiers strapped my trunk to its rear (which made me yearn for Hercules to rescue me). Basil jumped in beside me. I couldn't read his familiar, almost handsome face. "Where are we going?"

He pointed at an open slot, through which he issued orders to the coachman. The carriage lurched, the horses plodded, six soldiers marched on each side. Basil closed the slot. "You're safe, my love," he said.

I whispered. "My baby?"

"As long as you trust me, she's safe, too." Basil peeked inside the blanket.

The rocking of the carriage had quieted her, or perhaps it had been the drumming of my heart. She gurgled. His grimace set my teeth chattering. But, as I took in his pressed uniform, his polished medals, his square chin, I yearned to trust this solid man. "How did you get here?"

"I left St. Helena three days after you. Your ship had orders to lay over in Tenerife. Mine sailed directly here." He flicked my nose.

At his fond gesture, I drew closer. "Can you get a doctor for Joséphine? She's been ill."

"Soon. But I warn you, I won't be the one searching your luggage. Tell me now, what's not on Sir Hudson's bill of lading?"

Prescient Napoleon. He had made me memorize the information for his mother, made sure the *Clisson* manuscript was written in my hand. But Basil would expect contraband. I wet my lips. "I didn't tell Sir Hudson about three gold Napoleon coins. And a tiny silver spoon with an 'N' insignia, a snuffbox with his portrait on it, a handkerchief of his. They're sewn into my skirt so no one can steal them."

Basil gripped my elbow. "What else?"

I resisted the bread crust in my pocket. (He'd read my need as guilt.) "Everything else is mine. Napoleon has more reliable couriers than I ever was."

His grip tightened. "A lie will lose you the child."

I clutched Joséphine. "You'll find a manuscript I wrote. Just a silly novel—I never told you about it. And a tiny straw box Tobyson's father gave me, but nothing's inside it. They're on the manifest, but maybe someone will question them."

"You're sure? We're almost at the inn."

"How can I know what you might misinterpret? A jar of dried flowers . . . Do you care about that?" I cuddled little Joséphine. "Listen, I'm not going to endanger my baby, not for Napoleon, not for Charles, not for money, not for you."

"Fair enough." He gave a half smile. "What messages do you carry in your head?"

I covered my start with a kiss on Joséphine's nose. "How much farther? The carriage is making her sick."

He let it go. A flush spread to my cheeks. He still loved me.

THE INN WAS A SHABBY AFFAIR, sour from spilt beer. Basil engaged a parlor. The two leering men who pawed through my belongings were jailbirds, if not in their past, then in their future. They brought along a midwife to probe my body inside and out. (If not for Joséphine, I would have kicked out the wretch's last few teeth.)

They found nothing.

As I repacked my trunk, Basil (all smiles) dismissed the soldiers and examiners. He sent a boy to fetch a doctor. To demonstrate my domesticity, I suckled Joséphine. She rejected what I had to offer, though I concealed that from Basil.

When I ended the feeding charade, he went down on one knee, saying, "I'll make you happy, if you'll let me."

I had trouble envisioning that. Joséphine's health came first, Napoleon's mission to Madame Mère second. Basil, although enticing, must wait his turn. As I searched his naive face, guilt assailed me. "My dear friend, this isn't St. Helena, where such relationships are tolerated. Joséphine Napoléone and I, we'll ruin you."

He caressed my cheek. "We won't stay in England. Indeed, the government won't allow it. I'm to take you to Brussels. But first, here's the doctor."

At Basil's words, a none-too-clean, black-suited man entered our parlor. He clunked down a worn leather bag. "Dr. Greenwald," he said, as though testing the syllables for the first time. "Where's this baby I hear about?"

Eyeing the doctor's bag, which was large enough to transport my child, I unswaddled Joséphine.

"Dab of a thing." Greenwald chuckled. "Give her a tug on those hearty tits of yours, why don't you?" He pinched and prodded until Joséphine screamed. "Lungs strong enough. Child's fit to travel." He swiped a finger in her mouth.

I seized his sausage finger and twisted. "What did you give her?"

"Yow." He rubbed his finger. "Call it a prophylactic, if you know what I mean."

Basil hurried the doctor out the door.

"Who asked him about travel, anyway?" I wrapped my frail girl in her linen. "Joséphine and I are staying put until she's stronger. Can you find us a clean, quiet place? Not too expensive?"

"My dear Albine." Basil drew a sheet of paper from his jacket. "I would do anything to make you happy, but . . ." He smoothed the paper on the table.

I shook my head. "Beyond my English vocabulary. Read it to me."

"It's orders. We must board the packet to Belgium this evening."

"And if I refuse?"

"Don't, my love." His voice quavered. "Don't make me take the baby."

Napoleon

TAP, TAP. SCRATCH. TAP, TAP.

"Master—"

The Emperor's hand covered Tobyson's mouth.

Tap, tap. Scratch. Tap, tap.

There was no moonlight to outline the palm the Emperor expected to see pressed to his window. "It's Cipriani. Let him in before a guard catches him. Be a brave soldier."

As Cipriani swung himself over the windowsill, Tobyson backed into the Emperor's hug. The Corsican, lifting the bicorne from its shelf, plopped it on his head and settled into the Emperor's favorite chair.

The Emperor cupped Tobyson's chin. "Just an old friend playing games. Sit outside the door while I visit with this amusing fellow."

Tobyson, casting Cipriani a resentful glance, crept from the room.

"Put down my hat," the Emperor hissed.

"And here I thought you'd be happy to see me." Cipriani dropped the bicorne on the table. "Submarine's sitting off the horizon. We go tomorrow night."

"Ah, welcome news, indeed. One more adventure, eh?" The Emperor pressed his hand over Cipriani's heart. "Together at the start."

"Together at the finish." Cipriani removed the Emperor's hand from his chest and crawled out the half-open window.

Late the next night, Marchand, weeping silently, moved around the moonlit room, handing the Emperor his shirt, helping him pull on the white knee breeches they had darkened with tea, smoothing the green chasseur's jacket across his Master's shoulders. He tucked the oilcloth sack containing the manuscript and the etching of the Eaglet into a large pocket in the jacket's lining.

The Emperor tugged Hercules's knit hat over his ears. For the first time in decades, he was leaving the bicorne behind. His hand caressed its rough leather. Ah, well, wherever he ended up, they'd make him a new one.

Cipriani's dark form appeared in the doorway.

The Emperor grasped Marchand's trembling shoulders. "Remember, be the first to raise the alarm. Act frantic. Someone's kidnapped me. Search for a ransom note. Later, when it's over, give Tobyson my spyglass." As tears blurred his sight, he kissed Marchand and Tobyson on both of their cheeks. "Au revoir, my Chand-Chand. Au revoir, my son. We go, Cipriani."

Outside, they hid in shadows, avoiding the guards. When they reached the fence, the Emperor leaned against it. He jumped at the wood's creak. Cipriani yanked him to the ground.

A sergeant stepped out of the guardhouse.

The Emperor's warm breath rose in the moist air. He waved to disperse the cloud. Cipriani grabbed his hand and shook his head. Minutes passed.

Hercules emerged from his shed, called to the sergeant, and sauntered through his neatly planted rows, laughing, jesting, pointing at guards lazing on a bench. Under the cover of his noise, Cipriani and the Emperor reached the stone wall, where wood boxes improvised a ladder. The Emperor scrambled over. On the other side, Cipriani's wiry arms caught him midfall. They raced across the open road, into the bushes.

"Holding up all right, Master? Got to walk from here."

The Emperor nodded, damning the weakness arsenic had left in its wake. At least he'd learned to ignore the stitch in his side.

"Don't you worry. Mostly downhill." Cipriani's eyes shone like a girl's at her first dress party. "That was the tricky part. Pretty nice work, if you ask me, which you didn't."

The knots in the Emperor's calves loosened as they walked the ridge to the Valley of the Geraniums. He wondered how Toby was doing with the Balcombes in Australia. Beyond that point, the path twisted through a valley, over a hill, behind a house where a bull snorted as they crossed his field. When the path disappeared, they trudged through brush.

"Stop. Rest." The Emperor flushed. His voice had come out weak as a child's.

"No time now. The beach's not much farther." Cipriani took his arm.

They marched on. The slope leveled out; the thick foliage turned to low brush. The wind blew salt grit against his skin.

Behind them, something moved on the path.

The Corsican's hand clamped over the Emperor's mouth.

Cipriani's blade caught starlight.

The large thing on the path stepped closer.

Cipriani pushed the Emperor facedown on the ground and bent over him.

Hercules appeared out of the darkness. "Master? Trouble ahead. Damn me, I can't speak your French. Put the knife away, brother, or I'll break your arm."

The Emperor pushed Cipriani off his back. "What's he saying? I can't get all of it."

The Corsican waved his knife at the gardener.

Hercules spoke slowly. "No good. Don't go."

The Emperor bolted to his feet. "Mon Dieu, even I understand that."

Hercules gave a lopsided grin. "Go home."

"Why trust him?" Cipriani frowned. "The beach is just ahead. I say we go for it."

The Emperor searched Hercules's face. "He knows something. Ask him."

A voice called from the beach. "Eh, you got him? Cipriani?"

Cipriani tugged the Emperor's arm. "This way."

Hercules seized his other arm. "Solomon says no. Says it's a trap."

The Emperor shook off Cipriani. "'Solomon says no.' That I understand. What else did Hercules say, Franco?"

"Tell that giant to let us go." Cipriani's knife pricked the back of the Emperor's neck.

The Emperor flinched. "What's this?"

"Ah, surprised, my boy? Let's just say I've had enough of calling you Master."

"I never asked you to call me that." The Emperor flinched as the knife pierced his skin. Blood trickled to his collar. His fingers crawled up his jacket toward his chest.

"Nah, but you always thought you'd earned it. And maybe you had until your precious generals poisoned me. Think I didn't read your face that night? Think I don't remember, eh?" Cipriani jammed his thumb into the Emperor's kidney. "Tell your friend to let us go."

"For what, Franco?"

"You got balls to ask. What do you think? I've got a fortune riding on your ransom."

A cannon fired an alert from Lookout Point, far above them.

Another answered from the hills above Jamestown.

Cries came from the beach.

Hercules snatched Cipriani's knife hand. Cipriani cursed.

The Emperor's fingers found his pocket. He flicked open his stiletto.

Nearby, oars splashed as a boat rowed from the shore.

In the tangled mass of Hercules and Cipriani, the Emperor couldn't tell who was who. He couldn't pick out the Corsican's knife. Lanterns marched on the roads above as soldiers fanned out. They'd be there soon.

He saw an opening and drove his blade into Cipriani's chest, into the spot where, since they were boys, he'd laid his open palm.

The Corsican collapsed.

The Emperor caught his friend. He tasted Cipriani's blood.

Cipriani shuddered and went limp.

Hercules tugged Cipriani out of his arms and let the body fall. "Come on. Now."

The Emperor pantomimed carrying Cipriani.

"No," the big man said.

"Yes."

A third cannon fired its alarm.

Hercules threw Cipriani over a shoulder and took off uphill in limping strides.

The Emperor followed, fear driving his feet when his breath fell short. Before him, above him on the path, Cipriani's long arms dangled, his head bouncing against the giant's back. Halfway to the top, the Emperor fell to his knees, panting. "Stop. Stop. You're killing me."

Hercules took one glance at him, another at the soldiers' lanterns streaming down the hills. He concealed the body under brush while the Emperor caught his breath. The big man pointed to his chest, then to the hiding place. "Tomorrow." Hercules stooped, offering his back. "Climb up."

The Emperor hesitated.

Hercules mimicked a hangman's noose.

The Emperor climbed on.

Despite the weight upon his back, despite his uneven gait, Hercules moved silently and swiftly. With the big man supporting his thighs, the Emperor concentrated his strength in his arms, wrapping them over the solid shoulders to secure himself without choking the man. He patted Hercules's chest as he might a horse's neck, but unlike those horses he'd had shot beneath him in battle, this fellow knew the risks he took.

"Thank you, my friend," he whispered into the rough jacket that scraped his cheek. His legs hung where the Corsican's arms had dangled, his stomach pressed where his friend's head had bounced. Cipriani's blood stuck to his clothes.

This American who carried him had saved him. The Corsican who had been more than a brother had betrayed him. He who had conquered Europe couldn't distinguish foe from friend. Friend? The word crushed the breath from his lungs. He had none now. Had he ever?

He tilted his face to the moonless sky. Did the Eaglet think of him when he looked at those stars? "Forgive me, son," he mouthed. "Forgive me, Franco. I failed you both." Randall's face flickered in his memory. "Ah, yes, you, too." Parades of soldiers passed before his eyes.

In less time than it had taken to descend into the valley, Hercules returned him to the upper road. In the near distance, soldiers marched to a sergeant's ringing commands. Across the ridge, a carriage light swayed as horses raced toward Longwood.

The Emperor passed through the hedge to where Hercules's shed leaned against the fence. The big man pried off the planks. They hurried through the shed into the garden, and, creeping low, approached the kitchen. The door was unlocked. The Emperor turned. Hercules was gone.

Chapter 33

Albine

BASIL AND I FACED OFF over the parlor table where he'd laid the orders banishing me from England. "No more questions," he said. "We'll miss the ferry."

"No more ships for my baby until she's stronger," I pleaded. "I have safe passage. Read my papers. Hudson Lowe signed them. They're as lawful as yours."

"They promise safe passage to England, not permission to stay. Hudson Lowe tricked you." Basil gathered my belongings. "Look, I'm not an emperor. I can't give you power or riches, but I promise to take care of you and the baby. I'll reunite you with Tristan. Give you a peaceful home, a good night's sleep."

So many kinds of prisons . . . My hand searched out the bread in my pocket. "But you want to be married. I already am."

Basil freed my fist from its hiding place. He unfolded my fingers and brushed the crumbs from my palm. "When your husband returns, we'll buy you a divorce. Until then, we'll live as man and wife, no one the wiser. It wouldn't do in England, but on the continent, such arrangements are common. I love you. And, unlike you, my girl, I don't lie."

I jammed my hand back in my pocket. "Napoleon asked me to go to Rome to see his mother. She's blind, getting on in years. He wants me to assure her he's all right, despite the rumors about his health. An innocent visit."

"Innocent?"

"Except he wants to tell her he's well, which he's not. Will you take me to her when Joséphine Napoléone is healthy?"

He dumped my things in a sack. He had his back to me. "Yes, someday. Not right away. When it's safe for you and the baby, if you still want to go." He turned and held out his hands. "We can't miss the ship."

Something was wrong—I was sure of that. I swaddled Joséphine to my chest and strolled to the door, as though content to leave. Instead, I locked it and dropped the key in my pocket, among my precious crumbs. "I am the wife of a superb liar," I said. "I was mistress to the best liar of them all."

Basil collapsed into a chair.

"Until I hear the truth, we're not taking one step outside this inn. Yes, you can wrest this key from me, but if you try, everything's finished between us."

Basil rubbed his knuckles. "If we're not on the packet . . ."

"You will have failed in your mission. What exactly are your orders? Throw Joséphine overboard?"

He recoiled. "No, I swear."

On my chest, Joséphine whimpered. Perhaps she didn't like my tone. I touched her forehead. She was too warm. Distant church bells chimed. I counted. So did Basil. Five. "Did Hudson Lowe send you here?"

"Yes, but it was my idea. We don't have time for this. I'll explain later."

"You'll explain now."

"Albine, they planned to arrest you, take the baby. I convinced them there'd be an outcry, that I could remove you from politics. I've sold out of my regiment. By the time we reach Brussels, I'll be a civilian, on a stipend, enough with my inheritance—if we live a quiet, thriftful life—to keep us till we die." He crossed the room to take my hands. "I told Sir Hudson I was doing this for God, the

King, and England. That was the lie. I did it to keep you and your baby safe. To spend my life with you."

I said nothing.

He lowered his head.

"What more have you to say?" I asked.

"I love you." His square chin trembled. "I'll escort you to Brussels and Rome. When you're safe, if it's what you want, I'll say goodbye. I promise."

My constant Basil, my sacrificial lamb. I leaned against his chest. "You're not a good liar, but you tell the truth beautifully. I'll try to trust you."

ON THE SHORT FERRY TRIP to Dover and the longer one across the channel, Joséphine vomited. Her fever raged. I believed that doctor in Portsmouth had given her something evil. Once again, the winds, the tides, the gods fought against us. We landed at Ostend in pouring rain and traveled (no, bounced) overland to Brussels. Joséphine howled. We looked like war refugees when we arrived, but Basil moved us into the grand Hôtel Belle-Vue. There, our sheets were crisp, our baths hot, and food available at all hours. A last luxury, he said, paid for by the British government.

Joséphine grew languid. Doctors came and doctors went. Some made her sweat, some chilled her with ice. Keep her in the dark, bathe her in sun, feed her, starve her, leeches, mud packs, prayers, tears, curses. Mothers sing their children to sleep. I sang mine to Heaven's Gate. The Gate swung open.

My baby—sweet, innocent bundle of possibilities—whimpered. Then she was gone.

I wrote at the outset that this story was for entertainment. I draw the curtain here. Do not peek around it. The pain of losing Joséphine burns forever but burns in private. If public, I promise you, that pain would sear your world.

Napoleon

IN THE MORNING, TOBYSON COULDN'T stop chattering about the night before. The Emperor had barely left with Cipriani when Solomon sent an urgent warning to Hercules. There was no submarine, no rescue on the horizon. Hadn't Cipriani reported to the Emperor that the little boat had sunk in the Thames on its trial run?

The giant stooped to receive Napoleon's kiss on each craggy cheek.

"You retrieved the Corsican's body?" the Emperor asked.

Hercules shook his shaggy head. "Weren't nothing there."

"What?" He turned to Tobyson. "He's sure he had the right spot?"

"Master, he knows this island like . . . I don't know . . . like Monsieur Marchand knows the hairs on your head."

The Emperor lobbed a cushion at the boy. "Ask him *how* he knows it was the right spot."

Tobyson hugged the cushion to his chest. "He's sure. The plants were all trampled. There was blood and boot prints."

"But no body? No tracks, no blood leading away?"

"Nothing. No, wait, Master—not nothing. Give it here, Hercules."

Hercules handed a stiletto to Tobyson.

The Emperor closed his fist around it.

"Found it near the beach," Hercules said. "Only one there."

The Emperor brought it to his lips. It was not his mother's knife. It was Cipriani's.

When Hercules left, the Emperor sat before the fireplace, watching the logs smolder. Marchand hovered nearby. The Emperor looked up. "Get my writing box. And my clothes from last night."

"Oh, no, sire, I haven't had time to clean them—the blood."

"Yes, Marchand, the blood. I want to say goodbye to Cipriani."

The valet touched the Emperor's shoulder. "A traitor."

"Before he was a traitor, he was my oldest friend. Get me those clothes."

But that evening, when he picked up his pen, his first thoughts were not of Cipriani. He thought of his two wives: worldly Josephine, who betrayed him with other men yet stayed loyal in all that mattered, and "innocent" Marie Louise, who discarded him at the first signs of trouble. Long before Cipriani's latest scheme, life had treated him to as many kinds of loyalty as betrayal.

CLISSON: THE EMPEROR'S NOVEL

France's Northeast Border, 1791

As days passed between receipt of letters from Eugénie, Clisson wrote:

Dear Eugénie,

I am glad you share each day with Berville in discussion of what you call my misfortune. The wounds I experienced were a glorious sacrifice for the country I now accept as my own.

So, your mother has fallen for my sweet-talking friend? His gallantry must bring her pleasure. Truly, I wish your father a swift recovery from his distressing illness. I am thankful Berville abides with you to lend your family support.

I beg you write more often, Sweet Constancy. My health— nay, my sanity—depends on it.

Clisson

....

Eugénie,

One short letter? Only one, my love? Did you go all that time without thinking of me? It was interesting to hear how Berville enjoyed seeing the ruined abbey. I hope your groom accompanied you. Truly, I should rather you write of the books I suggested or how you fare with your new music teacher. These pastimes will do more for your character than jaunting through the dangerous countryside.

I must go fulfill the needs of our nation. Tell Berville he should be doing the same. The general says his name will be stricken from the officer lists if he does not return.

The weather here is frightful. It rains so much, I change my clothes twice in a day. A thousand kisses as hot as my passion, as pure as I trust your soul to be.

Your most faithful and trusting,
Clisson

....

Dear Eugénie,

I tremble for your sorrow. Your father was an industrious soul who could have been of great use to his reborn nation. I know his loss weighs upon you, particularly in these uncertain times.

My general will not grant me leave to visit you. Without Des Mazis, without Berville, I'm essential here. My devotion to my duty is such that I may not desert, as some have seen fit to do.

The trip to Paris seems unwise. Berville, as an aristocrat, will be in grave peril. By accompanying you, he adds to the hazard of your journey. Stay home. You are my wife. Obey me.

My most tender solace to your mother on her loss.

Clisson

....

Eugénie,

If you were witness, Mademoiselle, to the feelings that your letter inspired, you would be convinced of the injustice of your reproaches. Be sure that "the most feeling of women loves the coldest of men" is a sentence infused with such injustice that your heart disavowed it as your hand wrote it.

If all you can write is praise for Berville, do not write at all.

You hold my life in your hands. Make good use of it.

Clisson

....

Dear Eugénie,

It is 2:00 a.m. Everyone's prepared for death. The orders are given, the battle set. Blood will flow today. But you, Eugénie, what do you do, what do you say, what will become of you? I have heard nothing from you for three weeks.

Clisson dipped his quill into the ink.

The flap of his tent opened. The pen fell from his hand.

Standing in the opening was Amélie. Amélie Rose.

Clisson struggled to his feet, certain she was an apparition. She pushed back her hood. The specter had chestnut hair, hazel eyes specked with green, skin like peaches. Moonlight cast its halo around her, as if she, too, were a moon. He took a step. She rushed into his arms. How he loved the feel of those little teeth crushed against his own.

He pulled away. *This cannot be.*

He flicked a tear from her cheek. It might have dropped from his own eye.

"Are you really here?" he asked.

"I had to come."

He limped away. Instantly, she was at his side. "Sit. Your leg."

"Must you always be in command? I am fine." Still, he sat on the cot and pulled her next to him. His thoughts leapt. He grabbed her arm. "Not Eugénie? Eugénie's not dead?"

Amélie smoothed his hair, as Eugénie once had. "She lives, but I bring a message. She wanted to write. I told her this would be better."

Clisson's chest hardened into a shield. "She's gone?"

"Yes."

"With Berville?"

"Yes, with him." Amélie's eyes didn't waver.

He looked away. "Where? When?"

"They left for the coast last week. Her mother believes Monsieur LeGrand secreted money to business colleagues in the Nordic countries." She turned his face toward her. "They want Berville to be safe."

"They?"

"Eugénie and her mother."

"They're not coming back?"

"No."

"The mother, too?"

"I'm sorry. She encouraged it after Berville told them you weren't legally married."

"Good old Berville, pricking the soft underbelly of truth." Outside, the camp stirred. Someone pissed on his tent. There was a ribald laugh. "Berville saved my life."

Amélie lifted her chin. "So he told us. Again and again."

That debt was paid. Clisson's heart unfolded. He could talk to this woman about anything. He took her face between his hands. "And you? I heard your count fled to England."

A shadow passed over her face. "He, too, is not coming back. I have learned my lesson well."

"Poor Amélie Rose. What will you do?"

She gave a little frown. "I thought I would come to you."

"Aren't we both still married? How could we live in honor?"

"Oh, Clisson, when you return to the civilian world, you'll see what this revolution has wrought. Marriage no longer matters. In this new world, the best way to keep one's word is not to give it."

A drum sounded.

"The call to arms." He took her hands. "I must go, and so must you. This is not the time for us. We have little hope in this battle. You don't need to lose another lover."

"Then there is nothing else to say"—Amélie touched his cheek—"until after the battle. But if you live, we will meet again."

No one had ever left a tent with a more graceful stride. Clisson struggled to his feet, realizing she shouldn't walk the camp alone. Not on a day when men went to die. He opened the flap in time to see General Barras offer her an arm.

So be it. The lady had landed on her feet again.

On his cot lay his unfinished letter to Eugénie. Only moments remained before the battle. He reached for his pen.

As 1 wrote to you, Amélie arrived with news of your per-fidy. Nay, 1 lay that at Berville's door. You are trusting. 1 should have warned you to be wary. 1t will not surprise you that Amélie offered herself to me. But without you, Eugénie, 1 believe 1 will walk faster if 1 walk alone. 1 choose a solitary path to my end, which is likely to be today.

You once asked how you and Amélie differed in my love. 1 tell you now, in the last moments of my life, that Amélie's betrayals would have meant nothing because that is simply her nature. She is a butterfly who loves well but not deeply. She flits from bush to bush because she lives for amusement and pleasure. Your betrayal, Eugénie, on the other hand, is as deep and pure as your spirit. 1n your love, 1 tasted the grace that saves mankind. When you broke your oath, you shattered all honesty in the world. Rejoice in my death, curse my memory, and live happily. You have spared your children my ardent soul. Join Amélie among the merry widows.

Farewell 1 go to war, where 1 belong

Clisson

The call to arms sounded.

He folded the letter and called for an orderly to put it in his widow's box. Around him, friends clasped hands a final time. He alone among these men wished to journey beyond life's span.

He took his place at General Barras's side. Amélie was nowhere in sight.

The columns advanced on the field. The Enemy's cavalry charged the flanks. On the right, the French column broke.

The center was pushed back. Hand-to-hand combat ensued. At last, the center was victorious, but on the left, fresh Enemy troops launched into the battle. Smoke obscured Clisson's view.

He turned to General Barras. The general inclined his head.

Clisson bolted for his horse. He galloped to the reserve squadron. He seized their battle flag and yelled, "Hoorah!" The cavalry, sabers drawn, thundered in his wake into the cannon fire. Across the field they flew. His horse's hooves crushed the bones of fallen men. The Enemy quaked. Death prowled their ranks, choosing. He couldn't tell the smoke from clouds. All at once, a musket blew a thousand arrows through his chest. His stallion reared, wheeled, collapsed. The earth soaked in his blood.

Napoleon

THE EMPEROR REACHED FOR THE neat pile of soiled clothes Marchand had brought to him. He lifted the shirt to his nose. Cipriani's blood mingled with his sweat.

So many traitors, one after another. He had loved them all.

An hour later, Montholon knocked on his bedroom door. He handed the Emperor a small red silk sack. "The diamonds you gave me to hold, sire. They're safer in your possession." He swallowed. "Some are missing."

The Emperor raised his hand. "No explanation. Let us forget the past."

"Please, sire, I have not been honest."

"It's all right, Charles. From now on, you will be."

"Hear me out. I've concealed information that concerns you. That is, concerns Albine. I reported that she was on her way to your mother in Rome."

"Yes, yes. That wasn't true?"

"Not quite."

The Emperor leaned forward in his chair. "For God's sake, make a clean breast of it, will you, man?"

"The little one. Joséphine Napoléone. After the long voyage, she never was well again." Montholon hesitated. "The child is buried in Brussels, sire. Near where Albine lives with that British lieutenant Basil Jackson. She didn't visit your mother."

The Emperor pressed his hand over his heart, thinking it had stopped. No, no, it beat as stubbornly as before.

Poor little Joséphine.

Poor Albine. No, not "poor Albine." One more traitor on the bonfire of his life.

Chapter 34

Albine

As soon as I was strong enough, Basil fulfilled the first of his promises in an unexpected manner. Instead of waiting until Tristan's school holiday, Basil and I traveled to Switzerland to visit him. On arrival, I learned the difference between being frugal (as Basil was) and being stingy (as Charles was), for Basil paid Tristan's past debts and the next year's tuition.

Tristan, at fourteen, had his father's height, emaciated frame, and aristocratic nose (which overfilled his youthful face). His sole resemblance to me? The dissatisfaction so ably caught on the portrait inside my locket. Was he happy to see us? Let us say he was reserved, even surly, in confronting my emotion and Basil's generosity. Searching for welcome in his face, I encountered suspicion.

He turned his back on his benefactor's outstretched hand, demanding, "Why is this British man paying for my schooling?"

What was a Montholon to do? (Lie, of course.) "Oh, Basil handles my finances, dear," I said in an airy voice.

Tristan chewed a fingernail. "Does he have spending money for me? Do you know what it's like to be at school without a sou to your name?"

I wanted to swat that fingernail from his mouth, but we'd lived apart too long. "We couldn't send money from St. Helena."

Tristan paused from his chewing. "Then you shouldn't have gone there."

Basil counted out some coins. "With your mother's permission, I'll arrange a quarterly allowance."

Tristan snatched the money and went back to ignoring Basil. "What do you hear from Father? I haven't had a letter in more than a year."

I stared at Basil, who blushed. "I thought only mine got through."

Tristan observed the two of us through narrow eyes, as though he were soaking up weaknesses, probing for lies. Did those survival instincts come from his father or from me?

Basil, his own instincts on alert, beat a retreat, saying, "I'll leave the two of you to get reacquainted."

I told my son that the Emperor (still the world's most famous man) knew all about him, hoped to meet him, wished him health and prosperity. Tristan said he needed to return to his studies. He planned to stay with a friend over the next holiday; perhaps summer would be better for a visit with us. I swallowed hard, said nothing of his dead half sister, and begged him to write more often.

When I joined Basil in the waiting coach, he kissed my palm. "He's just a boy, my love," he said. "Give him time to be a man. You haven't lost him for good."

I flickered a smile. "No, not like Joséphine. This one can still grow to love me."

Basil wrapped his arms around me. I felt no need to search my pockets for bread.

Napoleon

THE EMPEROR WAS STARING INTO the fireplace when two small arms wrapped around his neck. He swiveled in his chair, his blurred eyes meeting Tobyson's. The boy brushed a tear from the Emperor's cheek, crawled onto his lap, and rested his head on his Master's shoulder. The sorrow inside the Emperor's chest mingled with the warmth of the little boy.

"Did someone hurt your feelings?" Tobyson asked.

The Emperor chuckled. "No one's ever asked me that. No, my son, old men's emotions lie close to the surface. A rare luxury of old age. Has our guest arrived? He's the son of an Englishman I met when I was young."

The Emperor hadn't dined with a stranger for two years, but this fellow claimed his father had attended military school in Paris with him and added some tale of a fencing match without buttons on the foils. To smile at a youthful memory lifted the Emperor's spirits.

He entered Longwood's reception hall, one hand against his painful side, the other on Tobyson's shoulder. The boy, who squinted less since they'd found him some wire-rimmed glasses, had grown to the perfect height for the Emperor to lean on. And at eleven years old, he'd learned to maintain a serious expression on his cheerful face, if he wasn't taxed too long.

The Emperor rested an elbow on the mantel. When Bertrand introduced the visitor, he guided the man's chin to the light. "You resemble your father. He was the first Englishman I ever met. So, he was at the Battle of Eylau? Trained in the French military, only to fight for the British and the Russians? Yes, there were many who did so. You will have met Las Cases, for instance. Ah, wait. He isn't here anymore.

"*Merci* for the wine you brought. I see the label was removed. Governor Lowe, searching for hidden messages, no doubt. He passes every moment in fear of my escape. Perhaps at one time he had reason on his side, but in my current state of health? No." He gave a small smile because he liked to show his straight white teeth.

"So, your father was at Eylau. My general, the good Bertrand, looks surprised. You see, I never talk about that battle." The Emperor took an uncertain step. "First we eat; then we talk."

Tobyson helped him into the dining room, where they ate in silence.

The Emperor put down his fork. "Eylau. Everyone talks of battles; a rare few ask about the aftermath when soldiers—fearsome war machines—become mere men. Gray smoke lifts, and, as its smell leaves with the wind, blood and flesh take its place. The cries 'Hoorah!' and '*Vive l'Empereur!*' are silenced. Dead and wounded blanket the earth, overflow the ditches. The soul is oppressed to see so many victims. Grown men beg for their mothers, imagine their wives at their sides, sell their souls for a sip of water.

"You said we won that battle? We lost twelve thousand men, the Allies fifteen thousand. Can you imagine so many bodies? No, no one can. Think of a herd of, say, eight thousand cattle; then, in your head, butcher them on an open field and stack up the meat. If that does not move your heart, then you aren't a man.

"Few know victory smells as bad as defeat. The stink was less that day because it was so cold." He pushed back from the table. "Bertrand? Do you remember? We came across a dog, a noble black hound with a muscular chest. I made the mistake of naming him Victoire.

"The animal, scraping his belly to the ground, approached Bertrand, who leaned to touch its bloodstained head. The dog snapped. It ran back and forth, leading us to a body that crawled. We approached the injured man, but the snarling cur held us off.

"'Shall I shoot him?' someone asked.

"'What, the man?' I demanded.

"'No, sire, the dog.'

"But shoot Victoire? That would bring bad luck. The man would die nonetheless. As he expired, we offered words of solace. Victoire howled into the night until a bullet silenced him."

The Emperor sniffed a juniper-scented handkerchief. "I still carry the smell of that battle in my nostrils. I tell you, a father who has lost so many of his children doesn't taste the joy of victory. No. Disrobed Glory shows herself as an ugly illusion."

He stood. "Some think my luck changed on the frozen steppes of Russia. No, it turned five years before. Since that day in 1807, I have always been at Eylau." Wincing, he pressed his stomach. Tobyson hurried to his side.

"Go," the Emperor said to the Englishman. "Tell them you are the last to have dined with the Monster of Europe."

He closed the door in Marchand's offended face and shuffled across the floor to unlock the writing desk. That last page rankled. It was not the Dead who changed the world. He tossed the final page he had written into the fire. "No, my brave Eaglet, not for you the saber and the drum. The next Napoleon must find a different way forward."

CLISSON: THE EMPEROR'S NOVEL

France's Northeast Border, 1791
The End

Clisson galloped to the front of the reserve squad. He seized their battle flag and cried, "Hoorah!" The cavalry, sabers drawn, thundered in his wake into the cannon fire. Across the field they flew. His horse's hooves crushed the bones of fallen men. The Enemy quaked. Death prowled their ranks, choosing.

All at once, a musket blew a thousand arrows through his horse's chest. His stallion reared, wheeled, collapsed. The earth soaked in its blood.

Clisson whirled to his feet. His eyes streamed from the smoke. His skin was scorched, his hair singed. The artillery rumbled in his heart, not his ears. He'd gone battle deaf. Cannonballs pelted like hail. Bullets sprayed. Ahead lay the bridge the Enemy held, its planks slick with blood. A soldier on his left crumpled, one more goose on the chopping block. Clisson grabbed the standard the fellow dropped. He shook the tasseled flag free and waved it high. He couldn't hear his own voice scream. "Follow me! To Victory! To Glory!" He charged forward. "To Destiny!"

Around him, Frenchmen lifted soiled faces. French eyes came alight in blackened skin. One by one, they picked up his cry. "Follow Clisson! All upon the bridge!" They leapt felled horses, dying men. In a surge of flesh, into raking bullet fire, an avalanche of souls cascaded in Clisson's wake. They screamed for victory. They screamed in pain. Frenchmen fell, but the human deluge couldn't be stanched.

The Enemy line quavered, buckled, broke. The ranks fled for their lives. The French surged to the far side. The bridge won, Clisson stood upon a cannon, the barrel warm through his boots. Around him flowed his cheering men. They gathered at his feet, pounding fists into the air. "For Clisson, France, and Glory!"

Drawn into the current of their jubilation, in the glare of their shining eyes, he mouthed, *I was born for this.*

This was where he belonged, at the forefront of men. Forget the arrows love drove through his heart. Let betrayal strengthen the betrayed. Forget Death's Glory. To play leaderless French-men like a violin, to conduct all France in his tunes, to lead it in a grand orchestration, that was a Destiny worth living for. That was a legacy to build a dynasty upon.

Until Destiny was through with him, he would not falter.

But if these brave men would follow him into Death, to what greater heights might he lead them? Notre Dame's soar-ing vaults burst from his memory. Someone, a man of no more worth than he, had built that lasting monument. To God, to Nation, it mattered not, as long as it withstood the centuries.

On the bridge, among the human carnage, a bloodied sol-dier crawled. The man scaled a comrade's corpse to reach the broken rail. He pulled himself upright and, stumbling over fallen soldiers' limbs, dragged himself into the victory cele-bration. Clisson jumped from the cannon barrel and caught the wounded man in his arms. He turned the man's face to his. "What were you?" he asked.

The soldier shook his head.

"Before the war. What were you then?"

The man's eyes cleared. A smile cracked the dirt on his face. "A farm boy. I ran away to join the war."

"Good fellow," Clisson whispered in the soldier's ear. "Follow where I lead. Together we'll win more than war's fleeting Glory. Yes, we'll fight like the Devil when we must, but the Glory will come from what we build. Live, my friend. Let us live."

Albine

ALTHOUGH NAPOLEON'S MADAME MÈRE didn't respond to my letters, ever-generous Basil took me to Rome. At the door of her mansion (which she called a palace, as though she herself had earned those royal honors), her familiar chamberlain blocked my entrance.

"Colonna, you know very well who I am," I scolded.

But Colonna, his posture ramrod straight, his black court breeches of the finest silk, his coat embroidered with gold thread, lifted a lip at my modest dress. "Yes, you are a schemer, and Madame does not receive schemers."

"My God, I come from St. Helena. Tell her my pass phrase, 'chestnuts in the cellar,' before you do the greatest injustice to Napoleon."

"No, Madame de Montholon. We anticipated your arrival." He closed the door. The lock clicked.

I reached for the brass knocker, fashioned in a bold Napoleonic "N."

Basil stopped my hand. "Enough of these Bonapartes."

"We must watch for her to go out."

"One more try, and then we give up?"

I nodded, and he led me away.

At the British embassy, Basil learned Madame Mère often drove to the Villa Borghese in an open coach that bore Napoleon's arms. For the next three afternoons, I waited on a park bench under tall poplars, until I spotted her.

She wore a cashmere shawl over her black silks and a black lace cap topped with a tiny black hat. Her cataracts hid behind a veil. Leaving Basil on the bench, I ran alongside the coach, calling out, "Chestnuts in the cellar, chestnuts in the cellar."

Letizia Bonaparte cackled. "Oh, all right, into the carriage with you. Let me feel your face." As her dry fingers traced my features, I beamed, my heart light at fulfilling Napoleon's assignment.

"Your beauty—what little you had—hasn't worn very well, has it?" She drew back her veil. "Once a hussy, always a hussy."

I cringed. "You feel the cares of motherhood, not debauchery. I gave birth to Napoleon's daughter, your granddaughter."

"So your letters claimed. And where is this wondrous child?"

"My precious girl died three months ago. She's buried in Brussels." My voice, my breath, my soul caught on those words I rarely spoke. "The voyage from St. Helena was too arduous—"

"Oh, your interminable lies." The old woman smirked. "Born on St. Helena? Bah! Napoleon escaped that place two years ago."

"What?" I gripped her hand, but she pulled free. "I left five months ago. I promise you, he was still there."

"I have proof." She seized my bodice.

I let her drag me close. Her juniper scent—achingly reminiscent of Napoleon—furnished a thin veneer over the stew of an old woman who rarely bathed. "What proof could you possibly have?" I whispered.

"Revelations, my girl. Something a godless woman like you would never understand. Napoleon ascended to the Heavens, carried to a safety where he shall be healed and brought forth again." Her dull eyes brightened. "These useless eyes saw it all. God gave me the power."

Poor Madame Mère. I yearned to stroke the knob on her cleft chin, so like Napoleon's, so like my little Joséphine's. Best if Napoleon never heard of her delusion. For his sake, I tried one more time. "I have a man who was there with me—"

She chuckled. "Of course you do. You always have a man, don't you?"

"But, Madame—"

"You hussy, you gave birth to a gravestone, if you gave birth at all."

"Madame, you are wrong."

"I? Wrong? Out of my carriage. Out!" she screamed.

My foot had barely touched the pavement before the carriage sped away.

Basil, who'd raced to my side, caught me midfall. "Now, Albine? Are we through with the Bonapartes?"

In that park, a myriad of paths opened before me. I took a faltering step. "Yes, Basil, yes."

Chapter 35

Tobyson

AT MORNING'S LIGHT, THE BUNDLE in the corner unwound into bespectacled Tobyson, dressed in the Emperor's green livery. He yawned, rubbed his chin, and stretched. When his glance came across the Emperor on the bed, he curled into a ball, eyes behind his glasses the only movement.

He didn't see why everyone still called the Master the Great One, when the dear old man sat on the commode chair for hours, soaked in the tub until his skin puckered, and coughed up every meal. Half an eye could see the spirit pushing its way out of his body.

If Tobyson was lucky enough to see that spirit rise, he'd do his best to catch it. A box that held this man's spirit—now, that could make a poor boy rich. He dreamed of owning a little farm. With a stream and chickens. And a kitten named Betsy.

He scrunched his nose. No, if he caught that spirit, he'd never sell it, no matter what riches were offered.

The Master stirred awake. Tobyson sprang to his aid.

Today the Master wanted to garden, but first a red sash had to be looped around his wide waist, Tobyson was careful not to touch the old man's belly, swollen to hold all its pain. When it hurt, the Master ranted of poison, blamed Hudson Lowe, and called out for long-dead Cipriani.

Tobyson tied a madras scarf around the Master's head, knotting it in front, à la Martinique. The old man caught hold of his hand, saying, "Martinique is an island different from this one. Warm and redolent of flowers and fresh fruit, with gentle winds and sensuous women."

"When did you go there, Father?" Tobyson held his breath for the answer.

"Never," the old man recited. "But I have tasted it on the skin of a woman, my wife Josephine."

He had uttered that speech many times, but Tobyson never tired of it. "Do you think, dear Father, you could tell me the story about Toby-Mahafaly again? And our friend Betsy?"

The Master rubbed his watery eyes. "Maybe tonight when everyone else is asleep."

Tobyson ran to fetch the straw hat his real father had made. He placed it gently on the Master's head.

A British soldier's silhouette passed the window.

"Quick, my son," the Master said. "Fetch the machine. We'll have ourselves a skirmish before breakfast. Ah, that my Corsican friend were here to enjoy the fun."

Tobyson went to the cupboard and dragged out the "infernal machine," as the Master called it with a laugh he wouldn't explain. It was just sticks and a spoon tied together into a tiny catapult capable of throwing peas. Tobyson was well drilled in this operation. He placed it on a spot marked on the table and crept to open the window. Holding their breath, nudging each other in anticipation, he and his Master waited for the sentry to reverse his path. At the last moment, the Great One shuffled into the next room to create a diversion.

The sentry came into view. Tobyson squinted through his glasses and let loose the catapult. Square hit upon the cheek. The soldier dropped his weapon and grabbed his face. Tobyson grinned. For the next few days, the Master would take pleasure in watching that bruise grow and fade. Maybe he'd issue another proclamation praising his artilleryman's prowess. Tobyson concealed the machine and went to get the gardening basket.

That night, his Master's vision grew dim. "My son, my son," he muttered.

Tobyson sat on the camp bed. He pressed the Great One's hand to his cheek. "Tell me, Father, what you want."

The Master hugged him to his chest. "I want you to know what kind of man I was. I want you to know what you can be, my Eaglet, no matter the odds against you."

"Monsieur Marchand says no unknown star ever rose higher than you," Tobyson whispered.

The Master's eyes cleared. He patted Tobyson's head. "You here, my little friend? Nice of you to keep an old man company."

Tobyson snuggled closer.

"You won't forget your orders, will you, Lieutenant T?" the Master asked.

Tobyson saluted. "No, General. I have the maps memorized."

The old, steely spark relit the Emperor's eyes. "But your destiny is your choice alone. Remember that."

Before dawn, the old man climbed out of bed. He wound the madras scarf around his head himself. Tobyson let him get out the door before he followed.

He found the Great One slumped in the garden, clawing at the dirt around the rosebush they'd planted to honor Josephine, the woman from Martinique. Tobyson whistled for the gardener. Hercules limped out of the shed, lifted the Master in his arms, and carried him into the house. He laid the Great Man of Europe on the camp bed, where Tobyson and Hercules watched him fall asleep. When his breathing grew fitful, Tobyson ran to fetch Monsieur Marchand.

The next day passed in a rush of doctors, whispers, and tears. Monsieur Marchand set up his own cot in the bedroom. Doctors came and went at odd hours.

At the Emperor's bedside, Tobyson sniffed back a sob. When no one was watching, he slipped into his mouth a bit of licorice he'd sneaked from the Emperor's bonbon sack. He blew the candy's scent onto the unconscious face. The Emperor's nose twitched.

Tobyson's twitched back. "Please don't go," he whispered.

Outside the bedroom door, floorboards creaked. The narrow, low-ceilinged room shrank as stout General Bertrand, in dress uniform, entered. General Montholon and a black-suited servant crowded in behind him. The two generals conferred while Marchand held a mirror below the Emperor's nose.

Tobyson peeked under the valet's sleeve. Fog clouded the reflection.

General Montholon narrowed his lips. "Word is out. Already a crowd gathers."

"Like vultures," said Marchand.

General Bertrand rested his hand on his sword hilt. "You speak of my wife, among others. You are upset, Marchand, but do not be impertinent. We shall move him to the larger room."

Marchand bowed, his mouth twisted.

Tobyson stole behind the curtain.

Each of the four men approached a corner of the bed. At General Bertrand's "Hut!" they seized the iron poles supporting the collapsible camp bed the Emperor had used at battle sites from Austerlitz to Leipzig. And on that same bed, although Tobyson felt disloyal to recall it now, the Master said he had spent a fitful night in a farmhouse near Waterloo.

As they lifted, the Emperor murmured. Monsieur Marchand, nearest to the Master's face, repeated for the others, "*Armée . . . tête de l'armée.*" Heads lowered, the four men carried the Emperor out of the bedroom, past the dining room's temporary chapel, into Longwood House's reception hall.

When Tobyson could no longer hear the men's footsteps, he emerged from behind the curtain. He eased the bedroom door shut, cringing at the *clunk* of the latch. From the center of the room, he contemplated the wall where the camp bed had stood.

"Our Father, who be in Heaven . . ." He cocked his head, the next word stuck on his tongue. The floorboards outside the room were silent, the adults busy settling the Master in the reception hall. Tobyson's eyes fixed on the shelf where the Emperor's bicorne hat stood. Ears alert for Marchand's footsteps, he inched toward the hat.

He lifted it slowly, the weight of the rough leather familiar from the thousand times he'd carried it to the Emperor. He lowered the bicorne onto his own head. A grin spread over his round face. He ran to the mirror.

Proof of the Master's words was reflected in the glass: these days, anyone—a poor Corsican boy, even a slave's son like he was—could grow into an important man. With the bicorne on his head, wearing his green uniform jacket, white knee breeches, and black boots, identical to those the Emperor wore, he, Tobyson, looked the part. And the Master had said Appearances Win Half the Battle. After a final look, he restored the hat to its shelf.

The time had come to be a Man of Action.

Crouching, he crept to the window. Hercules was in sight, his shaggy head down as he dug among the yellow everlasting daisies.

Tobyson pulled a key from his pocket. He unlocked the Emperor's desk, lifted its lid, and took out the metal writing box. He relocked the desk and slid the key beneath loose papers on the mantel. Crossing the room to a high nautical chest, he pulled open a top drawer. On his tiptoes, he searched beneath shirts and under-clothes until he found a red silk purse. He stuck it in his pocket and closed the drawer. The cold steel box from the desk tucked under his shirtfront, he sauntered past the servants' rooms, down a corridor, and into the garden.

Outside, a brisk trade wind rolled mist over the high plain. Rain was not far behind. Flagstaff Hill and the British bivouac hid under a cloud. The moist air chilled Tobyson's close-cropped scalp, but he couldn't risk going back for his own three-cornered hat. The distant patch of ocean he liked to scan for ships had disappeared behind fog. If he was lucky, the Emperor might leave him the spy-glass they had shared. He would beg Monsieur Marchand for it.

Tobyson whistled one sharp note. Hercules's head popped up. Tobyson raised his chin toward the far end of the garden, where white pickets joined a stone wall. Hercules grabbed his shovel and limped toward the corner.

The Emperor had lectured that the Enemy, seeing Bold Action, would not look for Subterfuge, so Tobyson strolled the garden, winding his way to the fence, sniffing flowers along the path. When Sergeant Kitts at the British sentry box caught his eye, he waved. The soldier turned away.

Hercules had started a hole under the spreading branches of a white-flowered ebony bush. His doglike eyes turned to the boy. "This about right?"

"Deeper." Tobyson pulled the box from under his shirt. "Two feet more. Like the first time we buried it for him."

Hercules dropped to one knee in the dirt. "Rain's coming fast—don't get your fancy clothes messed up in this mud. Way things going, you aren't getting any new ones, little man."

Tobyson wiped his eyes on his sleeve. "And you'll be out of a job."

"A strong man can always find work." Hercules patted Tobyson's back. "Don't worry. I'll buy you out and set you free if the Emperor's will ain't clear about it."

When the hole was deep enough, Tobyson wrapped his hands around the gardener's wrist. Hercules lowered him into the hollow so he could lay the box flat. He sprinkled a fistful of dirt upon it. As rain began to fall, the gardener hoisted him to the surface, shoveled in more dirt, and covered the loose ground with sticks and leaves. He pulled a rag from a back pocket to brush soil from Tobyson's breeches.

"That do it?" Hercules winked.

"All for the Eaglet now." Tobyson tucked his small hand into the gardener's huge, earth-blackened one. Sagging against the big man's hip, he removed his precious spectacles and lifted his chin to the sky. Rain rinsed the smell of death from his cheeks.

⤳

TOBYSON, BEARING A BOWL OF spring water from the Valley of the Geraniums, stepped around Father Vignali's makeshift altar and into the reception area. British officers ranged against the walls; four doctors debated restoratives; Madame Bertrand wept; the two French generals paraded. And in one corner, between the old coachman and the faithful cook, his friend Hercules leaned against a wall.

In the center, the Emperor, under the green silk tent that gathered at an eagle crest above the iron bed, lay as still as . . . Tobyson shoved the thought away. He slumped to his knees next to Marchand's bedside chair. Madame Bertrand and General Montholon crowded against the valet's back. They hung over his shoulder like vultures, as Monsieur Marchand had said they would. Father Vignali's prayers floated with incense from the dining room.

Monsieur Marchand added a drop of sweet Constantine wine to the spring water. Tobyson daubed the Emperor's mouth with a dampened sponge again and again. Above the Emperor's head, the doctors disputed in English and in French, but Tobyson didn't need grown-up knowledge to know the man on the camp bed had set one foot in the next world.

For two hours, no one spoke above a whisper. Tobyson's knees and back grew stiff. He wearied of the Latin drone drifting in from the next room. His Master deserved something more French than the priest's Roman prayers. After all, Monsieur Marchand had said he came from the People and that the People called him their Man. No matter that he started out a Corsican. Someone should sing a joyful song, but Tobyson didn't dare.

At dusk, a puff of breath burst from the Emperor's lips. His chest didn't expand to take another. The muscles in his face relaxed, and he looked like a young lieutenant.

His eyelids sprang open.

Tobyson leaned forward eagerly, but Monsieur Marchand shook his head. A light went out in Tobyson's heart. All was still until a wail filled the room. Tobyson realized it was his. He threw himself on the dead man's chest, his heart stretching to tug his Master back, but it was no use.

Napoleon Bonaparte, Emperor and General, Builder and Destroyer of France, escaped his exile on St. Helena to greet his Maker with his eyes wide open.

My time is done.

Let my Eaglet spin Your world.

Chapter 36

Tobyson

ELEVEN YEARS LATER, APRIL 1832
ONBOARD HMS *CONSTANT*
APPROACHING THE SOUTHERN COAST OF FRANCE

LAND! TWENTY-FOUR-YEAR-OLD Tobyson raised the Emperor's spyglass to capture his first sight of France. The mountains loomed more softly than St. Helena's cliffs. The Master had claimed they were gentler because they were older. Towns stretched along the shore, their buildings rising in colors of the sun: yellows, oranges, cinnamon, painted by men of passion, not cool Englishmen. His Master had said he could smell the Mediterranean when he shut his eyes. Now, with those gray eyes shut for more than a decade, Tobyson breathed the sharp scents into his lungs.

"Hercules," he asked the large man standing next to him at the ship rail, "does this country smell like the Master to you?"

Hercules grinned down at him. "Can't say as I remember."

"Eleven years, and I still can't forget. I hope now that we're away from St. Helena, he's not lonely in his grave." Tobyson turned the spyglass to the southern coast of France.

"Gonna miss that grave, aren't you?" Hercules rubbed Tobyson's head. "We'll do the job he asked of us. Then it's off to America. But mind yourself: here, you act like you belong to me, in case they don't believe those British freedom papers."

They landed at Nice. For two months they walked to Austria, following the route the Master had drummed into Tobyson's head.

In Vienna, an American giant and a Black youth couldn't hide in the crowds, so Hercules's flute backed up Tobyson's sweet tenor under Schönbrunn Palace's long, green-shuttered facade. They came away with plenty of coins.

"Always safer to appear poor," Hercules said. "And to look like we're not hiding."

But the big man's English became a problem, so mostly he rendered himself mute and let Tobyson hobble along on his French. The young man was so short and smiling that, despite his unusual skin color, no one thought him threatening or older than fourteen.

A month passed, and they still had no plan to enter the palace the Eaglet never left. They developed a penchant for a café where the owner spoke French and had taken a liking to Tobyson.

Tobyson stared at the café's empty tables. "Hercules, we must meet this second Napoleon, even if it means taking a chance."

The big man shrugged. "Ask the fellow at the café."

When Tobyson stopped talking, the fat proprietor pulled his mustache. "I must introduce you to Herr Doctor Wiehrer, who visits the palace daily. He'll be amazed."

That afternoon, Tobyson stood at the doctor's table, since a Black man couldn't sit in a café without attracting attention. Hercules sat on a low wall nearby, whittling a branch with the stiletto the Emperor had given him.

Tobyson brought him some bread and cheese. "Told the doctor the truth."

"Dangerous," said Hercules.

Tobyson pressed his friend's large hand. "He'll take us tomorrow to see the Eaglet. They call him a duke now, which I don't understand. Anyway, you'll carry heavy bags and I'll be a specimen for exchanging blood."

"Leeches?"

"Leeches."

"Nasty. All for the Emperor, I guess." Hercules bit into his bread.

The next day, they followed the doctor down the long gilt corridors into the left wing of the palace. Recalling the maze the Emperor had drawn for him, Tobyson knew he would be able to find his way out in a hurry. He plucked his friend's sleeve. "Hercules, we're going to the room where the Master once stayed."

At last, they stopped where four soldiers stood at attention. One opened a door, and the doctor led them in.

The room smelled like a stable that hadn't seen a shovel.

Tobyson's eyes widened.

Fifty candles flickered shadows on the tall, white-painted walls. Their dancing flames reflected on gilt filigree, shimmered on gold curtains, mottled the red marble floor. In all, an elegant contrast with tumbledown Longwood, where the Emperor had lived out his days. But the frail young man shivering on the bed didn't resemble the Master, who had been, even at the end, a force of nature. This Napoleon's eyes were a mild blue, his hair auburn curls, his chin as smooth as a child's.

A wisp of a man born for war.

The doctor put his jar of leeches on a table. He spoke in a hearty tone. "Now, now, today, use your French, Your Grace. We have visitors who don't speak German. Through them, I bring a different kind of medicine, one that may do more good than any in my black bag."

The Eaglet twisted away. "Good. I'll drink no more of your nasty potions."

The doctor pressed two fingers on the inside of the Eaglet's wrist. His lips moved silently. He lost his smile and stepped away to jot numbers in a little book. His voice softened. "No potions. These two people bring you words from across the seas and years. I leave you in their care." He patted Tobyson's shoulder. "Best if I don't hear what's said. You have two hours." He disappeared out the door.

Tobyson tiptoed to the bedside. "Your Majesty?"

"*Your Majesty?*" The young man's voice was high-pitched and cross. "No one calls me that. Who are you? And why's your skin that color?"

Tobyson took a deep breath. "Monsieur Eaglet, your father sent me."

"My father?" Two bright red spots lit the young man's cheeks. "Is this a trick?"

Tobyson motioned Hercules to join him at the bedside. "My friend and I come from St. Helena. We were with the Emperor at the end. He bade us come to you when we could."

"My father's end? And now you come to witness mine? Don't you understand? I'm dying—dying of consumption, I tell you. Oh, what's the use?" He turned his face into his pillow and coughed up a spot of blood. "Give me some water. I swear, I could drink an ocean."

While Hercules poured a glass of water, Tobyson removed the metal writing box from the doctor's satchel. He perched on the bed alongside the young duke's thin, febrile body. "Your father took great care to write this for you. We've come halfway around the world to bring it."

The Eaglet raised his head. He fingered the soft white pages and squinted at his father's cramped script. "But what does it say? The handwriting's impossible to read."

"Not for me." Tobyson straightened his glasses. "Listen."

The Eaglet's breath whistled through his parted lips. He smiled at the stolen *Plutarch* and turned his face to the wall when Clisson discovered his mother's perfidy. Tears coursed down his cheeks while Tobyson read about the mob's having killed Sergeant Lyons. "I had plans to run away. I was going to join the army as a soldier and earn my way up the ranks." His voice quavered. "I dreamed of leading men into battle."

"Hercules and I could help you—"

"Oh, if you could! But I'm not strong enough. My father would have despised me."

Tobyson took his hand. "I knew your father as well as anyone.

He loved you. He wished you to be strong, not just in war but in life, in love. That's why he wrote you this."

The Eaglet shook his head. "My life will be a blank between my birth and my grave. He would have loved my cousin better."

"Louis-N?"

"See? Even you have heard of him. Give this book to him."

Tobyson took the Eaglet's pale face between his palms. "Is there nothing you're proud of?"

The Eaglet hesitated. "I can drive a carriage with four horses."

Tobyson smiled. "Imagine that: the Eagle and the Eaglet out for a carriage ride. I can see the joy on your father's face. And I would be there, too, in my green jacket with epaulets, clinging to the—"

Angry voices sounded in the hall.

The door burst open. A young captain entered with his pistol drawn. "What's this? The guards say the doctor left. The Duke's not allowed to have visitors."

"Thank God you're here, Captain von Osthaus." The Eaglet pushed Tobyson off the bed. Coughing, he swung his feet to the floor. "No, no, don't call the guard. On your life, keep your pistol trained on that big man. And lock the door."

The captain aimed his barrel at Hercules. With his other hand, he turned the key.

Hercules backed against the wall.

"But, Eaglet!" Tobyson cried.

The Eaglet caught his breath. "Quiet, you. Don't move, or your friend dies. Captain, that man's dangerous. Keep your eyes on him. No, don't call the guards. You don't want to split the reward."

"Reward?" The captain's eyes darted between Hercules and the Eaglet.

"Ah, wait until you see. I have it right here." Breathing hard, the Eaglet padded in stocking feet to a tall dresser. He reached into the top drawer and swung around with a loaded pistol pointed at the captain's head.

The captain's mouth opened.

"If you want to see those fine children of yours," the Eaglet said, "you'll hand your pistol to my friend."

Tobyson removed the pistol from the captain's loosened grip.

Hercules grinned. "Well, I'll be damned. He's his father's son, after all."

The Eaglet gave a coughing laugh. He leaned against the dresser. "You two must leave. Can you find your way?"

Tobyson smiled. "Your father taught me every twist and turn of the palace's maze."

"Good. The captain and I are going to sit right here. But first, Tobyson, take this ring and put it in the good man's breast pocket. Captain, that's your reward, but, like many things in life, it can turn on you." He paused to catch his breath. "If you swear never to talk of what you've seen here, never to pursue these friends of mine, it's yours. If you breathe a word of what has passed here, I'll swear you stole that ring while I was sleeping."

"Bravo," said Tobyson. "You sound like your father."

The Eaglet grinned. "Hold the weapons, Hercules, while I talk with your friend."

Tobyson helped the Eaglet to a chair and knelt beside it. The Eaglet, grasping Tobyson's shoulders, spoke in a low voice. "This captain has debts and a large family. He won't say anything, but go quickly. Follow the river out of the city."

Tobyson rubbed his nose. "You won't come with us?"

"You saw that doctor's face. My life's over. Take my father's book to Louis-N. Tell him I ask him ... No, as the rightful Emperor of the French, I *charge* him with my family's legacy. He's Napoleon now." A cough shook his shoulders.

Tobyson hesitated. "When you see your father in Heaven, will you tell him I chose to fulfill his mission? Those exact words, please: 'I chose.' He'll understand."

THE NEXT MORNING, THE SUN cast amber light on their campsite near the Danube River. Hercules counted their coins. "No point in being sad, little man. Got to move on if we're gonna catch a ship to America before winter. After all these years, my heart aches for my own country."

Tobyson wiped his sleeve across his cheeks. "Bear with me a bit longer."

The big man sighed. "Where to?"

"Brussels and Madame Albine. She'll know how to find that nephew Louis-N." Tobyson's swollen eyes brightened. He tapped his chest where the Emperor's red silk purse lay hidden. "We'll give her enough diamonds that she never panics again."

Albine

AFTER JOSÉPHINE NAPOLÉONE LEFT ME for Heaven, I gave up my blue striped dresses for mourning clothes. Surprisingly, black and gray bestowed dignity (perhaps a touch of beauty) on my aging face. I wore my hair in a knot, displaying my scar to all who cared to look.

We lived a quiet life, which suited Basil's definition of "respectable." Did he make me happy, as he had promised? I fear a woman who has lost a child can never be what the rest of the world calls "happy." Rather, I learned contentment. Contentment far from the intrigues of Paris, in a placid village on the outskirts of Brussels, dwelling in a stone house, sleeping alongside Basil, puttering in my garden, polishing the furniture, chastising the maid. I baked our bread as penance for my past. Indeed, contentment formed a protective shield around my tiny world.

News of the Eaglet's demise pierced that shield. Without the slightest proof, I believed someone had poisoned the young man. (So many people wanted that dynasty suppressed.) The thought rekindled suspicions about the death of my Joséphine, another lost Napoleonic seed. My wounds inflamed, I mourned my daughter and Napoleon afresh. My grandchildren—two little girls Tristan had given me—wept at my weeping, their arms sweet garlands around my neck in place of (but never replacing) my lost Joséphine's embrace.

Those wounds were still tender when joy inflamed them again. On a soft September day, Hercules and Tobyson strolled into my rose garden, like apparitions conjured from the past. As battle-scarred compatriots do, we searched each other's faces in hopes of finding our own youth. Big Hercules was much the same (such crags couldn't change), though his large frame had become a burden on his limp. What a handsome young man my Tobyson was, with long lashes and a still-sweet, knowing smile.

Hercules, after an awkward hug, took up my discarded shears and deadheaded thorny branches I had missed. Tobyson and I clung to each other, murmuring half sentences.

"The straw hat your father made . . ."

"It fell apart . . . I have some pieces."

"Tossing balls in the garden—"

"I understand that much French," Hercules interrupted. "Trampled my lilies, you two scoundrels did."

"Galloping horses . . . but for you, Madame Albine, I wouldn't be here."

"Hot towels you carried the day Joséphine Napoléone was born . . ."

"Never been so scared. Till the day our dear sire died."

"At the end?"

"He was ready, Madame."

They told me life was hard on St. Helena after the Emperor died and the British troops left. It had taken a decade for Hercules to buy Tobyson's freedom. Such constancy between those friends.

They stole glances at my face. "Alas," I told them, "despite mountains of cucumber paste, age changes a woman—a grandmother, no less—more radically than it does a man."

"But you must agree she remains a most handsome creature." Basil hesitated on the porch, unsure (I could see) of his welcome. Indeed, Hercules and Tobyson stiffened.

I led him forward to shake their hands. "We must forgive each other. That's the greatest gift of love."

Basil kissed my cheek (not minding its soft wrinkles). "Best I leave you three to visit."

My old friends relaxed after he withdrew. To lighten the mood, I described how I made our bread every morning. They laughed at my downfall from court intriguer to bread baker, as I knew they would. "But truly, it's the small life that makes a person content," I insisted. "I ask you, was our Emperor ever happy? Ever content? No."

To my surprise, Tobyson shook out diamonds from Napoleon's red silk pouch.

I thumbed through the stones I'd once coveted. "I thought Charles had stolen these! But why didn't you use them to buy Tobyson's freedom?"

"Madame," Hercules said, "they would have arrested us as thieves. But, truly, the Emperor gave them to us, and you must share in his bounty."

"So you may always feel safe from poverty," Tobyson added.

I hesitated, wanting to rise above my old faults, but, seeing the pleasure it would give Tobyson, I selected three. (I'd keep them hidden, I decided, until I needed something fresh for Basil to forgive.)

"Madame . . ." Tobyson hesitated. "Your husband?"

"I saw Charles when he first returned to Europe." I picked up my shears and clipped a deadhead Hercules had missed. "As always, it's hard to tell what side he's on or where his funds come from.

He sells trinkets and papers from Napoleon. Some are scribbled pages, discards, I think, from that *Clisson* book you brought to the Eaglet. Do let me add the last pages to my manuscript. But if you want to see Charles, I'll give you his direction. He's become a great supporter of the nephew, Louis-Napoleon."

"Yes, chère Madame, we want to visit Louis-N, too."

"I warn you, Louis-Napoleon is not the man his uncle was, but then, who is?"

As often with old friends, our ties ran deep but narrow. I felt their urge to leave long before I was ready to let them go, but dusk was falling. I relented. "Come, we'll walk together as far as little Joséphine's grave. Hercules, would you cut us each a flower?"

First, I climbed the stairs to my bedchamber, where I extracted two precious items from my St. Helena mementos. To Tobyson, I gave the tiny straw box his father had made for me after I saved him from those horses' hooves. To Hercules, I gave the small jar I had brought from St. Helena containing dried everlasting daisies.

Tobyson

One Week Later
Near Chantilly, France

On an autumn day, Tobyson and Hercules rode in the cart of a jovial French farmer. Hercules stretched on the hay in the open back, his feet dangling over the cart's edge, while Tobyson sat on the bench, conversing with their benefactor. Overhead, the branches of plane trees met in a vault, casting dappled shade on the road.

"I love these trees," Tobyson said. "They're both beautiful and useful. Have they been here long?"

"Why, Napoleon planted them. Don't you know anything? He wanted shade for his marching army." The farmer chuckled. "Story has it, the general who was told to plant them protested, saying it'd be twenty years before they provided any shade. The Emperor answered, 'Then you'd better hurry up and get started, hadn't you?'"

Tobyson nodded. "That sounds like him."

The farmer stared into the distance. "These days, a lot of Frenchmen don't like to admit how much good he did the country, but every summer as I drive this road, I thank him for the trees. And for the canal that takes my wheat to market." He made the sign of the cross. "My two oldest boys died in Russia's snow, so my wife curses the Emperor's memory. But you know? My grandson went to one of the Emperor's schools. Now he wears a colonel's uniform. Someday he might be a general."

They rode on in silence until the farmer turned to Tobyson. "A poor farmer's grandson, a general. I tell you, anything's possible these days. Reform in France comes with violence, but still it comes, stuttering forward. I'm proud to say I cast my first vote in the plebiscites that made Napoleon our leader."

The farmer clucked to speed his horses. "There's talk of bringing his body back, talk of his nephew Louis-Napoleon seizing power. That young man's cut from his uncle's cloth, but, to tell the truth, I don't care about Napoleon's son or nephew, I just want someone, anyone, who will make our lives better. But why should you care about Napoleon?"

"My father once gave him a hat that he valued." Tobyson climbed into the back of the cart and lay down on the straw, his head against Hercules's arm. Soon he'd have to break the news to his friend that he wanted to stay in France. In America, they still had Black slaves. In France, a farmer's son could become a general, a Corsican boy a king. Who knew what he himself could be? He'd serve Louis-Napoleon, help him get back the Emperor's throne. He'd change his name to Toby, so that when he had a child . . .

The sunlight flickered through the leaves—the green, the shining, shadow and light alternating on his face. Comfort provided by a man he had called Father. The fleshy hand that used to rub his own head had left its imprint upon this land.

But the man he had loved as a father was not the one he'd heard described as tyrant, hero, god, and devil. It was as the Emperor had told him: monsters appear bigger when far off.

He shook his friend awake. "Come, we must get out and walk. I know the route. The Emperor taught me."

Author's Note

Inspiration

In 1795, TWENTY-SIX-YEAR-OLD Napoleon Bonaparte was a poor but up-and-coming general in the Revolutionary French Army. He lived in a Paris that, like he himself, was rife with possibility, brimming with intellect, and turbulent with revolution. His long-distance engagement to his sister-in-law's sister, Eugénie Desirée Clary, fizzled as their correspondence cooled to petulance on her side and brotherly advice on his. He had not yet met his passionate but unfaithful love Josephine. In a lull between army duties, he tried to write a novel.

His scribbles—mostly story summary, with an occasional line of dialogue—covered fewer than twenty pages, ending in the hero's glorious death. He named it *Clisson et Eugénie*. At some point, he removed the middle section—the part where the hero has a happily married life—and renumbered the pages. He scratched *et Eugénie* out of the title. He kept the manuscript secret all his life and carried it with him into exile on St. Helena.

I learned about *Clisson* in 1999. I immediately decided to expand the brief work into a full novel, ghostwriting it for an older Napoleon as he reflected on his youth. In my early teens, I had lived in France and retained a love of the country and a fascination with Napoleon. Thus began a long journey, which culminated in the book you hold in your hands.

Along the way, I researched hundreds of sources about Napoleon and traveled tens of thousands of miles. I visited Napoleon's childhood home in Corsica and his school in Brienne and, of course, took research trips to Paris. My greatest adventure was my trip to St. Helena Island, which remains one of the most remote spots in the world. The island didn't have an airport then, so I took the only option: a five-day voyage out of Cape Town, South Africa, on the HMS *St. Helena*, one of Britain's last mail ships. I stayed on the island for nine days, until embarking on a return voyage of five days on rough seas.

On St. Helena, the French lovingly maintain Longwood House, the Briars Estate, and the site of Napoleon's first grave. I don't believe in ghosts, but the day I stood alone in Longwood's reception hall, where the Emperor died, I was moved by the presence of a huge, tragic soul. I'd found the driving force for my novel.

Fact Versus Historical Fiction

FINDING NAPOLEON IS A WORK of historical fiction. While it's the result of deep research and based on historical events, the product is an imaginative interpretation of what *did* happen and what *might have* happened.

Napoleon Bonaparte

NAPOLEON BONAPARTE, HIS ERA, AND the personalities surrounding him are endlessly complicated and fascinating. Reportedly, more than sixty thousand books have been written about him, and every year more join the pile. He's both revered and reviled. Naturally, much of the record is written to promote its author's particular point of view, whether British, French, contemporaneous, or modern. Napoleon was an incredible propagandist, too. It's good to be skeptical as you read about him.

In this book, the basic facts are true: He was born in Corsica in 1769, went to military school in France, joined the French army during the French Revolution, became a general, and was ultimately the ruler and emperor of France. He was married twice and had one legitimate child, later nicknamed the Eaglet. Napoleon died in 1821 during his second exile, which took place on St. Helena Island in the South Atlantic.

He was, by the way, about five feet, seven inches tall, an average height for Frenchmen of his era.

Albine and Charles de Montholon

HISTORICALLY, ALBINE'S HUSBAND, **Charles de Montholon,** has been a prime suspect in any poisoning of or spying on Napoleon on St. Helena, on behalf of either the British or the French. Yet Napoleon trusted him. Back in France, before Napoleon's defeat, the two men had not been close, but the Emperor forgave him for embezzling and for claiming false accomplishments in battle.

While on St. Helena, Napoleon had an affair with **Albine de Montholon,** presumably with her husband's knowledge and permission. Napoleon is believed to be the father of her child Joséphine Napoléone, who died in Belgium shortly after Albine's return to Europe. After Napoleon's death, Albine and Charles never reunited, other than brief meetings. Charles never visited little Joséphine's grave in Belgium. Albine died in 1848, reportedly surrounded by her grandchildren at a ball held in her honor. I took liberties of omission and commission in imagining Albine's life beyond the thin historical record.

Lieutenant Basil Jackson

BASIL JACKSON WAS A BRITISH officer on Sir Hudson Lowe's staff who had a close relationship with the Montholons and probably an affair with Albine. Three days after Albine and her baby left St. Helena to return to Europe, Basil Jackson boarded a ship to join her there.

My Clisson *Versus Napoleon's*

WHILE I MAINTAINED THE ORIGINAL plotline, there are differences. In his *Clisson*, Napoleon covered his childhood in a paragraph. In my version, I drew on Napoleon's childhood legends to lead up to the point where Clisson becomes a young man, born for war, ready for love. In both versions, Clisson meets two women, is fascinated with the older, experienced one, and marries the younger, innocent one.

I adapted some of Clisson's romantic letters from correspondence the real Napoleon wrote to his lovers, including to Josephine. To project the Emperor's voice, I often used quotes attributed to him or drew on other material Napoleon wrote. The original manuscript ends with Clisson's death. In this book, Napoleon rewrites that ending.

Throughout it all, I strove to remain true to the spirit of young Napoleon's manuscript. In the end, I hope that the aging Emperor would have recognized my *Clisson* story as his own.

I recommend that those who are interested in the research, compilation, and translation of Napoleon's exact manuscript read *Clisson and Eugénie: A Love Story, by Napoleon Bonaparte*, translated by Peter Hicks, published by Gallic Books, London, 2009.

Elba Versus St. Helena

NAPOLEON'S EXILE ON THE MEDITERRANEAN island of Elba is better known—at least to Americans—than his final exile, on St. Helena. The first lasted only ten months. During that genteel exile, Napoleon was recognized as the Emperor of Elba, and the restored French king promised him a large stipend. Those funds never arrived, but news of French dissatisfaction with Louis XVIII's reign did. Napoleon saw an opportunity to recover his throne.

He evaded his English guards and sailed to France with four cannons, forty horses, and a thousand soldiers. They landed on the southern coast and marched five hundred miles to Paris, acquiring supporters along the way. The French king fled, and Napoleon reinstated himself as Emperor without firing a shot.

One hundred days later, his decisive defeat at Waterloo ended his second reign. Believing that the British would treat a deposed ruler generously (as was the custom), he surrendered to a British navy captain whose ship was blockading a port on France's Atlantic coast. The British refused him sanctuary and exiled him to remote St. Helena. He lived there until his death, five years later, in 1821.

Josephine Versus Marie Louise and the Eaglet

NAPOLEON'S FIRST WIFE, **Josephine de Beauharnais**, was the great love of his life, but they had a tumultuous relationship. They were married in 1796. Two days later, he left for war in Italy and she took a lover. He crowned her Empress in 1804 and divorced her in 1810, when it became clear that she wouldn't be able to provide an heir for the Empire. They remained good friends.

A few months after his divorce, Napoleon married **Marie Louise**, the daughter of the Austrian emperor. A year later, their son, later nicknamed **the Eaglet**, was born. During Napoleon's defeat in 1814, Marie Louise returned to Austria with the one-eyed Austrian **Count von Neipperg**, who reportedly had been sent by her father to seduce her. She and von Neipperg had three children before Napoleon's death. Napoleon never publicly spoke ill of her or acknowledged her infidelity.

As in this novel, Napoleon's beloved son, the Eaglet, never saw his father again after their farewell in 1814. He grew up as a pampered prisoner-guest within the Austrian royal court. He died of tuberculosis in 1832 in Vienna, at age twenty-one. The nickname the Eaglet became popular only after his death, but it would have been confusing to call him young Napoleon or use his title, the King of Rome, in this novel. Unfortunately, he never got to read *Clisson*.

Napoleon and Slavery

FRANCE RULED SAINT-DOMINGUE (HAITI), the western portion of the Caribbean island of Hispaniola, after acquiring it from Spain in 1697. A hundred years later, at the time of the French Revolution, the little colony was producing almost 50 percent of Europe's sugar and coffee. For decades, these riches had supported France's monarchs and wars.

That wealth came at a terrible cost to millions of enslaved Africans who suffered under unimaginable cruelty—perhaps the worst in the western hemisphere. In no way does this novel make excuses for that horror, or for the less violent but still appalling treatment of enslaved people on St. Helena.

In 1794, France's revolutionary government abolished slavery in the French Empire. However, many plantation owners (mostly white Europeans, but also free Blacks and mixed-race "mulattos") in Haiti and other colonies refused to free their slaves. Rebellions resulted in massive slaughter.

When Napoleon came to power eight years later, France's revolutionary government was corrupt and bankrupt. Above all, Napoleon needed money to stabilize France before its neighbors broke it to pieces. Haiti's wealth offered a quick solution, if the plantation trade could be salvaged. In 1803, Napoleon sent troops to restore order in Haiti. Initially, he wanted to do that without reinstating slavery, because a prosperous free Haiti would disrupt England's Caribbean slave colonies, but he quickly changed to supporting the slaveholders.

His efforts were a military and moral disaster. At every turn, the poorly equipped but determined rebel slaves defeated the crack French army, whose ranks were further decimated by yellow fever. Before long, Napoleon gave up on Haiti and the New World. Disillusioned, he sold the Louisiana Territory to the United States.

During Napoleon's "Hundred Days" rule before his defeat at Waterloo, he declared all enslaved people in France's colonies to be free. Clearly, he had failed to uphold the French Revolution's ideals of *liberté, égalité, et fraternité.*

While on St. Helena, Napoleon started up a friendship with the Balcombe family's **enslaved gardener Toby**. Reportedly, they spent long hours together. As in this novel, the Emperor tried to free Toby, but Sir Hudson Lowe denied the request. Toby indeed made a straw hat Napoleon wore. He also called the Emperor "the good gentleman" and "his king."

Additionally, there's an eyewitness account of an incident on St. Helena when Napoleon made several high-bred British gentlewomen step aside to let slaves pass on a narrow path, saying, "Respect the burden, if not the men." The women were deeply offended. I based the scene of his stopping British troops to **let slaves pass with their barrels** on that report.

On the other hand, the story of his plot to escape with Toby and Randall is purely my imagination. But, according to the historical record, for some reason, Napoleon gave Toby twenty gold Napoleon coins. And who knows what Napoleon and Toby discussed during those hours in the Balcombe family's garden? I hope, in my small way, this novel gives some voice to St. Helena's enslaved population, who are too often forgotten in Napoleonic stories. It does not excuse or justify Napoleon's, France's, or anyone else's participation in slavery.

Other Characters from the St. Helena Story

ALL THE CHARACTERS IN THE ST. HELENA portion were real people except **Tobyson, Hercules, Randall,** and **Miora**. As I mentioned above, Toby was a historical figure. His son, Tobyson, is a beloved invention of my imagination, meant to represent Napoleon's yearning for the Eaglet.

The character Hercules is fictional, although Napoleon called a large Englishman who lived on St. Helena by the same name. Readers of Napoleonic history may also remember Joseph Domingue, one of Napoleon's Black battalion commanders, whom he nicknamed Hercules. In *Finding Napoleon*, Hercules is a composite of other St. Helena residents who may have worked on Napoleon's behalf.

Napoleon's **Corsican major domo on St. Helena, Francesco Cipriani**, died suddenly "of a fever" (sometimes reported as appendicitis) in 1818. No one knows where on St. Helena he was buried. Napoleon had known him since their boyhood on Corsica. Although I've read accounts that claim he was Napoleon's half brother, he was not the younger brother of a butcher who was tortured to death in the citadel in Ajaccio, as in my *Clisson* story. That incident is fiction, except it's true that as a child Napoleon lived a couple of blocks from the citadel and liked to sneak away from school to consort with the French soldiers.

Napoleon's nephew, **Louis-N**, is Louis Napoleon, who became Emperor Napoleon III of France in 1852. He was the son of Napoleon's younger brother Louis and Josephine's daughter (Napoleon's stepdaughter), Hortense.

The upstanding valet, Marchand, is generally true to character, as are **General Bertrand and his wife, Fanny. Marchand's mother** cared for the young Eaglet in France and stayed in Austria with him until the Austrians forced her to leave. As portrayed, she smuggled a lock of the Eaglet's hair to St. Helena.

Las Cases and his son were among Napoleon's entourage on St. Helena. Hudson Lowe sent them home under a cloud of suspicion. Some say Las Cases wanted to leave because he planned to sell his Napoleon memoirs.

For simplicity, I left out of the novel various other members of the Longwood household, including General Gourgaud, who arrived with Napoleon and left in 1816; the strange Polish officer Pointkowski, who arrived in late 1815 and left in 1816; and numerous household servants and valets.

The British

ADMIRAL COCKBURN WAS IN CHARGE of transporting Napoleon to St. Helena on the HMS *Northumberland*. He was, as the book mentions, also involved in the burning of the American White House during the War of 1812.

Sir Hudson Lowe was governor of St. Helena from 1816 through Napoleon's death in 1821. History generally portrays him, as Wellington indeed said, as "a pettifogging bureaucrat." Napoleon's refusal to accept his authority or even to see him for years at a time, drove him almost mad. To his credit, he worked with the St. Helena slaveholders to reach an agreement that set free all children born to slaves after Christmas 1818. However, that partial emancipation led to decades of struggle for the remaining enslaved population.

Dr. O'Meara was an Irish doctor in the British navy who overstepped his loyalty with his devotion to Napoleon. Sir Hudson Lowe sent him home in disgrace.

Napoleon spent his first six weeks on St. Helena at **the Briars, the Balcombe family estate. William Balcombe** was a British merchant who probably passed messages from the Emperor to Europe. His spunky fourteen-year-old daughter, **Betsy**, spoke French and became a dear companion of the Emperor, who had always enjoyed the lighthearted company of children (probably because his own childhood had been cut short and because only with children could he relax from ceremony). There is no indication, other than propaganda, that the relationship was anything more than avuncular. Sir Hudson Lowe distrusted the Balcombe family and sent them away in disgrace in 1818. As an adult, Betsy wrote her memoir, *To Befriend an Emperor*.

The merchant **Saul Solomon** arrived on the island in 1790 and prospered, especially during Napoleon's exile. He undoubtedly smuggled messages for Napoleon, since he returned to the island in 1840 as an honored guest when Napoleon's body was reclaimed for France. His descendants ran emporiums on the island until the 1970s. To this day, Solomon's Emporium is still the largest grocery store on St. Helena's main street.

Events

NAPOLEON IS RUMORED TO HAVE wanted to throw himself into the battle to die at the end of Waterloo. His generals restrained him, although not Bertrand and Montholon. He said goodbye to **his mother, known as Madame Mère**, in a private meeting at Malmaison. She was not blind at the time, although she became so from cataracts later. During Napoleon's exile, she lived in Rome, where she fell under the influence of an Austrian mystic who convinced her that angels had rescued Napoleon from St. Helena.

The stories of Madame Marchand's sending a **lock of the Eaglet's hair** through the botanist Philip Welle, the arrival of a **bust of the Eaglet**, and Napoleon's triumphal **British troop review** are all based on reported events.

In 1803, the American inventor Robert Fulton and a British smuggler named Thomas Johnson built an operational submarine for Emperor Napoleon to use against the British navy. He never tried it in battle. Robert Fulton went home to America to work on steam power. There were rumors of **attempts to rescue the Emperor from St. Helena by submarine**, but no evidence exists that the plots advanced as far as this book imagines.

The **Emperor's baths**: Yes, he loved to soak in a hot tub for hours.

Arsenic and stomach cancer: Whole books and research papers have been written on this subject alone. Napoleon himself claimed that the British were poisoning him. In more recent years, clippings from Napoleon's hair have shown evidence of exposure to arsenic. Another reason arsenic has been suspected is that when Napoleon's body was exhumed in 1840 for its return to France, it was in eerily perfect shape—a condition attributed to arsenic, which acts as a preservative. Montholon is generally the prime suspect in any "inside job."

On the other hand, the arsenic might well have been natural to the environment, or it might have leached out of Longwood's wallpaper into the air. Others in Napoleon's entourage were also ill, but during the last two years of his life, Napoleon refused to leave Longwood House, so he would have had the most exposure.

While arsenic may have been an aggravating factor, most researchers today believe he died from stomach cancer or an ulcerated stomach. The French won't exhume his body, so we will never know for sure.

I chose to interpret the evidence of periodic arsenic exposure as **self-poisoning**, knowing Napoleon had poisoned himself after his first defeat, in 1814. For much of his life, he kept poison handy in case of capture. On St. Helena, he hoped his ill health would speed his return to Europe. To me, it seemed in line with his character.

I HOPE YOU ENJOYED READING *Finding Napoleon* as much as I enjoyed writing it. Please visit www.margaretrodenberg.com, for book-club discussion questions, more information about this novel, and tidbits about my literary life.

— MARGARET RODENBERG

Acknowledgments

ALONG THIS BOOK'S ROAD TO PUBLICATION, family, friends, and colleagues gave me encouragement to persevere, kudos for my triumphs, and sympathy for my stumbles. I am grateful to you all.

Much credit goes to my longtime critique group, Women of Words. Lorelei Brush, Raima Larter, Christine Jackson, Stephanie Joyce, Susan Lynch, Melanie Otto, and Pragna Soni, your love, wisdom, and support made *Finding Napoleon* a better book and me a better person.

I also thank my long-distance critique group, WordPardners, for inviting me in just when I needed you. Rex Griffin, Mike Torreano, Scott Hibbard, John Andrews, and Marilee Aufdenkamp, you keep me on my toes. I rely on your kind words and sharp critiques.

To my beta readers, including Heather Webb, Sondra Arkin, Alix Sundquist, Mary Tod, Sarah Helfinstein, Missy Craig, and Kathryn Johnson, thank you for the gift of your time. Your insights improved this novel in hundreds of small and large ways.

Throughout the years, publishing professionals have encouraged, improved, and promoted my writing. Without your recognition, Laurie McLean, Russell Galen, April Eberhardt, Rebecca Strauss, and especially Rachel Ekstrom, I might have thrown in the towel.

While researching this book, I enjoyed many Napoleonic adventures. I thank J. David Markham, Edna Markham, and my friends at the Napoleonic Historical Society for all you've taught me and the fun we've shared. For my unforgettable experiences on St. Helena Island, I thank Michel Dancoisne-Martineau, who allowed me private time in Longwood House. To Dr. David Karpeles, thank you for permitting me to hold Napoleon's original handwritten pages of *Clisson* in my hands.

Author Heather Webb deserves special thanks for her generous support, as do all the wonderful authors and Napoleonic experts who provided their praise for *Finding Napoleon*. Thank you, Sandra Gulland, Stephanie Dray, Allison Pataki, J. David Markham (International Napoleonic Society), Louis Bayard, Peter Hicks, Kathryn Johnson, Michelle Cameron, Scott Hibbard, and Mary Tod.

I thank the She Writes Press team, headed by the inestimable Brooke Warner. You shepherded *Finding Napoleon* through the publishing process and created a book I am proud of. I'm grateful to Annie Tucker for her careful edits, to Julie Metz for the book cover, to Tabitha Lahr for the internal design, to Samantha Strom for managing the process, and to Brooke for accepting the manuscript. Brooke, you are an inspiring powerhouse of a woman!

Most of all, I thank my most loyal and supportive reader, my wonderful husband, Bert Helfinstein. You were a perfect helpmate during countless research and conference trips. Your video- and photo-editing skills make my website shine. You buck me up when I'm down and put me on track when I'm floundering. Best of all, when I suggested that we embark on a monthlong voyage to St. Helena Island, you agreed (on the condition that, on the way through South Africa, we dive with great white sharks). Your companionship, advice, and support have been monumental. Your love is essential to my being.

About the Author

MARGARET RODENBERG'S passion for French history began when she lived in France as a young teen with her US Navy family. An avid traveler who has visited more than sixty countries, she journeyed more than thirty thousand miles to conduct Napoleonic research, including to St. Helena Island in the remote South Atlantic. She's a former businesswoman, an award-winning writer, and a proud director of the Napoleonic Historical Society, a nonprofit that promotes knowledge of the Napoleonic era. Her website, www.margaretrodenberg.com, reports on her literary life and Napoleon's presence in world culture. *Finding Napoleon* is her debut novel.

Author photo © Bert Helfinstein

SELECTED TITLES FROM SHE WRITES PRESS

She Writes Press is an independent publishing company founded to serve women writers everywhere. Visit us at www.shewritespress.com.

Beyond the Ghetto Gates by Michelle Cameron. $16.95, 978-1-63152-850-7. When French troops occupy the Italian port city of Ancona, freeing the city's Jews from their repressive ghetto, two very different cultures collide—and a whirlwind of progressivism and brutal backlash is unleashed.

Dark Lady by Charlene Ball. $16.95, 978-1-63152-228-4. Emilia Bassano Lanyer—poor, beautiful, and intelligent, born to a family of Court musicians and secret Jews, lover to Shakespeare and mistress to an older nobleman—survives to become a published poet in an era when most women's lives are rigidly circumscribed.

Elmina's Fire by Linda Carleton. $16.95, 978-1-63152-190-4. A story of conflict over such issues as reincarnation and the nature of good and evil that are as relevant today as they were eight centuries ago, *Elmina's Fire* offers a riveting window into a soul struggling for survival amid the conflict between the Cathars and the Catholic Church.

Estelle by Linda Stewart Henley. $16.95, 978-1-63152-791-3. From 1872 to '73, renowned artist Edgar Degas called New Orleans home. Here, the narratives of two women—Estelle, his Creole cousin and sister-in-law, and Anne Gautier, who in 1970 finds a journal written by a relative who knew Degas—intersect . . . and a painting by Degas of Estelle spells trouble.

The Nun's Betrothal by Ida Curtis. $16.95, 978-1-63152-685-5. Sister Gilda and Lord Justin are charged to resolve a conflict: Count Cedric wants to annul his marriage to Lady Mariel so he can marry Lady Emma; Mariel believes Cedric's half-brother Phillip, not Cedric, is the man she married at her wedding; and Philip and Emma are in love. Can Gilda and Justin complete their mission before their burgeoning passion for each other overwhelms them?